The Ticking

Ali Ives

Literary Wanderlust | Denver, Colorado

Published in the United States by Literary Wanderlust LLC Denver, Colorado.

www.LiteraryWanderlust.com

ISBN Paperback: 978-1-956615-27-2
ISBN Digital: 978-1-956615-28-9

Printed in the United States of America

Dedication

To my family, made and found. You fill my life with love.
And to the spot on the dock on the pond, where the frogs sing
and my mind finds rest.

My own little pocket of the universe.

Other Works by the Author

The Winding

Prologue

Ruins

The Maze stands abandoned. Locked in a pocket of the universe all its own, it is a timeless place, the once-great home of a god. The remnants of elegant staircases, twisting and ornately impossible, lie in the dereliction of crumbled mortar and cracked stone. The massive walls grow dusty, marred by lines of cold water leaching from the ceilings high overhead.

A breeze stirs the Gambler's pale hair as he picks his way carefully through the debris. Footprints paint a red trail behind him, tracing his barefooted path.

It never used to be so drafty. He's tempted to speak the dry thoughts aloud, if only not to feel so alone.

Then again, in the words of exasperated parents everywhere, that's what you get for leaving the door open. Or, in this case, doors. There are many doors in the Maze, taking every shape and size and design imaginable. Tall doors, short doors, plain, embellished, glass, wood, and metal. Most are never meant to be opened. Now none are closed.

The Gambler's path stops at one of the thousand doorways, and he stares into its depths. The act in and of itself is impressive: staring is a difficult feat when you don't have eyes in your head.

The Gambler is a god, though he would be the first to amend this claim with the humble clarification "of sorts." He prefers the term "demigod" or, more specifically, "personification of Choice." It is a title that denotes a certain degree of individuality, which the Gambler possesses in spades. From his eyeless face to his ever-bleeding knees, to the bloody trail of footprints he leaves in his wake, he sets himself apart long before he ever opens his mouth and his unearthly voice can be heard. It is the voice of ancient sorrow, beautiful and heartbreaking in equal measure.

The Gambler is a god, and the Maze is a god's home, and yet they are far from a match. This is another's abode, one no longer to be found here. The Gambler sighs and turns away from yet another open doorway. It had been foolish optimism to think that there would be anything here. Denken is long gone.

But gone where? Slender fingers trail over long cuts sliced into the stone wall, each digit matching a mark. *Claws,* he thinks. *He's angry.*

Another bitter non-surprise. Denken's rage threatens them all.

"Where are you?" he asks the empty air. Silence answers. Was this how it felt for his brother when he was the one missing? Had Denken searched the Crossroads, hoping for some sign of him?

If he isn't here, there is only one place he can be. It isn't a comforting thought. The human world is a large place for a demigod to hide in, especially if he doesn't wish to be found.

He can't hide forever. Another discomfiting thought. Denken's reappearance will be anything but peaceful. It is the case in every future the Gambler sees, smudged and blurry as his visions have become. They range from bad to terrible to unthinkable, and he doesn't know what to do.

All he knows is that there's no point in looking in an empty home. Denken won't be back here. Not unless they can stop this. Stop *him*.

"I'll save you," the Gambler whispers, and the promise is carried away on the wind. The moment arrives to leave this place, to return to the ticking passage of time.

Our story continues.

Chapter 1

Amends

Gloucester's phone rang. The chime wasn't remarkable, cutting through the quiet of the darkened break room of Zephyr Clocks, and yet the young man jolted awake as if he'd just been electrocuted. He sat up on the sofa bed, eyes wide and hair an unruly mess. Breathing unevenly, he stared at the phone on the coffee table like it was a foreign object.

In many ways, it was. Until a month ago, Mikalai Gloucester hadn't had contact with other people for a very long time, let alone access to a personal telephone. The six months he'd spent in solitary confinement had left him feeling frustratingly unaccustomed to many things that were previously mundane parts of everyday life. Upon his release from his cell, he quickly found that things like conversations, loud noises, crowds, and even his own complicated emotions were a lot more difficult to handle. Phones had also made that list, as it turned out.

Not that the one given to him by Antimony Jones got

very much use. "For emergencies," the reserved scientist had explained. It was important that they all be able to reach each other. Just in case.

There hadn't been many calls for him to expect, as there weren't many people who would have any reason to contact him. Really just Antimony and Zane Zephyr, the owner of the clock shop and his current housemate.

Seeing as the latter was sleeping right upstairs, it seemed unlikely she would be calling him. Something told him the Gambler wouldn't rely on phones to communicate, so it was probably safe to rule him out. Toby Mulligan, the former chief adviser to the late high minister and current interim lord of the city-state of Frettchen, was a possibility. He had grudgingly exchanged numbers as well, but Gloucester suspected the city would have to be literally collapsing around their ears for Mulligan to call him. For all their uneasy truce with the leading power in Frettchen, Gloucester knew the man saw him as nothing but an enemy.

It had to be Antimony, then. What could have her calling at this time of night? The first stirrings of foreboding began to overtake his sleepy consternation. Gloucester picked up the still-ringing phone and clicked to answer the call.

"Hello?" he said, voice pitched low and groggy with lingering sleep. He pushed his free hand through his hair, raking the tumbled black curls away from his brow. "Antimony?"

"Not exactly," said the lilting voice on the other end of the line. It was male and jauntily familiar. "In fact, not at all."

Gloucester held the phone away from his ear for a moment to stare at it. "*Finch?*"

"Got it in one," said Cassus Finch's cheerful voice. "Well, two, but I'm still flattered." Gloucester said nothing, and after a moment of silence, Finch spoke again, this time with an edge of uncertainty. "Gloucester? You still there?"

"What the *hell* do you want?" Gloucester demanded. Surprise was quickly transformed into anger as the shock wore off. When he'd last seen Finch two weeks before, the circumstances of their parting had been far from amicable.

Cassus Finch was a magician. Amidst this newly discovered world of demigods and hidden dimensions, his magic was perhaps not the most powerful or strange thing Gloucester had come across, but it was still hard to wrap his head around. Yet it wasn't Finch's proclivity for magic that was Gloucester's main concern. A fortnight earlier, he and Denken, the mischievous and powerful personification of Thought, had nearly killed each other in a violent, revenge-fuelled confrontation.

"How's your nose?" asked Finch now. The question held a timidness of which Gloucester couldn't easily judge the sincerity, which only darkened his mood all the more.

"Very recently broken," he snapped. "Almost like some two-faced, scheming bastard smashed me in the face with a big bloody gun." He had Antimony to thank for how quickly the injury had healed. Though not magical herself, her first aid kit was full of items enchanted with healing spells. Only yellowing bruises hinted now at what had been an ugly break.

"I never meant to hurt you." Finch must have realized how his words would come off as soon as they left his mouth because Gloucester barely had time to make a scandalized croak before he cut in to hastily amend the statement. "I just meant . . . Look, I'm sorry about how things went down in the church. That . . . You were never part of the plan. Not like that, anyway."

Gloucester glared at the blank wall opposite the sofa bed, wishing Finch was in front of him just so the scowl wouldn't be wasted. "Not like *what?* What part of the plan *was* intended? Just the part where you tricked me? Where you used me? I'm tired of people using me, Finch, so if you only called to ease whatever guilt you're feeling, then just forget it. Leave me alone." He paused, confusion worming its way through his righteous anger. "Wait, hold on. How did you even get this number?"

"Not easily," Finch answered. "But this is important, Gloucester. I need to talk to you. Face to face."

"Why would I—"

"I know I made a mistake, okay?" Finch interrupted. "But it's not one either of us can fix on our own."

"I'm not on my own," Gloucester pointed out.

Impatience was starting to outweigh any apology still coloring Finch's tone. "Dammit, can you not be so bloody contrary? I can help you. All of you. But not over the bloody telephone, so just say you'll meet me. Please."

Gloucester tried to remember if he'd ever heard Finch say please before. The secretive magician was amiable—or at least seemed so, up until the moment he let all hell break loose in the name of vengeance—but he wasn't the sort for sincere politeness.

It could be a trap. Well-founded paranoia made Gloucester want to shy away from the whole thing. He ought to just hang up the phone and go back to sleep, pretend like nothing had happened. Finch had used him for his own ends before. His vicious, half-baked plan had brought nothing but trouble, not only to Finch himself but the entire city. He wasn't to be trusted.

On the other hand, Gloucester couldn't see what possible motive Finch might have for playing him again. Perhaps he was being honest when he admitted to his mistake. Maybe he did want to help set things right.

Only one way to find out.

"When and where?" he asked grudgingly.

Finch's relief was audible. "There's a café in Uptown, walking distance from your mate Zane's shop. Hawke's Landing. Be there in forty-five minutes. I'll find you."

"Now?" Gloucester groaned. "Finch, it's the middle of the—"

But his protest was met with the click of Finch hanging up and the quiet ticking of the clockwork dial tone. Gloucester scoffed, then tossed the phone down onto his lap.

Sitting in the dark, he pondered what to do. He looked up at the ceiling. Upstairs, Zane was sleeping, or at least trying her best to do so. Sleep didn't come so easily these days.

Ought he to wake her? Doubtless, she would want to know about Finch's call, even if it was only to tell Gloucester off for not immediately hanging up on the magician. She would probably want to come with him, no matter how much she'd complain the whole time, pointing out all the ways this was a terrible idea. Zane was a pragmatist, and particularly grouchy when woken in the middle of the night, but Gloucester knew her complaints would be masking genuine worry. The young clockmaker was the first person he'd met after his release from prison who had shown that sort of guileless concern for his well-being.

Which meant a lot to him, but now wasn't the time for it. Perhaps it was foolish to go see Finch alone, but there were things he wanted to say that were just between them. He would do this on his own.

—

According to the hundreds of ticking timepieces Gloucester passed on his way out of Zephyr Clocks, it was just past 1:45 in the morning. Outside the shop, the streets of Uptown Frettchen had fallen under the spell of the late hour. The city was oddly muted, with only the most determined of night owls and sufferers of unfortunate work shifts still out and about. Despite the occasional holler or burst of laughter from one of the pubs, Frettchen seemed to be sleeping. Even the nighttime traffic sounded quieter to the ears than it did during the day.

Gloucester shrugged deeper into his jacket, collar turned up to shield the back of his neck from the chilly breeze chasing him down the sidewalk. Though spring had settled comfortably over the city, the nights were still cool. A faint mist of rain sparkled in the glow of the streetlamps, just enough to encourage the chill to seep past his layers of clothing.

It wasn't just the dreary weather he was hunching his shoulders against. Trepidation clung to him like an unwanted cloak, a feeling he couldn't shake. The moment he stepped out of the shop, it draped over him, whispering worries into the back of his mind and making him cast furtive glances over his shoulder every few minutes. He felt this way every time he left the safety of Zephyr Clocks, and it only seemed to be getting worse with each passing day. In the daylight hours, the hubbub of the city was overwhelming, yet when night fell, all he could think of was imagined threats lurking in the dark.

He was ten minutes away from the clock shop when a problem occurred to him: What sort of café would be open at this time of night? Most weren't known for their late-night hours, after all.

As soon as he spotted this issue, he wondered how in the world it had taken him so long to think of it. Deciding to blame the haze of sleep still pressing on the back of his mind, he slowed his steps until he came to a stop in the small pool of light from a street lamp, wondering what to do. Should he turn around? Maybe Finch was up to something after all, and the phone call had been nothing more than bait to lure him out of the safety of the clock shop. If this were the case, he couldn't fathom what the point would be. But he felt stupid nonetheless for falling for such a blatant ruse.

Yet something was still telling him Finch had spoken the truth. His request to meet at a café in the dead of night felt too odd to be a lie. If there was one thing Gloucester had learned of late, it was that nothing was stranger than the truth.

A clatter from the depths of a nearby alley shook him from his uncertain thoughts, and he whirled to face it, immediately on guard. Nothing greeted his searching eyes. Only darkness. *Probably an animal,* he told himself, nonetheless wishing he'd brought a weapon with him. Stray animal or not, it was a reminder not to linger anywhere too long. The streets weren't safe anymore.

So, go back or continue on?

Hoping he wouldn't come to regret it, he set off once more in the direction he'd been headed. Maybe Finch just wanted to meet *outside* the café. Gloucester repeated the name of the place in his head as he walked, searching the signs above the storefronts. *Hawke's Landing, Hawke's Landing, Hawke's Landing . . .*

There it was, a streetlamp away and across the road. A white stone building, its windows dark. Suspended above the door, a swinging sign painted with graceful brushstrokes suggested the wings and body of a bird as it swooped toward an equally simplified tree. "Hawke's Landing" was carved above it, letters painted gold.

Gloucester crossed the street, searching for any sign of Finch as he approached. The place appeared abandoned for the night. Tucking his hands into his pockets, Gloucester came to a stop just outside the door and stood with his back against the wall to wait.

The minutes slid by. Gloucester's mind began to wander, though the keen edge of wariness still couldn't be shaken. Only fools loitered alone in the night these days.

It came as a shock and an annoyance, then, that he didn't see Finch coming. One moment he was certain he was alone, glancing idly down the street to his left, and then the next, the sound of someone clearing their throat nearly made him jump a foot in the air. A hand tapped him lightly on the shoulder.

Resisting the urge to clutch at his chest, Gloucester spun to face the owner of the hand. Finch grinned at him, retracting the appendage and sticking it back into the pocket of the long wool coat he wore.

"Bit jumpy, aren't we?" he said by way of greeting.

At first glance, Finch looked exactly as Gloucester remembered. Taller than him by several inches, he had dark red hair cut short and sharp green eyes in a face full of freckles. A tattoo shaped like a sun decorated the left side of his forehead, half-obscured by his hairline. He was a handful of years older than Gloucester and handsome in a way best described as roguish.

"I've plenty of reason to be," Gloucester retorted. A look

in Finch's eyes hinted that he knew this well, though, and Gloucester held back the rest of the vitriol that had risen on his tongue. Upon closer inspection, the magician's smile was a thin mask over a much weightier bedraggledness that clung to his entire demeanor. He didn't look like he'd slept well in days, perhaps not since Gloucester saw him last. Dark smudges under his eyes stood out against the paleness of his skin.

"You look terrible," Gloucester told him.

"Cheeky." Finch snorted, but there didn't seem to be a lot of effort behind his glibness. "You look pretty good. Zane and Antimony still minding you?"

Gloucester frowned. "No one's *minding* me. I'm not a dog. What do you want, Finch?"

To his surprise, Finch ducked his head, the action almost shy. Timidness was not something he'd come to expect from the other man. Finch was silent for a moment, seeming to weigh his options, and when he looked up again to meet Gloucester's eyes, his expression was contrite.

"I'd like you to call me Cassus, for starters." The request escaped his lips quickly as if he were embarrassed to speak the words aloud. "Strikes me that you of all people have earned the right. And secondly, I want the same thing you want. To fix things. To fix my mistake."

Gloucester peered at him intently in the light of the nearby street lamps. He *looked* sincere. That didn't mean much, however.

Trust no one.

His mantra was hard to shake.

"Maybe so," he hedged. "I assume you have some sort of plan, then, Finch? Cassus," he amended. The correction was met with a tiny pleased smile from the redhead. Much to Gloucester's irritation, the sight of it caused some of the ice in his mood to melt, despite his best efforts to stay aloof. He cleared his throat, expectant—perhaps overly so—in his attempt to stay on track.

"Calling it a plan might be a stretch, but I've got ideas. Come inside and we'll talk through them. It's not safe out here."

It was a bleak sentiment, but an honest one. In the weeks since Denken killed the high minister in his church and disappeared, the city had fallen into a dark state that most of its citizens were struggling unsuccessfully to comprehend. How could they be expected to, when the poisoned root at its heart was supernatural and secret? Most of them were blind to a whole side of their world, even with it existing right under their noses.

Gloucester had stumbled upon it by accident, dragged into a mess he was still trying to understand. What he did know was Denken had changed things the moment he snapped the high minister's neck, sending out dangerous ripples that still spread through Frettchen now. The Gambler had warned of the consequences that came when his kind broke the rules that bound them, one of which forbade them from killing humans. Now they were getting to see just what those consequences entailed.

The breaking news of the high minister and lord of the city-state's death had caused a frenzy throughout the city two weeks ago. He'd been found in his bed, the news reported, having died peacefully in his sleep of natural causes. A controversial figure, the reactions were a mixed bag of horror, worry, and delight, and overnight it became all anyone was talking about. The media was in an uproar, bantering amongst themselves and with the public about the various illnesses and diseases that must have been the culprit. Mulligan had done an impeccable job burying the truth.

Yet before long, new causes for dismay arose. A series of murders, all seemingly unrelated, set everyone's already fraying nerves further on edge. Several bank branches were robbed. Shops were looted aggressively. Citizens attacked each other in the streets, stirred to violence at even the smallest offense.

A city in crisis, said the news reporters, faces grim and eyes fearful. A people struggling to hold their own after the loss of their leader. They urged everyone to take care of themselves and others and to work together to get through these dark and uncertain times.

They were inspiring words, but Gloucester wasn't sure they would be of much help in the long run. What was happening in Frettchen was more than the chaos born of politically unstable times. He remembered how it had felt when Denken caught hold of his mind and nearly succeeded in making him commit murder. The personification of Thought had powerful abilities in the art of persuasion.

Not just intentionally, either. Gloucester recalled the way the demigod's moods had affected the people around him, seemingly without his knowledge. When they'd been searching All Saints Shrine for the Gambler, Denken's easy confidence had begun to slip, and the desperation and fear hiding beneath it leaked out, infecting those around him. Gloucester remembered the feeling of despair bogging down his mind and the looks of fear and sadness on the faces of bystanders who couldn't understand why they suddenly felt this way. Considering the violence and rage stirring in Frettchen's collective consciousness, Gloucester feared to imagine Denken's current state of mind.

"Are you coming?"

Finch gestured for him to follow, reaching out to take his arm. Then he hesitated, seemingly thinking better of the action. Gloucester looked from him to the dark windows of the Hawke's Landing café.

"It's closed," he said, nonplussed.

"Looks aren't everything, mate," Finch replied, some of his old good humor returning as he winked. "Appearances can be deceiving."

He stepped up to the door of the café and moved his hands in a quick weaving motion, drawing a complicated symbol in the empty air. For an instant Gloucester felt the thrum of magic, followed by an audible click. Finch reached down and turned the handle.

The door swung open without protest. Gloucester opened

his mouth to point out that if Finch needed to talk so urgently he was breaking and entering places, they could have just met in the clock shop, but the magician hushed him and beckoned once more for him to follow. Scowling at his back, Gloucester did so.

Chapter 2

Hawke's Landing

What he found on the other side of the door stopped him dead in his tracks.

They were not, as he'd expected, standing on the threshold of a darkened shop closed up for the night. Though the view from the street had revealed only darkness inside, this was not at all the case now. Gloucester stared in awe at the brightly lit room, raising one hand to shade his eyes.

What appeared to be a deserted building was packed with people. They filled the booths and the tables, gathered around steaming cups of coffee, plates of pub food, and the occasional large pitcher of alcohol. Every sort of person imaginable seemed to be present, from snickering teens in one corner to a tiny old woman in a colorful headdress who was arguing loudly with the barista in one of the Southern languages. Gloucester recognized the hurried vowels and crisp consonants but wasn't well-versed enough to identify the specific tongue.

"What is this place?" he asked, turning toward Finch with wide eyes. "From out there it looked—"

"Empty as a beggar's pocket, aye," Finch finished, nodding. He eyed their surroundings with obvious fondness. "It's an illusion. Keeps out the riff-raff."

Assuming that meant the place was in some way exclusive, Gloucester looked around again, searching for some common feature all of the patrons possessed. Yet they varied in everything from gender to age to culture to class. The only demographic notably missing was children, but it was hard to say if that wasn't just due to the late hour.

Then it hit him. An illusion. *Magic.*

"They're all magicians?"

Finch grinned. "More or less. Magic's a bit more complicated than I reckon you've seen so far. Magicians are only one sort. There are loads of them here, of course, but there are also witches, soothsayers, and even a few enchanters. Some here aren't even any of those. Couldn't use magic to save their lives, they just know about it. There are always a few of those who weasel their way into places like this. Take your friend Antimony for example."

"Places like this?" Gloucester repeated. "Just what *is* this place?"

"What I said it was." Finch shrugged out of his coat, folding it over his arm. "A café. One where people like me can relax."

Gloucester stared around the room, trying to take it all in. The café itself didn't seem all that remarkable. He wondered if it ran a mundane business during the day. Its plaster walls and wooden tables gave no sign of being overtly magical. The lights hanging from the ceiling were encased in colorful stained glass but seemed to be powered by regular light bulbs, not any mystical glow.

Not that there weren't signs of magic to be found. Gloucester's eyes lingered on a rotund young woman with a shaved head, whose hands were surrounded by a soft kaleidoscope of lights. They danced around her tattooed fingers as she held an animated conversation with her friends. A few tables away from her, two cowled figures played some sort of game, moving the pieces on the board without ever touching them. Then there was the woman near Gloucester and Finch, who calmly returned Gloucester's gaze while the pen and notebook on the table in front of her busied themselves of their own accord, scribbling notes without her ever lifting a hand or looking their way.

Overwhelmed, Gloucester did his best to focus on Finch and tune everything else out. He generally tried to avoid crowds these days, and this one was especially mind-boggling.

"So, what did you want to talk about?" he asked.

Finch's smile dimmed. "You're handling the whole 'room full of magic' thing better than I thought you would."

Gloucester spared an instant to roll his eyes. "I'm learning to just accept things and not think about them too hard. So what do you want to talk about?"

Still looking a little put out, Finch led the way to a free table and gestured for Gloucester to take a seat. The magician sat down across from him, the last traces of humor leaving his expression.

"First off, I wanted to say sorry." The words came out in an awkward rush, like he wasn't used to apologizing. "I used you to get back at Denken. I know that. And I'm sorry I hurt you. I shouldn't have done things that way. Shouldn't have involved you. So . . . yeah, sorry."

There were a lot of things Gloucester wanted to say to that. Questions that pleaded for answers while simultaneously fearing them. Snarled retorts urged on by his wounded pride and stung feelings. Anger at the mess Finch had helped make.

Stay on track. The whole reason he'd come here alone rather than waking Zane was because of specific things he wanted to ask Finch. Yet now that he was here, he couldn't bring himself to raise the subject. So instead he stuck to the safe ground of bigger issues. When had angry gods and magic become less complicated than his own emotions?

He bit the inside of his cheek. "Forget about it," he said brusquely. "What's done is done. You wanted revenge. I get it." Eyes narrowing at the disbelieving twitch of Finch's brow, Gloucester pressed on. "You didn't drag me out of bed at this hour just to clear your conscience. You said you wanted to help. So what have you got? Do you know something?"

"I know plenty of things," Finch said, defensive. The conversation clearly wasn't playing out the way he wanted it to. "You've seen what I can do, you know I can help."

Gloucester offered a slow nod. "So you want to help. That's great, but you could have just told me that over the phone. This place is . . . it's impressive. There's no denying that, but is there a point to bringing me here?"

"Beyond impressing you?" Finch joked. His grin vanished again after a beat, and he sighed. "I wanted to offer my help, yeah, but that's not all. There's something I need to tell you, and I wanted to show you this place—these people—when I did."

"Okaaaay," Gloucester hazarded. This didn't sound like it was going to be good news.

"Ever since the High Minister's Cathedral, since Denken went rogue, you've noticed how things have been in the city. How everyone is acting. Feeling. How *you're* feeling." It wasn't a question. "Frettchen's the epicenter of a sort of . . . of spiritual calamity. One that's spreading out through the whole city. Ripples of Denken's wrath and fear, you could say. If he's not stopped, they'll continue to spread, beyond the city and out into the world, until everywhere is affected. And they'll only get worse."

Gloucester grimaced. Antimony had said something similar. The so-called consequences of Denken's cosmic rule-breaking.

"But that's not all," Finch continued. Grim, he drummed blunt fingernails on the tabletop. "There have been signs. Omens. Everyone here, every magical practitioner I know of, has seen them in some shape or form. There's more than Denken's anger to contend with."

Gloucester didn't want to know, but he forced himself to ask anyway. "What else is there?"

"His madness." Finch's full-lipped mouth drew into a hard line. He must have read the impatient confusion in Gloucester's eyes because he carried on without further prompting. "You remember when we were in the Maze, all of those doors?"

Gloucester nodded. The memory of Denken's bizarre home was firmly locked in his head. Funny, he thought, considering how his first encounter with Denken had wiped itself from his recollection. Too much for his human brain to take in, Denken had later offhandedly explained. A one-off effect, as it turned out. Perhaps the human mind wasn't as weak as Denken believed, acclimating quickly with repeated exposure to things like the Brothers, what Finch and Antimony called the demigods.

"When we saw those doors, they were all closed," Finch said, pulling Gloucester from his thoughts like a fish on a hook. "But now all the seers and soothsayers are dreaming of the same thing—doors swinging open. Hundreds of them. Thousands. It's being read in the cards, glimpsed in the vapors, whispered in the winds. Everything is saying the same thing. Those doors we saw aren't closed anymore."

"So?" asked Gloucester, coldness slinking up his spine. "What was behind the doors?"

"No one knows for sure. I'm not even sure the Brothers know. The Maze is home to Thought itself, though, and I think we all know how scary thoughts can be." Gloucester must have still looked confused because Finch's eyes narrowed in impatience. "All those dreams and nightmares, all that imagination, capable of creating miracles and monsters. Thought is a powerful thing. And dangerous. For every wonderful idea someone has, how many bad ones are out there? Or in here." He tapped a finger against his temple. "How many terrible creatures can be conjured up by our wandering, morbid minds?"

"You're saying . . ." Gloucester leaned forward across the

table. "You're saying that you think it's . . . what? *Imagination* that was locked up behind those doors?"

"Something like that." Finch smiled again, but it was strained. "We won't know for sure until we face whatever it is. The signs are all reading the same, though. Something worse is on the way."

Gloucester knuckled his brow, trying to sort out his thoughts. There really ought to be some sort of law against dumping things like this on a person so late at night. It was just cruel.

"All I know is, we can face this better together. With the Gambler and his lot working to stop Denken, I reckon we have the best chance possible, and I want to help—"

"So you've said," Gloucester cut in, a touch unkindly. The late hour was catching up with him.

"—but I don't want a knife in my back for my troubles," Finch finished, carrying on like Gloucester hadn't said anything at all, though a frown cut a downturn into the corner of his mouth. "I know what I did was bad, and if people are angry, that's, you know, *fair,* but I want to know if I'm gonna have to worry about the Gambler wanting a piece of me for trying to kill his brother."

"The Gambler doesn't seem like the sort that wants a piece of anyone," Gloucester said. "Can't say you're his favorite person— or anyone's—but I don't think he'll try anything. He's got bigger problems to deal with."

"You really know how to comfort a man, don't you, Gloucester?" Finch said dryly, but he was smiling again. "Talk to the others, will you? If they hear it from you, they'll listen."

Try as he might, Gloucester couldn't find any flaw in the earnest expression on Finch's face. He told himself not to be fooled again, but no matter how he turned things over in his head, he couldn't see how Finch had anything to gain from tricking them. He lived in the world, after all; it made sense he would want to protect it, whether he felt genuinely guilty about past misdeeds or not.

"I'll do my best," he said at last. "I imagine they'll be up for hearing you out, at the very least. Though I can't promise you Zane won't tear you limb from limb on sight."

Finch shrugged, apparently unfazed by this potential threat. "Fair enough." He chuckled as he watched Gloucester stifle a yawn. "Sorry to drag you out of bed. We magicians tend to be night owls. Though to be honest, I'm not sure exactly where you were sleeping. Does that clock shop have a spare bedroom?"

"Something like that," Gloucester said. Zane seemed apologetic when she presented him with the sofa bed in the break room, but Gloucester had slept on far worse. That she had given him a place to stay at all was more than he could ever have asked for.

He got to his feet, working up the will to leave the light and warmth of the magicians' café and return to the chilly darkness of the street. At least the reward of his bed waited at the end of it. Finch caught his hand before he could step away from the table.

"Wait! Here, so you know how to reach me." Turning Gloucester's hand so his palm faced upward, he traced his finger lightly over his skin. Though he was barely touching him, Gloucester's palm tingled, and he watched as numbers appeared in the finger's wake. It was a phone number.

"This isn't going to be permanent, is it?" he asked, pulling his hand free to inspect it. The numbers had an organic, handwritten quality to them, but were legible.

Finch snorted. "Just ink. Well, more or less. Don't worry." He shook his head in mock despair. "That was a neat bit of magic right there, and look at you, completely unimpressed."

"I like to make you work for it," Gloucester said absently, still eyeing the numbers scrawled across his palm. They didn't smear or fade when he rubbed his fingertips across them.

"Oho! I do love a challenge." Finch laughed. The sound, increasingly uncommon these days, made Gloucester smile.

"I'll talk to the others and get back to you," he promised. "I'll see you around, Finch. Cassus. Sorry." With a wave, he turned away.

He was halfway to the door when Finch called out to him.

"Hey!" The magician was still seated at the table. A strangely hopeful look lit up his face. "Can I call you Mikalai, then?"

"We'll see," he called back. Then he headed back out into the night.

Chapter 3

The Path Forward

"I still can't believe you did that!"

Zane's voice, full of alarmed disapproval, turned a few heads at neighboring tables. She and Gloucester were sitting at Purpurrot's Pies, a steaming pot of breakfast tea on the table between them. Zane shook back her hair like the mane of a disgruntled lion. Her eyes, almost the same pleasant brown hue as her skin, were flashing, and though she was normally quick with a laugh, no humor warmed her expression now.

"He didn't mean any harm," Gloucester insisted quietly, eyeing their onlookers and quite relieved when they all lost interest after a few seconds. "He just wants to help."

"So you thought it would be a good idea to go swanning off into the dark streets in the wee hours of the morning? Bloody hell, Gloucester! What were you thinking? Forgetting for a moment that the last time we saw Finch he beat the hell out of you and picked a fight with an unstable god, who knows what kind of trouble you could have run into out there at night? You know what it's been like in the city lately."

Gloucester knew that Zane's anger stemmed from heartfelt concern, but he couldn't help the annoyance her relentless scolding dredged up. Lately, her concern had started to feel more confining than comforting.

"I can take care of myself," he said. He bit back the desire to remind her he wasn't some helpless child. He'd trained with the best when he was a security agent, and he could hold his own in a fight.

Zane looked like she was battling the overwhelming urge to argue, but she held her tongue. Gloucester appreciated that, at least. He knew how foolhardy it had been to go out alone the night before. He didn't owe Finch—*Cassus*, he amended, trying to get used to the name—anything, certainly not risking getting attacked or whatever else might befall a person wandering the dark streets of late.

"It all turned out all right, didn't it?" he pointed out, knowing full well it was a weak defense. "We don't have to trust him, but his help could be really useful. We've seen his magic at work. It's a powerful weapon. Plus, he's well-connected in the, uh, the magical community? Seems that way, at least."

"He's not the only one." Antimony Jones appeared beside their table and slid onto the bench seat beside Zane. "We're talking about Mr. Finch, I assume? Zane told me about your late-night escapade with him." She offered him the tiniest of lopsided smiles. Coming from her, it equated to a wide, teasing grin. The faint warmth of a blush rose in Gloucester's cheeks.

Antimony showed no sign of noticing. Taller than both Gloucester and Zane, she was a willowy blonde somewhere in her early thirties. Her long hair was pinned into a bun, and combined with her pristine white dress, it made her look like she belonged in one of the business district skyscrapers, not in a pie shop in Uptown.

"According to Zane, Finch told you that the magic-wielders

of the city are sensing something on the way, right? Worse than the murders and other attacks?" she asked. Gloucester nodded, and she mirrored the motion. "It coincides with what I've heard. The oracle Orange Ianto told me much the same."

"Oracle?"

Gloucester was ignored. Antimony waved at a waitress to get her attention, then continued. "Still, even if his warning isn't exactly news, he could still be useful to have on our side."

Zane gawped. "Seriously? After everything he did? He—"

Antimony shook her head, politely cutting off Zane's protest. "I'm not denying he's dangerous. Or even that he's an idiot. He is powerful, though, and we need all the help we can get. Two weeks and we're still no closer to finding Denken. We need to end this before it's too late. Hi there, Murphy."

This last was said to the waitress who had just stopped beside their booth. Gloucester recognized her as Antimony's housemate. He'd only met Murphy briefly a few weeks before, yet she offered him as warm a smile as the one she gave Antimony and Zane.

"Hey, Antimony. Hi, Zane, Mr. Gloucester. How are you all today?" Even friendly as she was, a strained edge lined the question. It was a hard one to ask lately.

"Well as we can be," Antimony answered, not missing a beat with her usual coy approach to things. "Do you know if Purpurrot is around today?"

Murphy nodded, her chestnut hair bobbing around her chin. "She is, yeah. Last I saw, she was talking to Blei in the kitchen. Can I send along a message for you?"

"I need to talk to her if she has the time. Please tell her it's quite urgent."

Perhaps such a request from Antimony wasn't unheard of, because Murphy didn't question it, nor did she hesitate before agreeing and heading back toward the kitchens.

"How's the owner of a pie shop supposed to help?" Gloucester asked.

To his annoyance, this perfectly reasonable question was met with shared amusement from his companions. Antimony raised a hand to her lips to cover a smile, and Zane let loose a giggle that earned her a scandalized frown from Gloucester. Considering she'd been giving him a piece of her mind all morning, he wasn't very appreciative of her upswing in mood at his expense.

"What?" he demanded. "What's so funny?"

"Sorry," said Zane, visibly holding in more giggles. "Sometimes I just forget that you don't know these things. About magic and gods and the like."

Despite her mirth, she was trying for an apologetic expression. Gloucester held his grimace in place a moment longer for his dignity's sake, then relented.

"So this Purpurrot person's involved in magic too?" He was starting to wonder if he had been the only person in all of Frettchen oblivious to the existence of magic. "Is she a magician like Finch?"

Again it seemed he'd said something wonderfully droll. Antimony was no longer even trying to hide her smile, and Zane was grinning broadly as she shook her head.

"Definitely not like Finch," she said.

"She's a bit of a step above him," Antimony chimed in. Her smile was sympathetic, at least. "You'll see."

—

A few minutes passed with neither woman elaborating beyond that. Zane assured him that any explanation she gave would go on longer than it would take for this Purpurrot to appear, while Antimony merely worked her way through a slice of rhubarb pie in comfortable silence. Gloucester knew better than to push either one for answers: Zane would get annoyed, and Antimony would simply dodge any question he aimed her way. It seemed to be less trouble just to wait and see for himself.

Patience had once been a virtue of his. He'd always had a

talent for sitting quietly on the edges, watching and waiting. It took him a long time to get bored, and even then he'd been excellent at hiding it.

Solitary confinement had left its mark on that part of him too. While he could still force patience when needed, it wasn't as effortless as it had once been. As they waited for the pie shop proprietor to appear, his fingers tapped a silent rhythm against the tabletop.

He was staring aimlessly out the window when movement to his left claimed his attention, and Gloucester saw Purpurrot for the first time.

She glided through the morning crowds like a ship coming into harbor. Though she wasn't broad, she towered a head or more over her patrons, who all seemed to subconsciously move out of her way as she approached, parting before her. With her rich brown skin and ebony hair, she had the appearance of someone from the South Cities, especially clothed as she was in the region's silks. The cloth was dyed a deep violet and embroidered in gold. She was beautiful but in a quietly ferocious way. The beauty of a wild animal, not a flower. She was impossible to look away from, and Gloucester stared as she drew closer.

"Antimony," she said, stopping beside their table. "You wanted to see me."

Her voice had a strange cadence, a kind of melody, and it took Gloucester a moment to make the connection: she sounded like the Brothers. Denken and the Gambler had very different voices, but they both shared an unearthly quality that this woman possessed as well. Gloucester knew if he closed his eyes he would hear all sorts of things in her words beyond their meanings. The creak of trees, the crash of waves, the crumbling of stone, the singing of birds, and, more than anything, wild, turbulent music.

She's one of them.

"Zane, long time no see," she said, now turning to the

clockmaker with a smile before her dark eyes settled on Gloucester. "And this must be the one you told me about, Antimony. It's nice to meet you at last, Mikalai Gloucester." Her long hair, more loosely curled than Zane's, billowed around her shoulders as she cocked her head to the side, regarding him curiously.

Gloucester didn't meet her eyes for longer than it took to nod and murmur a greeting. Beyond the reeling revelation of another demigod, he'd never been fond of keen looks like the one she was leveling his way. It made him feel like he was being weighed and measured. Judged for usefulness or examined for weakness. When she finally moved her gaze back to Antimony, a weight lifted from his shoulders.

"It doesn't take a mind reader to know this is about Denken," Purpurrot said, making a noise at the back of her throat that might have been a laugh at her irony. "It seems as good a time as any to update each other on what we know."

She sat down at the end of the table, on a chair Gloucester didn't remember being there an instant earlier.

"What do you know about these omens the seers and magicians are talking about?" Antimony asked without preamble.

Purpurrot's sigh thrummed like the strings of a cello. "Orange Ianto's mentioned them to me too. And the Gambler, though his Sight has been marred by Denken's influence. The futures are muddled now, even for him. It's been driving him mad."

She seemed to sense Gloucester's confusion before he even had time to register feeling it. She smiled at him benevolently as she explained. "It's difficult for the Gambler. His powers do not extend to matters of his kin. None of their powers do. He cannot foresee the danger in the same way he would were the source human. It leaves him, *ha,* blind, as it were." She made the amused sound again.

"What about you?" asked Antimony. "What about your

powers?"

Purpurrot's expression shuttered, her eyes narrowing beneath long black lashes. They were an odd color, the irises an unnatural hue that changed with the light from periwinkle to dark violet. Gloucester found himself avoiding her gaze even more than he did those of other people. Something lurked in those eyes, a shadow in deep water.

"My powers are not what they were. Not for a long time now. You know that, Antimony." The hint of a warning darkened her words.

Antimony pressed the matter no further. Instead, she inquired, "Still no sign of Angus?"

"Who?" asked Gloucester. It was difficult not to get frustrated when Antimony and the others kept throwing names around like this.

"Denken and the Gambler's other brother," Zane explained in a whisper.

"What's he the personification of?" Gloucester asked, lowering his voice as well. Zane only hushed him as Purpurrot continued.

"Angus rarely strays from his Pocket when duty does not demand it anymore," she said. "The Gambler has been so busy searching for Denken that he hasn't put much thought toward anything else, and he is the only one now who could find Angus if he doesn't want to be found. Perhaps he doesn't yet know." She shrugged, her smile humorless. "Angus doesn't care much for Frettchen or Denken. He avoids both when he can. Maybe he hasn't yet noticed anything awry."

"Surely he would have noticed the Gambler missing for a whole year," Zane interjected. Though her voice held its usual level of confidence, Gloucester noticed she too was avoiding eye contact with Purpurrot's gleaming gaze.

The demigoddess hummed noncommittally. "A good question to raise if he shows his face."

Magical family politics sounded as complicated as human

ones. Combine that with an eternity of existence and Gloucester reckoned he'd identified the source of all their apparent lunacy. He imagined the three demigods he'd met all sitting down for a meal, like a normal family, talking about their respective days and complaining about the weather. It left him with the fleeting urge to laugh, which he hastily smothered. Now definitely wasn't the time.

"So what about these visions Finch mentioned?" he prompted, eager to steer the conversation back into territory that, while far from familiar, he could at least contribute to. "About all the doors in the Maze opening and releasing whatever was on the other side. Do you think he's right? Has something escaped?"

Any hopes that Purpurrot would scoff and deny this horrifying eventuality were promptly dashed. "It seems likely. Denken is the guardian of the Maze. With him out of control and loose in the world, no one is there to guard those doors." She propped her chin on a delicate hand and sighed. "The last I saw of the Gambler was several days ago. He was going to search the Maze. He'll be able to tell us for certain what's happening there."

"Several days ago?" repeated Gloucester, perplexed. The last thing they needed was to lose the Gambler again too. "Shouldn't he be back by now? And why didn't he check there first, right after Denken disappeared?"

"It's not so easy for the Brothers to go nosing around in each other's space," Antimony told him. "If they're not invited, it can be almost as difficult for them to get into each other's Pocket as it would be for us humans. The Gambler's been working to get into the Maze ever since the high minister's death."

"Oh," said Gloucester, mollified. "Er . . . all right then. Good."

"It was a fair question," Zane said, patting his hand. "You weren't to know."

Gloucester appreciated the sentiment, but he felt all the more foolish, like a child who needed everything explained to him. It was an irritating symptom of always being the least-informed person in the room when it came to . . . well, *any* of this. He missed his old life when there were at least a few things he'd been confident about.

"Do you have any idea what might have been behind the doors?" he asked Purpurrot.

"Some," she answered. For a long moment after, she was silent. Gloucester was on the verge of snapping when finally she spoke again. Her voice was measured, and he realized that she'd been thinking over the question, not being purposefully enigmatic. "In a word, imagination. In two, human creativity."

"Finch said something similar. Raw imagination, he called it. All the best and worst humanity can create."

"He's not wrong. He might not seem like the sort when you're face to face with him, but Denken's always carried the weight of a mighty responsibility on his shoulders. The safeguard against the darkness of humanity's collective mind."

"Which explains why he's bloody nuts," Zane muttered under her breath.

Gloucester had to agree. An eternity of keeping the nightmares of an entire world at bay would surely drive anyone mad, let alone a powerful, mind-reading demigod with the attention span of a toddler.

"So, if this . . . this imagination is coming, how do we stop it? What's it even going to *be?*"

What would raw imagination look like? How could such an abstract concept take concrete form? Would it? Or would it strike in the minds of Frettchen's citizens, like Denken's rage and fear were already doing, invading people's thoughts and turning them against one another?

"Good question," Purpurrot said, a little too lackadaisically for Gloucester's taste. "It's impossible to say until we come up against it. Or them. There are thousands of doors, after all. Stands to reason that would mean thousands of . . . things." She blinked owlishly at their unimpressed expressions. "What?"

"Please try to be a little more concerned about this, Purpa," Antimony said, settling her chin on her fist, elbow braced on the tabletop. Gloucester exchanged a glance with Zane. When Antimony Jones was telling you to ease up on the unaffected demeanor, you knew you had issues.

Purpurrot, however, offered only the faintest of apologetic smiles. "I'm sure we'll find out what forms the imagination will take before long."

"Er," said Zane. She was staring out the nearest window. "Sooner than we were expecting, I think."

Gloucester turned his head to follow her alarmed stare. They had a good view of the street outside from their booth. Normally it would be a peaceful scene on the other side of the glass, full of pedestrians wandering from shop to shop and a steady stream of traffic threading past. The pie shop was in Uptown, one of the higher-end parts of Frettchen's shopping district, filled with well-maintained streets and trendy shops. The area attracted crowds of all ages, from students seeking an escape from their studies to the elderly reading on benches in the shade of flowering trees.

There was nothing peaceful to be seen now.

The street clamored with screams as people crowded onto the sidewalks. Though they were all headed in one direction, their frightened gazes were locked over their shoulders, like they were being chased. A weight dropped in Gloucester's stomach.

"They're running from something," he said, lunging to his feet before the words were out of his mouth.

Zane was already out of her chair and dashing to the window. "There's some sort of light coming from the east end of the street," she told the others, craning her neck as she pressed her face against the glass, trying to get a better look. "Something must be on fire!"

"People don't usually run from a fire once they're out of it," Antimony observed, joining Zane and Gloucester by the window. Her knitted brow was the only sign of her concern.

"Not like this."

"Come on." Gloucester made a beeline for the door. "We have to check it out. It could be one of the—the, you know, the imagination monsters. Or whatever," he added, conscious of how stupid that sounded.

"Even if it's not, it could be another attack," Zane said, a step behind him. "Some poor bastard driven mad by Denken's whole thing."

Gloucester didn't waste time looking back as he and Zane reached the door, but just as he was pushing it open, he heard Purpurrot's beautiful voice, shaded with amusement. "They're a brave pair, that's for certain."

As they hurried into the panicked street, shoving their way as best they could against the flow of the crowd, Gloucester's thoughts lingered on the demigoddess in her pie shop. He wasn't quite sure what to make of Purpurrot. Antimony seemed to trust her, but he couldn't shake the memory of her apathetic voice, unfazed by everything happening in Frettchen. Surrounded as they were by fear and confusion, that disinterest was disconcerting. Maybe immortality drove everyone mad in different ways, he thought, as he and Zane raced toward the commotion at the end of the street.

The sight that awaited them was something from a nightmare. Searing flames bled skyward from the shattered windows of an old three-story building. The signs outside, orange in the firelight, proclaimed it to be a coffeehouse, with a stationery shop on the floors above. No doubt filled to the brim with flammable materials. The heat was so intense that it felt like running into a wall. Gloucester and Zane drew closer, squinting against the smoke and blinding light.

"Where's the fire brigade?" Zane yelled over the noise of the inferno. "A fire this big, they should be here by—*What the hell?*"

Her eyes had gone wide and her face bloodless in horror as she stared into the flames. Gloucester followed the line of her vision and reared back. Something was *moving* in the fire.

Something huge.

It rose up within the walls of the burning shops, its silhouette visible through the many windows, not blocking the firelight but made *from* it, a being of solid flame. The roaring of the fire suddenly seemed a lot more unnatural.

Gloucester gaped, mind skittering between shocked speechlessness and frantic, half-formed planning. "How do we fight *that?*"

"World's biggest bucket chain?" quipped Zane. Panic laced her humor with raw unsteadiness. "I have no bloody idea! But if we don't stop it, it'll burn down the whole neighborhood!"

Gloucester fumbled for his phone, eyes glued to the sight of the fire-beast. He dragged them away just long enough to punch in the number still scrawled across his palm.

Finch picked up on the second ring, but Gloucester didn't even give him the chance for a greeting. "I need your help. East end of Uptown. If you know any magic for dealing with fire, now's the time."

To his credit, Finch didn't dawdle asking questions. Silence carried over the line for the briefest of moments, then he said, "Got it. Uptown. I'll find you," and hung up.

—

The fire had spread to the neighboring buildings by the time Finch arrived less than five minutes later. He appeared seemingly out of nowhere, though whether by magical means or simply on foot, Gloucester couldn't say. Either way, he burst from the gathering crowd and hastened to Gloucester's side, barely sparing Zane a glance before nodding to Gloucester and staring up at the fire.

Flames billowed from all the windows, and a roasting wind rushed over them, even from their careful distance. Inside the epicenter of the destruction, they could still see the massive creature's fiery form. Finch stood motionless, watching its movements through the burning walls.

Then he swore. "Well, that's a problem."

Zane made a sharp noise like a scoff's louder, more histrionic sibling. "I'm glad we brought *you* in to point that out. Dead helpful, you are!"

Gloucester was caught between wanting to tell her off for the untimely aggression and voicing his agreement. Swallowing his impatience, he asked, "What *is* it? Do you know?"

It was Finch who scoffed this time. "No idea. Not specifically, at least. I'd place a sound bet on it being something from behind the doors, though."

Zane threw up her hands. "Thanks, sort of figured that bit out already."

"Patience, love," Finch told her, not quite managing to pull off the roguish grin he fired her way. His eyes lingered on the fire-beast. "Anyway, I don't exactly see you racing into the inferno to battle it."

He wrung his hands as he spoke. At first, Gloucester thought it an understandable case of nerves, but he soon realized it was nothing of the sort; he could feel the hum of magical energy building up in the air. If Zane noticed it too, it didn't stop her from snapping a retort.

"Course I haven't! What am I gonna do about it? Throw clocks at its head? Give it a piece of my mind? I'm not an idiot, Finch. I know when I'm up against something more powerful than I am."

"Lucky for us, that makes one of us," Finch said with the same forced lightness, as he stepped toward the burning building.

Chapter 4

Fire

The fire howled like a living, breathing thing. Perhaps the sound wasn't the flames, but the creature inside the inferno bellowing its fury. Gloucester raised an arm to shield his face against the waves of heat rolling across the street. The fire brigade had finally arrived, and though he could see the fear in their faces, they were doing what they could to stop the fire from spreading further down the street. It was obvious that they were avoiding the main building, where dwelt the beast at the heart of the fire. Gloucester couldn't hold that against them. They were brave enough to attempt their job in the face of a nightmare. What more could anyone ask of them?

What Finch was asking of *him*. He gritted his teeth as the magician—his hands glowing with a swirling, ghostly light—beckoned for him and Zane to follow as he drew closer to the fire. Common sense demanded he do the opposite. Gloucester's brain screamed at him to *run*, to be anywhere but here.

Maybe one day I'll learn to listen.

He wasn't sure what good he and Zane would be in a fight against whatever was inside the burning building. At least Finch had his magic. That felt like a weapon. Gloucester thought longingly of his gun, stowed safely away at the clock shop. Useless. Then again, what good would bullets be against a monster like this? Would *magic* even be enough to fight it?

"Trust me!" Finch called back to him as if reading his mind. He bit back a reply and forced himself to stride forward at Finch's flank.

Something very strange was happening to his ears. The roar of the fire and the hubbub of the frightened masses had both fallen quiet. The noise wasn't silenced, per se, but rather turned abruptly and significantly down. More than that, it seemed bizarrely slowed, like time itself had been caught in amber.

Gloucester looked around in bafflement. It wasn't his hearing that had gone wrong; the crowded street had ground to a near halt in a most unusual manner. People shouted and pointed in distress, but with sluggish movements like old footage played too slowly and quietly. A few feet to his left, Zane looked equally boggled. Even Finch halted his determined march to blink around in consternation.

"I'd appreciate it if you didn't take too long," said an orchestral voice behind them. "This isn't exactly easy."

Gloucester turned. Purpurrot stood at the edge of the crowd, dark hair tumbling around her shoulders and eyes fixed on the towering flames. Her hands were raised, long fingers splayed wide. Beside her, Antimony squinted in the bright firelight, grimacing up at the destruction.

Finch barked a laugh. "Demigods. Always complaining about how hard their lives are," he said, no longer needing to raise his voice to be heard. "Bloody typical."

"Mind your manners, magician," Purpurrot replied, and for the first time Gloucester heard an edge of displeasure in her voice. "And do your job."

If Finch made a rebuke, it was mumbled too lowly to be heard. He turned his back on Purpurrot, magic gathering more visibly around his hands as he resumed his approach. The flames were no longer spreading, slowed like the crowd of onlookers.

"We'll do what we can out here," Antimony called. "Good luck. And if you need to, run."

"That's not very heroic," Zane called back to her, trying hard to sound brash and unafraid.

"Not much use in dead heroes," Antimony said. Gloucester thought he saw fear in her expression too, but an instant later she looked as collected as ever. Putting it out of his mind, he started after Finch again, who was now almost at the door of the burning building.

"Here's to not dying," he muttered to himself.

—

It grew more difficult to breathe the closer they got, and by the time they reached the coffeehouse's door, Gloucester was wondering how they were supposed to survive long enough to confront the beast inside. Paint peeled from the wood of the door in the heat. Surely they would all suffocate before they even had a chance to get burned. His sleeve went over his nose and mouth, his eyes streaming from the smoke. Beside him, Zane was in a similar state.

Finch, on the other hand, appeared unaffected. He drew a deep breath entirely unhindered by smoke, then looked back at them and blinked in surprise. "Oh, right. Sorry about that. Sort of not used to working with people who can't work protection spells."

Zane looked like she would have something to say if she dared lift her sleeve from her face, but Finch paid her no mind.

"Here," he said and laid a hand on each of their shoulders.

A cool wind washed over Gloucester, chasing away the heat of the fire and the smoke burning his eyes and lungs. He coughed to clear the latter and found he was now able to breathe normally. He could still feel the heat and smell the smoke, but the effects of both were distant and harmless.

"There," Finch said with satisfaction. "You should be fine, long as you don't roll around in any fire directly. And the smoke will get to us eventually, so best not to waste—"

Anything further was cut off by a roar too guttural and wild to be natural. Gloucester squinted through the smoke and crumbling brick at the creature awaiting them.

"Yeah," he said faintly. "Let's hope this doesn't take too long."

"No time like the present," quipped Finch. He was either very brave or very good at faking it. Then again, in Gloucester's experience, the two went hand in hand.

Taking deep breaths that no longer clogged their lungs with smoke, they stepped through the doorway.

"Keep on the lookout for falling debris," Finch called over his shoulder.

"Yeah," agreed Zane. "I'll do that in between fighting the hell-beast from the mindscape. Bloody hell, we're all gonna die."

"We will with that attitude," Finch retorted, an unintentionally perfect imitation of Gloucester's mother. "Just do as I say and follow my lead. We'll be fine."

Gloucester wished he could share Finch's cocksure certainty. *I must at least share his idiocy,* he thought, resigned, as he gave a terse nod and followed the magician into the inferno.

Their quarry wasn't difficult to find. The inside of the coffee shop had been gutted, tables smashed and thrown against the walls. Shelves and displays from the upper floors had crashed down through the decimated ceilings, their contents burned beyond recognition. The floor was a treacherous mess of broken furniture and smoldering stationery. People's livelihoods clawed away by fire and monstrous talons. The barest jolt of amazement that the walls were even still standing passed through Gloucester's mind, but then he got his first proper look at the creature and all thought fell away.

It was a dragon. Or at the very least, it matched what Gloucester thought a dragon ought to look like. Long-necked and lizard-like, it was coiled in the center of the room on a massive pile of fiery debris, its mighty head angled toward them. Unlike how he'd always pictured dragons, however, it wasn't breathing fire. It was entirely made of it. From its flared nostrils to the tip of its scaly tail, it was composed of orange and red flame, burning white-hot at its core. Despite this, it looked distressingly solid.

It immediately brought to mind the giant shark made of shadows Gloucester had seen Denken conjure up when he was angry—his rage made into a semi-solid and terrifying form. Like the dragon, it seemed to carry the weight of a corporeal creature despite being composed of something as intangible as darkness. Any doubts he might have had that this monster belonged to the personification of Thought vanished.

Zane swore next to him, but he didn't bother looking her way; her attention was surely as locked on their enemy as his own.

"I don't know what I was expecting," said Finch. His light tone wasn't all that convincing. More than scared, however, he sounded thoughtful.

"Can you fight it?" Gloucester hissed. He clenched his hands into fists, half-raising them even as it occurred to him how stupid that was. He would never be able to beat a dragon that *wasn't* made of fire with his bare hands, let alone one that was.

What has my life become? This thought was quickly followed by the realization that those could very well be his last words, even if only to himself. In the back of his mind, the oddly calm voice that often appears in the heart of panic cast about for better ones.

"We can try," Finch said. He raised his own hands. Light still engulfed them, now a yellow so bright as to be almost white. It swirled around his fingers and wrists like darting, twisting snakes.

The dragon's head moved. It had ceased its roaring when they came in, and Gloucester wondered if they'd managed to surprise it or if it was simply waiting to see what they would do. It watched the movements of Finch's hands with one giant, unblinking eye.

Finch spoke a series of words in a language Gloucester didn't recognize and swept his hands in front of him. The light careened toward the dragon's face. The beast reared back, but it was either too slow or too large to get out of the way in time, and the magic struck it in the jaw.

A great billow of steam issued from where the spell hit its mark like a large bucket of water had been thrown against the dragon's fiery hide. An angry hiss arose.

"Well, that's encouraging," Gloucester heard Finch say over the dragon's ensuing fury. The magician backed up several paces, never taking his eyes off the dragon. He stopped between Gloucester and Zane. "I have a plan," he told them as quietly as he could in the din of destruction. "But I'm gonna need your help."

"Anything," Gloucester said promptly. They didn't have time to waste fretting about trust. Even Zane nodded without hesitation.

"Right then. Touch me," Finch ordered.

"What?" sputtered Zane.

Finch groaned, impatient. "*Touch me.* On the shoulder, the arm, wherever. I need to siphon magic into you."

As explanations went, this wasn't the most reassuring. Siphon magic *into* them? How was that supposed to work? Trying not to question what he was doing, Gloucester reached out and laid a hand on Finch's shoulder. On Finch's other side, Zane paused for only a moment before doing the same. In front of them, the dragon still growled its displeasure, clawing at its injured face.

As soon as Gloucester's hand touched the rough wool of Finch's coat, he felt the effect of the magic. It was like electricity, sweeping up his arm from his fingertips, neither tingling nor burning, but rather some sensation in between. Perhaps electricity wasn't the right comparison, but if not, then he wasn't sure what was. It didn't feel like anything he'd experienced before, and he fought the urge to leap back and break the contact. Instead, he tightened his grip and held on. At Finch's other shoulder, Zane was whispering a litany of colorful oaths.

"On my signal, let go and throw it all at the beastie," Finch instructed through gritted teeth.

"All what?" Gloucester asked. The sensation of magic was overpowering, making it difficult to think. He wasn't sure if he was whispering or yelling at the top of his lungs. The dragon roared, abandoning its injury and wheeling back to face them. It raised a clawed forefoot, ready to swipe them away like unwanted pests.

"The magic!" Finch shouted back. "Throw it *now!*"

He swept his own hands forward, and his companions, at a loss for what to do, let go of his shoulders and did the same, imitating his movements. Finch cried out the unintelligible words again, and Gloucester could *feel* them as they pulled the gathered magic from his body. Just as it had flooded into him, it was channeled once more through his arms, the opposite way this time, coursing through his muscles and bones to blast out of his hands toward the dragon. He heard an alarmed cry and didn't know if it came from Zane or himself.

The light of the magic was an eye-searing blue, so vivid Gloucester could still see it after he squeezed his watering eyes shut. Spots of color danced across his retinas. The dragon roared, and Gloucester cracked his eyes open to see it stagger backward, collapsing a wall as it writhed in pain.

"Do we have to kill it?" shouted Zane, her voice ragged. Gloucester was amazed he could even hear her over the ringing in his ears. "Can we send it back somehow?"

Finch laughed, loud and wild. "I'm not an expert in this, Zane. *No one's* an expert in this. You think I know what I'm doing? Hit it again! Gloucester, you're the stronger channeler—aim for its eyes, *now!*"

The buzz of magic still swirling through him, Gloucester swept his arms in the indicated direction. Under less dire circumstances, he would have felt stupid gesticulating like some mad conductor who had forgotten his baton.

Yet again, a great surge of magic rushed through him, and he gasped. He hadn't expected that much to be left. Perhaps a connection had been forged by the touch of his hand on Finch's shoulder, one that was maintained even after he let go.

Less thinking, more fighting! he told himself with a sort of hysterical sternness.

His singular attack on the dragon's eyes struck home. The dragon reared back onto its haunches and clawed once more at its face, which was so thickly engulfed in steam that it looked like its head had gotten stuck in a giant cotton ball.

In its panic, it exposed its underbelly. Finch, shouting directions to Zane, wasted no time before targeting the opening in the beast's defenses. Another blinding flash of light struck the dragon squarely in the chest, and it fell back with a crash.

Victory seemed near at hand. Unfortunately, the dragon's distress was making it flail, its fiery limbs wreaking wanton destruction. At this rate, it wouldn't matter what fireproofing spells Finch had cast on them, not if the ceiling collapsed on their heads.

The dragon's tail swept through the air like a burning battering ram. Gloucester ducked and felt the heat of it whiz over him, passing through the air where his head had been a second earlier.

A scream rang in his ears. Gloucester scrambled up to a crouch in time to see Finch and Zane tumble across the floor.

"Zane!" he shouted, bounding to his feet and racing over to them. "Cassus!"

"I'm okay," coughed Zane, wincing as she tried to get up. Her sweater was smoldering, but she appeared otherwise unharmed. "I think I'd be charcoal if it wasn't for that spell making us fireproof, though."

Finch was slower to recover. His sense of humor was the first thing he regained, however, and he offered Gloucester a dazed grin. "You called me Cassus," he said amidst a fit of coughing. He groaned, one arm wrapped around his ribs as he struggled to sit up.

"Are you okay?" Gloucester asked.

"I'll manage," Finch wheezed. He latched onto Gloucester's shoulder and levered himself up into a sitting position, staring past him at the dragon. "Looks like I'm not the worst off."

"Is it dying?" Zane asked, her face pinched in dismay. She caught Gloucester's expression and squared her shoulders. "It's not evil. I don't think, at least. It's just an animal."

"It's a figment of imagination," Finch cut in, still coughing and wincing. "And whether it's dying or not, we're next if we don't get out of here."

He was right. Vestiges of the ceiling creaked ominously overhead, and the heat grew more oppressive with each passing minute. *Finch's spell must be wearing off,* Gloucester thought, because the smoke was also starting to burn his eyes and lungs again. He stifled a coughing fit of his own, trying not to breathe too deeply. Magic or not, they'd all fall victim to the fire if they lingered much longer.

"If it's still alive after this, we'll deal with it then," he said, words muffled by a sleeve over his mouth. Zane, too, was covering her face to keep the smoke out of her lungs, one hand clamped over her mouth and nose. Her eyes were bloodshot. "Let's get out of here."

Gloucester hauled Finch to his feet, pulling one of his arms across his shoulders for support. Finch was still lucid, but he leaned heavily on Gloucester as they staggered toward the door, Zane leading the way. Gloucester couldn't help but wonder whether Finch's fireproofing spell had also been keeping the fire itself at a distance, as the flames filling the coffeehouse now encroached upon them in a much more urgent way than before. A dangerously loud series of cracks issued from the splintering ceiling beams. As they neared the door, another wall crashed down, laden with colorful mugs and a once-cheery blackboard menu.

"Run!" Zane shouted, the word nearly lost in a cough.

They dashed for the doorway, Gloucester beleaguered under Finch's weight but too desperate to even notice the burden. They burst into the sunlight of the outdoors but didn't slow down, wanting to get as far away from the collapsing building as possible.

They were barely halfway across the open ground between the fire and the crowd when the building finally gave up the ghost. In a great gust of smoke and heat, the last remains of the walls and roof caved in, crashing in on themselves in a deafening collapse. Gloucester, Finch, and Zane threw themselves to the ground, the act half done for them by the expanding force of the destruction. Gloucester collided with the street, heat at his back, and everything went dark.

Chapter 5

Ashes

For an indeterminate amount of time—seconds or years; in his daze, Gloucester couldn't tell—the world ceased to be anything more than the ringing in his ears and the rough texture of the pavement underneath him. His face stung, as did his palms, arms, and knees, where he'd skidded when he landed. All told it was a small price to pay for not turning into a human barbecue.

He suppressed a wince as he rolled onto his back, gasping for breath. The air was gray with ash, dust, and debris from the explosion mingling with the choking clouds of smoke from the fire. As he blinked blearily around, Gloucester watched the fire brigade descend on the shop's burning remains. Other than that, it was difficult to tell what was going on. Purpurrot's spell had broken, and chaos reigned amidst the smoke and steam.

Flopping onto his side in a dizzy attempt to get up, Gloucester collided with another form. The rough wool coat was immediately recognizable.

"Finch?"

The other man wasn't moving. Gloucester rolled him onto his back, where he lay, face smoke-stained and eyes closed.

"Cassus!" Gloucester ducked his head to Finch's chest, listening for a heartbeat.

There was one, beating steadily. He was just unconscious. Gloucester sat back, relieved. Underneath the grime from the fire, several cuts adorned Finch's face, and Gloucester guessed he would soon have a sizable goose egg or two. But there were no signs of serious injury beyond his lack of consciousness.

Zane stumbled over. "Is he all right?" She sunk to her knees beside them, trying unsuccessfully to clear the smoke from her lungs.

"I dunno," Gloucester answered. His voice, like hers, was raw, passing painfully through his throat on its way to his tongue. "I hope so."

He nearly jumped out of his skin when someone laid a hand on his shoulder. Looking up, he met the slightly reddened eyes of Antimony.

"We need to get out of here," she said. There were smudges of soot on her pale cheeks and brow, but otherwise, she was unscathed. Behind her, Purpurrot loomed over them all. "The police are already here, and we don't have long before they realize it's us they really want to talk to."

"The high minister—I mean, the lord of the city-state's security team will be here soon too," Gloucester said, lumbering to his feet as he heaved Finch's unconscious body over his shoulder. It still felt bizarre to remember that Toby Mulligan was in charge of the city's secular affairs now, as well as the security force of which Gloucester himself had once been a part. Mulligan was a clever man, though, and Gloucester had no doubt that the moment news of this unnatural fire reached him, he would make the connection to Denken and come in search of answers. Gloucester wasn't keen on being hounded for information, especially when he was still desperately trying to figure it all out himself. And frankly, he would be happy to go the rest of his life without ever hearing from Mulligan again.

"Let me help with that," said Purpurrot. She glided forward, and before he could argue, she pulled Finch from his grasp and hefted him onto her shoulder as though he weighed nothing at all. Gloucester panted his thanks.

"What about the dragon?" he asked, pointing back at the charred husk of the coffee shop. Purpurrot and Antimony blinked in unison.

"Dragon?" the scientist repeated. "Is that what it was?"

"Fascinating," murmured Purpurrot, eyeing the wreckage with investigative interest. Except . . ."I don't think the beast is a threat anymore."

Gloucester followed her gaze. The fire no longer roared with the same unnatural fury, and he could find no sign of movement beyond the completely mundane flames.

"So it's dead?" Gloucester asked, raising a hand to shield his eyes and squinting. "I can't see it. Would it just vanish if it died?"

"No idea," Purpurrot answered. She had the decency to at least look a little apologetic. "Maybe it's dead, maybe it just went back to the Maze, tail between its legs. All I can tell is that it's not here anymore. And neither should we be."

They hurried from the scene, trying to look inconspicuous. Easier said than done when one of them was a seven-foot beauty carrying an unconscious man like a sack of potatoes. The rest of them were earning stares too. Gloucester wondered how it seemed to the time-slowed crowd, to watch them run into the burning building. Regardless, many people had seen them run *out* of the flames. A murmur passed through the crowd, like a wind rustling the canopy of a forest. Gloucester did his best to ignore it, but he felt the weight of a hundred eyes on him.

"If only Finch were awake," grumbled Zane, casting her own eyes around uneasily. "He could, I dunno, make us invisible or unnoticeable or something. Like Denken did back at the church. Useless bastard." There wasn't quite as much venom in her insult this time. Gloucester guessed the fight with the dragon was still very much at the forefront of her mind. Finch had been far from useless.

"I'll do what I can," Purpurrot said over her shoulder, sounding surprisingly miffed. Gloucester remembered the curtness that had entered her tone back in the pie shop when Antimony asked about her powers. Was she self-conscious about them? Looking at her, it was hard to imagine her being self-conscious about *anything*. Yet she'd said that her powers were weaker than they'd once been. Perhaps that rustiness was a sore spot.

Shifting Finch's limp weight more comfortably over her shoulder, she let go of him with one hand and swept her arm in a wide gesture.

A strong, stirring breeze rushed over the crowd, tugging at coattails and ruffling hair. As it gusted over them, it seemed to take something with it; each person who had been staring at them blinked and looked away, apparently forgetting they were there at all. Denken had done something similar back at All Saints Shrine, as Zane had just described. He had been able to make them all blend in, altering onlookers' perceptions just enough to make them think nothing was amiss. Whether Purpurrot was doing the same thing now was hard to say, but it certainly felt in the same vein.

Either way, it was working. They passed through the throng of people without so much as a second glance. They headed back toward the pie shop, with Zane, Antimony, and Gloucester hurrying to keep up with Purpurrot's long stride. She had a commanding gait and, like Antimony, she walked with a graceful sway of her hips. Together they looked like a pair of particularly impatient runway models.

In contrast, Gloucester and Zane moved with increasing unsteadiness. By the time they reached the front door of

Purpurrot's Pies, the effects of Finch's protection spell had faded completely and they were coughing again, throats raw from the smoke they'd inhaled before it was cast. Once they were inside, Zane collapsed gratefully onto the nearest chair.

The shop was now devoid of customers, leading Gloucester to assume Purpurrot had cleared them all out before she left to join the fray. He was as grateful for that as Zane was for the chance to sit down. He'd had enough of staring faces for one day.

"You know," he said after a few minutes of silence, wherein he'd been trying to catch his breath, "I've never fought a dragon before, but that wasn't as bad as I would've expected."

Purpurrot looked at him from where she stood over Finch's body and smiled. She'd laid the magician down on the bench seat of a booth and had two fingers pressed to his left temple, against the sun-shaped tattoo that disappeared into his hairline.

"That was just the first. A creature of thought, unaccustomed to this world. It wasn't at its full strength. Unless we can find Denken and close the doors in the Maze, the beasts will keep coming, each one stronger than the last." She noticed the looks on their faces and added, "You all did very well, though."

"Thanks." Zane sighed, leaning back in her seat and pushing her hair from her face with both hands. "Something to look forward to—bigger and scarier monsters."

"I didn't say bigger, just stronger. Though definitely scarier," Purpurrot said lightly, taking her fingers away from Finch's temple.

"Not helpful, Purpa," Antimony said. She nodded at Finch. "How is he?"

"He'll be fine," Purpurrot replied. The strength of the relief that swept through Gloucester surprised him. It seemed suddenly easier to breathe. "He channeled a lot of magic back there," Purpurrot went on to explain. "That's no easy task for a human. Plus, he nearly got blown up."

Gloucester eyed Finch's still face. The man was a mystery to him. It seemed strange to think the same person who just saved their lives had been the one smashing him in the face with a gun only two weeks ago, eyes cold with furious vengeance. In turn, it was difficult to think that either of those scenarios had played out with the same person who, when they'd first met, had genteelly called him "friend" as he held a gun to his head. More and more, Gloucester was learning that no one was who they seemed.

But maybe, he thought, that wasn't always a terrible thing. People were complex and ever-changing, but not always in a bad way.

Now wasn't the time to be ruminating on human nature, though. He shook himself from his thoughts, looking away from Finch and back to his other companions.

"So what now?" Zane asked. "Monsters like that are just gonna start popping up all over the city? There's gotta be a way to stop them before they appear. I mean, what happens if something attacks but we can't get to it in time? Or more than one thing shows up at once?"

"If they're only going to get stronger, Zane is right, we've got to find a way to head them off, not just face them as they come." Gloucester glanced around at the others. "But how? Is that even possible?"

"It is," said an unmistakable voice from across the room, laden with a millennium of sorrow. Everyone spun toward the door to the kitchens, where a tall figure stepped into the light.

The Gambler had returned.

Chapter 6

Past Lives

In comparison to all of their smoke-stained faces and dirty clothes, the white shirt and pale hair of the Gambler were pristine. Yet the tired frown on his eyeless face gave the impression *he'd* been the one battling dragons, not them.

"Gambler," breathed Antimony. "You're back."

The Gambler nodded solemnly, a greeting and acknowledgment of the obvious. Then he swept his blind stare over them all. "We can close the doors and send the invading monsters back." The ghost of a grimace crossed his face. "But it won't be easy."

"When is it ever?" Zane asked dryly. "We live for the challenge."

"Hm," said the Gambler. "I'll explain what I can, but first I need coffee."

Gloucester blinked, wondering if he'd misheard the eerie immortal. No one else seemed to find the comment odd.

"Really?" he asked.

The Gambler sighed. "Desperately."

—

Ten minutes passed, and Gloucester's hope that once caffeinated, the Gambler would provide the perfect solution to all their problems was quickly deflated. In lieu of his promised explanation, the Gambler exchanged a meaningful look with Purpurrot—*How is that possible?* Gloucester wondered, musing on how someone with no eyes could do so much looking—and then the pair excused themselves, disappearing in the blink of an eye. Even Antimony was miffed by this.

She now sat at a table by herself, one high-heeled boot propped on a chair and her expression far away.

"I hate waiting," grumbled Zane, kicking her feet. She was sitting on the table of the booth where Finch lay, her legs dangling over the edge. Gloucester sat on the other bench seat next to her, frowning at nothing in particular. He nodded in agreement.

"I mean," Zane carried on, encouraged by his silent commiseration, "we just fought a dragon. A *dragon.* And we saved the Gambler's life! We shouldn't have to sit here waiting to hear what his plan is."

"Maybe he hasn't got one," Gloucester suggested. "Not really. Could be that's what they're working on now."

"If the Gambler says he's got a plan, then he has," Antimony said, speaking for the first time since the demigods made their exit. "Trust him."

With that, she got to her feet and left, vanishing out into the street with little more than a farewell and brusque request that they contact her should the Gambler and Purpurrot return. Gloucester stared at the door long after it had fallen closed behind her.

"Why does she trust him so much?" he asked eventually, unable to hold the question in any longer. It had been clamoring inside his skull for several minutes, and as soon as he spoke it aloud, he knew he'd been wondering for much longer than that. He thought of Antimony's determination in her search for the Gambler, the way she hadn't seemed to care about anything other than his welfare.

He half expected Zane to refuse to answer, but she took a deep breath and said, "Antimony and the Gambler have known each other for a long time. They've been through a lot together." She paused, clicked her tongue, then added, "Well, *she's* been through a lot, at least. The Gambler just sort of weathers everything pretty effortlessly. Other than being kidnapped, of course. We both know how that turned out."

"How did they meet?"

"Oooh, is it gossip hour?" said an unfamiliar voice from somewhere behind Gloucester. He started, turning so quickly that he nearly gave himself whiplash.

A woman watched them from the door to the kitchens, wearing a flour-dusted apron and an amused smirk. Her thick ash-blonde hair was pulled back into a high ponytail, tumbling over one shoulder. She idly twisted the tips of it around her fingers.

"Hi, Zane," she said cheerfully. "I'd heard you were back in the picture. Finally missed us all too much, eh? And your friend's the former drone, right?" She waved at Gloucester, unfazed by his indignant frown. Then she gestured at Finch's prone form. "Who's the dead guy?"

"Hey there, Blei," said Zane, whose smile suddenly looked a bit weary. "That's Finch. He's a magician. And he's not dead, just knocked out." Finch gave a well-timed snore to support this. Zane snorted. "Gloucester, this is Bleifrei, the chef here. Blei, this is Mikalai Gloucester. He's not a former *drone,* he's a former security agent."

"Exactly," said Blei. "A drone. Still, from everything I've heard, you sound like a solid fellow, so I suppose I approve." She gave him a thumbs up.

"Uh, thanks?" Gloucester managed. Sometimes the sheer amount of strange folk Zane knew amazed him. He couldn't help but wonder what might have happened if he hadn't sought her help that night he escaped the high minister's mansion. Nothing good, he suspected. Bad as things were at the moment, at least he wasn't locked up anymore. At least he had friends.

He vaguely recalled seeing Bleifrei the first time he'd been to the pie shop. Zane had pointed her out as the chef, but at the time Gloucester didn't have reason to think she was anyone of import. Now all sorts of questions bubbled up in his mind. How did someone end up working for a demigod? It seemed like she was in the know about who and what her employer was. Was she magical too?

"You're welcome," Blei said. It was impossible to tell whether she was being sardonic or not. She carried herself with such an unwavering air of wry amusement that it sufficiently masked any other emotions she might be feeling.

"So," she went on, sitting down at the table Antimony had vacated. She propped her feet up on the back of another chair. "You want to know about the mystery that is our dear Antimony Jones."

"Er," stammered Gloucester, feeling like a child caught with his hand in the cookie jar. He was nosing around in business that wasn't his own; he couldn't blame this Blei person if she called him out on that, especially if she was one of Antimony's friends. "I was just curious."

"His life got turned upside-down to save the Gambler," Zane said. Gloucester glanced at her, surprised by the interjection. "He helped Antimony and the rest of us when he didn't have to. He could have run. So maybe we owe him some answers. I think Antimony would understand that. And if not . . . well then, I'll take the blame." She folded her arms across her chest in a way Gloucester had learned meant she wasn't prepared to budge.

Blei laughed, rocking her chair backward to balance on its two back legs. "I never said I wasn't happy to share the story. I love stories!" She fiddled with something as she spoke, a small shiny object that reflected the light as she turned it. Looking more closely, Gloucester saw it was a hairpin, a delicate butterfly with wings of blue metal. She didn't seem to even notice she had it in hand as she launched into her tale:

"Antimony met the Gambler about a year or so before I met her, at least as far as I remember it. I was already working for Purpurrot when the Gambler brought her here for the first time. She was different back then. A lot less happy."

"*Less* happy?" Gloucester couldn't help the exclamation. Antimony broached "cheerful" at best with her moods. Zane hushed him, while Blei raised one eyebrow in an impressive arch before continuing.

"She had reason to be. See, she met the Gambler at the worst moment in her life. The day her husband died."

Gloucester had to bite his tongue to keep from interrupting again. Antimony had been married? He'd had no idea. There had been no sign—

Except there had been. The weight of realization settled over his shoulders, and he looked down at the clothes he was wearing: a slightly too-big sweater and jeans rolled up once at the bottom hem. Clothes that Antimony had given to him. He'd wondered where they came from when she first presented him with a change of clothes but didn't ask about it because Zane shot a silent warning look his way like he would be crossing some sort of line. Now he knew what that line was. He shifted uncomfortably in the borrowed clothes.

"I didn't know," he said. "That's awful. Did . . . Why did the Gambler show up to a death? That's not a choice. Unless . . . Did he . . . ?"

He trailed off, but Zane shook her head briskly. "It isn't that. He was sick. Antimony told me once when we were working together. The Gambler didn't show up when her husband died." She hesitated, and when she spoke next, her voice was lowered and melancholy. "He showed up before. The Gambler, he . . .

well, he shows up for important decisions. The ones that make a difference, you know?"

"The Gambler didn't come to Antimony's husband," Blei added, sending Zane a vaguely annoyed glance. It seemed she didn't appreciate having her story taken over by someone else. "He came to Antimony."

"What choice did she—" Gloucester started, but looking from Blei to Zane and seeing the somberness in their expressions, realization dawned.

"He'd been in a coma for weeks," Blei said quietly. "The doctors told her there was no hope. It was just a matter of time. But the choice was hers."

Gloucester was silent for several minutes, thinking it all over. Not only did that solve the mystery of the spare clothes, but he thought that perhaps it explained a lot about Antimony too. He felt a pang of sympathy for her. He might not know what it felt like to go through the death of a spouse, but he knew what it was to have everything that was your life taken away from you.

For far from the first time in the last month, his thoughts turned to Jeb. There had been days in the last two weeks when he'd stepped out the door of the clock shop, intent on returning to the apartment where he and Jeb had lived. Now that Mulligan had called off the search for him, it would be safe to go back there.

Yet he'd never made it more than a few meters down the sidewalk before he lost his nerve. He had the same problem whenever he started to dial Jeb's number into his phone. He couldn't settle on what was stopping him. Maybe a lot of things. He hadn't seen Jeb in seven months. He didn't know what he might have been told to explain his disappearance. Did he still live in that apartment? Was he even still in Frettchen?

Did he still love him?

So many questions flooded Gloucester's mind whenever he thought of his old life and the man who had been the love of it. One in particular nagged at him, sliding under his skin and pulling at his thoughts: Did *he* still love *Jeb?*

He had. He'd loved him more than he could say in his halting, bashful attempts at romance. Jeb had been his friend, his lover, his confidante. He'd been his future.

A future that was jostled out of the picture and replaced with something else the day he was arrested and locked away. As much as he wished they hadn't, those six months had changed everything. They'd changed *him.* He didn't feel like the same person he'd been before the fateful day he stumbled across the Gambler. He'd reluctantly come to the conclusion that his old life wasn't something he could return to.

Certainly not now, with Denken on the loose and his monsters descending upon the unsuspecting city. That was the other factor, far less confusing, that always stayed his hand when he was tempted to reach out to Jeb. It wasn't the right time. There was too much else to do. Stopping the destruction of Frettchen and possibly the world was a bit more urgent than reconnecting with his ex.

Still, his thoughts lingered on lost love, and the sympathy he felt for Antimony grew stronger.

"Why did she and the Gambler stay in touch?" he asked. "I mean, if he appears to, to everyone who has a big decision to make—" He paused, a frown forming. "Hang on. If he appears every time someone has to make a hard choice, how come he's not common knowledge?"

Blei shrugged. "No one but the Gambler knows why he chooses to show himself to some and not others. Maybe it's something in those futures he sees. I reckon he saw the futures with Antimony and knew there was something important there for him."

Unconvinced, Gloucester looked to Zane, but she just held up her palms, indicating she had no better explanation to offer. On the other bench seat, Finch offered another snore, equally unhelpful.

"As for Antimony's motives, *weeellllllll,*" Blei went on,

drawling the word. "I'd say no one knows save for her, either. You can ask her, if you like, but I doubt you'd get much of an answer."

Gloucester doubted he would too. One of the few things he knew about Antimony was that she didn't like talking about herself. He nodded and murmured his thanks, not pressing further. They fell back into silence as they waited.

Chapter 7

Patience

An hour passed, according to the clock on the wall, which was aptly designed to look like a pie. The time went by mostly in silence. After a quarter of an hour spent humming to herself, Blei grew bored and returned to the kitchen. For their part, Gloucester and Zane just rested, trying to regain their bearings after the morning's excitement.

This had its pros and cons. On the one hand, Gloucester's head cleared and his lungs grew less sore since he was out of the smoke. On the other, the quiet and calm amplified his awareness of the aches and pains he'd sustained. His skinned palms, elbows, and knees stung, red, and bloody. He felt a raw spot on the side of his face too, the pain of which was hard to ignore now that he didn't have a dragon to face down.

He was almost envious of Finch, who had slipped into a peaceful sleep where he lay on the bench seat of the booth if the gentle snoring was anything to go by. Gloucester was sure he would have aches of his own to contend with once he woke up, but for now, he appeared untouched by any discomfort or worry.

Though it was quiet inside the pie shop, the hubbub down the street could still be heard, muffled by distance and walls. The high keen of sirens blared, and the flashing lights of law enforcement passed by on several occasions.

He had no doubt that the police weren't the only ones investigating the scene. Mulligan was no high minister, but he'd stepped into the position of lord of the city-state with smooth grace and efficacy. No matter how much he disliked him, Gloucester knew Mulligan worked hard to keep the city running as close as possible to business as usual. He was probably one of the only things keeping the wolves at bay after Frettchen lost both of its major leadership positions in one fell swoop. The other regions had surely taken notice of the abrupt power vacuum.

"Mulligan will want to talk to us, sooner or later," he said, breaking the silence at last.

Zane made a face. "Ugh, you think so?" Both hands above her head, she tried to wrestle her hair into a bun. "How d'you know?"

Gloucester watched another police car pass the window. Civilian traffic had trickled down to nothing; they must have closed the road off.

"Procedure," he answered simply. "Follow the best leads. I figure the way Mulligan sees it, something weird and magical going on in Frettchen? We're the people to call. I didn't get the impression he knew anyone other than the Finches when it came to magical stuff."

"Fair point," Zane conceded. "So what should we do if he comes looking for us?"

"Maybe we should just tell him the truth," Gloucester suggested. The look Zane gave him made him laugh tiredly. "I don't like Mulligan, but if he can help—"

"Never tell anyone you don't trust the whole truth," came a sleepy voice from the bench seat nearby. "They'll just strangle you with it later."

Finch was awake. He sat up slowly, grimacing and clutching at his ribs with one arm, while the other levered against the tabletop for support.

"I don't care who's in charge, the city leader and their black-clad army aren't gonna be our friends. And if you lot are wanting a happy ending for the Brothers when this is all sorted, you'd best keep in mind that isn't in the cards as far as Mulligan's concerned. Denken killed his precious boss. Do you really think he has any plans to let him live after that? And don't think he's much fond of the Gambler, either. Or us, for that matter. And we're all plenty easier to kill than the Brothers."

It was a lot to say for someone who had just regained consciousness. At the end of his speech, Finch looked a bit short of breath. His face was very pale, his freckles and tattoo standing out more than ever. He rested his back against the cushioned seat.

"Cassus!" Gloucester said, so relieved to see him awake and lucid that he paid little mind to his pessimistic contribution to the conversation. "You're awake. Are you all right?"

Massaging his temples, Finch managed a smile. "I seem to be. Though, gotta say, I was waiting and waiting for the kiss to wake me from my slumber and, lo and behold, it never came. You've got very little grasp of romantic clichés, you know that?"

"Kissing sleeping people is creepy," Zane told him. Finch ignored this reasonable criticism and wagged an admonishing finger at Gloucester, who raised his eyebrows at him, secretly fighting the color that threatened to rise in his cheeks.

Don't get fooled again.

"Since when do you call him Cassus, by the way?" asked Zane, looking from Finch to Gloucester with a frown.

"Since he asked me to," Gloucester said, shrugging with the sort of forced nonchalance that comes with concealed defensiveness.

"I thought only your friends were allowed to call you Cassus," she reminded Finch shrewdly. "Are we your friends now?"

"*He* is," Finch retorted. "Leastways, I like to think so. You? Still up in the air."

"Oh really?" Zane's voice was acidic. "Not for me, mate. And if you think all's forgiven just because you helped us fight that fire dragon, you've got another thing coming."

Finch looked unimpressed. "What happened with Denken wasn't my fault. I didn't make him kill the high minister. He would've done that no matter what."

"You didn't make things any better, though, did you?" Zane accused. "Maybe if you hadn't riled him up further, the Gambler could've reasoned with him. Maybe all of this wouldn't be happening. And what about Gloucester, eh?" She jabbed a finger in his direction. "No one *made* you beat him up, did they? No one *made* you trick him, just so you could—"

"Zane." Gloucester raised his voice just enough that they would hear him over their argument. "It's fine." He appreciated Zane's indignation on his behalf, but he didn't want to hear it. He didn't feel like listening to people talk about him like he didn't have a voice of his own. "Thanks," he told her sincerely nonetheless. It felt strange, but nice, to have someone who so staunchly had his back after all this time.

"It's not fine," Zane grumbled, but she didn't argue further.

To his credit, Finch did nothing to rebuke her comments, sending Gloucester a hard-to-read look and running a hand through his short red hair. "Back to the point, we need to figure out what the plan is before the friendly folk in black suits come knocking on our door. Speaking of . . . are we in a pie shop? Oh no, this is that demigoddess's weird bakery, isn't it? Where is she?" He looked around, as though he might have simply missed the towering Purpurrot during his initial inspection of the room.

"She's off with the Gambler. Planning our next move, I

hope," Gloucester said. Finch raised his brows.

"The Gambler? How much did I miss while I was snoozing?"

—

It didn't take long to fill Finch in on all that had happened since they fled the fire. Gloucester let Zane do most of the talking, though he chimed in whenever her voice grew strained. The pair of them were both sounding distinctly more gravelly than usual.

Finch made for a good audience, quiet and patient as he listened. Gloucester supposed that when you'd grown up with magic as an integral part of your life, you felt less of an urge to interrupt fantastical stories with exclamations of incredulity.

"Yeah," Finch said when the story came to a close. He let out a long sigh through his nose. "Things aren't looking great." Leaning back against the plush lilac fabric of the bench, he winced, still sore.

Gloucester snorted. "Understatement of the year." It was a weak attempt at humor, but he was struggling to see anything funny in their predicament. "You know, a year ago my biggest problem was keeping journalists off the high minister's back and whether it was my turn to cook dinner or not."

Gods, but he missed that.

"Oh, and he cooks too." Finch laughed lightly. Despite the severity of the situation, he didn't seem to be having much difficulty remaining upbeat, even as he cradled his ribs.

"I'm twenty-six, of course, I cook," Gloucester shot back. Still, it was momentarily easier for him to find a smile too.

"Flirting later, please." Zane gave up trying to tame her tangled hair, and the ash-coated curls bounced around her face as she sat back, huffing. "I don't know where Purpurrot and the Gambler have gotten to, or whether Antimony's coming back at all today, but we should at least be trying to figure out our next move."

"Right," Gloucester agreed, faint color rising in his cheeks again. "Before the Gambler showed up, we were talking about how we could stop the monsters from escaping the Maze, rather than facing each one as they attack. I was thinking . . . would it all stop if we got Denken back to the Maze? Would that close the doors again? Or . . . I dunno, put him back in his right mind, so he might do it himself?"

He hadn't any idea how any of this god stuff worked. All he knew was the troubles had started with a single moment and a single being: the high minister's murder at the hands of Denken. If Denken going rogue had set this chain of events into action, could setting him back on the right path undo it?

Finch scratched his chin. "Mayhaps. Their Pockets are where they go to replenish their strength. Spend too long in our world, cut off from their own spaces, and . . . well, you get this." He gestured around at the pie shop.

It was a valid point, Gloucester supposed, but he couldn't help wondering if Purpurrot could slow time over an entire crowded street, just how powerful had she been at full strength? It was an off-putting thought.

"Denken's powerful right now, but he's not in control. If we could get him back to the Maze, it might provide the stability he needs to regain that control." Finch frowned, hands twisting in slow motion in front of him. No feeling of magic rose in the air, though. Gloucester guessed that he was simply working out knotted muscles in the wake of their battle. "Could be that without a solid grip on his powers, he *can't* get back into the Maze. He'd need the help of one of his siblings to take him there."

"Which I am more than happy to do."

The Gambler had reappeared. He was tall, but with Purpurrot standing next to him, he hardly appeared so. Below the smooth skin where his eyes should have been, his mouth was set in a determined line. He held a large mug in his hand, and the pleasant scent of coffee reached Gloucester's nose.

"I believe that idea is our best course forward. We both do," he added, nodding solemnly up at Purpurrot, who had gone back to looking generally unfazed. She finger-combed her hair back and twisted it into a thick braid.

"It isn't a plan yet, but it's a direction, at least," she said. "Every victory starts with figuring out which way you're going."

"Inspiring words," Finch quipped, in the light-hearted tone of his that made it hard to tell if he was being genuine or not. Hazarding a guess, Gloucester would lean toward the latter. "As pleased as I am that we've all agreed I'm right, it leads us to the next problem. How do we find Denken?"

"That is the tricky part." The Gambler's sigh weighed on Gloucester's chest like the memory of heartbreak. Being around demigods was exhausting.

"Hold that thought," Zane cut in. Then she spoke into the phone raised to her ear. "Antimony. They're back. We're trying to figure out how to deal with Denken himself. He's—hm?"

They all watched her in silent curiosity. Zane's brows knitted as she cut herself off mid-sentence, listening intently to whatever Antimony was saying on the other end of the line.

"That's—really?" she said, while the rest of them squirmed in suspense. "Okay. I'll tell them. See you soon."

She hung up, pocketing her phone and then recoiling in surprise at the sight of everyone's stares.

"What was that about?" asked Gloucester.

Zane slid off the table and jerked her thumb toward the front door. "Antimony says she has an idea about how to deal with Denken."

"She can find him?" Finch asked eagerly, but Zane only shrugged.

"She didn't specify. Just asked that we meet her at her laboratory as soon as possible." She tugged at the hem of her sleeve, a sure sign that she had a lot on her mind. Whatever Antimony wanted to show them, Zane wasn't taking it as a definite reason for hope. Gloucester knew Zane always tried to stay grounded, but this didn't strike him as an encouraging sign. Finch looked as confused as he felt.

Purpurrot and the Gambler, on the other hand, appeared entirely unbothered. The Gambler was even smiling. Though the expression was restrained, it was unusual on his normally solemn face. And yet, the furrow of a frown carved itself between his brows.

"This will be interesting," he said.

"Do you See?" Purpurrot asked, peering at him keenly. On the surface, it seemed like a silly question to ask him, but something in the way she stressed "see" made Gloucester think she wasn't talking about what was right in front of him.

"That's the funny thing," he said, still smiling. "I can't. I can see Antimony smiling. I can feel her pride, but I cannot see what she is showing us."

"So, not eerie at all, then." Finch wore a smile of his own, but something less jovial lurked in his eye. Zane huffed an uneasy laugh in agreement.

"If she's smiling and proud, then it can't be bad," Gloucester pointed out. "Right?"

"I'm sure it's well-intentioned, whatever it is," Purpurrot said. "It's just . . . Antimony isn't always the best judge of the types of things to be proud of. At least when it comes to her work. It can be . . . ill-advised."

"A polite way of saying 'mad scientist,' I take it," Finch drawled.

"Politeness is easier for some than others." Purpurrot sniffed. "Whatever it is that Antimony wants to show us, she considers it important. That's good enough for me. Let's be on our way."

The Gambler nodded mutely at her shoulder.

"Try not to have all the fun without us slow mortals," Zane said. She tossed her thumb over her shoulder at the street outside again. "Some of us can't just transport ourselves instantaneously from one place to another. We have to make do with cars."

The demigods nodded in solemn understanding, apparently in pity of such hardship. Then they vanished. Gloucester stared at the empty air where they had been standing.

"That must be handy," he mused.

"And a pain in the ass for the rest of us." Finch got to his feet with a groan. "Saints above, I feel like one giant bruise," he complained, holding himself stiffly. "Next monster we fight, someone else can take point."

"I'd say fair enough, but you're one of the few of us actually equipped to fight those things," Gloucester replied sympathetically. "Sorry about that."

"'Sorry,' he says, after fiendishly beguiling me with flattery." Finch's smile was cheeky as he clapped Gloucester on the shoulder, winced at the movement, then gestured to the door. "All right, Zane, Silvertongue, let's go see what the mad scientist has made for us."

Chapter 8

Gear

To avoid the traffic caused by the closed-down street, they had to take the long way back to Antimony's lab, which was conveniently located in the basement of her townhouse. When Finch, squashed in the cramped backseat of Zane's tiny car, pointed out how odd it was for a scientist to work out of her own home, Zane merely shrugged, never taking her eyes off the road ahead.

"Antimony likes her privacy," she said. "If it wasn't for the pie shop, I'm not sure she would ever leave her house. Murphy takes care of most things like groceries and other errands."

"Doesn't sound like a simple case of liking her privacy to me." Finch snorted. "Sounds more like agoraphobia. What do you think, Gloucester?"

Gloucester shrugged. Though he, like Zane, didn't shift his gaze to look back at Finch, it wasn't responsible driving that held his attention. He stared out the passenger's side window, watching the world go by and trying his best to ignore the discomfort of being in the car. Small spaces never used to bother him. In the wake of his imprisonment, however, the limited space of any car, especially Zane's very small one, set his teeth on edge.

"You all right, mate?" asked Finch. Gloucester could feel Finch lean closer to his shoulder, concern bleeding through the flippancy.

"I'm fine," Gloucester told him, eyes still fixed on the scenery on the other side of the window. Watching the movement of the car helped, he'd found. "Just tired. And eager to see . . . whatever it is Antimony wants to show us."

"Hm, me too." The seat creaked as Finch leaned back again. "It's a shame the godly ones will already have been there for ages by the time we get there. We'll have missed their reactions to whatever the devil it is. They were probably like 'Oh my.'" He dropped his voice to a comically exaggerated monotone. "'I cannot fathom this. You've saved us all, Antimony Jones.'"

Gloucester chuckled, finally turning away from the window to smile over his shoulder at Finch. Even Zane snorted a laugh, her lips twitching.

"Sounds like them," she admitted, steering the car around the corner onto Antimony's street.

The quiet residential street was deserted. When Gloucester had first come here, children played in the small yards out front of the houses, surrounded by people walking their dogs and neighbors visiting on each other's porches. Now the sidewalks were empty and the doors all closed. A feeling of trepidation hung heavy here, even more so than in the busier parts of the city. Despite the epidemic of violence in Frettchen, people were still going to work, still running essential errands. Here, though, here was where they *lived*. Here was where their children slept. And so the fear ran stronger, defensive and stifling.

"There's something about streets like these," Finch mused, peering out at the houses lining the road. "I don't much like them. Too perfect, that's the problem. They feel like they're hiding secrets."

"Secrets hide everywhere," Gloucester said. By now he could easily pick Antimony's house out from the others, even before Zane pulled up to the curb in front of it. Red brick walls and a blue-painted door rose up from a colorful flower garden.

"How enigmatic of you to say," Zane remarked, amused. Gloucester, who hadn't intended to be anything of the sort, made a face at her, which she countered with one of her own. In the backseat, Finch rolled his eyes.

The moment of humor didn't last. As they got out of the car, their smiles waned.

"No time like the present." Gloucester sighed, trying to pay no mind to the stirrings of foreboding in his chest. "Let's see what's what."

They could hear voices as soon as they stepped through the door. Antimony's housemate, the waitress Murphy, greeted them on the doorstep. She must have been advised to expect them, as they didn't even have a chance to knock before she was ushering them inside.

"They're in the lab," she told them. "Just follow the sounds of arguing." Anxiety shone brightly in Murphy's hazel eyes, and she didn't make any move to join them on their way to the basement laboratory. This did nothing to assuage Gloucester's mounting nerves.

It did indeed sound like there was an argument going on. The voices were raised enough to be heard through the floor, though the words themselves were muffled into indistinct noise.

Or maybe it was only one person arguing, Gloucester amended, listening closely. There was no mistaking Purpurrot's voice, even when he couldn't tell what she was saying. Though there seemed to be occasional pauses in her speech, no responses were audible.

"Sounds like the arguing is a bit one-sided," Zane whispered.

"Something tells me that whatever it is Antimony wants to

show us, Purpurrot's not a fan," he muttered back.

They made their way cautiously past the doorways to the kitchen and the living room, down a carpeted corridor lined with paintings of flowers. At the far end, they reached a door. Though it was closed, the raised voice was obviously coming from the other side.

"Here goes nothing," Gloucester said under his breath. He reached forward and pulled the door open.

A flight of stairs greeted them on the other side, leading downward. Gloucester was reminded of the door they'd all traveled through just a couple of weeks prior when they descended into the basement of All Saints Shrine. At least this staircase was illuminated by a light issuing from somewhere at the bottom. It made for a much more inviting sight. However, Purpurrot's anger was even louder now that the door was open.

Gloucester led the way down the stairs. As the distance between them lessened, he could hear Purpurrot more clearly.

" . . . dangerous!" she was saying scathingly. "Not to mention, just . . . just *wrong!*"

Antimony responded, sounding waspish but still too quiet for her words to be discernible.

"It won't work!" Purpurrot snapped in reply.

Then came silence. Gloucester had stopped in his tracks halfway down the staircase, put off by Purpurrot's fearsome tone. In the newfound quiet, he could feel something in the very air change and knew without seeing that Purpurrot had left. Like the Brothers, she carried with her a presence that weighed on the minds of any in her company. Gloucester wasn't sure if he felt relief or loss in its absence. There was something almost intoxicating about being around the gods.

Zane stepped past him, reminding Gloucester that they had pressing things to do.

"Um, hello?" she called out as they reached the bottom of the flight. "The . . . er . . . the mortals have arrived!"

A long moment of silence reigned, but before any of them

could break it, Antimony appeared through a door that opened from the hallway they'd just entered. She was more red-faced than usual, the color bright on her high cheekbones.

"There you are," she said briskly. Foregoing any proper greeting, she beckoned for them to follow her before turning on her heel and going back into the room out of which she'd just stepped. The three of them hesitated, then moved forward as a group to enter the room in Antimony's wake.

Gloucester had never been inside a laboratory before. In school, he'd excelled in other classes, like history and geography, but he'd never had much of a mind for science. He understood the appeal of the curiosity the subject was based on, of course. Science was about asking questions and the constant search for answers. It was just all the nit-picking procedure and complexity that couldn't hold his attention.

And yet, Antimony's lab was fascinating even to him. Tall glass-fronted cabinets lined the walls, containing everything from biological specimens to microscopes to miniature perpetual engines. The latter filled the air with a hum on the edge of hearing. It reminded Gloucester of the feeling he got when Finch used his magic. Several long tables, some metal and others wood, took up the middle of the space, while a desk piled with papers covered in minute handwriting was wedged into one corner.

When he thought of a mad scientist's laboratory, he imagined a visual cacophony of shining glassware and mysterious machines. He pictured beakers of strange concoctions bubbling and massive gears turning in the kind of industrial clockwork used in large factories.

Taking in Antimony's clean and organized lab, he supposed it was a fairly juvenile preconception to hang onto. Even if she *were* a mad scientist, he doubted Antimony would be so imprudent as to leave her equipment lying around when not in use. And really, open beakers of unattended chemicals were just a hazard.

Clean or not, one thing in the room did look out of place, and it drew all of their attention. On a wooden table in the center of the room sat a young woman. The ceiling lights bathed her like warm sunlight. She was kind-faced and smiling shyly, but at the sight of her, the three newcomers froze in shock.

With a resigned sort of bewilderment, Gloucester wondered if he would ever become accustomed to the weirdness of the world as he'd come to know it since his release from the high minister's custody. Would there come a day when his desensitization was enough that things like gods and magic were nothing more than another everyday occurrence? Or when what he was looking at now wouldn't baffle him?

If Zane's gasp or Finch's quiet oath were anything to go by, the chances seemed slim.

It wasn't the woman's kind face that was strange, but rather everything surrounding it. Though the skin of her face was freckled and golden-brown, it contrasted sharply with the pale white of her throat. This wasn't a case of an unfortunate tanning session, but rather two entirely different complexions. Indeed, two different *skins,* stitched neatly together. The same phenomenon marked the even harsher contrast where her neck met her chest, which was a dark brown. The stitching was even and precise, with no sign of redness or infection, or even bruising. How extensive this mismatched flesh was would be difficult to gauge, the majority of her body concealed beneath what appeared to be a long flannel nightdress.

Yet as she turned her head inquisitively to look from the three of them to Antimony, her patchwork skin wasn't even the most remarkable thing about her. The back of her head glinted in the lights, and Gloucester's stomach did an unpleasant flip as he realized that she had no back to her head at all. At the top of her crown, her short brown hair ended in an unnaturally straight line, along with her entire skull. Where the back of her head ought to have been, a convex sheet of plexiglass took its place. Gloucester flinched, expecting to see exposed blood and brain.

Only there was none. The woman's head was far from empty, but in the place of organic matter, it contained a whirring, clicking mass of metal gears.

"Er," said Zane, effectively summing up Gloucester's thoughts.

"Sorry, is she an automaton?" Finch asked, managing a touch more eloquence even amidst his blatant incredulity. He looked wide-eyed from Antimony back to the strange woman. "Are you an automaton?"

The woman looked to Antimony, unsure, then regarded Finch again. "I'm me," she said after a moment of contemplation. This seemed to satisfy her, at least, and she beamed. "Who are you? What's an automaton?"

"She is and she isn't," Antimony cut in. She hadn't given them the chance to answer either question, but this was perhaps because she saw the expressions on all of their faces and aptly read the situation. Now was a time for answers, but not from them. "She's a clockwork-automated organic-hybrid artificial intelligence."

"Catchy," Gloucester said faintly.

Antimony offered him the shadow of a smile. "Her name is Gear."

"I wonder why," Finch pondered, lightly sarcastic. In the silence between their words, a faint clicking could be heard above the whir of the perpetual engines. It came from the mechanism in the back of Gear's head, making her sound like one of the clocks in Zane's shop.

"You actually did it," breathed Zane. She stared avidly at Gear, not in horror or disgust, but in awe.

"You knew she was making a . . . this?" Gloucester asked. He couldn't tear his eyes away from Gear, who was smiling back at him. She didn't seem to mind her questions going unanswered.

"Well, yeah," said Zane. "Antimony's been working on Gear for *years*. I never thought I'd see her finished. I didn't think it was possible."

"Oh ye of little faith," Antimony hummed. Despite the dryness of the joke, she looked happier than Gloucester ever remembered seeing her. It wasn't so much in her face as it was a feeling, brightening the room where she stood. She moved forward to lean her hip against the table Gear sat on, regarding her proudly.

Gloucester opened his mouth but didn't know which of a dozen questions to ask first. How was this possible? That was a pretty obvious one. How did Gear work? Was she a machine or a person? She seemed so . . . real. Why had Antimony spent years working on this? What had motivated her? Was magic involved? And why, as miraculous as this was, did Antimony think this would help them against Denken?

He was starting to feel like a gawping fish, so he forced himself to ask the easiest question to articulate: "How?"

Antimony looked pleased that he'd asked. Gloucester got the feeling the normally reserved scientist was bursting to talk about her achievement.

"A lot of work. A lot of trial and error. Add that to some advanced biological experimentation and sophisticated clockwork, and here she is." She was grinning, which was such a bizarrely out-of-place expression on her that it was rather a relief when she replaced it a moment later with a gentle grimace. "And yes, okay, maybe a little bit of spellwork, but hey, magic is science unexplained, as they say. The important thing is she works. She's alive!"

"I think it's a good thing!" Gear piped up. Her voice was uncannily human. Did she have a throat, Gloucester wondered? Vocal cords? Lungs? How much was machine and how much was human? How much was magic? Though he was adept at holding his tongue, he'd never been able to hold back the countless questions that burst through his mind when presented with something new. And this? This was *very* new.

"That's a healthy way of looking at life," Finch told Gear,

offering her a wink. Sobering, he turned his attention to Antimony. "This is all very brilliantly weird of you, but how's this supposed to help us against Denken?"

"Hold on," Zane cut in before Antimony had a chance to reply. "Where's the Gambler?"

"Here," said the demigod's unmistakable voice. It came from the corner behind them, and they all spun to see the Gambler lurking in the shadow of the tall shelves against the wall. His eyeless stare was fixed on Gear, and he stood so still that Gloucester hadn't noticed him in the slightest until he spoke. He offered them no greeting, only continued to regard Gear in his impossible way.

"Um," said Zane. "Are you all right?"

The Gambler was silent for a moment longer. Then he gave himself a little shake and cleared his throat. It was such a bashfully human thing to do that it was quite jarring to see from a being like the Gambler. Finally, he dragged his attention away from Gear to turn a knitted brow Zane's way.

"I am just . . . surprised."

Gloucester didn't think he'd ever heard the Gambler so off-kilter, not even when they rescued him after a year in captivity.

"Purpurrot didn't sound like she approved of Gear here," Finch said. His gaze narrowed as he eyed the Gambler. "What about you?"

The Gambler was back to staring at the automaton. She smiled and waved.

"She is remarkable," the Gambler said quietly. He waved back and Gear giggled in delight. "She should be impossible." His tone was very different from Purpurrot's. No trace of disapproval to be heard.

In fact . . .

"Are you *blushing?*" Flabbergasted, Zane stared at the demigod with as much disbelief as she had previously leveled at Gear.

She was on to something. Though it was less blatant on

his face than Antimony's, a distinct scarlet tint colored the Gambler's cheeks. He coughed again and looked away, suddenly deeply intrigued by the pattern of lilacs on the wallpaper beside him. Finch made a noise suspiciously like a laugh.

"I am just surprised, that's all," the Gambler insisted, a little too quickly to be convincing.

A thousand questions still buzzed in Gloucester's head like bees in a hive, but he tried to voice the ones of most immediate importance. "What can she do?" he settled on. Then, worrying this might seem presumptuous, he added, "Against Denken, I mean. How is she supposed to help us?"

He wasn't sure if it was rude to ask about the woman as though she weren't capable of giving answers herself. But, well, she wasn't *real,* was she? She was a machine. She wasn't a *person,* not really.

Except his certainty faded the more he watched Gear. In spite of her strange appearance, she seemed uncomfortably human in her expressions and movements. Though she hadn't said much, her words sounded like a human speaking.

If Antimony—or indeed, Gear herself—was offended, they didn't show it. The scientist simply looked pleased to talk about her creation, and perhaps a little relieved that no one else was yelling at her about it. Gear continued to smile at everyone, clockwork clicking steadily.

"The Brothers are powerful." Antimony nodded at the Gambler as she launched into her explanation. "They're the embodiment of extremely vital components of human nature, of all living things, even—love and choice and thought. As such, they have tremendous influence over all of us and our world. You've all seen it in action, especially from Denken. He's dangerous, not only because of his strength or his intelligence or his viciousness. He has power over the mind itself. He can influence the way you think and how you feel. He can plant an idle thought in your head and then magnify it a hundred times over until it's all you think about. And he's even more powerful and dangerous now that he's lost control."

As far as pep talks went, Gloucester had heard better. He wanted to press her to get to her point, to answer his question, but he bit his tongue. Antimony wasn't exactly a chatty person, so if she was saying all of this, it was for a reason.

"Denken's powers make it too risky for us to fight him outright ourselves. He'll be on the lookout for the Gambler, and if any of us humans came up against him, we'd be hard-pressed to resist his tricks. We all know what he can do. What he can make people do."

Gloucester shifted uneasily. He remembered all too well the sensation of Denken in his mind, playing with his free will. He'd nearly committed murder at the demigod's behest, and the sheer effort of resisting had been brutally painful.

"That's where Gear comes into it," Antimony went on. Moving to her creation's side, she patted her gently on the shoulder. "She's smart and capable, but most importantly, she's not human. She thinks and feels, but not the same way we do."

This seemed like a harsh thing to say about someone, especially when the person—automaton?—was sitting right there in front of them. Realization of what Antimony was saying swept over him, however, and thoughts of impoliteness fled to the back of his mind.

It was Finch who spoke aloud what Gloucester was thinking: "She's immune to his powers?"

"I'm almost positive," Antimony replied, the closest to giddy that Gloucester had ever seen her. A lightness filled her voice, her mood buoyed since Purpurrot's angry departure, despite the gravity of the conversation. The unusual levity in her demeanor made her seem suddenly younger.

"*Almost* positive," Gloucester said. "So you're not actually sure of anything, really."

This earned him a reproving look, no matter Antimony's high spirits. "I'm sure of a lot of things, Mr. Gloucester. This just isn't one of them. Not one hundred percent, at least. Call it a very strong hunch. A hypothesis. One that gets tested today."

"Well, if Purpurrot's reaction was anything to go by, I'd say you were onto something." Finch leaned back against the door jamb. He'd recovered from his initial awe and fallen back into more characteristic flippancy.

"It wasn't that," the Gambler said, giving his head a slow shake, like a disapproving owl. "It might be a factor in her distaste, but it's not the main reason Purpurrot is uncomfortable with this. This . . . woman . . . Gear, she is life without nature. For Purpurrot, that goes against everything she is."

"Only because she chooses to see it that way," Antimony said. She crossed her arms, lips pursed. "Nature isn't about playing by the rules all of the time. It's about *life*. It's about creation and finding a way to survive and exist, no matter what."

This seemed like a very personal point she was making. Everything from her raised chin to her stubbornly planted feet communicated that criticism would not be greeted kindly.

"Good point," said Zane, so firmly that Gloucester was quite unsure whether she actually agreed or had simply learned to smile and nod when she needed to. "So, you weren't sure whether, er, Gear here would be immune or not until she met one of the Brothers, right? So now that she has, what's the verdict?"

All eyes turned to the Gambler, who responded with an enigmatic smile. "I cannot see the futures surrounding her. It is very . . . odd."

"I like your voice," said Gear, beaming at him. "I've never heard one like it. Though, I've only heard a few. But yours is interesting."

The Gambler looked touched by this unexpected compliment. His smile became less mysterious and more bashful again. Gloucester fought the urge to laugh at the sight. A snort to his right told him Finch hadn't bothered doing the same.

"Thank you," the Gambler said. He recovered his composure quickly as he addressed the rest of the room. "I believe it's safe to say she negates our powers. Or at least is immune to them herself."

"That's great!" Despite Zane's momentary relief, her brows were soon drawing together again. "So what do we do with her?"

A pregnant pause stretched out as everyone digested this question. Antimony, swept up in the excitement of showing off her scientific success, apparently hadn't thought that far ahead.

"We can't just throw her at Denken," Gloucester said. "She doesn't strike me as a fighter and, I mean, I wouldn't want to make anyone face an angry Denken unprepared."

The smile Antimony turned his way was soft. "Your concern is nice. But she's immune to the Gambler, which means she's immune to Denken. He wouldn't be able to get in her head like he can with us. His shadows shouldn't hurt her. And even with his strength . . . well, Gear's tougher than she seems."

Bit of a low bar to clear, Gloucester thought. As he watched Gear swing her bare legs lightly against the edge of the table, the delicate gears in her transparent head reflecting light, very little about her seemed tough.

—

"Well, can't say it's quite what I was hoping for."

An hour or so later, Finch, Zane, and Gloucester were gathered around the counter island in Antimony's kitchen, the midday sun bright in their eyes.

Finch was the one who broke the quiet, staring broodily down at the countertop. No one had spoken since Antimony shooed them back to the main floor, saying she needed to catch Gear up on everything to do with the city's predicament. In truth, Gloucester wondered if she'd simply grown impatient with them not being as awed by her plan as she'd hoped they would be. She'd let the Gambler remain, after all.

"You can't tell me you're not impressed," Zane said. "She created life! A *person*."

"Loads of people can do that," Finch said. "And the method's a lot more fun."

"Maybe if you're into that sort of thing," Zane retorted. "In all seriousness, though, I mean it. What Antimony's done is dead impressive. She's been working on Gear for as long as I've known her. That's *why* I know her. She came to me for my expertise in clockwork."

"You worked on Gear with her?" Gloucester asked, eyebrows raised. As weird as he found the whole thing, he couldn't deny it was extraordinary.

Zane shrugged a nonchalant shoulder, but she looked pleased with herself. "A bit. Mostly I just worked on the early stages with her. It didn't seem to be going anywhere, though, and eventually, I needed to go back to my shop full-time. I guess I sort of ended up thinking it wasn't anything more than Antimony's pipe dream." She grew quiet for a moment, lost in thought. "I wonder how long Gear's been up and . . . you know . . . *sentient*. I suppose it would explain some of the weird sounds I've been hearing from the laboratory lately."

"I thought she just had a cat," Gloucester admitted.

Finch's laughter was mocking, but his smile was genuine. "Big cat."

"A big cat might be more useful." Gloucester sighed.

"Oh, come on! Not you too," Zane huffed. She rounded on Finch in a half-joking accusation. "You're a bad influence on him. Gloucester's known about magic for less than a month, and already you've got him all unimpressed and wise-cracking when faced with something genuinely amazing."

Gloucester frowned. "I'm not a little kid," he said. Zane was just teasing in her frustration, but it nettled him. "Stop talking about me like I am."

Zane sat back in her seat, face pinched, but before she could reply, Gloucester hurried on. "It's not that I'm unimpressed. You're right, Gear's amazing. I just don't see how she's going to be useful, even if she is immune to Denken's powers. He'd still put up one hell of a fight, and Gear doesn't seem like much of a brawler."

"That's true," Zane admitted grudgingly. She crossed her arms, expression turning thoughtful once more. "I mean, yeah, when Antimony called, I was kinda hoping she'd show us some . . . I dunno, anti-Denken weapon or something. But if Gear's unaffected by the demigods, that's something, at least. More than any of us can claim, that's for sure."

Though Gloucester knew how loyal Zane was to Antimony, it sounded like she was trying to convince herself as much as the two of them.

"Maybe she can be a—a distraction," she suggested. "So that the Gambler can get close enough to Denken to . . . to—"

"To what?" Gloucester asked. He stared down at his feet. One jittered anxiously, and he couldn't seem to make it stop. Getting up, he started to pace. "Does anyone know what we should do if we find Denken? How we should fight him?" He found no answer in either of his companions' faces. "I mean," he went on, lowering his voice, "what if we have to kill him? What if that's the only way? Is it even possible?"

Zane shook her head, but it was Finch who answered. "I'm not sure. They've survived this long, so something tells me they're not easy to put in the ground. And even if it were possible, I don't reckon that's in the Gambler's agenda."

"*You* tried to kill him," Gloucester pointed out quietly.

"Yeah, and see how well that turned out." Finch tipped his head back, offering a surly stare up at the ceiling. "It wasn't my best plan. Dad was . . . It was Denken's fault, what happened to my father. I just wanted—I needed to do something. To make it right."

"Killing doesn't do that," Zane said. Finch's eyes narrowed, but he didn't look down.

"I know that," he said testily. "I was angry."

He was *still* angry. It was no longer a boiling rage, but Gloucester could see it in Finch's eyes and the hard line of his jaw.

And so he should be. Two weeks was no time at all to dull the pain of a father's death. Two *years* wouldn't be enough. Nor would it be enough time for Gloucester to forget the burning fury Finch had wielded when he'd gone up against Denken and when Gloucester had tried to stop him, turned on Gloucester as well.

Finch didn't strike him as someone who allowed himself to wallow, though, at least not in times like these. After all, it had been he who reached out to Gloucester, wanting to help, not the other way around.

"Maybe Gear will surprise us," Gloucester said, cutting in before Zane could respond to Finch's edged words. "You never know. Before today I wouldn't have thought a living person made of clockwork was even possible, so who knows what she could be capable of. It doesn't mean we should totally rely on her either, though." He stopped pacing, staring out the window at Antimony's sun-filled garden. "One plan's good, but it'd be better to have more. Especially since we have next to no idea how this is going to go down."

"Which sounds great," Zane said with a sigh. "Except that none of us *have* a plan."

Chapter 9

Restless

In the wake of Antimony's reveal of Gear as her secret weapon, what followed were several days of frustratingly little progress. It quickly became apparent that none of them even had a clue how to *find* Denken, let alone a solid plan to act on if they did.

Little progress did not imply uneventfulness, unfortunately. The day after Gloucester and the others were introduced to Gear, a shooting in the city's business district sent another reverberation of terror through Frettchen's streets. *Such nice people,* everyone whispered of the culprits. *It's like they just lost their minds.*

The night after that, a street down by the docks was destroyed. No one knew how it happened. The new lord of the city-state was terse and opaque in his statement to the press the next morning, eyes tight with stress behind his horn-rimmed glasses. He called for the citizens of Frettchen to be brave, and to look out for and after each other, but gave no answers to the journalists' demands for explanations. People whispered that this would never have happened under the old lord of the city-state, the old high minister. He had been cold and controlling, but he had protected them, hadn't he?

Lord Mulligan couldn't protect them, the whispers accused. The fear, both unnatural and earned, weighed heavily on the populace and began to boil into anger. People were *dying*. Innocent Frettchennians were no longer safe in their streets or their beds.

The city was nearing a breaking point. Gloucester could feel it, like the electric charge of magic in the air. It made the hair on the back of his neck stand on end, a familiar feeling of unease prickling between his shoulder blades. If this wasn't stopped soon, things were going to get out of control.

Despite their fight with the dragon still fresh in his mind, he couldn't help but feel useless. Stewing in his thoughts was about all he did now, and it made the anxiety that had been building for weeks even worse. He was relegated back to Zane's shop to wait until he was needed. Zane, too, was effectively side-lined, though she stayed in daily contact with Antimony and relayed everything she knew back to Gloucester. The Gambler and Purpurrot came and went like flitting spirits, searching for Denken to no avail, while also trying to keep the rising number of attacks under control, or so he was told. It was hard not to lose his mind with worry and the crushing weight of his restlessness. He wanted to be out there *doing* something.

Finch was as busy as the demigods. He at least spoke directly to Gloucester, who came to expect a nightly call from him. He was gathering the other magicians and magic-wielders of the city to fight against all the monsters escaping from Denken's Pocket. Each night Gloucester heard the weariness in Finch's voice deepen. Magic seemed to be effective against the creatures, but it was dangerous and exhausting work.

And how Gloucester longed to be a part of it. He was reaching his wit's end, shut away from it all. The clock shop felt more and more reminiscent of his old cell. Only this time it wasn't a locked door and an armed guard caging him within. It was his own helplessness. He had no money, no home, no plan for how to fix any of this. In his cell, after months had passed, it began to feel like the outside world no longer existed. Like the cell was all there was, without time or place. Here and now, he almost missed that. Now the world outside was all too real. And in equally real peril, but he had *no idea* what to do about it.

Don't miss it. Don't you dare let yourself miss that, he told himself every time his thoughts veered that way. That cell and the people who stuck him in there had ruined his life.

Change came a week later, on a warm but overcast day with a drizzle of rain dampening the streets. In spite of the weather, the clock shop was busy with customers perusing the shelves and vying for Zane's attention. Gloucester offered to help out, but Zane turned him down, shooing him as kindly as she could back to the break room that had become his living quarters.

She claimed she had things under control, but Gloucester wasn't sure whose benefit she had in mind. Being in groups of strangers put him on edge. Zane had probably picked up on that and was once again doing her best to protect him in her own way. She was scared too, and surely feeling as helpless as he was. Unfortunately, it left him annoyed on top of restless, and resentful of her as she continuously shepherded him away from any useful task.

That afternoon, he was diverting his nervous energy into exercise when he was interrupted by the sudden appearance of Finch in the doorway.

Caught off-guard, Gloucester looked up mid-push-up. Nothing in Finch's countenance suggested urgency, but it was the first time he'd shown his face in the clock shop, which immediately set off alarm bells in Gloucester's mind. He pushed himself up enough to gather his legs under him, then got to his feet.

"What's wrong?" he asked, glancing around as if the danger

might pop out from behind the door. His shirt, damp with sweat between his shoulder blades, felt chilled against his back, amplifying the tingle of unease dancing up his spine.

Finch leaned against the doorframe, eyeing him with amusement. "Hello to you too."

"Hello," Gloucester said. His initial alarm was fading now, overtaken by curiosity. "What's wrong?"

Finch threw himself down on the sofa bed, pulling a face at the creak of old springs. "So this is where you've been staying, eh? Can't say it's the lap of luxury, but it could be worse." He looked around the room, surveying the pale green walls and framed paintings of wildlife.

"Yeah," said Gloucester. He grabbed his towel off a chair and dabbed away sweat from the back of his neck. He was suddenly uncomfortably conscious of the stains under his arms and the mussed state of his hair. "It could. Why are you here, Cassus?"

"I wanted to see you." Finch shrugged as he leaned back against the pillows at the head of the makeshift bed. His hair blended in against the dark orange fabric. "You're a welcome sight after a day battling demons."

"Demons?" Gloucester's eyebrows shot upward.

"Close as I can tell. Shadowy things, glowy eyes, big long claws. A group of us went after a pack of them in the public library off Hammond Street. You wouldn't believe the mess they were making." He grimaced.

"With the books?"

"The librarian. Though the books too, I suppose."

They both went quiet. Finch didn't seem perturbed by the break in conversation, his eyes drifting closed as he settled himself more comfortably where he lay. Gloucester, however, felt each passing second like a growing itch, a clock ticking away in the back of his mind. With each second that ticked by, there could be someone out there in danger, and he was in here. Useless. His fingers clenched around the towel draped over his shoulders.

"Is there anything I can do?" The question burst from his lips, and he hated the note of almost-pleading in his voice. Finch opened his eyes and peered at him with an air of confusion.

"For the librarian? Doubtful. She was pretty damn dead."

"With *any* of it!" Gloucester exclaimed, throwing the towel back onto the chair. "Demons and dragons and who knows what else, and I'm sitting in here twiddling my thumbs while other people fight them. Isn't there anything I can do?"

Finch sat up, regarding him sympathetically. It didn't make Gloucester feel any better, nor did it stir up any hope for the magician's reply.

"I dunno, mate. This is all magic and, well, that's not exactly your forte. You're a decent channeler, but you've no training. You're not a magician." He shuffled forward to sit on the edge of the bed and patted the blanket beside him, inviting Gloucester to sit down too. Grudgingly, he did so. Heaving a heavy sigh that had a lot more to do with impatience than wistfulness, he pushed both his hands through his hair.

"So I'm just supposed to sit here and wait for other people to save the world, all the while doing nothing to help," he grumbled. He dropped his hands to his lap and leveled a resigned glower at a cuckoo clock hanging on the opposite wall. Zane had yet to start repairs on it, and its leaf-shaped pendulum hung motionless. A broken tool waiting to be given back its functionality.

It wasn't about being a hero. The attention of people he didn't know always left him ill at ease, and his pride had never demanded recognition for things he didn't feel he'd earned. What did bother him was the powerlessness. He knew about the danger they were all in, and he wanted to be able to help stop it.

"No one could accuse you of not being helpful whenever you can be, Gloucester." Finch squeezed his shoulder, eyes kind. His hand lingered for a moment before he moved it away, leaning forward with his elbows propped on his knees.

Gloucester wasn't convinced, but he offered Finch a small smile nonetheless. "You can call me Mikalai. If you want."

His smile grew at the surprise on Finch's face.

"Really?" Finch sounded like he genuinely hadn't expected this, but it was clear he was pleased. "You sure? I mean, Zane doesn't even—"

"Zane doesn't care one way or the other," Gloucester said. "Seems like you do. So if you want to call me Mikalai, I don't mind."

"It's a nice name," Finch said, smiling meekly. He seemed afraid Gloucester would retract his permission if he wasn't careful. "That's a Nordlander name, isn't it?"

Gloucester nodded. "My mum's from there. So am I. I lived in the Nordlands until I was twenty and I moved down here. Mum and Dad are still there."

"Do you get along with them? Or did you leave because they found out you were—"

"Gay?" Gloucester finished. He shook his head with a laugh. "No. No, they already knew. They were pretty used to the idea by the time I left. No, I just wanted to see a bit of the world. Maybe get away from the long winters for a while. I'm from a little town in the mountains, so Frettchen was a pretty big change."

"You don't have much of an accent."

"My dad's Frettchennian. I grew up speaking both languages. Sort of nixes the accent either way, for the most part."

"Bilingual." Finch hummed appreciatively. "That's hot."

"What about you?" Finch's accent was impossible to miss, but Gloucester wasn't sure where it traced back to. "Where are you from?"

"All over, at this point," Finch said. Catching the look Gloucester gave him, he laughed and added, "One of the West Isles originally. A wee spit of rock and trees called Cyclops Stone." He pointed at one of the paintings on the wall, which depicted a coastal scene, sunlight sparkling off the water and the only land a colorful stone outcropping guarded over by a small thicket of trees. "Looks a bit like that."

"Never heard of it," Gloucester admitted. The smattering of

islands known as the West Isles was hard to accurately map. While some were big enough to have small cities or communities of their own, many were barely more than rocks in the ocean. Save for the very largest of them, most were little known and even less minded by the mainland cities.

Finch waved a hand, swatting away Gloucester's apologetic tone. "I'd be more surprised if you had. I'm not sure even the neighboring islands have heard of it. It's not exactly known for its contributions to modern society."

"How old were you when you left?" It wasn't pertinent information, but Gloucester found himself interested in the answer and the conversation in general. Some of his nervous energy was simmering down, and for the first time in several days, he was able to think about something other than Denken and his monsters.

"Ummmm . . ." Finch took a minute to think it over, making Gloucester chuckle at the show he made of scratching his chin while squinting up at the ceiling. "Let's see . . . about five, maybe? Six? We'd traveled a bit before that, but we always came home again. Until Mum died. Then we packed up for good." The smile twitching Finch's lips faded away. "I've never been back."

In his mind's eye, a tiny Cassus Finch, round-faced and innocent, stood on a shoreline like the one in the painting, crying over a mother and home lost together. He blinked it away to regard the man in the present, far from innocent but just as human.

"Maybe now's a good time," he suggested, only half-joking.

"Why, 'cause a stark raving demigod with an axe to grind with me is rampaging through the city with a bevy of beasties?" Finch snorted, shaking his head once. "Nah, this is too important. Plus, loath as I am to admit it, I helped bring this about. Gotta make it right." His smile returned, wearier than before.

Sitting this close beside him, Gloucester saw that the sun tattoo on his forehead didn't end at his brow, but rather extended onto the scalp beneath his red hair. He wondered if it went full-circle and if it was there for any reason beyond decoration. Was it magical in some way? What other tattoos did he have? He'd seen parts of one on Finch's arm, the tentacles of an octopus wrapping around his elbow.

"It's brave of you to stay," he told him.

As soon as he said it, it seemed like a very silly comment to make. Finch gave a laugh and Gloucester looked away, annoyed with both of them.

However, Finch's next words weren't to tease Gloucester, as he'd expected. "Not really. This madness will spread if we don't stop it. Even if I did a runner, it'd catch up with me eventually, no matter how good at hiding I was." Gloucester glanced over at him quickly as a hand came to rest on his knee. "*You* could run, though, you know. I doubt Mulligan would waste the effort to chase you. You could start over. Or go home to that little town in the mountains."

Gloucester thought about it. He thought of home, the smell of wood smoke, and winter in the air. He could go back there. Start over, as Finch said. It might not be easy—he'd have to build his life back up again—but it would be far away from everything bad that had happened to him here in Frettchen.

"I don't think I can," he said finally. "I can't just run away."

"Now who's the brave one?" He patted Gloucester's knee. "I'm glad you're sticking around." He paused, his smile spreading into a wry grin, before adding, "Partly because I'm pretty sure you're the only one who can stand me. Even the other magicians and mages, uh, tend not to take kindly to me."

"They're just jealous," Gloucester joked. "Of your rapier wit."

"Ah, I was hoping it was my stunning good looks."

Gloucester laughed. "That too."

"Aha! So you admit it!" Finch moved his hand from Gloucester's leg to clap triumphantly. He leaned smugly back against the blue tartan fleece of the blanket. "You think I'm stunning."

"Well, you've left me stunned on occasion," Gloucester retorted. "Throttling a person will do that."

He saw Finch's smile fall away and immediately regretted his words. Finch didn't seem offended so much as wary, but he wasn't laughing.

"Sorry," Gloucester said, looking away again and feeling quite foolish. "I didn't mean it like that . . . or, well . . . I'm not very good at jokes. Even before . . ." He cleared his throat. "Anyway, sorry about that. Didn't mean anything by it."

When he risked a glance over at Finch, the other man's expression was solemn, not angry.

"If I could take back all of that, I would," Finch said, his voice barely above a whisper. He sat up again and reached for Gloucester's hand, fingertips brushing across his knuckles. On Gloucester's palm, the digits of the phone number still emblazoned there tingled. "I wasn't thinking straight. I just . . . saw the opportunity and I took it."

"Including kissing me," Gloucester said. "As a way to distract Denken from seeing what you were thinking."

"That wasn't supposed to . . . That wasn't planned. Not that the rest of it was all that planned out, either." Gloucester wasn't sure he'd ever seen Finch so uncomfortable. He couldn't look Gloucester in the eye for long, shifting where he sat like he was resisting the urge to get up and run. "The opportunity arose and . . . I knew a little about how Denken's power works. I've met mind-readers before, though none as powerful as the personification of Thought himself. Surface thoughts are the easiest to read, which also makes them the most distracting. And the more emotional they are . . . the more passionate . . ." He was blushing, color rising in his cheeks beneath the peppering of freckles.

"Mission accomplished," Gloucester said, trying to ignore the twinge of pain in his chest. It was stupid to be hurt by this. He stared down at his hands and tried to will his emotions under control.

"Glou—Mikalai," Finch said. "It wouldn't have worked if the emotions weren't real. Denken would have seen through it if I hadn't actually felt anything about the kiss. About you."

Gloucester wasn't sure what he felt. Too many different things, all mixed up together. "That's supposed to make me feel better?"

Finch's expression was still, but Gloucester thought he could read a tiny flinch in his eyes. "I'd hoped so."

The silence that asserted itself between them wasn't a comfortable one. Gloucester wished he could find an excuse to get up and leave, or summon the wrath to insist that Finch do so. Instead, he sat, frowning down at his hands in his lap and trying to think of what to say.

"I don't know what I feel," he confessed.

"That's okay. That's fair. It's . . . complicated."

"What isn't?" Gloucester grumbled. "My life used to be so simple."

He could feel Finch's eyes on him. "Do you miss it?"

Yes. He wanted to shout it, to snarl and cry and fight until he had back what he'd lost. Some things weren't so easily returned, however. Sometimes going back wasn't an option.

"Yeah," he answered, with less certainty than he liked. "I miss what I had."

Finch said nothing for another long moment, and the room filled with only the ticking of clocks. Several of them were on the walls, in various states of repair and regulation. A couple of dismantled time pieces were spread out across the tabletop on the other side of the room, where Zane had been working on them between customers. Gloucester found it strangely calming to watch her work; he had no idea how all the little pieces fit together, but Zane handled them all with a careful and deft confidence, fixing what was broken and putting the pieces back together again.

"I know things are . . . well, frankly pretty horrible right now." Finch scoffed a laugh at his own words. "Even setting aside all of the bloody madness with Denken, things must be weird for you. Complicated. But maybe complicated isn't all bad, eh? Maybe there's some good to be found too?"

He half-raised his hand with a hesitance unbefitting the normally confident magician, moving to pat Gloucester on the shoulder again. Or maybe it was his face he was reaching for.

Either way, the gesture was cut short when Zane's voice rang through the ajar door, louder than usual and catching both of their attention. "I'm coming in," she announced. When she didn't immediately show her face, Finch rolled his eyes.

"We're decent if that's what you're worried about," he called back to her.

"Hey," chided Zane, sidling through the door. "Just trying to be considerate." She peered at the pair of them. "So what are you up to, then? Has something happened?"

"Just came to visit, that's all." Finch seemed to notice for the first time how close he and Gloucester were sitting, and he got to his feet with just enough composure so as to not be overtly hasty. "But I'd best be off. Fight the good fight and all that rubbish." With a parting smile at Gloucester and a jaunty nod to Zane, he swept past them and through the door. They listened to his retreating footsteps and the distinct tinkle of the chimes above the front door as he left the shop.

"Sorry, did I scare him off?" Zane asked, staring after Finch with an expression of conflicting amusement and concern.

Gloucester frowned too, thoughtful. "I dunno. I don't think much scares him."

"Lucky him."

Gloucester got to his feet, suppressing a sigh. He didn't know what to make of Cassus Finch. He was a flippant, joking enigma with a lot of power Gloucester didn't understand. It made him fascinating. *And dangerous,* he reminded himself. He'd thrown them into harm's way to serve his own interests before; they had nothing to guarantee he wouldn't do so again.

Nothing, save for the earnestness in his voice as he confessed his regret. Could that be trusted?

I have no idea, Gloucester thought, frustrated with trying to navigate the murky waters of human emotion.

"Judging from your face, the conversation didn't go too well," Zane said, blowing a tendril of hair from her face and crossing her arms. "What did you talk about?"

Gloucester's frown deepened as he glared down at his feet. "A little bit of everything. And I'm not really sure how it went, all in all. Mostly I'm trying to remember if people were this hard to understand *before* I spent six months completely alone."

Zane's laugh wasn't without sympathy. "Who knows? Probably. People are weird, it's just a fact of life." She was quiet for a moment, watching him. "He seems to really like you," she added tentatively. When Gloucester responded only with a noncommittal hum, she pressed on. "Do you like him? For fear of sounding like a gossiping teenager."

"More like a teenager's mother," Gloucester retorted. He knew she meant no harm by her curiosity, nor by her caution, but he wasn't entirely sure himself what he felt, let alone what Finch might be feeling. "It's complicated. There's so much going on. Honestly, I feel crazy most days, so whether someone *likes* me or not is sort of the last thing I'm thinking about."

"Probably for the best." Zane nodded sagely. "Anyway, I just came to check on you, since there's been a lull in the customers finally. I doubt it'll last, though, so I'd best get back up front before anyone else comes in. You staying in here?"

She seemed to make the decision for him, a quick smile flitting across her face as she stepped back through the door before he had a chance to say anything. "I'll be in the front if you need me," she said. The door clicked shut behind her.

Gloucester stared at it. In the moment of it closing, he'd heard the all-too-familiar slamming of his cell door, so clearly that he didn't know how it was only imagined. His gaze jumped around, half-expecting to find bare white walls and a thin cot instead of a table covered in clock parts and a fold-out sofa. Old fear trickled through him like telltale water through cracks in a dam.

This isn't the same, he told himself, staring at the door again. *I'm not trapped. I'm not a prisoner.* And yet when he reached out for the doorknob and twisted it, the relief he felt when the door swung open was strong enough that he wondered just what he'd been expecting. *You're not a prisoner. You're not.*

These reassurances weren't helping. The walls seemed suddenly too close, looming over him. He pushed a hand against the ajar door, afraid that this time it wouldn't budge and the open doorway was nothing more than a fantasy of freedom.

What if this, all of this, was nothing more than a dream-turned-nightmare, and he would wake up any moment back in his cell? It was a fear that still haunted him every night when he closed his eyes. What if this time was the time? The day the dream ended.

He stepped through the doorway so hastily that he stumbled, letting out a breath he only now realized he'd been holding as the door proved to be real. He wasn't stuck. This wasn't in his head.

He needed to get out of here.

He barely heard Zane's startled voice as she called his name. He certainly paid it no mind, pushing past the handful of customers in the shop. Faces he didn't know stared at him, and he refused to look too closely. The only thing that mattered was getting out of here. Getting away.

The wind chimes above the door jangled as he pushed it open, and then he was outside on the sidewalk.

Chapter 10

Harmony and Discord

The air seemed fresher than usual, and Gloucester breathed in great lungfuls of it, trying to clear his head. He knew this wasn't normal. This wasn't how he was supposed to react to things. Knowing that did nothing to calm him, though. If anything, it made it all worse with the added stress and frustration at his own oddness.

"I used to be normal!" he snapped at no one in particular. A passing trio of women gave him alarmed looks and hurried their strides to put some distance between them and the angry, wild-eyed young man who had just burst from the clock shop.

The chimes tinkled again and Zane exited her shop, face set in concern. "Gloucester? What happened? What's wrong?" He flinched at the hand she laid on his shoulder, making her step back. "What's wrong with you?"

I wish I knew.

"I need—I need to get out of here. Get fresh air." His head

felt like it was spinning, as everything was suddenly too much. Too much to do. Too much to fight. To fix. To think.

He left Zane gaping on the sidewalk. He was walking quickly, almost running in his desperation to be away. The irony of the contradiction to what he'd told Finch earlier wasn't lost on him. He wasn't running away, he tried to assure himself as his feet followed a path that hadn't been laid out by his conscious mind. He was just trying to clear his head.

With no money for a taxi, he took the bus, enough loose change in his pockets to at least cover that fare. Then he was walking again, feet slapping on concrete sidewalk and the bubbling panic in his mind simmering into white noise. Soon he was thinking of nothing more than the act of setting one foot in front of the other. The tightness gripping his chest relented, allowing him to breathe again.

When the realization of where he was headed finally dawned on him, he was three-quarters of the way there. He'd left the busy streets of the shopping district behind and now walked along a sidewalk in the shadow of tall apartment buildings, their gray facades sprouting out of tree-lined grounds behind short stone walls. Balconies jutted out from each floor, some sparse and others dotted with color, decorated by their owners with flower-boxes and lawn chairs.

The path he traced was a familiar one. He used to walk it all the time. As he got closer to his destination, he searched the faces of everyone he passed, for once not avoiding eye contact. In each face, he looked for familiarity, for recognition. Some were nothing more than strangers who met his eyes briefly before moving on. But others . . .

He heard his name murmured a few times as he passed by people whose names didn't come to mind, but whose faces he knew. The woman who had lived two floors above gasped at the sight of him. The man who worked at the nearby bank did a double-take. Two twenty-somethings who had always been waiting at the bus stop when he was on his way to work whispered to each other, pointing surreptitiously. Others he knew paid him as little mind as the complete strangers did, perhaps never having noticed he'd been gone. More and more, though, he saw recognition in their faces that mirrored his own. They knew him here. Or they had, once.

Finally, he reached the end of his path. The morning's drizzle had dried up, giving way to a weak sun that peeked through the clouds and cast shadows down from the tall buildings lining the streets. The shadow of the building Gloucester stopped in front of engulfed him as he stared up at the tiers of balconies sprouting from the red brickwork. Just as he had a few weeks ago, hidden in an alleyway across the street, he counted silently, shading his eyes from the sun with one hand.

Seven up. Five from the corner. The window of his old home was dark, and he could see no sign of movement from within. Not that he could see much of anything from this distance and angle.

No knowing if he's home until you get there, he thought, pretending the trepidation that rocked through him didn't exist.

His feet, which led him so effortlessly back to this place, had stopped in their tracks, and it was suddenly a trick to get them to move again. Gloucester continued to stare up at the window. Once that had been home. Could it be again?

He'd scarcely taken two steps toward the main doors when a ruckus just across the street caught his attention. Blinking, he looked over. He thought of the dragon forged of fire, of demons with burning eyes and dreadful claws, even of Denken himself, with his shark's smile and bottomless stare.

What he saw was none of these things. A young person, their short brown hair and smooth-skinned face giving no solid indication of gender, was stumbling across the grassy lawn outside the apartment complex on the other side of the road. As far as Gloucester could guess, they had just burst through the doors, which were still swinging on their hinges. In the person's hand was a long wooden bat. Even from where he stood,

Gloucester could see the blood. Two prone figures already lay near the bat-wielder's feet, and a crowd was gathering with urgency, shouting out in fear, confusion, and anger. Gloucester thought he heard a child crying but couldn't see one amongst the milling crowd of adults. Swearing none too quietly, he abandoned his path and dashed across the street.

"Get away from me!" the youth with the bat shouted, their words growing distinct as Gloucester drew closer. They swept the bat in wide vicious arcs, not allowing anyone within two meters without being struck. The anger in their voice was augmented with terror. Gloucester could feel it like heat emanating from them, rolling out in waves over the fearful crowd.

"What's happened? What's wrong?" sobbed an elderly woman, clutching at the side of her face, where an angry smear of bruises spread darkly across her skin. One of her eyes was swollen shut. "I don't understand!" Her cries were nearly drowned out by the others' shouts.

"Quiet!" barked Gloucester, bellowing the word to be heard above the tumult of the crowd. A few people looked his way, but the person with the bat and the stricken old woman paid him no mind. Several others were too busy yelling to notice him. "LISTEN!" he shouted, coming to a halt as close as he dared, fists clenched at his sides. "LISTEN TO ME!"

This drew more attention. "Why the hell should we?" someone shouted back.

"Who are you?" demanded the person with the bat. They pointed it at him aggressively, their chest heaving with each ragged breath. "Who are you? Leave me alone! You're just another—"

"Quiet!" Gloucester snapped again. The crowd had ceased yelling, at least for now, and he was able to lower his voice a little. He took a deep breath, did his best to ignore the many eyes on him, and focused on the angry pair staring at him down the length of the bat.

"You're scared, right?" He held his hands up slowly,

placatingly. "Terrified. Maybe that's not new. Maybe you're scared a lot. I get that. But today's worse, right? *You're all scared.*" He spared a glance around at all the others. "More than you've been in a long time. Maybe ever. But you need to *calm down.* Don't let that fear win."

"What the hell do you know about it?" the bat-wielder growled, but they seemed less certain, and some of their rage had subsided.

More than you'd ever guess. "You don't want to hurt these people," Gloucester said, a calmness he didn't feel layered in his voice as professionalism took over. He'd been trained for situations like this. "They're not going to hurt you. They're *not.*" His voice was firm as he again surveyed the onlookers, a warning in his eyes. "Just put the bat down."

The old woman with the battered face nodded, her cheeks wet with tears. "Please," she begged. "Please, Harmony, just put it down."

Harmony no longer looked sure of anything, their face frightened as they stared from Gloucester to the old woman. "Gramma . . ." they said hesitantly. "What—? Did I—?" The bat lowered as their eyes widened, taking in the sight of the bruises on their grandmother's face.

The woman shook her head, hands pressed to her mouth. "It doesn't matter," she said, voice muffled by her fingers. "It's okay, Harmony. It's okay."

The bat clattered to the sidewalk, bouncing a little and then rolling away from Harmony, who threw themselves sobbing into their grandmother's arms. Gloucester saw the momentary flinch in the old woman's expression before she pulled her grandchild into a tight embrace, whispering comforts and consolations.

"That lunatic would've killed us!" shouted a gruff voice in the crowd. A middle-aged man in flannel and jeans shoved his way forward and snatched the bat up from the ground. "They can't just get away with it." He pointed the bat at Harmony. Gloucester heard the stirrings of agreement amongst the gathered people.

"It's sorted now," he said tightly, stepping between the newcomer and Harmony, who was still huddled in their grandmother's arms. "Just leave it, all right? It's over. There are people who need tending to." He gestured at the people unlucky enough to have been struck by Harmony's bat, now picking themselves up off the ground, groaning.

"Over?" The bat swung to point at Gloucester's face once more. "Like hell it is! What d'you even know about it? Who the hell are you?"

"Someone who doesn't want to see a load of people beat each other to death with a bat," snapped Gloucester, losing his patience. "Just drop it!"

"Mikalai?"

Everything about the voice was familiar: the depth of it, the pleasant cadence, even the tone of surprise. Gloucester was blindsided by the cascade of memories that washed over him. Unthinkingly, he turned his eyes away from the man in front of him, searching for the source of the voice.

THWACK!

If the memories had hit hard, they had nothing on the bat.

Chapter 11

A Door Closes

The sky, clearing from gray into blue, danced drunkenly in Gloucester's vision. Trying to stop everything from spinning, he narrowed his eyes with a wince and several choice words. He wheezed, struggling to pull air back into his lungs.

Pale sunlight was blocked out by the appearance of a face in front of his own, staring down at him in open concern amidst dozens of long, dark braids.

"Mikalai? Can you hear me?" The face looked away again, turning stormy in anger. "Get back, the lot of you. And *you*. Drop the bat or I'll bloody well shove it where the sun don't shine!"

Gloucester heard the clatter of wood hitting concrete, then the patter of a dozen feet retreating. The face above him turned back to meet his gaze.

"Jeb . . ." Gloucester murmured. "Hi."

Jebediah Thaly offered him a smile that had once meant everything to him. "'Hi'? You've just been clobbered with a bat and all you can say is 'hi'? I daren't even bring up the fact that I thought you were *dead*."

The smile didn't last long. A moment later, Jeb was back to staring at Gloucester in wide-eyed disbelief as he eased him to his feet. Gloucester swayed on the spot. He felt breathless from the blow the bat had landed across his back, but he was able to stay upright. He barely noticed his own dizziness anyway, preoccupied with the man keeping a steadying hold on his arm.

"Like you *ever* daren't—" he started to say, before stiffening when Jeb's words fully sank in. "You thought I was dead? Did they tell you that?"

Jeb frowned. He was still staring at Gloucester like he couldn't believe his eyes. "The high minister's agents? Yeah. I mean, they told me when you went undercover in the Nordlands last fall. Then a month later, they told me you'd been killed in the line of duty."

Well, that's one mystery solved. What Jeb was told to explain his disappearance had been one of the most persistent questions on Gloucester's mind, but now that he had the answer, it didn't give him any of the satisfaction he'd hoped for. Mostly he just felt sad.

"Last I'd heard, though, ghosts weren't vulnerable to being hit with blunt instruments," Jeb went on. "Which sort of leads me to believe things are a lot more complicated than that. Especially when it sounds like you had no idea what they told me. What the hell happened, Mikalai? Where have you been?"

Wondering where to possibly begin, Gloucester said nothing for a long moment. He didn't care that he was staring at Jeb as openly as Jeb was at him. Taller than Gloucester by several inches, Jeb's regal features, long braids, and kind eyes made for as handsome a sight as he remembered. The casual grace he always exuded was the same as ever, even as Jeb gaped at him. Gloucester had always admired that grace, even envied it. Everyone liked Jeb almost instantly upon meeting him. There was just something about him. Gloucester had never been able to mimic that social ease.

A fact evident now, as he realized just how long he'd put off the requested explanation when Jeb further prompted him with raised eyebrows and an impatient "Well? Where were you? You vanish for months, your work tells me you died, and then one day you show up out of nowhere, only to get beaned with a bat. What the hell, Mikalai?"

"It's—"

"If you say it's complicated, I swear you'll be missing the bat," Jeb snapped.

"It *is* complicated," he said, quickly adding, "But I'll try to explain," when Jeb crossed his arms and opened his mouth.

Ought he to tell him the truth of it all? About the Gambler and the magic and the threat the city was under? Part of him desperately wanted to. Jeb was in just as much danger as everyone else in Frettchen. He was asking for the truth, and he deserved to hear it. Once, Gloucester had shared everything with him. Now, though . . .

Would Jeb even believe him? Could he blame him if he didn't? What if he thought he was merely a traitor trying to escape justice? What if he thought he'd lost his mind? He didn't want to lie to Jeb, but what good would the truth do if he didn't believe him?

Perhaps the middle path was the best one to take. Tell the truth, just not the whole story.

"They lied to you," he said.

"Oh really?" Jeb's dark brows strove to disappear into his hairline. "I've reached that conclusion already, but I'm glad to hear it."

Gloucester gave him an exasperated look but forced himself not to rebuke him. Jeb had earned the right to a little pithiness. He just hated that it was aimed at him. "Seven months ago, I saw . . . something I shouldn't have. One of the high minister's secrets. They arrested me for it. Locked me away."

Jeb looked dubious. "The high minister's dead. So is that

why you're free now?"

Sort of, Gloucester was tempted to say. "He let me go because he needed my help. Someone was trying to kill him, and he didn't think he could trust any of his people."

"Someone was trying to—wait, wait, wait, are you saying . . . They said the high minister died of natural causes. Was that a lie? Was he murdered?" Jeb's eyes widened again when Gloucester nodded. "Bloody hell, Mik, what did you get yourself caught up in?"

Though the crowd had dispersed, Gloucester could see curious faces watching them from the windows of nearby apartments. "Can we talk about this somewhere more private?"

Jeb hesitated, then nodded. "Yeah. Yeah, of course."

—

Upon first glance, the apartment was as Gloucester remembered it. The same paisley curtains in the windows, sewn by Jeb's mother, and the same paintings of Nordish woodlands on the walls. The same mismatched table and chairs in the kitchen visible from the entryway. The smell was even as he remembered, the undefinable scent of home, and he took an involuntary moment to stand in silence, trying to pretend the last seven months hadn't happened.

He noticed the differences slowly, small inconsistencies from what he remembered. Different jackets hanging by the door and a different armchair in the living room, in place of the ugly but delightfully cozy one he'd bought second-hand when they moved in the year before. Here and there he spotted other things, pieces of furniture and odds and ends that weren't the same.

"You've, uh, redecorated a bit," he said. He felt odd, standing here like an interloper in a place that had once been home. Jeb was watching him, and Gloucester couldn't help but think that he was looking at him like he didn't think he belonged there anymore either.

"A bit, yeah," Jeb said. His arms were crossed tightly over his chest again. Not exactly the reunion Gloucester had been hoping for. He looked tired, crow's feet crinkling the corners of his eyes, another change from what Gloucester remembered. "Looking at your stuff, thinking that you'd died, some of it was sort of difficult to be around."

Gloucester blinked, looking around again. Indeed, there was a distinct shortage of his own possessions to be found. "Did you—?"

"It's all in storage," Jeb told him quickly. "I can give you the, uh, the information. So you can pick it up or . . . whatever you want."

That didn't sound like an invitation to move it back into the apartment. He nodded mutely, unsure what to say. Talking to Jeb had never felt hard before.

Jeb saved him the trouble. "So you said you were arrested, then released to . . . help with an investigation? One that ended with the high minister's death? What happened? And why didn't you call or come back before now? Why did they lie about you being arrested?"

It was a lot of questions, and all of them valid. Gloucester struggled over which one to answer first. "I think . . . they lied because they never intended to let me go. I think they were planning on just making me disappear."

"Why not just have you killed, then?" Jeb looked apologetic as soon as he asked the question. "Sorry, but from what you're telling me, it's starting to sound like something they would do."

"No doubt. Maybe they thought I could still be useful somehow." Gloucester didn't think it would go over too well to say the vision of an eyeless demigod had convinced the high minister to spare his life. "Which I guess turned out to be the case. Look, it's sort of a long story, so just let me tell it best I can, all right?"

Jeb looked impatient and more than a little overwhelmed, but he nodded. Taking a deep breath, Gloucester launched into his story.

He told Jeb as much as he dared. He explained how he'd stumbled upon a prisoner the high minister was hiding away, who was being tortured and used for political gain, and how he'd been locked away immediately after getting caught, with no trial or chance to reach out for aid. He hesitated then, wondering if there was a point in trying to put into words what those six months in solitary confinement had been like. He decided there wasn't. He'd never been much good with words, and he wasn't at all sure how he would describe the time he'd spent in that cell.

Instead, he skipped to the first assassination attempt on the high minister's life and how that had prompted the paranoid politician to command his help. He did his best to avoid any mention of magic as his story unfolded, which he knew left some gaping holes in the tale, but what could he do? He didn't want to be stuck trying to convince Jeb of the existence of magic when he was already explaining everything else. Rather than telling him about the headache that had nearly made him a murderer, he made do with describing how he'd managed to escape when he realized that the high minister was going to betray him. On the run, he hadn't dared approach anyone from his old life, not wanting to put them in danger and also knowing it would be the first place the minister's people would look for him.

"I tried to stop the assassins anyway," he said, winding down the incomplete story. "But I couldn't. He still died."

Jeb, who had been silently engrossed for the whole story, let out a low whistle. "Good riddance, from the sound of it. Not that things have been all that great since he died." He grimaced, scratching his thumb across his chin. "I guess that could be said for the old bastard—he might have been a corrupt, cold-blooded bully, but he kept the city together. It feels like all of Frettchen has been falling apart since his death."

"Yeah," said Gloucester, biting his tongue on the truth he wanted to speak aloud. "It does."

"He died two weeks ago, though. Why didn't you contact

me? Why come back now and not then?"

Gloucester pondered the possible answers. True or false, they all felt like excuses.

"I was scared," he admitted at last. He tried for a smile. "Stupid, huh?"

Jeb reached out and patted him on the shoulder, yet even his touch didn't feel the same. It carried compassion and sympathy, but hesitance too.

"Nah, I get it," he told him. "I can't imagine what six months in solitary confinement must've been like. And then thrown right back into a case . . . Nah, it's understandable that you're overwhelmed. Hell, *I'm* overwhelmed. Emotions can be tricky."

Gloucester nodded in fervent agreement. His eyes swept over the apartment again, searching for signs of old comfort within the pastel blue walls. This used to be his sanctuary. Their home together. Longing pulled suddenly and sharply at his heart. They'd been happy here.

The living room, like the entryway, had an open doorway into the kitchen, and from where he stood, Gloucester could see a portion of the small dining table, the countertops and cabinets, and a good view of the fridge. The latter caught his eye. Jeb was a talented photographer and, as Gloucester remembered it, the fridge was bedecked with photos. They weren't all the same as before, though. Sure, he still spotted the ones of Jeb's family, his childhood dog, and a postcard from an old friend living in one of the South Cities, but most of the pictures surrounding these were new. Gloucester stepped away from Jeb's comforting hand on his shoulder and into the kitchen to take a closer look.

Gone was the photo of them at the summer Flower Festival, smiling amidst the garlands of pink and yellow blossoms, Jeb in a leather jacket dusted with petals and Gloucester's lashes dark with eyeliner. Nor was there any sign of the photo from Gloucester's twenty-fourth birthday, when they'd only been dating a few months and Jeb said his smile in it made it his favorite photo. Pictures of them at the apartment, out with friends, on holidays, all gone.

And in their place, a face he didn't know.

There weren't many, but Gloucester saw enough of the same smiling young stranger that he knew it wasn't a coincidence. His fingers brushed lightly over one. Jeb's arm was around the man's shoulders, and they looked happy and *right,* like two puzzle pieces fitted together.

"You met someone." His voice sounded distant in his ears. The breath slipped from his lungs as a sigh, and he felt a piece of him tugged out with it. He looked over at Jeb, who had the grace to hold his gaze. His eyes were sad.

"You were dead, Mikalai."

Gods, but he wanted to be mad at him. Gloucester thought he might feel better if only he could bring himself to scream and shout and rage against the injustice of the world, the betrayal.

But he couldn't. Not to Jeb.

"Yeah," he said, dropping his hand away from the photos. "I suppose I was."

"If I had known . . . We only started . . . I mean, I waited, and I know that it was too fast, but—"

Gloucester shook his head, looking away from the faces smiling at him from the fridge door. "It's not your fault, Jeb. You don't have to apologize. There was no way for you to know. They lied. It's what they're good at."

Jeb stuck his hands in his pockets, and Gloucester wondered if it was perhaps to keep himself from reaching out. Saints knew *he* wanted to.

It wouldn't be right anymore. That was taken from you too.

"What will you do now?" Jeb asked. "Where will you go? If you need money or—"

"I'll figure it out," Gloucester said firmly. "I'm staying with a friend at the moment. I have some stuff to sort out. Then . . ." He shrugged.

Jeb bit his lip as if physically holding his words back as much as his hands. When at last he spoke, it was only to say, "I'll get you the storage information. Wait here."

He disappeared into the hallway, heading for the bedroom. Gloucester stayed rooted where he was, avoiding looking at the fridge door. Frozen smiles and happy gazes taunted him. This wasn't his home anymore.

After a few minutes, Jeb returned with a slip of paper and a key in his hand. He sat down next to Gloucester where he'd taken a seat on the sofa.

"Here," Jeb said, offering him the paper and the key. He tossed his head absently to flick his braids over his shoulder, a familiar tic that Gloucester had always found effortlessly attractive. "This is the location and number. The key will get you in. You can keep your stuff there as long as you need."

"Thanks," Gloucester murmured, eyes on the key in his hand. "But I can't really . . . I don't exactly have money right now. They froze my accounts and—"

Jeb laid a hand on his shoulder. "Don't worry about it. *Really*," he insisted when Gloucester opened his mouth to protest. "Who knows how long I would've kept paying for it anyway. I don't mind keeping it up until you have someplace to put everything."

Gloucester hesitated, then nodded. As much as he didn't like the idea of Jeb paying for the upkeep of his belongings because he couldn't take care of it himself, he was grateful. He would have hated to lose all of his worldly possessions on top of everything else.

"I'll figure something out soon," he promised. "It won't be long-term, you paying for it." He closed his fingers around the jagged edges of the key, feeling them dig into his skin.

"Thank you," he added after a moment, voice scarcely above a whisper. "For holding onto it. Even when you thought . . ."

"Mikalai, this wasn't your fault. I don't blame you." Jeb seemed to realize that his hand was still on Gloucester's shoulder, and he yanked it away, an unhappy redness flushing his cheeks. "I'm the one that should be apologizing. I—"

"No." Gloucester shook his head hard enough to dislodge the curls of hair tucked behind his ears. "It's not your fault either. I can't blame you for moving on. You thought I was dead. The only people to blame are the high minister and his cronies, and I think they've gotten what was coming to them."

"Good," said Jeb, the certainty in his voice leaving no room for debate.

"I just—" Here Gloucester's impassioned words faltered. "It wouldn't be fair to either of us," he said after a moment's silence, dragging in an uneven breath. "To try to go back to where we were before . . . before everything, no matter how much I want to. I wouldn't ask that of you." The words escaped him very quickly, tumbling from his tongue before he could change his mind about saying them.

Until he'd arrived here, sat down on the couch that used to be his, and saw the sympathy in Jeb's brown eyes, he hadn't realized just how badly a part of him wanted all of this back, nor how large a part of him it was. He'd told himself it wasn't possible, that it was an unattainable past, but that part of him had still hoped. He struggled to let go of it, when all he wanted was for this to still be his haven, to curl up in their bed and stave the world off at the door.

It wasn't his place to take refuge in anymore, though, and it wouldn't be right to try to take it back.

Jeb watched him, a silent intensity lighting his eyes. Gloucester bit his lip against the urge to lean forward and kiss him, to return to that familiarity too. That sense of home. Of love.

"I'm so sorry this happened to you, Mik," Jeb said at long last, voice little more than a sad whisper.

"I'll survive." He tried to force a nonchalant smile but didn't quite manage it. *I ought to ask his name,* he thought morosely. The man who had taken his place. Yet what would that achieve? Surely it would only make Jeb uncomfortable and defensive while encouraging Gloucester's sullenness. It wouldn't make either of them feel better.

I'll ask him next time, he told himself. Would there be a next time? He wasn't sure. Remaining in touch with Jeb and watching him be happy and fulfilled with someone who wasn't him felt like misery. On the other hand, he didn't want to sever another tie to his old life. Jeb had been a major part of his life here in Frettchen in the last few years. The thought of just leaving that behind was as intimidating as it was sad.

"I should go," he said, turning the key over and over between his fingers as he summoned the will to get to his feet.

"You don't have to," Jeb replied. "If you want to stay a little longer, I can make coffee and we can talk."

About what? They used to talk about anything and everything. They would have conversations that lasted hours, laughing or debating or simply venting to each other's sympathetic ear. Now his head was deserted of things to discuss. He didn't want to know how Jeb's life had progressed while his had fallen apart. Nor could he share the truth of all that had happened to him.

"Thanks," he said, offering Jeb a weak smile. "But it's okay. I'll be all right." He pushed himself up off the couch.

Jeb followed suit, still eyeing him fretfully. "Are you sure? According to your own story, it sounds like you could be in danger." He gripped Gloucester's arm. "Maybe you should, I dunno, get out of Frettchen for a while. You could go back to the Nordlands. I'm sure your parents—" He caught the look on Gloucester's face and gaped. "Oh bloody hell, you haven't said anything to them yet? Mikalai, they think you're *dead*. They're devastated!"

Guilt swarmed through Gloucester, enough to make him sick to his stomach. Just thinking about what his parents must be feeling in the wake of their son's supposed death made him want to call right then and there and tell them everything was okay.

Except that everything *wasn't* okay. He knew if his mum and dad found out he was alive, they'd be on the first train to

Frettchen. The last thing he wanted was more people he cared about in danger. If they could manage to stop Denken and his chaos before it spread beyond the city-state, then his parents would be safe and sound up north.

"I can't tell them yet," he said. When Jeb turned incredulous, he held up a weary hand before any protest could be given voice. "There's still a lot of fallout from this whole mess. I don't want them caught up in it. Not until I know it's safe."

He'd expected Jeb to argue further or, at best, nod in grudging understanding. Instead, his dark eyes fixed in an odd expression. Gloucester couldn't tell if it was curiosity or concern.

"Why did you come here today, Mikalai?" he asked.

Gloucester often wished, especially in Jeb's presence, that he was witty and eloquent. He wished he had charm and confidence that would make answering such a question easy. He imagined giving some meaningful reply that would tug at Jeb's heartstrings, and he would fall into his arms, moved to happy tears as they remembered all that they'd had together. That was ridiculous, though, least of all because of his lack of verbal grace.

"I missed you," he said, ducking his head. "I've missed you for seven months, but when I was finally free, when I was able to do as I pleased and go where I wanted, I . . . I couldn't. Like I said, I was scared."

It still sounded so pathetic out loud. What must Jeb think of him, spouting such cowardice?

What does it matter? He's got someone else now.

"So what changed today?" asked Jeb.

"I'm not sure," Gloucester confessed. "Everything got to be too much, and next thing I knew, I was on my way here. I guess . . . this place used to be where I could always go to feel safe, you know?"

Jeb lowered his gaze. "Yeah, I know. I'm sorry."

Gloucester forced a smile, shrugging a shoulder. "Don't be. Life is weird for me right now. It's probably for the best. And, well, you know how the saying goes. Life is what it is."

Jeb nodded slowly, face still down-turned. After a pause, he fixed Gloucester with a look of near-palpable worry. "You'll be okay, though? You're sure you're safe?"

I'm sure I'm not. It wouldn't be the most productive thing to admit out loud.

"I'll be okay."

It was only a matter of strides to the front door, which was for the best, as every one of Gloucester's steps was accompanied by another heavy weight settling onto his heart. He'd known things between him and Jeb would be strained, but he was still getting used to exercising a wide range of emotions again, and heartbreak was a new one for him.

"Thanks," he said when they reached the door. "For talking to me today."

"And for stopping a man from beating you up with a bat?" Jeb's smile didn't look like his heart was really in it.

Gloucester laughed just as weakly. "Yeah, that too. And for everything before . . . Just for everything."

"You too. Take care of yourself, Mikalai. I'm really glad you're not dead."

He opened the door and Gloucester forced himself to step through it. On the other side, he turned back for one last look at the apartment and the man smiling sadly back at him.

"Me too," he agreed. "Be well, Jeb."

He did his best to wear a smile of his own as the door closed.

Alone in the corridor, he didn't move for a long moment. The click of the latch felt like a slap, stinging his heart and stealing his breath away. The flat wooden surface of the door stared back at him, and Gloucester gloomily considered that he hadn't felt this alone since leaving his cell.

"You know what they say," said a voice in his ear. "When one door closes . . ."

While the proximity of the voice was cause enough for alarm, it was the voice itself that made Gloucester whirl to face it. He couldn't mistake it, not in a million years. Smooth, warm, and alluring, it was a beautiful poison pouring into his skull.

"You!" he gasped, stumbling back until his shoulders thudded against the wall. Black eyes and a too-wide, sharp-toothed grin filled his vision.

"Long time no see, Mik," said Denken. "I'd like a word."

Gloucester scrambled for a weapon he didn't have, desperately trying to tear his gaze from Denken's stare, but Denken's eyes were like tunnels, swallowing him up in darkness.

Chapter 12

Heart to Heart

Gloucester's head was spinning even before his senses properly returned. In the dark, empty void of semi-consciousness, he felt it: the unnerving sensation of back-and-forth, as if he were slowly swinging his head from side to side. The closer he came to waking, the more certain he was that the feeling was baseless.

Groaning, he opened his eyes. The brightness that greeted him made him squeeze them shut again with a wince. After a few seconds, he tried again, squinting cautiously.

He was in a room with walls of stone so white they shone, stretching high up toward a vaulted ceiling in the same blinding hue. Though the architecture struck him as similar to that of the Old Cathedral or All Saints Shrine, there wasn't a window in sight. Blinking to adjust his eyes to the bright surroundings, Gloucester tried to turn around.

His movement halted in a jarring manner, and the final

walls unconsciousness had erected around his senses crashed down. He was tied up.

More specifically, he was bound to a pillar at his back, arms pinned to his sides. Though the ropes weren't tight enough to be painful, they didn't allow him an inch to budge. The cords emitted a faint golden light that would have been pretty under different circumstances.

"Shit." He looked around wildly. "Denken!"

"No need to shout." The sultry voice issued from behind him, but no matter how he tried to crane his neck, Gloucester couldn't see the personification of Thought.

"What do you want?" he snapped. Denken clicked his tongue in mock disapproval.

"How cliché. And rude, I should add. People usually start conversations with 'hello,' you know. I'm aware you're out of practice with the intricacies of social interaction, but come on. That's a pretty basic one."

"People don't usually start conversations by tying the other person up." Gloucester tugged at the ropes binding him. They held fast.

"Depends on the conversation."

Denken finally stepped into view, gliding out from the corner of Gloucester's eye to stand in front of him.

He didn't look the same as he had three weeks before when he'd appeared in the high minister's interrogation room, grinning and full of carefree menace. Nothing was carefree about him now.

Yet some things remained unchanged. The general shape of him was as Gloucester remembered: slim of stature, with tousled black hair and wide eyes. He still commanded the same stifling aura of taking up more space than he physically possessed. The smile was different, though, as was the look in his eyes.

The wide grin, lined with teeth too pointed to be human, no longer conveyed any humor. Now it looked hollow and mask-like, pasted across his face but never reaching his eyes. Eyes as dark and deep as the dead of night, when the world seemed to cease in its physical existence, persisting only as sound and smell and memory. In that darkness, monsters lurked. Ebony filled not only the iris and pupil but extended where the whites of Denken's eyes should have been.

Gloucester had seen the demigod's eyes like this before, back in the High Minister's Cathedral. It was something he'd hoped never to see again. He looked down at Denken's hands, and sure enough, his fingers stretched to unnatural lengths, tapering into talons. None of this, he reflected, was looking very good for him.

"What do you *want,* Denken?" he asked more cautiously this time.

Denken crossed his arms, exaggerating a frown as he stared down at his needle-sharp fingers drumming against his bicep. "Your help. Of a sort."

"Of a sort?" That didn't sound promising. Not that Gloucester expected any interaction with Denken to be sunshine and rainbows.

"Of a sort," Denken repeated in a self-satisfied way. It was the most cheery thing about him, however. His clothes were rumpled and torn, and he seemed agitated, almost jittery, a beast on the verge of frenzy.

A shark that's smelled blood in the water. Gloucester immediately regretted the comparison. As far as comforting thoughts went, it wasn't one.

The tattoo tracing from Denken's left hand to his throat, a pattern of intertwining lines, was as it had been when the demigod lost his temper before, extending farther than usual, climbing up over his chin to stretch vertically across his face. It seemed to move even as Gloucester watched it, winding eternally—and making him sick to his stomach.

"You really know how to ask a guy for help," Gloucester said.

"Who said anything about asking? Asking implies you have a choice. You're already helping me, whether you like it or not." Denken waggled his eyebrows, but even that looked menacing.

"Do you like it?"

Gloucester tried to kick him, but Denken easily sauntered out of reach of his limited mobility.

"I'll take that as a hearty 'no,'" the demigod snickered.

"If I'm doing so much to help you, do me a favor and tell me what it is I'm doing." Gloucester grudgingly stopped struggling, but he made a silent vow not to miss any opportunity to give the bastard a good kicking. "It's not like I can do anything about it anyway."

Denken wagged a finger under Gloucester's nose, clicking his tongue reprovingly. "That would be a textbook villain mistake, now wouldn't it?" he said, then laughed.

While Denken's voice was seductive, his laughter held power of a different sort. The sublime made into sound, it stormed through Gloucester's skull and right into his brain. He wanted both to cover his ears and to let it sweep him away. When at last Denken stopped laughing, Gloucester sagged in relief.

"Then again, I don't like to think of myself as a villain. It's a good rule to live by, so remember that. Never condemn yourself to villainy. If you see yourself as the villain, then that's what you'll be. See? Self-fulfilling prophecy."

With his wide black eyes and empty grin, it was difficult to determine what Denken wanted from him. Agreement? Applause? An argument?

"So does that mean you'll tell me or not?" Gloucester demanded.

"Why not?" Denken shrugged. The movement was no simple rise and fall of his shoulders, but instead, a fluid, complicated motion Gloucester was quite certain he would be physically incapable of mimicking. Which was a shame, because he'd never seen a more effective demonstration of nonchalance.

"I have a few things to work through," Denken went on, inspecting his nails, his casual air ruined by the fact that said nails were four-inch, needle-like claws. "In my, hah, spare time sort of thing. People to have words with."

"Like we're having words?" snarked Gloucester.

"Hush now," Denken ordered. Gloucester was infuriated to find he had no choice but to comply. The power of Denken's voice was irresistible. "Good lad." His smugness made Gloucester try to kick him again. Still out of reach, the demigod paid the effort no mind as he continued with his explanation. "You are annoyingly difficult to get a hold of. Did you know about the protection spells on Zane's shop and Antimony's joint? Something tells me you didn't, else you likely would have been a bit more prudent. Instead of, oh I dunno, gallivanting across town to rekindle old flames. Tough luck with that, by the by. He was hot. It's for the best, though."

"That's none of your business," Gloucester growled, barreling through the walls of silence enforced by Denken's command.

Denken threw up his hands in a placating gesture, though the accompanying burst of laughter undermined it considerably. "Oh, doubtless. Luckily, I really don't care. I meant that it's for the best *for me*. See, this is about the other man who cares about you." When Gloucester stared at him uncomprehendingly, he gave an impatient huff. "Tall, red hair, drawing on his face? Ringing any bells here?"

Realization dawned. "Cassus? We barely know each other."

"And yet you're using his first name. What was it that he said? Something like, 'Only my friends get to call me that!'"

A shiver ran down Gloucester's spine. Denken's voice had changed into an uncanny imitation of Finch's.

"So?" he said gruffly, refusing to be cowed. "We're friends. He's trying to make things right after everything that happened at All Saints."

Denken's eyebrows climbed, and when he spoke, it was with his unnatural voice once more. "Oh, is he? What a coincidence! So am I." This was said with a smile that had nothing to do with friendliness and quite a lot to do with teeth. "And I'd say you're more than friends. Or at least headed that way. Please don't dismiss my mind-reading, Mik, it's disrespectful. If you want, I can describe some of the things you think about him. I'm good at detail. Graphic, you could even say. You were unconscious for quite a while there, and unconscious minds are easy to explore. It's like snooping around somebody's attic—messy, but you never know what treasures you might find."

Gloucester glared at him. He'd almost forgotten about Denken's mind-reading abilities, on top of his dangerous powers of persuasion and hypnosis. Knowing the demigod could read his thoughts like words on the page of a book was uncomfortable, making him second-guess every thought that passed through his mind.

"Please don't," Denken groaned. "That's really annoying."

"Then get out of my head," Gloucester snapped. "There's no point to this anyway. What was your plan? To get revenge on Cassus when he rides in to save me like some fairytale knight in shining armor?" He barked a derisive laugh. "If that's what you're hoping for, then you picked the wrong damsel. He's not gonna risk his life for someone he barely knows."

"Why not? You did. Humans are funny like that. And I might not be able to read the magician's thoughts as easily as some . . ." He looked squarely at Gloucester, eyebrows raised. " . . . but I know how he feels about you. He'll come."

"If you want revenge on him so badly, why wait all this time for it? Why not snatch him off the street?"

Denken seemed to find him effortlessly. It didn't only raise the question of why he hadn't struck at Finch more directly, and sooner, but also why he hadn't targeted any of them in the weeks since the high minister's death. They'd been sitting ducks, clueless as to what Denken's plan might be and powerless to stop it.

"The little magic-monger is why," Denken answered. "He's made himself untraceable. That takes powerful magic, too. I'd almost be impressed if it weren't so annoying. As for the rest of your merry little gang, well, I think you're better protected than you know." He scoffed in amusement at Gloucester's nonplussed expression. "I would've expected as much from Purpurrot's little retirement home—she's never liked any sort of mischief, the old stick-in-the-mud—and I wasn't gonna get my hopes up with Antimony. She's been friends with the Gambler for too long. She's learned some tricks. But oh, how I thought Zane's little clock haven would be *easy*. Did dear Cassus even tell you when he set up the wards?"

Gloucester's confusion must have been evident on his face because Denken burst into laughter again. "Didn't think so. He's a sneaky bastard, isn't he? I'd ask if that's your type, but handsome Jeb doesn't seem to have a sneaky bone in his body."

"Leave Jeb out of this!" Gloucester said hotly. "You said it before, he's got nothing to do with anything."

Denken shrugged. "You're right. And don't worry your little head about him. Why would I bother him anyway? He's done nothing to me."

"Neither have I!"

To Gloucester's surprise, Denken didn't have a flippant remark or a cruel laugh to greet this point. Instead, a more serious look flickered across his face. "No, you haven't, have you? In fact, you got yourself beaten up trying to save me." For a bizarre moment, Gloucester thought the demigod was about to thank him.

But the moment soon passed, and then Denken's off-kilter smirk was back to full strength as he reached forward to pat Gloucester on the shoulder in the mockery of a kind gesture.

"Unfortunately, this isn't about you. This is about tying up loose ends with the magician. Far as I can tell, you're the only person he halfway cares about. If his dad was still alive, you'd be off the hook, but . . . tough break."

"So what's the plan? You're gonna lure him here and then . . . what? Kill him?" His stomach turned at the thought.

"Yep."

"All of this started because *you* killed someone. You can't just—"

"All of this started because Cassus Finch and his father kidnapped my brother to sell to a despot. Don't pretend otherwise." Denken wore no smile now. "Do you think I *wanted* this to happen? Do you think I *like* this?" The white walls at his back dimmed as shadows crawled up them. "I wanted to save my brother. Someone I love. Someone who had been captured like something to be hunted, like *game,* to benefit the whims of a puny, pathetic human who dreamt of being bigger and more important than he was. At least he had ambition," he sneered. "What did the Finches do it for? What was their glorious reason for stalking the Gambler like a beast? Money. Money and some sad need for validation on the father's part. Proof that everything he'd devoted his life to was possible. He threw away everything in his life to study me and my kin, and what was the best way he could think of to honor that? To throw one of us in a cage. For *money.*"

His disgust was so potent that Gloucester felt it seep into his mind. It made him want to agree, to curl his lip and curse the Finch name. He fought the feeling back, knowing it wasn't his own.

Not that, objectively speaking, Denken didn't make a valid point. "If you think I'm gonna defend him or make some sort of rationalization for what he did, you're wrong," he said as evenly as he could manage.

"I didn't think you would." The sourness curdling Denken's tone receded somewhat. He cocked his head to the side, his black eyes making the movement all the more birdlike. "You're not a hard one to read. Too honest. Funny trait to find in a security agent. I'd be tempted to joke that's why you aren't one anymore, but we both know that's not the case. I've seen it in here." He reached forward to tap Gloucester's forehead. The claw felt like the tip of a knife brushing against his skin, too gently to draw blood but inescapably threatening. "You tried to rescue him. Before I'd even figured out who'd taken him. Why'd you do that?"

Gloucester dared not move his head away from the razor's edge of Denken's finger. "Why don't you tell me, if I'm so easy to read?"

Denken regarded him for a long moment, then lifted his finger away. "Surface thoughts are easy to read. Things you think a lot, emotions you're feeling, memories you're dwelling on. Other things, deeper thoughts, they're trickier. I could delve into them, dig past the surface, but . . ." He trailed off for another long pause. "I don't want to."

The confession was quiet and matter-of-fact. Denken was still watching him with unreadable eyes. Gloucester stared back at him.

It was the demigod who eventually ended the silence risen up between them. "You didn't have to try to rescue the Gambler all those months ago. You could have gone back to your post and pretended you'd never seen anything. You didn't. You tried to save him, a person you didn't even understand, let alone know. And then, when you were pulled back into it when you had the chance to run, you didn't. You went to try to save him again. Why?"

The single word tugged at Gloucester, a loose thread on the sweater of his mind. It was a question he'd asked himself numerous times before. Why had he? He'd lost everything trying to save the strange being he discovered in the High Minister's Cathedral.

"I dunno," he said finally. He couldn't see the point in lying to Denken. "It was just the right thing to do, I think. I couldn't just leave another person in a situation like that."

Denken stared at him intensely for several minutes, much to Gloucester's discomfort. He fixed his own gaze a little over Denken's left shoulder, no longer able to maintain eye contact. He could still feel the weight of Denken's appraisal, however, and it set his teeth on edge.

He was about to demand something be said, just to end the silent awkwardness, when Denken spoke.

"And me? You tried to stop Finch in the church when he could have killed me. What made you do that?"

Gloucester wished he had a good answer to this question too, but again all he had was the truth. "I don't know about that either. Everything was happening so fast. I wasn't even thinking." He tried to think now. It felt bizarre to be mulling over past motives at a time like this, tied to a pillar who-knew-where, while a half-mad demigod paced in front of him. Still, the question nagged at him. He wasn't sure if it was the power of Denken asking it that drove him to search for a proper answer or if he needed to find one for himself.

"Right or wrong, you were trying to save your brother," he said. "You went about it all wrong, but that doesn't mean you didn't have cause to be angry. I know I would be if someone had hurt my family. And then Cassus . . . his father died. Right in front of him, because of you. Yeah, he did plenty wrong, both of them did, but that doesn't change the fact that it was his dad. Him being so angry makes sense too. I guess . . ." He tried to shrug, but his bound arms made it difficult. "I guess I just didn't want anyone else to die."

Denken made a face. With his eyes and teeth, it made him look quite frightening. "Pah, that's a boring enough answer to be true." His demeanor was exaggeratedly disappointed, but something else lingered behind the facade.

"So what now?" Gloucester asked.

He drew in a quick breath as Denken stepped closer, laying a fearsome hand on his shoulder.

"You're bait, Mik. You do what bait does—stay right where I need you and be tantalizing." Denken laughed his terrible laugh again, pulling his hand none-too-gently away from Gloucester's shoulder. The talons tipping each finger sliced through his shirt like hot knives, and he hissed as blood welled up from the long cuts left in their wake. Nausea twisted his gut. He hadn't eaten much that day, and his empty stomach and unpleasantly eventful day were proving to be a miserable combination.

"Be good and you'll even survive this," Denken told him with false cheer. "I owe you that, life for life."

"And what happens once you have your revenge? What's your plan then?"

No answer came. Denken simply flickered out of existence like a shadow banished by the light. He was there one moment and gone the next, leaving Gloucester alone in the vast white hall.

"Denken!" he shouted. No reply returned to him but the echoes of his voice bouncing off the walls.

It was far larger than his cell had been, this strange, windowless place, but trapped there alone, Gloucester felt the old fear and claustrophobia seeping back in. "Denken!" he shouted again, panic roughening the edges of the name. "Don't do this! DENKEN!"

Cassus, don't fall for this. Stay away. Please.

Chapter 13

Multifaceted

Stark-white walls blinded him, bright as the sky on a sunny winter day. The world spun, a spiral of cold stone, smooth and hard as ivory.

Red, spattered in arcs. Lines tracing like the trails of dragging fingers. Against the white stone, it stood out like a beacon.

Brown eyes, so dark as to be almost black, wide and earnest and sad. He knew those eyes. He'd seen them full of fear and pain, confusion and amusement. And something else, something he wasn't sure of yet.

Then they changed. The darkness spread, leaking like spilled ink until no color remained. No warmth, no emotion. Eyes that were black and staring.

Shining more brightly even than the walls, teeth glinted as a shark's grin swept everything else away. "Finch," it said. Its call trumpeted the clarion of war. And in its wake, the whistle of the falling blade.

Cassus Finch awoke with a start, breath catching in his chest and making him gasp like a drowning man. He sat up in bed.

Just a dream. Just a dream. The same stupid mantra he'd told himself all his life. Sometimes it was even true.

He dragged a weary hand over his sleep-crusted eyes, squeezing them shut as he latched onto the vestiges of the dream, committing it to memory before it could fade. This, too, was habit. As was the journal he found himself reaching for on the nightstand beside his bed. Recording his dreams had always been for his father's sake, though. He needn't worry about doing it now. There was no one to let down if he didn't.

He could always tell a prophetic dream. They felt different from the regular sort, and not just in their lucidity. Something about the experience was unlike anything else. He'd been having them for as long as he could remember, and to this day he couldn't think of an apt description to convey what it was that set the sensation apart.

Whatever it was, it always left him feeling sick. With shaking fingers, he reached past the journal and picked up the glass of water just beyond. Bringing it to his lips, he took an uneven sip, coughing and swearing when some of the water went down the wrong way.

Prophetic dreams were nothing new to him. He'd inherited the ability from his mother, a hedge witch, whose magic had run through her veins, not just been learned from books like his magician father. Of late, however, the dreams had become a near-nightly plague. They were rarely helpful, more often than not too enigmatic to decode. Other times they would warn of events too late to actually change.

Sometimes, though . . . Sometimes one came along that was stronger than the rest. These dreams carried with them the hope of altering the course of the future. He didn't know what determined these lucky few. Surely it wasn't importance, at least not as far as his own interests were concerned. The death of his father had come un-forewarned, leaving him digging through memories and journal entries of half-forgotten dreams in the aftermath, searching for some sign he had missed or misread. Flashes of fire, the feeling of loss, the sensation of concrete beneath his body, and a voice shouting—had these been signs he'd simply not recognized at the time? They'd been scattered among regular dream nonsense, and none had carried the weight of prophecy, but he knew he would never be able to fully forgive himself regardless.

This dream was different, though. It stuck in his mind like the clinging tentacles of an octopus, refusing to relinquish its grip. White walls, red blood, and two sets of eyes, one pleading and one plotting. The images spun across the landscape of his mind on repeat.

He swore again, knuckling his forehead. What did it mean? Nothing good; even without the sickness unsettling his stomach, he would have been able to discern that. He knew both pairs of eyes in the dream. Denken's eyes were unmistakable and unforgettable. And the others . . . well, he'd been staring into them only hours earlier.

Denken and Mikalai . . . Nothing good could come of that combination.

The red spatter of blood, like paint flung on a wall.

"Oh shit," he breathed, the leaden weight in his gut plummeting. He threw himself out of bed and hurried to get dressed. No time to waste.

—

Hours had passed since Gloucester stormed out the door of the clock shop, and Zane Zephyr was growing increasingly worried. Perhaps "stormed" was a bit strong, but he certainly hadn't been happy, and with each passing minute, Zane told herself off more and more for not following after him.

For all that they'd only met the month before, Mikalai Gloucester had become a soft spot for Zane. She couldn't help wanting to look out for him. Maybe it was knowing what he'd been through, or his quiet, slightly awkward nature. Maybe it was just the damned unease that had been eating away at her for weeks now, ever since the showdown in the church. She found herself worrying about everything and everyone, but Gloucester most of all.

Where the hell would he go? She'd asked herself this a dozen times in the last hour. The day passed into evening, which darkened into night, and still no sign of him. Zane wracked her brain for any clue as to where the former security agent might be. She'd tried calling his phone, only to follow the ringing to the break room and find it lying on Gloucester's makeshift bed. Now, staring out the dark front window of the shop with a forgotten cup of tea in her hand, she'd long given up telling herself not to worry.

"Gloucester, you bastard, where the hell are you?" she muttered, chewing on her thumbnail. The pieces of a dismantled clock were laid out neatly on the desk in front of her, but she hadn't been able to focus on work in hours. Why hadn't he taken his phone with him? He was smarter than that. He knew how dangerous the city was nowadays. Zane was determined to give him a piece of her mind about his lack of prudence the moment she knew he wasn't dead in a ditch somewhere.

She jumped and nearly dropped her lukewarm tea when the door banged open, jostling the chimes above it. Zane looked over at the newcomer, full of desperate hope, but it wasn't Gloucester standing in the doorway. It was Finch. Zane's mood sank even lower.

"Please say you're here to tell me where Gloucester is," she said, setting the tea aside. Hands on her hips, she moved out from behind her desk to confront him unobstructed.

Finch shook his head, and Zane was disheartened to see that he looked as worried as she felt.

"He's not here, then?" he asked.

"No. He left right after you did." Her eyes narrowed in

suspicion. "What did you say to him?"

Finch balked, affronted. "Nothing!" He rolled his eyes when she remained incredulous. "Well, obviously not *nothing*, but nothing that would make him head for the hills. Maybe it was you," he went on, shifting the blame.

"Me?" Zane squared her shoulders. After a tense afternoon and a worry-filled evening, she was feeling all too ready for an argument. "What did *I* do?"

"Oh, I dunno!" Finch threw his hands up in the parody of a shrug. From the mounting ire in his tone, he was as eager for a fight as she was. "Maybe kept the man who was locked up in solitary confinement for months squirreled away in your back room and not let him do anything useful?"

Despite her anger, the telltale discomfort of guilt pulled at her insides. In her mind's eye, she saw again the look on Gloucester's face when he'd rushed out the door, full of confusion and near-panic. And maybe, just maybe, a spark of accusation aimed her way. She knew she'd been encouraging him to stay away from the fight, but she'd never intended to make him feel trapped. She just wanted him to be safe.

"I didn't—it's not like that! Gloucester and I don't have any magic. We're not gods or magicians or even mad scientists. What are we supposed to be out there doing? I wasn't squirreling him away! I was just trying to keep him safe."

"By shutting him in another tiny room by himself? That's— look, nevermind. That's not important right now. Do you have any idea where he might have gone?"

The honest-to-goodness urgency in Finch's voice kept Zane from arguing further. Something was definitely wrong.

I should never have let him leave alone.

"None," she said, biting her lip. "I don't even know where he lived before . . . you know, everything. He said once that he lived with his boyfriend, but I have no idea who that was or where they might have lived. When he left, he seemed . . . I dunno, restless, I guess you could say? He gets like that sometimes.

Usually, that's when I find him pacing or exercising. I hoped he'd just gone for a walk to clear his head. Only, then he didn't come back and . . ."

She trailed off, shrugging unhappily. She ought to have asked Gloucester more about his life pre-arrest. Though he wasn't opposed to answering questions, Gloucester never seemed keen to start conversations on the subject, so for the most part Zane had done her best to ignore her curiosity when it came to her impromptu roommate. Now she was wishing she'd been nosier.

"Do you think he's in trouble?" she asked.

She expected another biting remark, but Finch nodded, expression grave.

"Yeah," he said. "I do."

He'd had a dream about Denken and Gloucester, he explained, and not just a common nightmare. Zane listened as he laid out what he called a prophecy, doing her best to swallow back her dubious nature. Since meeting Antimony a few years before and subsequently being introduced to the magical side of the world, she'd witnessed all sorts of strange things and encountered all kinds of bizarre people. Yet she had a pragmatic streak too wide for her own good, as people had told her more than once—and not always in such kind terms—and she still couldn't help but greet much of magic with incredulity. She'd crossed paths with one or two hedge witches before, not to mention the odd soothsayer and even an oracle, so it wasn't like the concept of a prophetic dream was unfamiliar to her.

Even so, having someone stride into her shop and declare he'd just had a dream warning him that her friend had been kidnapped by an angry demigod was a lot to wrap her head around. Particularly when that someone was Cassus Finch, shady magician and, in her opinion, established ne'er-do-well. When she thought of soothsayers, she imagined someone demure and enigmatic. The only enigma about Finch was why Gloucester put up with him. He was brash, sardonic, and certainly not to be trusted.

"You're sure this is real?" she asked. Finch made a strangled growl of impatience.

"Yes! Okay? I know what I'm talking about. So instead of questioning every bloody thing I say, let's try figuring out where Denken might have taken Mikalai, all right?"

It took self-control not to snap back at him, but Zane needed no further reminder of how important this was. "Okay," she said. "Okay, let's think . . ."

—

Across town, the automaton named Gear had discovered something new: boredom.

Generally, she liked discovering things. It was quite easy, as there was very little that wasn't new to her. Just the other day, she had discovered stairs, the concept of math, spiders, and the word "curlicue." That was a good day.

Today hadn't panned out to be quite so rewarding. Antimony had left the house mid-afternoon—times of day being another concept of which Gear was recently made aware—and she wasn't back yet, though the sky outside the window had long since darkened to night and Murphy had headed up to bed, leaving Gear to her own devices.

She supposed she could sleep too. She'd given it a try and found herself capable of the phenomenon. It had been a lot of fun the first time, so exciting that it had been rather difficult to actually fall asleep. The novelty had faded, though. Not because it wasn't interesting, but because everything else was too. How could she sleep and let the world pass her by with so much waiting to be discovered?

Only, now she wasn't discovering much at all. Over the last several days, she'd explored every nook and cranny of the house, but Antimony had asked her not to leave on her own, so she wasn't sure what to do with herself. Maybe sleeping was the way to go after all. She didn't feel like it, though. She felt no semblance of the yawning, bleary-eyed weariness Murphy had displayed when she bid her goodnight.

Gear was watching her own reflection in the kitchen window when the telephone rang. The sound made her jump, staring around wildly for the source of the shrill noise. She'd heard it before, but only once when it wasn't muffled by the floor and distance between the kitchen and the basement. Sitting in the same room, the ringing was a lot more alarming.

Finally spotting the device, Gear got up from her chair and wandered over to it. When she explored the upstairs for the first time, Antimony had explained to her what the telephone was but had requested she not play with it. She'd gone on to explain that it would be easy for Gear to accidentally connect with a stranger and get herself into trouble. She hadn't said anything about what to do if someone called *them,* however. Usually, Antimony or Murphy was there to answer it. Gear listened hopefully for any indication that Murphy would answer upstairs, but the phone just kept ringing.

After a few more rings, she couldn't take it anymore. Feeling an uncomfortable fluttering in her stomach—another new sensation, and not one she liked—she reached out and picked up the receiver. "Hello?" she said into it like she had seen Antimony do.

"Antimony?" a voice asked through the phone. It sounded so much like the person was right next to her that Gear peered around the room. No one was there. Just her and the telephone. "Antimony, is that you?" said the voice.

"Um, no. I'm Gear."

"Oh!" The voice paused for a few seconds before speaking again. "Gear, hi! It's Zane. Do you . . . do you remember me? We met a few days ago?"

Gear wasn't certain why this was a question, but she thought back over the last several days nonetheless. There had been a day when she met several new people. There was the tall, angry woman, who hadn't seemed very happy at all to meet Gear and who'd spoken loudly, swinging her arms a lot before leaving.

There was the man with pale hair and no eyes, who had been quiet and kind and somehow seemed to stare avidly despite his obvious physical disadvantage. She'd thought that perhaps it was normal for some people to not have eyes, but then everyone else she'd met had them, so maybe the man was just special. He felt special, and she smiled at the thought of him.

Then there were three others, who came in as the angry woman left. A woman with a round face and curly hair, who had stared at her with wide, dark eyes, but spoke kindly. A tall man—though not nearly as tall as the angry woman—with hair in a color she hadn't seen before and freckles like her own. And finally, another man, with dark hair and eyes and a sad turn to his mouth. Was Zane one of them?

"Hello? Gear?" said Zane. "Are you still there?"

Gear shook herself, realizing she'd been silent for too long. "Oh! Oh, yes! Which one are you?"

"Which one?" The voice managed to convey a mounting sense of impatience. "I'm the woman with the curly hair? Wait, I guess Purpurrot has curly hair too . . . The not really tall one? I met you along with Finch and Gloucester. Redheaded fellow and a guy with black hair? Do you remember?"

Gear nodded. She remembered that well.

"Hello?" Zane definitely sounded annoyed now.

"Hi!" said Gear, though she wasn't sure why this conversation seemed to be going backward.

A faint thud came from the other end of the line. Had Zane smacked her head against something solid? Gear eyed the phone with some concern, but before she could ask if Zane was all right, her strained voice came through the receiver again.

"Is Antimony there?" she asked.

"No," Gear said. "Just me. And Murphy, but she's sleeping. Do you sleep?"

"Do I—? Yes, of course. That's, that's not important right now. Look, Gear"—Gear looked around obligingly, but saw nothing new—"I really need to talk to Antimony. Do you know where she is? She's not picking up her portable phone."

Gear frowned thoughtfully. Zane sounded upset, and if there was one thing Gear had learned about herself over the course of her short existence, it was that she hated when people were upset. The desire to help made her clockwork spin faster.

"Um, ummmm," she hummed, thinking. For a moment the only noise was the quiet *click-click* of her gears. "She said she was going to see someone. An orange person."

"Orange Ianto," said Zane, relieved. Gear didn't know what an orange Ianto was, but she was glad to hear Zane sounding a little happier. "Thank you, Gear."

Gear beamed. Antimony had explained the words "thank you" to her, and she quite liked the concept. "Can I help you with anything else?" she asked, rather hoping the answer would be yes.

"Nah, that's it. Just . . . if Antimony gets back before I can get a hold of her, let her know that I called, all right? Tell her it's important. Tell her Denken has Gloucester."

"Okay!" Gear replied with a resolved nod, smiling broadly. She felt very useful and quite liked the sensation.

"Thanks again, Gear. I'll talk to you later." With that, Zane hung up, the line going back to a whirring tone with a click. Gear listened for a few minutes more, but nothing changed, so eventually she placed the receiver back down on the main body of the phone.

"Tell Antimony Denken has Gloucester," she repeated to herself. "Denken has Gloucester, Denken has Gloucester, Denken has Gloucester. This is fun!"

—

Antimony Jones had scarcely turned her phone back on when it rang, the sound loud in the quiet of the street outside Orange Ianto's shop. The Oracle had a stringent no-phone policy that one had better abide by if there was to be any hope of help from her at all, so Antimony had thought nothing of switching the machine off when she arrived hours earlier. Now, though, she wondered if she ought to have requested an exception to Ianto's rule.

"Hello?" she said, raising the phone to her ear.

"Antimony!" Zane's voice was animated in its relief. *"Finally."*

Antimony frowned, the only outward sign that her heart was plummeting. Something must have happened to spur the anxiety lacing Zane's words. "What's wrong?" she asked.

"I tried to call you a bunch of times, but the call wouldn't go through, you must have had your phone off—which I guess makes sense, 'cause Gear said you were at Orange Ianto's . . . Oh yeah, I tried your place and Gear answered, which was a bit of a trip, so—"

"Zane," Antimony cut in. "Just tell me what's going on. Has there been another attack?"

"Sort of." Now that her voice was calmer, Zane's worry was more clear than ever. "It's Gloucester. We think something's happened to him. Because of Denken."

"We?"

"Finch and I. He had this dream—it's sort of a long story . . . or maybe not, I guess, if you know a lot about prophetic dreams already, but—"

"Zane!"

"Right, right, sorry. Kind of frazzled here. Anyway, Finch had a dream and now he's convinced that Denken has Gloucester as some sort of hostage or something. He says he saw blood and eyes and some sort of stone room. Normally I wouldn't worry about that kind of nonsense"—Antimony thought she heard a muffled protest from Zane's end of the line—"only, Gloucester left earlier today and hasn't come back. I'm worried Finch is really onto something."

"Prophetic dreams are a common phenomenon amongst people who use a lot of magic. Finch would know best if the dream's legitimate. You don't think he has any reason to be lying?"

"Why would he?" Zane said, lowering her voice. Antimony guessed that Finch was in the room with her. "Not about something like this, at least."

"And you have no way of getting a hold of Gloucester? What about the phone I gave him?"

"He left it here. He was sort of . . . weird when he left. Weirder than is usual for him."

Antimony hummed in thought. Gloucester was a quiet fellow, but no wilting flower. Denken's mental influence was weighing on the minds of everyone in Frettchen, exaggerating fears and pushing people's thoughts to dangerous extremes. Antimony could feel its effects on her own mind, like a whispering in her ears whenever she stepped out of the safety of her warded home or the protection of the pie shop. Chances were Gloucester had also been frustrated by his relative uselessness in the face of the Denken threat, making him all the more vulnerable to the demigod's influence. And now it could well be his downfall. Had Denken stumbled upon him by chance and taken the opportunity to attack, or had Gloucester walked into some sort of premeditated trap?

"Do you think he's still alive?"

She could hear the fear in Zane's voice, though the clock worker was doing her best to conceal it.

"If Finch's dream is anything to go by, then yes." Not that being Denken's prisoner was much better, considering the state he was apparently in. The Gambler's prediction of what Denken was going through hadn't been a pretty one. Best not to mention that aloud, she decided. If they wanted to rescue Gloucester, they needed level heads.

"I shouldn't be dawdling out in the streets," she said, casting a glance around her dark surroundings. It was only a short walk to her parked car, but it didn't do well to carry on with divided attention like this. Gloucester's predicament was a dire reminder of that. "I'll be back at my house in a few minutes. Can you meet me there?"

Zane agreed and they both hung up, leaving Antimony thoroughly alone in the abandoned street, the loudest sound her own thoughts. They drowned out the traffic on nearby streets and the distant tolling of the cathedral bells.

—

Something was wrong. The Gambler could feel it in his bones.

Of course, a lot was wrong since Denken's terrible mistake, so much so that sorting through it all was nigh on impossible. The futures were muddled and frantic, changing as quickly as ever, but lacking the clarity to which he was accustomed.

Denken was the root of that problem. The Gambler had never been able to see the futures for his kin, any more than Denken could command his thoughts or Angus could manipulate his emotions. They were immune to each other. It had never been cause for concern before, but now the Gambler found himself longing to abandon that immunity, if only to see what the futures held in store for the human world. Denken was too entangled in it now, at least in Frettchen. Left on the path he was treading, that entanglement would spread to cover the whole of the Lower Lands, followed by the entire world.

Not that he needed his prescience to know things were growing worse. This night more than ever he felt a juddering unease rolling through him, and it was for that reason he found himself standing in front of Antimony's door.

He pushed the door open and entered silently. The bloody footprints his bare feet left would fade with time, never lasting more than a few minutes. He paid them no mind. Antimony had never complained.

The Gambler took in the sight of the dim front hall. Without eyes, he didn't see the world in the same way humans did, limited by light and shadow and the ticking clock of age. His perception was a mental one, his senses spreading throughout the room like tendrils of ivy.

Was Antimony home? His mind searched for the familiarity of her presence in the house. It was late enough that she might be in bed. While it was possible for him to sleep, the Gambler had never felt much of a desire to do so. Denken loved to nap, he recalled, though the fond thoughts of his brother were soured immediately as he wondered where Denken was now and what he might be getting up to. Did he know that the creations of imagination were terrorizing the city? Or had he retreated somewhere far away, leaving the rest of them to deal with the consequences of his misdeeds?

No. The Gambler dismissed that idea almost as soon as it occurred. No, Denken was nearby somewhere. He could feel it. Which meant the personification of Thought had to know about everything that was happening. This only led to another question: Did the monsters he'd unleashed horrify Denken, or was he encouraging them?

A sound in the kitchen stopped him in his tracks, halfway to the stairs leading to the floor above. He looked over just as a young woman with a bright smile rounded the corner eagerly.

"Denken has Gloucester—oh! You're not Antimony." Gear's smile faded as she got a proper look at who stood in the hallway.

"No, I'm not," he replied with a smile of his own. He found it surprisingly difficult not to smile around Gear. "I'm the Gambler. Um, if you don't remember." Had he just stuttered? What was *wrong* with him?

"I didn't," Gear said. "Remember your name, I mean," she added quickly. "I remember you, though."

The Gambler was momentarily stunned by how far his heart could sink in a matter of a few seconds, only to be buoyed back up again at the same dizzying speed.

Only then did her initial words sink in, and down went the Gambler's heart again. "Did you say Denken has Gloucester? You mean to say that Gloucester is his prisoner?"

"I think so. Zane didn't say very much about it, but she was unhappy." She appeared more bothered by that than by Gloucester's capture. *She understands unhappiness,* the Gambler thought. *That makes sense to her.* It was likely that Gloucester's kidnapping was a lot more abstract for the automaton.

"Antimony told me about Denken. He doesn't sound very kind. Will the Gloucester person be okay?"

Perhaps not as abstract as he'd assumed.

The Gambler cast about for a comforting answer to her question. Denken had always been unpredictable, and now he was more dangerous than ever. Whether he'd taken Gloucester for a reason or not, the former security agent was in grave peril.

"Yes," he said with a lot more confidence than he felt. "We will get him back safely."

Hopefully. He was accustomed to the uncertainty of the futures, but he hated this, not being able to read the odds. He tried to focus his mind's eye on Gloucester, to get *something.* He caught glimpses—white walls, mostly, and Gloucester's sad eyes—but nothing that lasted longer than a few heartbeats. It was maddening to be so powerless. He felt like he was back in the high minister's prison, in that room with its enchantments and wards stripping him of his powers. He did his best to pull his thoughts away from memories of the place.

"Are you okay?"

The question chased away his cluttering thoughts like butterflies in the wind, and he regarded Gear quizzically. "Me?"

Gear nodded, and when she spoke, he could hear honest concern layered in her voice. "You look sad. I think. It's harder to tell what you're feeling. Even more difficult than Antimony. Murphy is easy. You can always tell what she's thinking from the look in her eyes. I guess that's why you're hard to tell. Why don't you have eyes?"

It wasn't the first time by far that he'd been asked that question. Yet Gear's bluntness and innocent curiosity made the Gambler laugh. He cut himself short when Gear winced.

"Sorry," he apologized. "My laughter can be . . .

overwhelming."

"It's very loud," Gear said faintly. "But loud in a . . . a different way. I'm not very good at describing things yet."

"No, no," the Gambler said, smiling. "I think that's probably a good way to describe it. I'm sorry if it frightened you." He was accustomed to that too. His voice, like those of his family, took getting used to, and there were few humans who stuck around him long enough to get to that point.

"It's not bad," Gear assured him. "It's very beautiful. I hear a lot in it, but I'm not sure what most of it is. I could listen to it for ages."

If he'd had eyes in his face, the Gambler would have blinked in surprise. That was quite possibly one of the nicest things anyone had ever said to him. He offered her a wider smile.

"Thank you," he said. "And I do have eyes. They're just not here." He pointed with the index and middle fingers of his right hand at the empty sockets beneath his eyebrows.

"Where are they?" Gear asked, utterly enthralled by this twist.

The Gambler cupped his hands together. Long and slim, his fingers were as angular as the rest of his features. He held his hands together for a moment, then yanked them away from each other, as if releasing an eager bird from his grasp. Only, what flew out from between his palms wasn't feathered or beaked. His eyes, their irises the warm color of amber, leaped through the air, spinning this way and that.

It was far from a normal sight for anyone to witness, and the Gambler wasn't sure what to expect of Gear's reaction. Would it frighten her? Disgust her? Or perhaps the worst prospect: Would she not find it impressive in the slightest?

His fears were brief, as Gear clapped her hands in delight. "That's amazing!"

It would occur to him later, in a moment of terribly human delayed realization, that it probably didn't take much to impress Gear. She no doubt thought all sorts of things were impressive.

Not only the usual sorts of things that everyone agreed were amazing; no, it was more likely Gear found just about everything astounding, from the sky to basic technology, to food and language, architecture, and art. With that in mind, her reaction to his eyes wasn't much to feel touched about.

He did, though, and grinned more broadly than he had in a long while, despite the grave news so recently related to him.

"Is it normal for eyes to fly?" Gear asked, watching his eyes orbit his head with fascination. "Can mine do that?"

"No," the Gambler said, a little hastily lest Gear think to try anything. "My eyes are special."

"They're very pretty." Gear giggled as one of them began to orbit her head instead. She kept trying to turn to keep her own eyes on it, but it moved faster and faster until it was nearly a blur and she was laughing outright.

"This is hardly the time for optical illusions."

Antimony stood in the doorway, hands perched on her hips and the faint crease of a frown between her brows. The Gambler knew her, and so he knew that such an expression from her was tantamount to passionate disparagement from anyone else. His smile faded, and the flying eyes returned to a much more sober orbit around his own head.

Gear didn't blush, but the clockwork in her head suddenly ticked much faster than before, somehow managing to sound flustered. "Oh, Antimony! Hi! Denken has Gloucester. I was told to tell you that. Does it help?"

Antimony's hard look softened as she turned her gaze to Gear. "Yes, Zane managed to get a hold of me after I left Ianto's. She's on her way here with Finch."

The Gambler was careful to keep his usual calm expression, but inside he felt an unhappy twinge at the magician's name. He knew Cassus Finch was trying to make better decisions, to make right all of the mistakes he and his ill-fated father had made. That was admirable. Yet the Gambler couldn't—and *wouldn't*—forget that the Finches were the ones who hunted him down, who turned him over to the high minister to be treated like a resource, a *thing*. That was a difficult misdeed to forgive, and an impossible one to forget.

Gear, on the other hand, seemed excited at the prospect of reuniting with the people she'd met the week before.

"People are coming here now?" she asked, looking eagerly to the door. It appeared she wasn't yet familiar with the concept of travel time.

What was it like, he wondered, to be so new to everything? He couldn't remember feeling anything other than old. Eternal. He and the world had grown up together. If there had ever been a time when he looked upon it and felt the awe of newness he saw in Gear's eyes, it had long since disappeared into the shadows of memory.

Perhaps that was why it was so fascinating to see Gear experience it. Despite her newness, she was a quick learner, and kind, ready to adapt and experience and feel. She was passionate in an all-inclusive way that was refreshing. The Gambler found himself excited to watch her discover the world.

"I'm putting the kettle on," Antimony said, slipping out of her jacket and hanging it on a hook. "Would you two let me know when they get here?"

She disappeared into the kitchen, leaving the Gambler and Gear alone in the entry hall once more.

Chapter 14

Coming Together

Zane wasn't sure what she was feeling as she climbed the steps to Antimony's door and knocked. Terrified, mostly. Finch was a step behind her, casting a wary glance around the sleeping street.

At least they were doing something. They were taking action, moving forward. Better that than sitting around at home doing nothing more useful than fretting. Doing nothing was no better than abandoning Gloucester. In the short time she'd known him, it surprised her how much she'd come to care about him. She refused to abandon a friend.

The Gambler answered the door, like the world's most unsettling butler. Past his shoulder was Gear. The automaton caught Zane's eye and waved happily.

"There's someone who has absolutely no clue what's going on," Finch murmured in her ear. The observation was amused, but after a painfully tense car ride with the man, Zane knew he was still just as upset as she was.

"Come in," said the Gambler. He beckoned them to enter the house, stepping to one side. "Antimony's in the kitchen."

"The perfect place for devising intricate rescue plans." Finch's smile didn't reach his eyes.

"Let's hope we can come up with another one that's just as good as the last," Zane replied.

"Just as good?" Finch scoffed. "Mayhaps you don't remember, but the last one involved several people dying."

"Yeah, but those people weren't part of the plan," Zane retorted. She knew it was a weak point as soon as she made it.

Finch sighed. "Really comforting."

They entered the kitchen, greeted by warmth and light and a tautly smiling Antimony, who turned toward them with a tray bearing a steaming teapot.

"Right," she said, setting the tray down on the table by the window and gesturing for them to sit. "Tell me everything. And then we'll see what we can do."

—

As it turned out, announcing the planning of a rescue was much easier than actually figuring it out. The group hit a wall soon after Finch explained his dream, as they all failed to think of a way to locate where Denken might be keeping Gloucester. Now that the way back to his Pocket was closed to him, he had to be somewhere in the human world, but that didn't narrow the possibilities down to a helpful degree. Hopeless panic stirred in Zane's head, spinning her thoughts into further disarray.

Turning an empty teacup between her hands, she jumped when Finch jolted upright in his seat.

"Wait, I completely forgot!" Bizarrely, he was grinning. "I can do it," he said. He still held a full mug of tea in his hands, though it had long since cooled. "I can find Mikalai."

"How?" Zane asked. "You said you only saw fragments of the place in your dream. How could you ever—"

"I can't track down Mikalai himself, not without something of his, a lock of his hair or a favorite possession—"

"Creepy," Zane interjected under her breath.

"—but there's something else I can track that'll lead us right to him."

"What's that?" Antimony didn't share Zane's dubious tone. She eyed Finch curiously from where she stood by the counter, fixing the Gambler a cup of coffee.

"Me. Or my magic, to be more precise." When they greeted Finch's statement with bemused silence, he sighed. "I used a spell on him when we met up last week. The night before that big fire dragon tried to set the whole of downtown ablaze."

"What sort of spell?" Zane asked, extremely suspicious.

"Nothing nefarious or improper. What are you, his mother? I gave him my phone number. I wrote it on his hand with a little bit of magic. When I saw him this morning, I noticed he still had it. If it's still there, so is the magic that put it there. Any magician worth his salt can track his own spells. Everyone's got a slightly different . . . I dunno what you might call it. Feel, maybe. Scent or taste or what have you. Only a fool wouldn't learn to recognize their own."

"That's . . . weird," Zane settled on. The look Finch sent her made it clear he knew she'd been considering a few other words for it. She wanted to ask if Finch had never heard of these things called pens, but held her tongue. If what he said was right, this would be the thing that could get them to Gloucester.

"It gets the job done. Denken is willing to bet I would find out he has Mikalai, so it's not a push to assume he knows I'll figure out a way to find him. He'll be expecting us," Finch said. "You can lecture me on how terrible and creepy I am once this is over."

"It'd be a waste of breath," Zane said, but she left it at that when she caught the look Antimony was aiming her way. Behind the scientist, Gear hovered, her fretful eyes flicking between Zane and Finch. This had to be the source of Antimony's impatience; Gear was easily upset by others' foul moods and, as they'd come to learn, Antimony was sensitive to her creation's happiness. Which only made Zane question this plan all the more. Walking right into the lion's den was hardly going to be a happy night out.

"All right," she relented. Best to focus on what they *could* do, rather than worry about things out of their control. "So you can find him, but then what? How do we get past Denken? He wasn't exactly easy to face last time, and that was when he couldn't even use all of his power. How do we combat his, you know, mind fuckery?"

"Blocking spells," Finch said, still smiling broadly. His idea for locating Gloucester seemed to have rendered him temporarily immune to worry. Zane rubbed her forehead, confused and more than a little annoyed.

"What do you mean, Blocking spells?" she asked.

"Defensive magic," he explained airily. "A bit like the ones I cast over Zephyr Clocks."

Zane leaped to her feet, furious. "You *spelled* my shop?"

"You're welcome," Finch shot back. "It's probably what stopped Denken from attacking Mikalai right from the get-go. Or you," he added as an afterthought.

This was a fair point, but the anger was difficult to shake, even when she knew, grudgingly, that it wasn't entirely justified.

"Don't just . . . do magic on people's places without their say-so," she grumbled, hating the petulance she heard in her voice. She sat back down. "It's rude. You could have just told me you wanted to do it."

"I'll bear that in mind."

His flippancy made her want to smack him, but Zane didn't need Antimony's warning look to hold herself back. They couldn't afford to waste time on petty arguments. Gloucester's life was on the line.

Finch turned slowly on the spot to sweep his gaze over everyone.

"In that case," he said when his eyes met Zane's, "I'm gonna have to ask you to bear with me one more time. Because if we're gonna be walking right into Denken's lair, then we shouldn't go without some sort of protection."

"Like weapons?" Antimony asked. She handed the Gambler his coffee and took a seat at the head of the table, crossing her legs primly.

"Not exactly. I'm thinking shield, not sword." When they all eyed—or in the Gambler's case, socketed—him rather impatiently, he rolled his eyes and explained, "Blocking magic isn't just good for safeguarding *places*. I can't build walls against all of Denken's powers, but since the showdown at the church, I've been looking for magic that can be used against him."

"Like the spells on my prison," the Gambler said, taking a slow sip from his mug. A wince flickered over Finch's face.

He's scared of him, she realized.

Maybe we all ought to be, whispered another thought in the wake of the first. She liked the Gambler, despite his reserved and eerie nature. But Denken was proof of how dangerous the Brothers could be, and she hadn't forgotten that the two were just that: brothers. Family. When push came to shove, which side would the Gambler take?

Don't think like that, she scolded herself in the privacy of her mind. She forced herself out of her ruminations on trust and made herself focus back on Finch, who was speaking again.

"I can do a fairly simple Blocking spell that works as a ward against mind magic. It's not perfect—it's designed to combat the powers of human magic-wielders, like enchanters or mind-mages, not Thought itself. But it should keep him from sneaking up on us, at least. Just keep your guards up. If we're not careful, he could still hit us with his hypnosis."

Zane dragged a weary hand over her face. "Comforting," she said.

Finch chuckled, but there was little humor in it. "I do my best."

Chapter 15

Opting Out of the Waiting Game

Laughter rang out through the unsettling space of the windowless hall. It echoed against the tall white walls, making it impossible to pinpoint its exact origin.

It wasn't Denken's laughter. Of that, Gloucester was certain. It lacked the inimitable quality of the demigod's voice.

The source of the laughter soon came into view, rounding the corner of Gloucester's peripheral vision and slinking forth to stand in front of him. Gloucester drew back in horror. The creature was of a sort he couldn't identify, animalistic in appearance, but emitting the too-human laugh. Moving on all fours, its long, bony limbs ended in human-like hands and feet, awkward and oddly jointed as they twisted to fit a quadrupedal stance. Its body was emaciated, almost skeletal, with razor-sharp shoulder blades jutting through the skin of its back. A long neck protruded upward, strung together from bare muscle and sinew, red and raw.

Despite the noise it was making, nothing humanoid resided in its face. Six eyes, yellow and with slits for pupils, glared balefully at Gloucester, set into a head like that of a horse gone terribly wrong. The teeth visible in its gaping mouth were pointed and plentiful. Gloucester wanted to flinch away from the horrendous sight but feared what would happen if he took his eyes off it.

What could it do to me then that it can't do now? This thought was the opposite of comforting. He was tied up, unable to defend himself even if he weren't completely disarmed. If the nightmarish beast wanted to attack him, it wouldn't make a difference one way or the other if he was watching it.

This sort of cold logic became easy to ignore when under the reign of fear. Still, he kept his eyes locked on the creature as it paced back and forth in front of the pillar to which Gloucester was bound. All the while, it never stopped laughing.

Until it was joined by another laugh. Though it wasn't as raucous, it quickly drowned out the monster's amusement, until at last the cowed beast fell silent. The second laugh continued, filling the air like a physical thing, weighing down on Gloucester until he thought he might suffocate in it.

"You should forgive the beast," came Denken's voice, riding the wave of his laughter, which continued to echo off the walls a little too long to be natural. The compulsion in his words made Gloucester want to oblige, but he fought it off as best he could, countering it with his own anger. Denken didn't seem to care, nor even really to notice.

"They don't usually get much cause for laughter," the god went on, sauntering into view. The now-silent monster ducked its head, looking like it would rather flee than laugh now. Denken eyed it and tutted sympathetically, but his flippancy was clear as day.

"Maybe you should take better care of your pets," Gloucester said scathingly.

Denken laughed again. Gloucester flinched as it crashed

over him.

"Stop it," he tried to shout, but it came out as a barely audible plea, grated through his clenched teeth. To his relief, Denken fell silent, though a smirk tugged at his lips in a way that made Gloucester want to break his nose.

"You wouldn't be the first," Denken said, crossing his arms over his thin chest. "Humans seem to love a good wallop on the nose. But trust me . . ." His voice, warm and amused one minute, turned suddenly chilly. " . . . every single one of them regretted it. Seems unlikely you'd be the first not to." He smiled widely, all of his teeth on display. "Plus, you're tied to a pillar. You have noticed that, right?"

"Don't read my thoughts!"

"Don't think so loudly, then."

"Would if I could!" Gloucester's temper had not improved after hours spent tied to a column in the middle of . . . wherever he was.

Denken had little concern for his anger, however. He turned away to address the cowering monster. "Off you hop," he told it, his terrifying smile still in place.

The creature scurried out of sight. Gloucester could only assume that the door out of the hall was behind him somewhere. Either that or Denken and his beasts could simply come and go without the need for a physical entrance. Considering what he'd seen of Denken's and the Gambler's abilities, this was entirely possible. Could the imagination beasts willingly transport themselves from one place to another as well? They were popping up all over the city, apparently out of thin air, but it didn't seem like they had much choice in the matter of their destination. Perhaps they were simply deposited at random when they were pulled from behind their doors in the Maze. Maybe the laughing beast simply had the misfortune to materialize here of all places.

Which reminded him. "Where are we? This isn't the Maze, is it."

"Oh? You're awfully certain about that." Denken went silent, head tilted to one side so dramatically that it was practically resting on his shoulder. Then he clicked his tongue, pseudo-disappointed. "The Gambler is such a gossip. So he told you I can't get back to my home. Have the lot of you been busy, then? Plotting and planning? It's adorable."

"He wants to help you," Gloucester said.

"He wants to save his precious humans. Not me."

"I think he wants to do both."

Denken regarded him, head still tilted to the side. It was impossible to guess what was going on behind the pure black eyes. "Yeah, you do, don't you? For someone who's been through so much shit, you're very trusting. That's not going to end well for you. It never does. Trust me." He seemed to find the irony funny, giggling as he tipped his head properly upright once more. "Even if that's what the Gambler wants, it's not what he's gonna get. This isn't headed for a happy ending, Mik."

Gloucester opened his mouth to argue, hopeful that Denken was at least listening. But before he could think of a convincing thing to say, Denken stepped closer, holding a claw to his lips for silence.

"Especially not for the handsome Mister Finch," he said. His smile turned wicked and spread across a face no longer his own. The shape of his jaw, his nose, his eyes, everything shifted in an instant. His hair grew shorter, changing smoothly from black to red, freckles appearing like constellations on pale skin, and Denken's odd contrast of black and brightly colored clothing unfolded into a long wool coat over a loose shirt and slacks.

"What do you think? As good as the real deal?" The voice matched the face now staring cheekily at Gloucester, but no strange magic could hide the power Denken possessed. He wore Finch's form, perfect to the last detail, save for two:

The eyes meeting Gloucester's were not the ocean green that was always so good at catching his attention; instead, they were the solid-black shark's eyes Denken had had before. It was a jarring effect, even more so than usual because of the face in which they now resided.

The smile, too, was wrong. It curved across the false Finch's lips, which pulled back to reveal teeth serrated and deadly.

Denken reached out his hand and brushed his fingers across Gloucester's face. "Hey, baby," he murmured.

"Get off me," Gloucester snarled. "You're not him."

"Ooh, touchy." Denken smirked, still wearing Finch's appearance like a mask. "You should work on that temper, Mik. It'll get you into trouble one of these days." Laughing, he turned and slid back into his own form as he strode away. He offered an impertinent parting bow before vanishing out of Gloucester's field of vision.

"Prick," grumbled Gloucester, not knowing or caring if Denken was still within earshot. He waited a few more minutes, breath shallow in his chest, but nothing reached his ears and he guessed that he was alone once more. He let out a long, shaky sigh.

The image of the black-eyed Finch haunted his thoughts, smirking at him every time he closed his eyes. Could they all shape-shift, these mysterious gods? What *couldn't* they do? Before, he'd been led to believe they were incapable of murder, but Denken had thrown that theory right out the window. So were there really any rules binding them? There had to be. Or was that just desperate hope?

Of course, the revelation that Denken could shape-shift would have been cause for more urgent concern if he hadn't already kidnapped him. Gloucester felt a twinge of shame. He'd been stupid enough to let his guard down, to wander streets he knew were dangerous, while unarmed and distracted. It had probably been mind-numbingly easy on Denken's part.

Weeping and moaning about that won't help me now.

Rather than wallowing in regret over things he couldn't go back and change, he ought to be looking forward. This was a trap for Finch, which meant that Denken must have found some way of letting the magician know he had been taken. Otherwise, this whole thing would be pointless. And if Finch learned he was in trouble, chances were the rest of his friends would too. Knowing Zane, she wouldn't rest until she could rescue him.

This meant there was only one thing to do: escape before that rescue could take place and all of his would-be rescuers walked right into a trap.

That sort of determination only got you so far, unfortunately. He'd gotten quite practiced at escape attempts over the course of his stint in solitary. Emphasis on "attempts." He'd never gotten far, and after a while, they became more of a way to pass the time and combat the worst of the boredom than legitimate hopes for freedom.

Now it had nothing to do with boredom. Lives depended on Denken's trap not succeeding.

Gloucester tugged at the ropes binding his arms. Those were the first problem. He could worry about the potentially door-less room and unknown location once he was no longer tied up.

He'd been struggling against his bindings for several fruitless minutes when laughter once again trickled through the air. It started out faint, then crescendoed until it filled the whole room. For a second Gloucester's heart stuttered, thinking Denken had returned. It only took a moment more to realize it wasn't the sound of the demigod's amusement, but that of the creature he'd interrupted.

The fearsome beast lurched back into view, staring at him with all its wide eyes, toothy mouth gaping. It was difficult not to read its appearance as overtly threatening, but it continued to do nothing more than watch him and laugh. Gloucester began to wonder if that was simply its default expression. He thought of the fire dragon and the pity and regret in Zane's voice at the prospect of killing it.

"Hey," he said quietly. The beast turned its head to the side, reminiscent of Denken. Gloucester tried again, this time doing his best to offer a passably believable smile. "Hi there . . . uh, you. Hello!"

Not the most eloquent conversation starter, but then again, he didn't have a lot of experience addressing six-eyed monsters. The beast's laughter stopped. It was now focusing the entirety of its attention on him, head still cocked to one side.

"Can you understand me?" Gloucester asked. The monster only stared. Gloucester's hopes, which hadn't been very high to begin with, sank even lower.

Then the beast nodded.

"You can?"

Another nod.

Gloucester took a deep breath, mind whirling as he tried to think of what to say next. Bits and pieces of plans, most of them ridiculous and doomed, careened through his mind. If only some of those fragments would coalesce into a cohesive idea . . .

"Is Denken your master?" he asked, buying time. The beast paused, perhaps thinking the question over, then nodded.

"Tough break," Gloucester told it. "Never mind," he added when the creature tilted its head again. It trilled a breathy chuckle, which sounded like a question. It didn't understand. He thought back to the way it had cowered in Denken's presence. "Do you like your master?" he asked tentatively. When it only stared at him, he went for something a little simpler: "Does he scare you?"

The beast gave a near-silent chuckle and nodded again, the motion quick and sharp, like it was afraid of being caught.

Gloucester's mind raced, an idea beginning to form. A really *stupid* idea, but what were his options here? There weren't many, and none of them seemed good.

"What if you could get away from him? Be free? Would you like that?"

Again the beast stared at him in seeming incomprehension. Gloucester huffed a frustrated sigh. How was he supposed to simplify this in a way the creature would understand?

Then the beast nodded again, the same single, nervous motion.

"You would? You want to escape?"

Another nod.

Here goes nothing. "Will you escape with me? If you help me get away from here, I could help you get far away from Denken. You could be free."

The beast breathed heavily, panting in what seemed to be anxious excitement. With each breath, giggling laughter escaped it. It took a few steps forward, and Gloucester forced himself not to flinch. His brain was screaming at him not to trust it, that this was a trap and Denken would storm back into the room, alerted by the treachery of Gloucester's own thoughts. How did you combat someone with a power like that?

By shutting up and trying. The monster stopped right in front of him, looming as tall as two men, its wide eyes fixed on him in a manner that could only be described as expectant.

"Will you help me?" he asked.

The beast nodded.

Gloucester's breath spilled out of him in a rush. "Thank you," he said, voice dropped to a whisper. "Can you . . . I dunno, bite through the ropes or something?"

The beast didn't have a particularly expressive face, yet somehow it managed to convey a very pointed look as it held up its bizarrely human hands.

"Right," said Gloucester. "Right, sorry. I guess you can just untie them. Um, in theory, I mean. It's not some sort of magically impenetrable rope or knots or something, is it?"

The ropes that once bound the Gambler in his prison had thrummed with power, and could only be untangled if you cut through them at just the right spot. Though they hadn't proven too difficult to take care of on the Gambler's behalf, he knew that the bindings' enchantments had stopped the Gambler himself from being able to break free. Was it possible that these were the same?

The beast shuffled around to stand behind the pillar. Even as a tentative ally, it was disconcerting to have the strange creature lurking out of sight. Gloucester shivered. The intimidation of it all wasn't combated in the slightest by the murmurings of laughter accompanying each of the beast's breaths.

Numb as his arms were from being pinioned at his sides, he could feel the slight tug against the ropes as the creature got to work. He envisioned it picking delicately at complex knots, slowly untangling them like someone working on a tactile puzzle.

It came as a surprise, then, just how quickly the puzzle was solved. The pressure holding him against the stone pillar fell away with a twang like a snapping guitar string, and Gloucester stumbled forward, falling to his knees with a gasp. Maybe there *had* been something magical in the rope, he thought, because the moment he was free of it, the feeling in his hands returned. As soon as it did, he missed the numbness; his fingers ached and prickled with returning blood flow. He winced and cradled his hands against his chest.

The beast shuffled around to crouch in front of him again. It, too, was massaging its hands, which were bloody and blistered. Not such an easy spell to break through, after all.

Gloucester nodded down at the creature's injuries, grimacing. "I'm sorry about that," he said. "Thank you."

It could still be a trap, he reminded himself. This place, wherever it was, didn't seem like somewhere to meet many friends. Not to mention the beast had already been upfront about who its master was. Could this be some cruel game of Denken's design, to curb his boredom or satisfy his pernicious whims? It was difficult to assign reason to Denken, who seemed to do many things for no grander reason than because he felt like it.

Better to be caught trying to escape than just wait around for a rescue. Better to do something than wait for them to fall into Denken's trap.

If only he had more information. Where was he? Was he even still in Frettchen? How were his friends supposed to find him?

Had Denken sent them some sort of message with a location and demand, like a hostage-taker contacting his negotiator? Who would he contact? It made the most sense for it to be Finch, but would the others hear of it too? He thought of Zane's worry and Antimony's kindness. They'd all come together to rescue the Gambler. Would they do the same when it was Gloucester's life on the line?

So many questions, Mikalai, echoed the words of his mother. *Sort through them one at a time, so you can ask the right ones.*

What now? That was a good one to ponder. Even better: *How do I get out of here?*

For the first time since waking up, Gloucester was able to see behind the pillar. Unfortunately, all that greeted him was more of the same: white stone walls, carved with an intricacy that would be beautiful if it weren't standing between him and freedom.

Wishing he had a weapon of some sort, he tried to think things through. The lack of a door made sense in Denken's case; Gloucester had seen the gods vanish right on the spot on more than a few occasions. Yet he'd had to get Gloucester in there somehow. Gloucester wasn't sure Denken could transport *him* through walls, at least not in the human world.

Working through this theory only spawned more questions. The Gambler had been certain Denken was trapped in the real world, but could Gloucester afford to have the same certainty? It wouldn't be the first time the personification of Thought had dragged him home to the Maze. The Gambler spoke like his brother's powers were diminished, but if anything, they seemed to be unleashed. This didn't feel like the Maze had, though, so he allowed himself some hope.

This didn't look like anywhere in Frettchen either, however. Turning in a slow circle, he craned his neck to peer up at the ceiling far above. He didn't know the city as well as many who had grown up there, but the room he stood in had to be big enough that the building itself would tower over those surrounding it.

Something Finch had said during their rescue of the Gambler came back to him then. The magic the Finches used to contain and conceal the Gambler had been powerful enough that his prison could have been hidden anywhere, even somewhere as small as a confessional, despite appearing to be a massive hall from the inside. If humans could perform magic that mind-bending, someone as powerful as Denken would be able to as well. This place could be in a shoebox for all he knew.

"So, that was bloody useless," he griped. The beast watched him silently, and he waved away its look with an irritated apology. "Sorry, just . . . thinking. Which is probably a bad idea with your boss lurking about, isn't it?" He tried to clear his mind. Unfortunately, this just resulted in him thinking more than ever. He swore under his breath. "I should probably just stop wasting my bloody time and get out of here, eh?" he said to the beast, mildly affronted when it nodded emphatically.

There will be time later for over-sensitivity. The beast was probably just as desperate to get out of there as he was. Especially now that it had helped him. It probably would have been better off just leaving him there and—

"Wait," he said, holding up a finger. "How did you get in here?"

The beast pointed at a bare patch of wall on the far side of the room. Gloucester inspected it. It was built of carved white stone, just like everywhere else.

"Great." He walked over to it. "And for those of us who *aren't* magic? How am I—"

He trailed off as his hand touched the stone. He'd expected the cold sensation of marble beneath his fingertips, but his fingers passed *through* it, sinking into the wall itself. It felt like he was pushing his hand through a heavy curtain.

Shocked, he looked back at the beast, who gestured encouragingly. It was uncanny to see such a human action taken by something so ferociously animal in appearance. Still, he knew it meant well.

Okay, he *hoped* it meant well.

Please don't be a trap.

Taking a deep breath, he stepped forward through the wall.

Chapter 16

Hyenas and Sharks

His hope that freedom would be waiting beyond the strangely non-corporeal wall diminished with every step Gloucester took. He'd emerged on the other side to find himself at the top of a spiral staircase carved of dark, roughly hewn stone, its steps descending into the shadowy depths below. It was a stark contrast to the brightness of the room he'd escaped, and he stood blinking for a moment, waiting for his eyes and brain to adjust.

It was a moment too long, as the beast appeared through the wall a few steps behind Gloucester and collided with his back, nearly knocking him down the long flight of stairs. He caught himself against a mercifully solid wall at the last moment. His bleeding shoulder scraped against the stone, and he rocked back on his heels, swearing colorfully but quietly in Nordish. He was on edge, and the sudden push, unintentional though it had been, made him want to snap at the creature. It wasn't its fault, though, and Gloucester—through sheer force of will—managed to rein his temper in.

"Careful," he ground out.

The beast snorted a laugh and held its hands up apologetically.

Gloucester eyed it while he tried to regain a normal heart rate. In the back of his mind, he couldn't shake the nagging reminder that Denken could return at any moment. The beast seemed just as ill at ease, shuffling its feet and turning its grotesque head this way and that, on the constant lookout for enemies.

"Do you have a name?" Gloucester asked it. He wasn't sure what exactly he hoped for in response. It wasn't like the beast had shown any indication that it could make sounds other than an impressively wide range of laughter. He supposed it could always write the name down. Except that he had nothing in his pockets with which to write, and somehow he doubted the beast had a pen on its person.

One wasn't necessary, as it turned out. The beast shook its head, the motion tugging on the exposed tendons in its neck.

"I should call you something," Gloucester said, as he stepped away from the wall. "As long as that's all right with you. Just makes things easier, you know?" When the beast didn't argue or shake its head, he took it as a sign of consent. "You're always laughing, so how about 'Hyena'?"

The beast blinked at him. The fluttering of its six eyelids wasn't entirely in sync, making it look all the more unbalanced.

"It's a kind of animal," Gloucester explained. "They live out on the plains between the South Cities and the eastern deserts. They make noises sort of like laughter. It's not an insult or anything, don't worry."

The beast seemed to consider it. Then it shrugged.

"Hyena it is," Gloucester said, attempting a smile and almost succeeding. "C'mon then, Hyena, let's get out of here."

—

As soon as he started down the steps of the spiral staircase, things became more complicated. Between one stair and the next, the world shifted. He found himself not at the top of the flight but in the middle, with stone steps coiling away from him in both directions. It left him with the uncanny feeling he'd been descending the stairs for some time, though he knew he'd only just begun.

Hadn't he? Certainty wavered. Perhaps he *had* been walking for a while now. He tried to remember, but the only memory presenting itself was of stepping away from the wall. Then how did he get here?

It's a trick. Magic or an illusion or something. Don't think about it. He wants to screw with my head. Don't let him.

It was one thing to tell himself to remain unaffected, but another entirely to actually do so. As Gloucester made his way down the spiraling steps, his nerves mounted. The only sound beyond his own breathing and footsteps was the muted clamor of Hyena. Though it was putting effort into sneaking quietly, the creature didn't seem capable of lasting silence. Each of its movements was accompanied by an undertone of breathy laughter, creaking bones, and the *slap-slap* of its bare hands and feet on the stone floor.

They'd been descending for a long time—or perhaps mere seconds—when things really started going wrong.

Whispers crawled into Gloucester's ears, so subtle at first that he scarcely noticed them, mistaking them for Hyena's perennial amusement. Yet they grew louder, filling the air like a ghostly choir. The words themselves were indistinct, but the tone was angry. Taunting. He thought he heard his name called out amongst the slurring crescendo, making him stop in his tracks and look around. He didn't spot anyone besides Hyena, who shook its equine head. *Not me,* it seemed to say.

"Great," said Gloucester, forcing his feet to continue on to the next step. "So it's just in my head. That's—"

Denken.

Here he was, thinking he was going mad when the real culprit was obvious.

"Get out of my head!" Gloucester shouted at the walls and thin air. It was a foolish move—he didn't actually want to attract Denken's attention—but anger was bubbling together with fear in his mind.

Soon shadows danced in his periphery, to join in with the whispers tormenting him. Hyena finally fell silent, or perhaps was simply drowned out by the murmuring ghosts. *Were* they ghosts? Gloucester tried to catch sight of what feinted and darted in the corner of his eye, but all he got for his troubles was a crick in the neck. On the edge of his vision, the shadows moved like living things.

No, he realized, dull horror coiling snakelike around his innards, *they* are *living things.*

One of the shadows solidified, stepping forward where there was no chance of missing it. Gloucester gaped at the sight of his own face staring back at him.

"What is this?" he said, shifting into a defensive stance. He didn't know what to expect from . . . well, himself.

It's not me. There's only one me. It's just a trick.

"Denken," he whispered, caught between wanting to shy away from the doppelganger and wanting to pummel it for stealing his face. He compromised, standing his ground but making no move to attack. His twin showed no reaction to the personification of Thought's name, merely staring back at him in unblinking solemnity. Gloucester's stomach twisted.

"What is this?" he demanded again. "Who are you?"

In retrospect, the answer was sort of obvious. Sure enough, his shadow self simply replied with "Mikalai Gloucester."

"Are you trying to be funny?" he asked it peevishly, only to have it turn away, paying him no more mind.

"Rude bastard." Gloucester suppressed a shiver. His false self strode up the stairs, and after a moment it disappeared out of sight, its footsteps fading away. Gloucester stared after it.

Was he meant to follow?

Like it was reading his mind, Hyena shook its head. Gloucester agreed; following an apparition, even one that looked like himself, had "trap" written all over it. *Especially* one that looked like himself.

"C'mon," he said. He cast a final uneasy glance up the stairs before continuing their descent.

The air felt strange. Not heavy, *per se,* but charged. It was difficult to tell amid the persistent murmur of whispers, but he could imagine a hum in the air, vibrating against his skin.

Magic.

For several reasons, this was an uncomfortable thought. Magic had done him few favors in the time since he'd learned of its existence. The least harmful spell he'd encountered was the little charm Finch used to inscribe his phone number on Gloucester's hand. And even that had left him with what he was beginning to worry was a permanent tattoo. A week had passed and the ink was still there, as clear as the moment it had been scrawled. If he got out of here in one piece, he was going to have a serious discussion with Finch about it.

"I would have lent him a pen and some paper, but *nooo,* he had to be showy with magic." He continued down the stairs, clenching his fist around the inked numbers. Hyena's laugh tipped upward at the end, a wordless question. Gloucester shrugged off its curiosity. "Sorry. Just thinking aloud."

Talking to himself. Not a habit he wanted to fall back into. In his cell, there had been no one else to talk to. Even the guards had avoided eye contact and conversation whenever they delivered his meals or escorted him to the showers. After a while, he'd started voicing his thoughts just to fill the silence. Sometimes he thought he would have forgotten the sound of his own voice if it hadn't been for his self-directed conversations.

Of course, it had done a good job of convincing all the guards he'd lost his mind. They said solitary confinement did that to you.

The whispers were getting louder, some of the voices heightening in pitch to become eerie whistles, like bird calls in the woods. The sound brought Gloucester home. Not to the apartment with Jeb, but the mountains of Lalune, the Nordland town where he'd grown up. Outside of the major cities, the northern region of the Lower Lands hosted a handful of mid- to large-sized towns and even more small villages and hamlets. Lalune wasn't all that small, but it was encased by the woods that grew at the mountains' roots. At night, as a child, he would lie in bed and listen to the birdsong. It had always been *normal*. If he'd had a good day, he'd find comfort and peace in the sounds. If the day had gone badly, it was just annoying.

Birdsong had never been *frightening* before. It felt like a violation for it to be used in this place, no doubt to put him on edge.

Is it Denken pulling the strings or is it just me? Perhaps Denken's mere presence in the building was the power source, and the mind games were nothing more than Gloucester's own fears bringing themselves to life.

He wasn't sure what to think about that, but the notion that Denken might not be lurking around the next corner, playing Gloucester like a fiddle as he conjured cruel tricks and illusions, made him feel at once uncomfortable and relieved. Again his gaze dragged back over his shoulder to the spot where his other self had disappeared around the curve of the stairs. Had he— it?—vanished the moment he was out of sight? Or was it still around, a doppelganger with thoughts and feelings of its own?

I hope not. This is complicated enough already. Gods know what I'd do with two of me.

Before long he had to plug his ears. It did nothing to muffle the din, however. It was all in his brain, not in his ears. Eventually, he couldn't take it any longer.

"Shut up!" he shouted at the very air surrounding him.

To his amazement, it worked. As if cowed into obedience, the whispers and whistles fell silent. The sheer absence of noise was so relieving that for a moment all Gloucester could do was close his eyes and sigh deeply, able to think clearly again.

Which led his mood to change a moment later, face pinched with worry once more.

"I shouldn't have—Denken could have—" He snapped his mouth shut, then turned a bemused look at Hyena. "I've not exactly been at my most stealthy best. Where *is* Denken? Is he not even here?"

Did Hyena know much about its master's plans? Perhaps not, if it was so willing to betray him. Or maybe that was *because* it knew exactly what Denken had in store.

The massive beast shook its head, many eyes darting to and fro. Gloucester wasn't sure if this meant that Denken wasn't lurking or if Hyena simply didn't know one way or the other.

Before he could press further, a distraction even odder than his own doppelganger presented itself.

What had been a seemingly bottomless staircase an instant earlier became the flat marble floor of a large room. Or perhaps it was a very small room. It was frustratingly difficult to say; despite its towering walls and distant ceiling, something about the place set off Gloucester's claustrophobia, like the walls themselves were pressing inward and invading his space.

He'd been here before, or somewhere very much like it. As he stared around at countless doors hanging open expectantly and impossible staircases set into ancient stone, it nearly convinced him he'd gone back in time. He could almost feel the bite of metal handcuffs around his wrists, could almost hear Zane's voice and see Finch's surly expression, countered by Denken's unflappable grin.

The Maze.

It couldn't be, though, could it? They had to be in the real world. The Gambler had been so certain that Denken *couldn't* return there. So how had they ended up back in that timeless place? Had the Gambler been wrong?

No, he thought, catching sight of a flicker in a window set high in the wall. The perfect blue sky visible through the glass had vanished for a brief moment, replaced by the glimpse of someone's grimy eavestrough, shadowed by night. *The Gambler was right. This is still real. The real world. He's making all of this himself.*

He's making a new Maze. Right here in Frettchen.

A realization like that ought to have hit him like a ton of bricks. It certainly carried the appropriate weight and consequence. Yet for Gloucester, the thought wore through him slowly, a mounting sense of unease blossoming into fear.

If he wants to recreate his little world right here, what does that mean for the rest of us?

Would the recreation of the Maze take over the human world? Surely two such places couldn't exist on the same plane. Would it just make everything worse?

Maybe it'll fix everything, he thought hopefully. The feeling didn't last longer than a few beats, dissipating like smoke in the wind.

Maybe it'll mean the end of everything.

"It's not finished."

The tone would have been light if it were any other voice, but it was compounded by a symphony of sensation, irresistible and unmistakable.

Gloucester swore. He leaped away from the breath tickling his ear, only to stumble right into Denken's hands. The demigod held him fast in what could almost have passed for an intimate embrace, if not for the unshakable grip of his arms, as immovable as those of a statue. Denken's chest was flush against Gloucester's back, and he rested his chin on his shoulder.

"Someone's been wandering where he ought not," Denken sing-songed.

The hold on Gloucester's arms tightened, and Denken turned them both on the spot to look at Hyena. The beast stood frozen, a deer in headlights. It wasn't laughing now.

"Who's a naughty, naughty thing, then?" Denken cooed. His

breath brushed the side of Gloucester's face. The scent of a sea breeze filled his nose, salty and cold.

For all its ferocious appearance, the beast cowered before the demigod and his prisoner. It raised its hands in supplication.

"Oh yes, I'm sure you're *very* sorry." Denken's sharp fingers dug into Gloucester's ribcage. Gloucester gasped a ragged breath, biting his lip to keep the sound of pain from becoming anything more than that. "Knowing that eases the sting of your betrayal more than you could know."

Out of the corner of his eye, Gloucester could see a glint of pearly white he knew was Denken's smile. He must have been grinning especially widely for it to be visible so far back in Gloucester's peripheral vision.

Not good. Not good, not good, not good, not—

Snap out of it.

Tempting as it was to give into panic, Gloucester forced his mind to clear.

"There's no need for this, Denken," he said in his most calm and rational voice, the one all security agents were taught to use when negotiating with potential threats to the lord or lady of the city-state. It was meant to soothe and reassure the assailant, so they could deal with the situation without spooking the person. Denken only laughed.

"Oh really?" the demigod murmured in his ear. "Well, praise be! I'm saved! Tell me, then, Mik—why isn't there need?"

Gloucester was keenly aware of the press of Denken's fingers against his sides. One wrong word or move and he would be skewered.

"The Gambler, all of us—we want to help you. You did what you did to save your brother. That's understandable. If we all work together, we could—"

He was forced into silence as Denken interrupted with another, louder burst of laughter. The first time had been overwhelming, but this time was *painful*. High and low all at once, it rumbled like a storm through Gloucester's chest while simultaneously jarring his eardrums with its shrillness. He instinctively tried to lift his hands to cover his ears, but his arms were pinned to his sides by Denken's hold. Gritting his teeth, he had no choice but to wait until the laughter subsided.

"If we all work together," Denken repeated. The mimicry was eerie, pitched too high in mockery but still uncannily like Gloucester's voice. When Denken continued, his voice was his own again, no humor in it to soften the dangerous edge. "The humans want me dead. And what good are you lot anyway? You think if we all hold hands, this will suddenly be undone?" He lifted one hand from its grip on Gloucester's ribcage and gestured vaguely. Gloucester wasn't sure if he was indicating himself or the room they stood in.

"Better to work together than to fight alone," he ground out.

"Do you think so? Do you think it's that easy? *Life doesn't work that way, Mikalai Gloucester.*" His words crashed over Gloucester, making him shout as tears welled in his eyes. "It's not fair or kind or hopeful. It's just *this.*"

He spun Gloucester around to look him in the eye. His stare was bottomless and impossible to turn away from.

In the depths of the darkness, Gloucester saw things. Shadows moving, stars burning out, feet running through the nighttime forest. The whispering rose back up in Gloucester's ears, taunting and warning and crying out for help. He heard the march of war, the light footsteps of a dancer, and the urgent pleas of those about to die. The world drained away to nothing. Nothing existed outside of the tenebrous gaze, not even himself.

Red-hot pain broke him free. It exploded through his left hand, starting between the first and second knuckles of his fist and splitting up his arm like splintering bone.

Clarity slammed back into place, and he clutched his arm to his chest, staggering away as Denken let go of him. The demigod's clawed hands went to cover his mouth, red streaming between his fingers.

"*Ow.*" Denken lowered his hands and spat out a mouthful of

blood and several serrated white teeth.

The pain in Gloucester's hand was blisteringly sharp, and he risked looking down at it. Another pointed tooth was embedded deeply into the skin between his index and middle fingers. Blood welled up from the torn flesh, and when he tried to move his fingers, all he could manage was a weak wiggle of his pinky and ring fingers.

"What did I say about punching me in the face?" Denken said, blood on his lips. "I warned you, Mik, didn't I? You really should have listened."

He took a step forward. Shadows were gathering around him, blurring the contours of his form and bleeding out into the surrounding space. Though it had yet to take on a distinct shape, Gloucester caught the hint of an undulating tail and triangular fin.

Denken's cloak of living shadows wasn't the only thing gathering; Gloucester could feel the now familiar sensation of magic building in the air, making the hairs on his arms and the back of his neck stand on end. Time, already so odd there, seemed to slow to a crawl. Gloucester found himself thinking of the woman at All Saints Shrine, Yvette Jacoby, and the way things had felt as she walked into the room with a bomb strapped to her chest. It was the same feeling now. The uncomfortable deep breath before the plunge, the final seconds on the clock before time ran out.

"I really didn't want to hurt you," Denken said as he advanced another step. Gloucester retreated two steps of his own, falling into a defensive stance he knew wasn't likely to do him any good. The punch had been a lucky hit born from the element of surprise.

A shrieking bellow made both of them falter. Gloucester jumped and Denken whirled on the spot. He gave an inhuman cry of his own an instant later when the heavy bulk of Hyena tackled him, and they went down in a tangle of limbs and gnashing teeth.

Gloucester took the opportunity to dodge around the fight and run headlong for the nearest door, an unadorned slab of wood that seemed starkly drab in comparison to the extravagant ones nearby.

When he reached it, however, his feet slowed. Instincts and logic alike urged him to keep moving. To take advantage of the monster's daring sacrifice.

Was that what it was, a sacrifice? Was Hyena really going to risk its own destruction just so Gloucester could escape?

Not if I can help it.

Trying not to think about what a mistake this might be, Gloucester turned away from the door and ran back to Hyena's side. The beast was on top of Denken, but the Thought god was a writhing frenzy of teeth and claws, his indistinct yells more animal than human.

"Hyena, come on!" Gloucester reached his uninjured hand out toward Hyena's, fingers splayed.

A few of the creature's eyes rolled to focus on him, and Hyena wasted no time before grabbing hold of the offered hand. Gloucester pulled with all of his might, nearly toppling them both over when Hyena pulled itself out of the fray and shot forward like a cork sprung from a bottle. Under vastly different circumstances, it might have been funny.

"Run!" Gloucester shouted, spinning on his heel and making another break for the door. Pressure built in the air like a storm front closing in, and as he ran, Gloucester waited for the lightning to strike.

It felt like a miracle when they reached the door unscathed, bolting through it and slamming it shut behind them. Whatever awaited them on this side couldn't be worse than what they'd just left behind. In the seconds before the door shut, Gloucester had looked back, and the sight wasn't one he would forget any time soon:

Shadows writhed like living things, seeping across the floor and up the white walls, coating the pristine surfaces in roiling darkness. In the midst of it all, Denken rose to his feet. Blood still smeared red across his lips and teeth, and his hair and clothing whipped in a rising wind. At the center of it all, no darkness was as deep and furious as the eyes that met Gloucester's. Over Denken's head, shadows coalesced once more into something massive. Gloucester had seen it before, so he did the best thing he could think to do. He ran.

"You can't run from me," Denken's voice called out, only marginally muffled by the door.

"We can try," he said, and though the words were barely a murmur, he somehow knew Denken heard them.

"Run!" he barked at Hyena again. The beast broke into an ungainly loping sprint down the hallway. Gloucester dashed after it.

They were a couple of meters down the corridor when a resounding crash blasted in Gloucester's ears. He flinched but forced himself to keep moving. *That'll be the door.*

A hand closing around his wrist made his already hammering heart stumble, but it was only Hyena, who had slowed its stride just enough to fall within arm's reach. Its hand, though human in shape, was twice the size of a grown man's, and its fingers encircled Gloucester's arm with room to spare. Hyena sped up again, nearly dragging Gloucester off his feet as it towed him along.

Something strange was happening to the corridor the further along they went. It took Gloucester a few minutes to recognize exactly what it was, but as soon as he did, fear wrenched his stomach.

The hallway was getting smaller.

The trick was in its subtlety. No sudden change occurred, just a smooth and gradual sense of the walls shrinking. Gloucester had the uncomfortable feeling of gazing through the wrong end of a pair of binoculars, distorting the view and shrinking it down.

He swore loudly, panic rising like bile in his throat. It was too small, the walls closing in. They were going to get stuck. Rats in a trap for Denken to find. The ragged jolts of breath escaping his lips got sharper, fear flooding his mind.

Hyena's head whipped up suddenly, eyes even wider than usual as it gave a piercing shriek of laughter. Gloucester winced, forced to slow his pace when the beast did. Not following suit would have been painful; Hyena had yet to loosen its hold on his wrist. If anything, it was holding on more tightly than ever, and any attempt to continue would surely end with a dislocated arm.

"What?" he hissed, at once grateful and anxious to be pulled from their claustrophobic path. Standing still wasn't much better, though, and he danced from foot to foot, eager to get moving again. "Do you have an idea?"

The urgent tug of Hyena's hand, sharp enough to be painful, gave the distinct impression that the creature wouldn't have wasted any time explaining even if it could. It jolted the both of them to the side, lunging for the smooth stone of the wall. Even with the memory of his recent escape from imprisonment, Gloucester flinched, flinging out an arm to shield himself from an impact that never came.

This wall seemed thicker than the other, catching Gloucester and Hyena like insects in amber just long enough to stir further panic in Gloucester's chest, before spitting them out the other side with a loud crash.

Chapter 17

The Plan

"Remember back when I hated our other plan?" said Zane, staring around at the dark city street as she clambered out of Antimony's car. "Well, I hate this one even more."

There were five of them in all. Amid the slowing whir of the perpetual engine, Antimony moved around the hood of her car to stand next to Zane on the sidewalk. Finch followed with the Gambler, who moved wraith-like through the night, his bare feet silent. Last out of the car, gazing around in avid fascination, came Gear.

"It's not perfect, you're right," Antimony said. "But we haven't got the time to come up with something better."

She was looking around as well, though less eagerly than Gear and with more composure than Zane. The clockmaker was always a little jealous of the other woman's ability to keep a cool head in dire situations. Of course, until recently, dire situations had been so few and far between that it had never really occurred to her as a trait to envy.

Ah, the good old days.

"You're sure this is the place?" Antimony asked Finch.

The magician had been noticeably closed-mouthed ever since they set out on this mission, speaking up only to direct Antimony once they'd gotten in the car. For once, Zane didn't think his stoicism had anything to do with brooding. Finch was concentrating; the faint hum of magic had been emanating from him for the better part of an hour. She'd never been that good at sensing magic, so the fact that she could feel it now meant Finch was probably channeling a pretty powerful spell.

"Absolutely." Finch's eyes were locked on the dark windows of the house directly in front of them. The place was abandoned, if the boarded-up windows on the first floor and the weed-stricken garden were anything to go by. "I'd know the feeling of my own spells anywhere."

Antimony nodded, satisfied with this response. "Right then, Finch, we'll follow your lead."

Finch had the grace not to look smug as he led the way up the front steps of the house. They creaked sagging protests beneath his feet. His hands were half-raised, tentatively feeling around for something in the space before him. He was also muttering to himself as he climbed the steps, the words in another language that rolled and lilted, unfamiliar in Zane's ears. Whether it was some magical dialect or merely Finch's native language, she couldn't say, but the spell seemed to be working. With each step, Finch strode forward with more purpose.

At the front door, he stopped. The rest of the group jumbled around him, looking up at their run-down destination.

"He's definitely here," Finch said.

"Are there wards?" Antimony asked. "Protection to keep us out? There are some pretty nasty magical deterrents out there."

"I know," said Finch. "I've used most of them." His eyes narrowed at the door. "It's not a ward here, though. It's a different sort of magic. It doesn't feel like a wall around the place or a lock on the door. This house feels . . . full. To bursting. Like it's filled up to the windows and doors with something. Something that's taking up more space than it should."

"Sounds like Denken." Zane tried to keep her words light, while nerves twanged through her like the plucked strings of a banjo. "I guess we've come to the right place after all." She eyed the door. It looked so innocent. "So the door's not even warded shut? That sounds like a trap to me."

"I reckon it *is* a trap," Finch said. "For the idiot he expects to come rescue the fair security agent in distress. A trap for me."

The women and the Gambler all leveled looks at him, save for Gear, who was inspecting the half-dispersed fluff of a dandelion in the weedy garden with great interest and didn't seem to be listening to the conversation in the slightest.

"You think this is all about you?" Antimony asked, thin eyebrows rising. "That's a bit self-aggrandizing, don't you think?"

"Mayhaps," Finch said with an unabashed shrug. "Doesn't make it not true. Whatever bone he might have to pick with you lot, it doesn't really compare, does it? Unless any of you also tried to kill him?"

No one answered, and Finch smiled grimly. "Right then, that settles it. Now, how about we end the inquisition and rescue Mikalai before he gets old or dies of boredom listening to Denken prattle on, eh?"

"I'd get offended on his behalf," commented the Gambler, "but it seems disingenuous to claim he doesn't prattle. Denken loves prattling."

His words were touched with fondness before the memory of where they were and who they were going up against apparently reoccurred to him, and his smile shrank away to nothing. The mood emanating from the demigod in its wake was a complicated storm of sadness, anger, worry, and fear. Zane tried her best to block it all out. Tonight would be dangerous enough without the Gambler getting in all of their heads. It was difficult to concentrate when she was stuck trying to ignore the immortal's infectious mood.

Apparently Antimony felt the same way.

"Gambler, get a hold of yourself," she told him gently.

"What's wrong?" Gear asked, catching up with them and eyeing their grim expressions anxiously. Dandelion seeds dusted her hair with bits of fluff. "Everyone looks upset."

Zane peered at her in the darkness. Did she not feel the effects of the Gambler's moods the way the rest of them did? An emotional Gambler was easier to be around than an upset Denken, but the weight of his feelings still hung heavy in the air. If Gear was immune to that, then maybe this plan wasn't as doomed as she'd worried it might be.

"It's nothing." Antimony patted Gear on the shoulder. "We're just worried about Gloucester. It's about time we went and rescued him, I think."

"I think so too!" Gear agreed.

"Right then," said Finch, clearing his throat. When everyone turned his way again, he rolled his shoulders and gave his hands a quick shake. They were glowing a faint blue. Most of the time Finch's magic showed no visual appearance at all, making itself known through a faint feeling and low sound in the air. The only times Zane had seen it as a visible light were when he'd conjured attack spells. She supposed that tracked, all things considered. They all had to be ready for anything. Zane longed for a better weapon than the crowbar clutched in her hands, but it was the best thing she could find on short notice. Hopefully, she wouldn't have cause to use it.

"Here goes nothing," Finch said, quietly enough that Zane reckoned he was talking to himself. He raised his hands toward the door, palms facing outward, stopping when they were only centimeters away from the surface of the wood.

Silence kept for a moment, wherein all of them, even the Gambler and Gear, seemed to be holding their breath. Then came a click and the door swung inward, creaking on its hinges.

For a split second, Zane thought she saw a dark and dusty interior, but then bright light filled her vision. Squinting, she shielded her eyes.

What lay beyond the doorway was neither dark nor dusty. Nor should it have been possible to fit within the dimensions of the old house. As they all crowded cautiously around the door, Zane couldn't help but feel like a mouse peeking out of its hole and into the relative massiveness of a house.

Towering white walls of stone rose far higher than the outside of the building, so pristine that the simple act of light reflecting off of them created the blinding effect. Despite the late—or possibly early—hour, Zane wished she'd brought her sunglasses.

"Well, that's unexpected," she said, too dazed to think of anything more clever.

"I like this place!" Gear enthused.

Neither Antimony, the Gambler, nor Finch looked very surprised by this strange turn of events. The scientist and the demigod stared impassively into the brightness, the light washing out the color in their faces. Finch looked more grim.

"Of course," he murmured.

"Is it safe to go inside?" the Gambler asked him.

Finch snorted. "Probably not. Here there be monsters. But if you're asking if we'll get zapped to dust or if the air will turn to stone around us the moment we step foot inside, then no. Not as far as I can tell, leastways. And I reckon you should be fine just about no matter what. If there's one thing I think we can all be certain of, it's how much your brother loves you."

The Gambler nodded solemnly, as if it were not a comfort but a weighty responsibility Finch had laid upon him.

As Finch had predicted, nothing happened when they went through the door. Though this was undeniably preferable to any number of possibilities Zane's imagination had supplied, it draped over them such a blanket of unease that she almost wanted the other shoe to drop, just so it would no longer be dangling over all of their heads.

The expansive white hall stretched out to the left and right of the doorway. It was reminiscent, in an exaggeratedly grandiose way, of the nave of a church, and Zane wondered if it was a purposeful nod on Denken's part to All Saints Shrine and all that had happened there.

"The air feels funny in here." Though Gear still seemed blissfully obtuse to the danger they faced, she had lowered her voice to a whisper. It seemed her instincts were correctly reading the situation even if her artificial brain was not.

Does she even have instincts? Zane wondered.

A question for another time.

"The air here is so full of magic, my head feels like it's stuffed with bees," Finch grumbled. "I can feel it humming like mad. It's dead distracting."

"Better get used to it quickly," Antimony warned. "Distracted is not something any of us want to be in here. If Denken knows we're coming—"

"Hold up," Finch interrupted. "One, he does know we're coming. Like I said, he's counting on *me* showing up. Not out of the realm of possibility he'll be expecting you lot too. And two, can you show a *little* more trust in my Blocking spells, please? I'm not a novice here, you know." He tapped a finger against his temple.

Zane's earlier reluctance aside, they'd all allowed Finch to perform the spells before they left Antimony's. Loath as she was to feel any sort of gratitude toward the magician, Zane had to admit the effect wasn't just noticeable, it was *remarkable*. Suddenly, she had become aware of just how much worry had been weighing on her every thought, and more than that, just how much of the miserable feeling had been Denken's influence. Once the ward was in place, it felt like a balm placed on her very thoughts. They were quieter and calmer than they'd been in weeks.

Whether the spell would protect her from a more direct attack from the demigod was still to be proven, but the only way to know would be to run afoul of Denken, and she was eager to avoid that.

"So where to now?" Antimony asked. Though quiet, her voice echoed off the vast white walls and cut through the tension permeating the rescue party. She turned her head from side to side, looking down the length of the huge corridor that stretched away from them in either direction. The group was silent for a moment of contemplation, then they turned as one toward the Gambler.

He shrugged, no small amount of irritation in the gesture. "Normally I would see the futures, the different possibilities depending on which way we went and which was most likely to lead us to success. This place, however . . ." He made an annoyed noise in the back of his throat. "This place was built by Denken. It's like a piece of him. Of the Maze. I can't see much of the futures of Frettchen of late, but here I can't see anything at all. No visions, no probabilities. Nothing." He grimaced. "It's awful."

"Welcome to the mortal world," Finch said dryly.

The Gambler's grimace deepened, emphasizing the melancholy cast of his features.

"Oh, cheer up," Finch said, rolling his eyes. "We're sort of on the clock here. Let's just pick a direction and hope, seeing as the personification of Uselessness doesn't have the lucky answer."

The Gambler didn't look at Finch, likely in a bid to keep his temper in check. It was for the best. Even setting aside the fact that they didn't have the time to waste, Zane didn't want to see what would happen should the Gambler really lose his temper.

"Let's go this way," Gear said, her bright enthusiasm sounding rather forced now. She pointed down the hallway to the left, but not before trotting to the Gambler's side and taking hold of his hand.

As she started down the chosen path, the Gambler trailed

a step behind her, visibly alarmed. Perhaps not in a bad way; he didn't pull his hand free, and soon enough he fell into step beside her. The pair of them left bloody footprints and a faint clicking in their wake, along with their bemused companions.

After a few seconds, Finch shook himself out of it. "Ehhh, I've seen weirder."

He strode forward to catch up with the strange duo. Antimony and Zane exchanged a look, then followed.

They walked for what seemed like days, or perhaps only five minutes. Time felt strange here, Zane noted uncomfortably. She was a good judge of time, a knack she'd had even before she entered officially into the realm of horology. Be it from the angle of a cast shadow or nothing more than a gut feeling, she could usually pinpoint the time within a margin of ten minutes.

Here, though . . . Here time didn't feel right. Zane mentioned this to Antimony as they walked side by side, and the scientist shrugged a shoulder. Before she could respond, Finch offered an answer.

"Remember the Maze?" he said, falling back next to the two women. "Denken's home? There's no time there, as the stories go. The Brothers exist in Pockets of time as well as space. Way I reckon it, this feels like home to him. Well . . ." He paused, then continued. "Home-*ish*."

Zane's face pinched in consternation. "So there's no time here? It's, what, frozen?"

"Nah," said Finch with a dismissive wave of his hand. Silver bangles glinted on his wrist. "My guess is it's just slowed. Could be the magic stretching the inside of this place so much bigger than the outside is so powerful that it messes with our heads. Or Denken is."

Another discomfiting thought. Zane looked uneasily over her shoulder, afraid she would see Denken's wide grin. Was he here somewhere? He had to be, surely. Especially if Finch was right and this was a trap.

All right, listen here, she reprimanded herself. *If you're just going to think things like this, maybe just stop thinking. This isn't helpful.*

"There are no doors," Antimony said suddenly. She was walking a few steps ahead of Zane and Finch now, watching the backs of the Gambler and Gear. When she half-turned toward the straggling pair, she wore an odd smile. It was wan, which was typical of Antimony, but it caught Zane's attention for the oddity of its timing. What was there to smile about here of all places?

Antimony pointed ahead with a slender arm. "It's just the same hallway, on and on. Makes you wonder, doesn't it? Are we being led in circles or right into the trap?"

"It is a bit too easy, isn't it? I feel like a lobster, taking the easy path into the trap." Finch nodded ahead at the Gambler. "Far as I reckon, he'll be able to lead us to Denken, even with his powers muted. They have a feel for each other, provided there's no magic acting as a block. And if we find Denken, we find Mikalai."

Zane pursed her lips. As far as she was concerned, this plan made their previous rescue seem professional. At least then they'd been up against humans. Clever, manipulative, ambitious humans, but limited in their power. Things weren't going to be so easy if they went toe-to-toe with someone like Denken.

"And then what?" she asked.

"Haven't really thought that far ahead just yet," he admitted, expression haunted. He clenched his fist, and bright sparks of magic leaped around his fingers. Preparation for the fight they all knew was coming. "I nearly beat him last time. We'll be all right."

Zane wanted to point out that Denken might not fight the same way now that he'd broken the unwritten rules of his kind. No doubt Finch was already thinking about that. What could they do? They couldn't just leave Gloucester to whatever fate Denken chose for him.

There's no way you're allowed to die, Gloucester. She

clenched her fists. Unlike Finch, she had no magic to summon, just a crowbar that would likely do nothing against Denken's powers. *Not before I get a chance to yell at you for being so reckless.*

Up ahead, the Gambler and Gear stopped abruptly, though Zane couldn't spot anything new about the white walls and marble floors. The other three caught up with the pair, crowding around them with wary curiosity.

"What is it?" Antimony asked.

"It feels different here," the Gambler whispered.

"Different how?" Finch glanced around. "Like Mikalai is near? Or like Denken's somewhere around?"

The Gambler gave his head a single sharp shake. Zane wasn't sure if it was meant as a response or if he was trying to clear his mind.

"I'm not sure," he admitted. "Perhaps both." Catching the look on Finch's face, his voice took on a bone-chilling edge. "Trust me, Cassus Finch, no one is more annoyed than I about the state of my abilities."

Finch actually appeared cowed for once, and he remained silent rather than offering a pithy retort. The Gambler regarded each and every one of them with his impossible gaze.

"Be careful," he warned. Before any of them had a chance to point out that this was stating the obvious, he continued on. "The wards you have cast on your minds will keep Denken from reading your thoughts—at least, provided he does not get his hands on you physically—but he can still cause a lot of trouble. If you have any thoughts that seem strange or out of place, thoughts that just aren't like you, then know they might not be yours. Don't trust them."

"Our own thoughts?" Zane didn't know whether to laugh or cry.

"Good to know," Antimony said, calmly and quietly cutting ahead of any further complaints.

This left Zane to fret in surly silence as they edged along, moving more slowly now as the Gambler tried to follow whatever it was he sensed. Zane kept glancing over her shoulder. Was the feeling they were being watched just because of her nerves or something more?

The question beckoned another in its wake: How could they fight someone who could so easily get inside their heads? She was childishly tempted to plug her ears, to try to physically block Denken's powers from breaching her skull. Every time she thought something, no matter how banal, she worried it was a trap, a cuckoo bird in the nest of her mind. The Gambler's warning, meant to further arm their defenses, only made her jittery.

A few minutes later, as far as Zane could tell, the Gambler stopped in his tracks again.

"What is it?" she asked, echoing Antimony's earlier question. She and the others gathered around the Gambler once more.

"Here," the Gambler said distantly. He seemed almost in a trance for how single-mindedly focused he was. He walked up to a bare patch of wall, his no-eyed stare unwavering as he faced the stone.

"Here?" repeated Gear. "What's here?"

Gear meant the question in honest curiosity, but Zane found herself thinking the automaton had a point, even if she didn't realize it. What good were empty walls?

"Remember where you are," the Gambler warned. The barest trace of his lingering impatience reverberated through all of their minds like a history of regrets. Zane made a mental note to start bringing headache medication with her wherever she went. "Nothing here is necessarily what it seems. Bear in mind what these walls look like from the outside."

Zane still didn't understand how this was supposed to help them find Gloucester. It was just another eerie reminder that Denken was probably toying with them. If nothing here was as it seemed, did that mean that even if they found Gloucester, it could still be nothing more than a ruse? What if they never found him?

The world, as it turned out, had a magnificent sense of timing and an enthusiastic desire to prove Zane wrong. She had scarcely thought these questions when her intended retort to the Gambler was cut off before it could even begin.

With a thundering crash, the wall that had been subject to the Gambler's scrutiny exploded.

Or rather, two figures barreled through it, tumbling into the endless corridor. The small group of rescuers scrambled back, with the exception of the Gambler, who had stepped out of the way several seconds before the newcomers appeared. They hadn't crashed through the stone itself, Zane realized but rather had fallen *through* the wall, leaving unblemished white stone where she'd expected rubble and dust. The bang accompanying their sudden appearance seemed to have come from the air itself.

That was a mystery to investigate later, though. Zane's attention was focused entirely on the people who had just about flattened the lot of them.

One of the figures was not a person at all, but a beast so monstrous that Zane's heart tried to leap out of her chest, hammering against her ribs and chasing the breath from her lungs. It was an exhalation echoed by some of the others—she didn't look to see who. The creature's huge body was all jagged bones and taut skin, with long, gangling limbs and a neck that looked flayed. The angry red of exposed muscle turned to pale gray flesh at its head, pulled so tightly over the bone that it seemed little more than a skull with eyes. Far too many eyes, in fact: there were six, yellow and slitted like those of a snake, all rolling wildly in their sockets as the beast looked around at them. Its mouth was lined with sharp teeth, and the sound rolling off its tongue wasn't a growl, but desperate, breathless laughter.

The second figure was tiny in comparison: trim, agile, and wearing clothes Zane remembered from that morning.

"Gloucester!"

The former security agent whirled to face her. Like the beast, his eyes were wild. Large patches of his shirt were stained dark, and blood dripped from his left hand. He opened his mouth, heaved several uneven breaths, then shouted something in what Zane vaguely recognized as Nordish and threw himself straight at her.

Chapter 18

Escape

It wasn't the strange travel through the wall that shook Gloucester the most. That honor rested on the narrow shoulders of Denken, whom he'd spotted approaching in the instant before Hyena barreled through the semi-corporeal wall.

Thought was a dangerous thing. Denken had never looked more terrifying than he did at that moment, stalking toward them, shrouded in shadow so deep and dark that it consumed everything it touched. The air thrummed like a thousand angry insects.

And most terrifying of all: the massive spectral shark, born of living shadow. It cut a path through the air above Denken's head, angry maw gaping. That would have been scary enough, with its sharp teeth and predatory approach, but something was as wrong with it as with its master. In the glimpse Gloucester caught of the shadow beast, it seemed to be . . . Perhaps malfunctioning wasn't the right word for it. It wasn't a machine on the fritz, after all, but a creature of sorts. Yet the edges of the shark's form shivered and jolted, as though charged with electricity that could overload at any moment.

The vibration of magic was still faintly discernible on the other side of the wall where they emerged, tumbling into another corridor and just barely managing to stay on their feet. That was the first thing Gloucester noted.

The second was that this corridor was much bigger than the one they'd left behind. That wasn't a very high bar to clear, but this hallway did it with gusto, not simply larger but towering to heights that matched the room in which Gloucester had been imprisoned.

The third thing he noticed was that they weren't alone. He and Hyena had nearly careened right into a whole group of people. Wide-eyed and out of breath, Gloucester realized he knew them. His friends had come to the rescue after all.

Or to the slaughter.

The buzzing in the air mounted steadily. Denken was just on the other side of the wall, a wall he had built. Getting through it would surely be no obstacle for him. In his attempt to avoid his friends being put in danger, Gloucester had led Denken right to them.

"He's coming! Run!" he shouted, too urgent and afraid to pay any mind to which language he was using. Nordish was quick and fluid, lending itself naturally to bouts of high emotion. Zane and Finch, standing closest to him, looked flummoxed as they stared from him to Hyena.

There isn't time for this. Gloucester threw himself at the pair of them.

"Run!" He managed it in Frettchennian this time.

That, they understood. He grabbed Zane's hand—wincing as his bloody knuckles knocked a crowbar from her fingers—and a handful of Finch's coat and kept running, hardly caring whether they were running alongside him or if he was dragging them in his wake. He could hear Antimony, her voice uncharacteristically loud, urging the others to run.

Gloucester risked a look over his shoulder as he ran down the corridor. He didn't care which direction he was headed in, provided it was away from where he was. Only the Gambler remained motionless, still standing at the innocuous patch of wall Gloucester and Hyena had come through.

"Denken."

The soft voice reached Gloucester's ears clearly, despite the distance growing between himself and the Gambler.

"There's no time!" he shouted. If the Gambler was planning on negotiating with his brother, he was in for a severe disappointment. If anyone could do it, it *would* be the Gambler, but Gloucester doubted even he would have any luck with Denken's current state.

The Gambler didn't move. "Keep running. I'll buy you all some time. *Go.*"

Any desire to argue, already weak with desperation and fear, couldn't survive the stress of a boom like a cannon as the wall exploded outward. Unlike when he and Hyena—already ages ahead of them all, galloping along on its hands and feet—had crossed through, now the wall itself burst into the corridor, showering the floor with bits of stone and mortar. None of it struck the Gambler, who stood silently amongst the dust and debris.

"Go!" he called again. Gloucester stumbled under the force of the command before heeding it, and he didn't look back again as he and the others fled.

—

The corridor seemed to stretch on forever. Panic clawed its way up Gloucester's spine. How were they ever going to escape? For all he knew, Denken could have them running in circles, tiring them out until he decided to pounce.

Still, he forced himself to keep running, even as his lungs burned and a stitch in his side screamed its disapproval. Beside him, Zane was gasping for breath, her eyes fixed firmly ahead. She and Finch seemed to be searching for something.

He wanted to ask if they knew the way out, but speaking took more breath than he was willing to spare. It was an unnecessary question anyway. If Finch or Zane or any of the others knew the way out, it wasn't like they would keep it to themselves.

On Finch's other side was Antimony, quick on her feet despite the low heels she wore. Gear ran hand in hand with her, but the automaton's attention was fixed behind them, and she looked on the verge of breaking away and heading back.

"We can't leave him here!" she cried. "I don't think it's safe!"

"The Gambler will be okay," Antimony said, voice ragged.

"Promise?" In contrast, Gear wasn't the slightest bit out of breath.

"He'll be okay," Antimony assured her again, tugging her along. Gloucester didn't miss that she hadn't actually confirmed the promise.

"Look out!" Zane yelled.

Ahead of them, a massive shape galloped down the hall in their direction. For an instant, Gloucester thought Hyena had doubled back to urge them on. But no, the cacophony of this beast wasn't laughter and slapping feet, but a loud, dry clattering. And though it too towered, it was quickly apparent that this was a completely different monster: the bare bones of a huge skeleton bore down on them. It ran on all fours, reminiscent in shape of a wolverine or bear, its skull broad and tipped in massive canines. Its bleached white jaws gaped open, letting loose a deafening roar. In its hollow sockets, blue flame flickered.

"Oh, what the fuck?" Zane's shout was nearly lost in the skeleton's roar. The group skidded to a halt.

"Cassus!" Gloucester looked to the magician, the only one who could combat such a monster. Finch shook off Gloucester's grasping hand and raised his own, magic gathering around his fingers. The skeleton would be on them in seconds . . .

A howl of laughter cut through the air. The skeleton slowed, distracted, and the lanky bulk of Hyena careened past it. The laughing beast scrambled to a stop between the other monster and the group of humans, teeth bared and eyes rolling wildly. It gave another shriek of laughter.

Heart thundering, Gloucester watched the two creatures face off. The skeleton had fallen silent, caught off-guard by Hyena's sudden appearance. Or maybe it was more than that. Though neither seemed capable of speech, they were staring intensely, and he couldn't help but feel that some sort of conversation was being had.

"Finch," Antimony hissed. "Do something."

Finch raised his hands again, but Gloucester caught hold of his shoulder. "Wait!" He ignored the others' incredulous looks, his attention on the beasts. Hyena was panting, giggles chasing each heaving breath, but it wasn't backing down. Behind them, Gloucester heard the crack of stone and the crash of godly voices. The Gambler's peace talks weren't going well.

C'mon, Hyena, he silently urged. *We need to get out of here.*

The skeleton lurched a single step forward, then hesitated again when Hyena hissed furiously and rose onto its back legs. It splayed its too-human hands wide. The message was clear: *You'll have to go through me.*

The skeleton gave a final, uncertain roar. Then it retreated. It clattered back the way it had come and, after several long strides, vanished.

"What the shit," said Finch. He let out a gusty breath. "What just happened?"

"Hyena saved our lives, that's what." Gloucester glanced over his shoulder and immediately wished that he hadn't. Darkness was clawing up the walls, drawing closer at an alarming rate. "Let's go!"

They set off running again, Hyena leading the way. It had dropped back down onto all fours and soon put a fair bit of distance between itself and the breathless humans. Then it slowed, letting out a triumphant laugh.

Gloucester could see why. A set of doors rose high against the wall. The exit? How the hell were they going to get the damn things open?

"Everyone, get out of the way!"

Sweeping his hands up, Finch launched into a spell, spewing words in a melodic language Gloucester didn't know.

The air vibrated more violently than ever, spreading out from Finch in near-palpable ripples. Then he slammed his hands forward, shoving the spell like a physical force.

The doors blasted open. Finch's hands dropped back to his sides, sparking with blue light. The air was thick with the sensation of magic.

And growing thicker still. Shadows enveloped the walls, floor, and high ceiling of the once-bright corridor. Whispers accompanied the moving darkness, wrapped up in screams and tangled with the terrible cry of battle horns.

"Go, go, go!" Gloucester shouted, shoving Zane and Finch out. Antimony, Gear, and Hyena were already ahead, dashing through the broken door frame and into the darkness on the other side. Gloucester threw himself through the doorway last.

He barely had a chance to gawp at his surroundings, which were profoundly mismatched to what lay within the building, before a second blast, much stronger than Finch's spell, rocked through the corridor he'd just escaped and buffeted him to the ground.

He tumbled down a short flight of steps and onto the hard concrete of a sidewalk, half-landing on Finch. Finch grunted at the impact but seemed too out of breath to say anything more. The house—for indeed that was, impossibly, what it was—still shook after the force of the explosion, wooden beams and brick walls creaking and cracking ominously.

"The Gambler!" Gear cried. On her feet, she headed straight for the broken doors. "He's still inside!"

"There's no time!"

Antimony's words were curt, especially for addressing Gear.

Her hair had fallen out of its bun, large portions of it trailing down over her shoulders in tangled strands. Gloucester dizzily thought that he'd never seen her so disheveled.

"The Gambler will be fine," she said, gesturing furiously for them all to get up. "But we won't be if we hang around here much longer. Now come on."

They all scrambled to their feet, coughing and hissing pained breaths. Gear couldn't seem to drag her eyes away from the impossible house.

Gloucester, meanwhile, was only too eager to get away from it, and too dazed from exertion and injury to devote much thought to the Gambler's predicament.

"C'mon," Zane said, laying a gentle hand on his arm. "Let's get you home."

Chapter 19

Comfort and Doubt

Dawn crept over the horizon as Antimony pulled her car to a stop outside her house. The sky, ebony when they'd left Denken's lair behind, grew lighter with the pale hues of morning, tinged in orange and pink. It promised a fantastic sunrise, but none of the car's occupants were in the mood to appreciate such things.

Morning had properly arrived by the time Gloucester sank into a chair in Antimony's kitchen two hours later. He bit his lip to hold in a groan at the movement. Now that things had calmed down, his body was eager to remind him of the many gashes, bumps, and bruises he'd accumulated since leaving the clock shop the morning before.

A shower, change of clothes, and a good hour spent with Purpurrot's healing powers plus a well-stocked first aid kit had left him feeling a lot better. Still, he ached all over. They'd pulled Denken's tooth from his hand, and Purpurrot had mended the worst of the damage, but his knuckles were still buried under a thick coating of charmed bandages. In his uninjured hand, he turned the tooth over and over. It looked no different from the sort you could buy on necklaces down at the docks. He stowed it away in his pocket.

"You want to talk about it?"

The question made him jump, which was painful. Looking over at the counter by the sink, Gloucester found Finch staring at him. He'd shed his wool coat and rolled up the sleeves of his thin shirt, revealing the trailing pattern of tentacles on his left arm. If Gloucester were to hazard a guess, he would say the design spread over Finch's entire upper arm and shoulder. He had been curious to ask about it ever since he caught his first glimpse but now wasn't the time. He had a question of his own to answer.

If only it were an easy one. Part of him did want to talk about everything that had happened. On top of the hope that it might help him make sense of things, there was information he needed to share, not just with Finch but with the entire group. Denken was trying to rebuild the Maze. A concrete place warped with magic right there in the regular world. Who knew what effect that would have on reality?

On the other hand, it hadn't been a good twenty-four hours, neither physically nor emotionally.

"Honestly?" he said. He could hear the strain in his own voice. "I don't even want to *think* about it."

"You will, though." Finch moved away from the countertop and came to sit next to Gloucester at the table. The dark smudges under his eyes were more noticeable than ever, and his skin had taken on an unhealthy gray pallor. "Better to talk about it now than dwell on it 'til it eats you alive. How about this? I'll cast the same Blocking spell on you that the rest of us have—" He paused to tap a ringed finger against his own brow. "—and while I'm doing that, you can get things off your chest."

Zane had explained the Blocking spells on the car ride over, managing to sound both peeved and grateful at the same time. More magic cast on his mind wasn't a comforting notion, but if Zane trusted it, then Gloucester was willing to give it a try. Anything to keep Denken out of his thoughts.

When he didn't argue, Finch murmured his thanks and carried on with a touch of hesitance. Gloucester guessed he wasn't accustomed to conversations like this.

"We'll need to know what happened anyway," he said. Shuffling his chair to better face Gloucester, he raised his hands to either side of Gloucester's temples. "So what happened? Are you . . . are you all right? And, pardon my asking, but what the *hell* is the beastie that came with you?"

"Hyena?" Gloucester said, frowning. Finch's fingertips tickled against his face, a feather-light touch that tingled even before he felt the magic begin to gather. "Oh, he's all right. Or she. Or neither, I'm not really sure. It's hard to translate laughter, and frankly, I didn't actually ask about that."

"Neither did I," Finch said dryly. "A little off-track there, mate. Long day and all that, I know, but try to focus, yeah? So what is . . . Hyena?"

Gloucester shook his head, not in denial but in a weary attempt to do as Finch had requested and focus. The magician clucked his tongue at the motion, his fingers pressing more firmly on the sides of his face. Bashful, Gloucester chuckled and tried to stay still. The shower and healing had done wonders, but his brain and body were calling out for sleep.

"Sorry," he said, rubbing one of his eyelids and stifling a yawn. Finch whispered a spell, but his steady gaze made it clear he was still listening. "I dunno. One of those imagination monsters. I called it—them?—Hyena 'cause they're always laughing. They don't seem to mind. They helped me escape. Actually . . ." A thought had just occurred, one that he knew he probably should have considered earlier. "Where *is* Hyena? Did they come along with us?"

The drive back to Antimony's had been a bit of a blur, but he felt like he ought to have noticed the beast hitching a ride.

"We thought they were gone for a bit," Finch answered, after finishing his quiet chant and lowering his hands. The effects of the spell quickly settled on Gloucester's mind. His head already felt noticeably lighter despite his weariness. "I'd lost sight of them by the time we left Denken's little place of worship, but when we got here, they were sleeping in the garden. No idea how they knew where to go. Don't you remember?"

His expression softened when Gloucester shook his head. "When you went to get yourself cleaned up, Antimony convinced them to move into the basement. I reckon it's a bit cramped for them down there, but better than them being out in broad daylight. Gear's with them now, though I couldn't tell you who's the worse company."

"The Gambler?"

Finch nodded, a shadow in his eyes. "She's worried about him. Last I heard, Antimony was assuring her that Denken would never hurt him, but she didn't seem much comforted."

Gloucester gingerly touched his bandaged hand. His shoulder, at least, was more or less healed, but the pain was still fresh in his memory. His thoughts were clearer in the wake of the ward, dredging up questions. "Do you think Antimony's right?" he asked.

"About this? Yeah, I reckon so. That's not what I'm worried about when it comes to the Gambler." Finch settled his chin on his hand, then moved it away again, crossing his arms over his chest and tapping one foot. Despite his obvious fatigue, he couldn't seem to sit still.

"You think he'll side with him. With Denken," Gloucester said quietly.

"Wouldn't you? If it were your brother? The Gambler knows that everything Denken did was to save him."

Gloucester thought about it. He had no siblings, so he imagined his parents. What would he do if they were ever in a similar position to Denken, an emotional train wreck and out of control? Or if they had been like the Gambler, imprisoned and tortured for months? Hells, Gloucester himself knew what solitary confinement could do to you. He felt it every day like some core part of himself had been damaged, and that was after only six months.

The Gambler had endured twice that. And his brother had led the charge to rescue him. With a plan that was malicious and half-baked, yes, but Gloucester couldn't deny he'd been passionate in his pursuit of the Gambler's freedom. Surely the Gambler would be thinking about that and everything else binding the Brothers together after however many eons they had existed. Against that, would his loyalty to the world and to humans hold fast?

"He knows Denken needs to be stopped," he said slowly. "He's been fighting just as hard against the rising trouble as any of the rest of us."

More than some of us, he added in the privacy of his own mind. He wasn't about to derail the conversation with self-pity.

"Aye, he has," Finch said. He leaned forward, dropping his voice to a conspiratorial whisper. "Have you ever thought about *how* we stop Denken?"

Gloucester opened his mouth to answer. Then he closed it again. He thought for a moment, running through his mind all the conversations they'd had in the weeks since the high minister's death. "Something about . . . we have to get the monsters back to the Maze, don't we?"

"That'd be Step One, but it would still leave us dealing with Denken himself. Who, you know, might not take too kindly to having all of his pets sent away. Which leaves us with a very unhappy demigod. We've been there before."

Gloucester frowned down at the table as he turned it all over in his head. Tiredness weighed down on his mind, making him feel slow and stupid. At least with the ward, a great deal of his simmering anxiety had fallen away.

Finally, he raised his eyes to meet Finch's again. "So . . .

what? You're suggesting we kill him?"

Finch didn't answer, but his silence spoke volumes. Gloucester shook his head.

"He was trying to save his brother—" he started.

"And now he's ending the world. How many people are dying because of him? Because he doesn't care about the humans who get in his way?"

"How many died because you and your dad caught the Gambler?"

As soon as the words left his mouth, he regretted them. Hurt and guilt flashed through Finch's expression before something closed behind his eyes.

"I know my mistakes," he said. "I'm not trying to pretend they didn't happen."

An apology was on the tip of Gloucester's tongue, but he held it back. As Finch said, his and his father's involvement had led to terrible things for many people, including Gloucester himself. He wasn't about to be the one offering apologies.

Still, it counted for something—more than Gloucester was certain he wanted to admit—that Finch was trying to atone. It was between him and whichever of the higher powers he believed in to sort out whether that was enough to counter what he'd done, but it was better than nothing.

He liked Finch. More than he knew he ought to. Something about the flippant redhead ensnared his attention. He was clever and powerful and interesting. Not to mention handsome, which was always a nice bonus. What he wasn't, however, was completely trustworthy.

"I don't even know how you would kill someone like Denken," he said, deciding it best to get the conversation back on track. "Can the Brothers even die?"

"Everyone can die," Finch replied, but he didn't sound entirely convinced.

Gloucester thought back to the Gambler's prison in the church and the look on Finch's face as he pointed his spelled gun at Denken. He'd been prepared to kill him even then, so it made sense that his feelings wouldn't have altered in the intervening weeks. Would he have succeeded if Gloucester hadn't stopped him?

Another question strode to the forefront of his mind and clamored for an answer: If the personification of Thought died, how would that affect the world? It struck him as a pretty important thing to find out before they tried anything rash.

It wasn't like they had many options, though. They couldn't just do nothing and allow the world to fall under the sway of Denken's infectious depravity. What if, when they faced off against him, killing him was the only option they had?

"Better you than me to put that idea to the Gambler," he said. "Something tells me he won't take kindly to it."

"If he even comes back." Finch stared moodily out the window. A songbird in the garden trilled its morning requiem to the rising sun. The pleasant ambience didn't seem to bring Finch any comfort.

"He will," Gloucester asserted. Deep down, however, doubt whispered. Who could he really trust?

Yourself. Just trust in yourself to do what's right.

If only he had any clue as to what that might be. He scrounged around for a change of subject, too tired and conflicted to dwell further on the topic of the Gambler's loyalty. Better to think of other things. He had something else he'd been meaning to say to Finch anyhow.

"Thank you," he murmured, then realized how abrupt the words probably seemed out of context. Finch looked away from the window to face him, bemused, and Gloucester hurriedly explained, "For the ward. And for coming to Denken's lair. For the rescue."

"You seemed to be doing just fine on your own," Finch said in return. The anger burning in his eyes had tempered. He was left looking weary beyond his years. Something else hid in his expression too, something softer. He reached out to gently lay his hand over Gloucester's uninjured one. "I—We would never have left you there. No one's going to abandon you."

"Thanks," Gloucester said again. The word was harder to get out this time, clinging to his throat. He coughed, uncomfortable with the surge of emotion. He had so desperately hoped that none of his newfound friends would come to his rescue and fall into Denken's trap, and yet he was realizing now how much a part of him had truly feared they wouldn't.

Finch's hand was still on his. His fingertips were callused, the rough texture brushing against the back of Gloucester's hand as he turned it over, exposing his palm. The phone number Finch had scrawled there a week ago still showed clearly, and the magician made a quiet sound that may have been a chuckle. He traced a finger over the numbers, the ghosting touch eliciting a shiver down Gloucester's spine. The sensation wasn't unpleasant but carried with it a sense of intimacy to which he was no longer accustomed.

"This did it," Finch told him, smiling down at his palm. "We wouldn't have found you without it."

Speaking quietly, he told Gloucester about his dream, about the plan he and the others had hastily put together, and how the lingering magic of the spell inked on his hand had been enough to lead Finch to him. When he finished, Gloucester stared down at his hand, digesting this new information.

"Is it permanent?" he asked.

Finch blinked, then a small grin broke across his face and he chuckled. "That's *still* what you're concerned about?" He clicked his tongue in disbelief. "You're an odd creature, Mikalai Gloucester."

Gloucester watched the movement of the fingers across his palm. Finch wore two rings on his hand, a silver band on his littlest finger, and an ornately carved gold one on his index. Distantly, he wondered if they had some magical function or if Finch simply liked jewelry. "So I've been told," he said. "Though not usually in those words."

"Good. I'm not really one for quoting others. If I tell someone something, I want it to be my words, not someone else's."

"Was there something else you wanted to tell me?" Gloucester raised his eyes from their hands to meet Finch's gaze.

"Was there something else you wanted to hear?"

Gloucester released a sharp sigh through his nose, impatience wearing the flirtation thin. Though he'd had a chance to calm down since their escape from Denken's clutches, he could still feel the effects of the near-death experience, his mind at war between leaden exhaustion and a frenetic jitteriness.

"Look, you risked a lot coming to save me. You must have known it was a trap, but you came anyway. I don't know if that means anything or if you were just eager to take another stab at fighting Denken, but I just—"

The rest of his words were stolen by the kiss Finch pressed against his lips. His fingers tightened around Gloucester's hand, and his other hand found its way to the back of Gloucester's skull, tangling in his hair and pulling him closer.

Gloucester hesitated for only a moment. The sudden contact made him want to flinch back out of instinct, but as the initial alarm faded, he sank into the kiss. Finch's soft chuckle tickled his chin as he pulled away just enough to catch a breath, with no apparent intention of moving any farther back than that.

Good, thought Gloucester. His bandaged hand was clumsily caught up in the front of Finch's shirt, the light blue fabric rumpled beneath his fingers.

"Should I take this as a thank you?" Finch murmured into the scant space between their lips, his own curving into a smile.

Gloucester laughed just as quietly in return. "If that's what you want it to be."

He closed the distance between them again.

In all honesty, he wasn't sure what this was. A thank you or adrenaline or a longing for closeness. Maybe something more than any of that.

For now, he didn't care about the reason. The only thing at

the forefront of his mind was the desire not to stop. It was an escape from everything that had turned his life upside-down, from the worries that plagued every waking thought. Right now all he was thinking about was Finch—*Cassus*—and the simplicity of that felt like a breath of fresh air.

Approaching footsteps made them break the kiss, both quickly sitting back. When Gear rounded the corner a moment later, her smile of greeting faded at the sight of them.

"Hi!" she said, still managing an enthusiastic tone, but looking between them with some concern. "Antimony asked me to come find you. Is everything all right? Your face is sort of red. Is that a thing faces are supposed to do?" The question was aimed at Gloucester alone because Finch was somehow utterly composed.

Bastard, Gloucester thought fondly.

He cleared his throat, adopting what he hoped was an innocent expression. "What, erm, what did Antimony want? Can it wait?"

Gear shook her head, the glass of her skull reflecting the light from the window. "I think it's important. She wants to talk to everybody."

Gloucester resisted groaning outright by masking it behind a yawn. He didn't want important meetings and complicated plans. As the moment passed, he didn't even feel like continuing his intimately good time with Finch. Mostly he just wanted to sleep.

"We'll be right there," Finch told Gear. "I take it we're meeting in the . . . ?" He trailed off expectantly, but Gear only smiled back at him, clearly not picking up on the less-than-subtle hint. Finch's eyebrows twitched, but it was the only sign he gave of annoyance before he tried again. "Where does she want us to meet?"

"Oh," said Gear. She eyed Finch a little dubiously. Gloucester supposed it had sounded to her like Finch left his sentence hanging for no reason. With her so new to the world, they probably all seemed like baffling contradictions and unpredictable puzzles. "The living room." She pointed over her shoulder.

"Right, thanks," Gloucester told her, half-heartedly stifling another yawn. "We'll be right there."

Chapter 20

Circles

They were soon all gathered in Antimony's living room. It was a fairly spacious area, but with everyone packed into it, it felt distinctly cramped. Gear sat down on the sofa, joining Zane and Antimony, the latter of whom was perched on the couch arm. Finch leaned against the other arm, his back to the sunlit window.

The claustrophobic atmosphere wasn't helped by the presence of Purpurrot. Besides her looming height—even while seated on the floral-patterned armchair in the corner—her mood was overwhelming. The demigoddess's beautiful face was set in a grim expression, and the very air in the room felt heavy and charged. Though he knew her overbearing presence likely wasn't intentional, Gloucester stood on the far side of the room, keeping the door close by. Not that he could just turn and leave if things got to be too much, but it was comforting to pretend it was an option.

He'd been pretty certain what this meeting was going to be about. Sure enough, he'd scarcely stepped through the door before he was being asked to recount what had happened from the moment he left the clock shop to when he and Hyena nearly trampled his rescue party almost a day later.

Clearing his throat, he began to speak. As had been the case several weeks prior when he shared his story with Zane and then again with Antimony, it felt odd to talk this much. Everyone's focused attention was on him, and he wasn't sure where to look. His eyes skipped from one intense face to the next, until eventually, he settled on the empty air a little to the right of Zane's head, doing his best to pretend he was just giving a report like he would have back in his life as a security agent.

No one interrupted him, save for the occasional murmur of shock or sympathy, mostly from Zane or Gear. Purpurrot's face was unreadable. Antimony and Finch were impassive for the most part, though the latter gave away a few instances of emotion, a muscle twitching in his jaw when Gloucester described his interactions with Denken.

He left out all mention of Jeb, instead describing how he'd wandered the streets out of a need for some fresh air and a clear head. His old life felt distant and separate from this strange new one, and he was reluctant to bring them together, afraid his past might somehow be tainted by the madness of it all. It was over now anyway, he thought gloomily. Now all he had were fond memories. They were his own, and he didn't feel like sharing them with anyone.

After he finished, the room was silent. Gloucester coughed, throat dry after so many words, and crossed his arms over his chest as he waited for their response.

Purpurrot eventually broke the silence. With a sigh that echoed the mournful calls of woodwinds and the howls of wolves, she dragged a hand over her face and sat back. "Another Maze, here in the human world . . . That *idiot*." Her mouth twisted. "If he succeeds . . ."

"If he succeeds, then what?" Zane peered at her from the couch, bottom lip caught between her teeth.

"It would destroy the world," Purpurrot said. Her demeanor, typically so aloof to the problems of humans, betrayed something suspiciously like concern. Her brow was faintly creased, and her painted nails scratched distractedly across the fabric of the chair's arm.

"How?"

Though Antimony's question was quiet, it carried the weight of what they were all thinking.

Purpurrot shrugged fluidly, mouth an unhappy downturn. "Even I can't say for certain. My guess would be what's happening now, but accelerated and unstoppable. Raw imagination and thought spilling out across the world, consuming everything it encounters. Denken is trying to rebuild his own realm over top of this one, but the two can't coexist like that. The Maze would be a virus, spreading and destroying until it was all that remained."

Stifling silence rose up once more as they all digested this grave prediction. Finally, Finch cleared his throat.

"Well, that's motivation enough to stop it, I reckon."

Gloucester surprised even himself by laughing, though the amusement was short and dry. "Yeah, just about. But how?"

Their conversation in the kitchen was replaying in his mind. Would destroying Denken be the only way to stop him? And was that even possible? Surely killing a god, even a demigod, was no easy feat. It seemed likely that the only ones who might possess that level of power would be those unwilling to do the deed: the other immortals.

This raised another question, but before he could ask it or receive an answer for the one he'd already posed, Gear put it forward herself:

"Where's the Gambler? He'll know what to do. We shouldn't have left him behind!"

It was more than Gloucester would have said on the subject,

but he followed Gear's bright-eyed gaze to Purpurrot and Antimony, wanting to know the answer.

The last they'd seen of the Gambler hadn't boded well, a solitary figure facing down his raging brother, unarmed save for the powers he possessed. Gloucester wasn't even sure those could be used against another of the Brothers. Had he been hoping to talk Denken down? Would Denken have listened?

Purpurrot said nothing for a long time, but the look on her face held the silence, not even the fretful Gear or skeptical Finch prompting her to answer sooner. Antimony was also looking at her, and Gloucester thought he saw the same worry and uncertainty they all felt lurking in her expression, her affection for the Gambler splintering her usual calm stoicism.

"I don't know," Purpurrot said finally. She rose to her feet, towering over them all. "But I will find out. I don't think Denken would purposefully harm his brother, but he's not in control of himself or his powers right now. Who knows what he might be capable of in the heat of the moment? It's a miracle that he didn't kill *you*," she added to Gloucester. "He must have really wanted to keep you alive."

"Dunno why," Gloucester admitted. "His trap would have worked just fine with me dead, as long as Cassus still thought I was alive to be rescued."

Why *hadn't* he killed him? Denken's questions about him trying to save the Gambler might hold the answer. Had gratitude stayed the demigod's hand? It wouldn't be the first time Denken had unexpectedly showed him mercy. Before that—weeks before—Denken had pulled him out of harm's way in the High Minister's Cathedral after Gloucester stopped Finch from shooting him. *Would* Denken have killed him so easily? Maybe he still had more control over his actions than they thought.

For how long, though? How long before the personification of Thought completely lost his mind?

"I'll go to Denken's lair," Purpurrot announced. Her unearthly tone brooked no argument. "I'll find the Gambler."

"No need," said an equally powerful voice.

The Gambler stood in the doorway, light from the hallway softening the edges of his figure and casting him in a semi-silhouette. Gloucester heard several gasps around the room and was certain that one was his own.

Purpurrot showed little more reaction than a swift turn of her head and the slightest widening of her striking eyes, but her voice was laden with relief like joyful gospel. "Joujou! You're all right!"

"Joujou" was a nickname Denken had used too. Gloucester wondered what significance it held. It sounded a bit like the Nordish word for "toy," which made little sense to him. Then again, nicknames were often like that. Little secrets and shared moments between friends and family.

"I am," the Gambler confirmed. He appeared mostly unharmed, if ruffled. His white shirt was no longer pristine, smudged with soot and grime, and torn down one sleeve. His face was the same as ever, save the fast-healing remnants of several long, thin scratches.

Like fingers, Gloucester thought.

"How'd you get away?" he asked. The agent in him couldn't stop from asking the question. Things weren't adding up. "What happened with Denken?"

The Gambler's eyeless gaze settled on him. "I escaped. Narrowly."

"Is Denken—" Finch started, straightening up from his lean against the couch, but the Gambler was shaking his head even before the question was out of his mouth.

"He lives. With no change to his plans, unfortunately. He intends to rebuild his home here in the human world, starting with Frettchen."

Finch's eyes narrowed, but he held his tongue.

"So how can we stop him?" Antimony was noticeably more at ease now that the Gambler had returned, though it was only through this contrast that Gloucester could see just how tense she had been.

Purpurrot tapped her chin with a fingernail the color of amethyst. "We'll have to contain him until we can figure out a way to get him back to the Maze. If we get him there, it might heal his powers and get them back under his control. This false Maze cannot heal him. It feeds off of his powers, not into them."

Containing a wrathful, half-crazed demigod sounded like an impossible task. Gloucester thought of Antimony's plan, and his eyes sought out Gear. She was the only one in the room who didn't look grim. In fact, she was smiling widely, staring at the Gambler with apparently nothing more on her mind than the joy of seeing him safe. Could the automaton really be the key?

Finch, he noticed, was also eyeing Gear. The magician then turned to the rest of them again.

"Whatever we do and however we do it, we have to act quickly," he said. "Things are barely under control now, even with all the capable magicians in the city on high alert and Mulligan and his goons keeping the monster attacks hush-hush."

The Gambler nodded. "It's true. Time is of the essence. We know where Denken is now, at least. He won't risk moving, not with his new Maze already started there. That will be the center of it, just as All Saints Shrine was the epicenter for the troubles we face now."

"All well and terrible, but we're going in circles here," Zane said. "*How* do we stop him?"

The Gambler and Purpurrot wordlessly consulted each other. The goddess shrugged. "The plan is a work in progress."

"Great," said Zane and Finch together. They flicked each other annoyed glances at the unintended unison.

Antimony leveled a long look at the pair of them, then addressed the immortals. "We use Gear like I proposed. She can't be affected by his powers."

Purpurrot looked like she very much wanted to say something, expression souring. Even the Gambler was shaking his head.

"To what end, Antimony?" he asked. "He might not be able to overpower her with his manipulations, but she cannot overthrow him physically. She's still flesh and blood, in part at least, and Denken . . . He's already killed once. There's little stopping him now from repeating the crime."

Antimony's pursed lips suggested discord, but Gloucester could see she had no counter-argument. She took a deep breath.

"Fair enough." From the sound of it, the two words pained her to say.

"So we're fucked."

Everyone looked at Zane. She glared at them all, arms crossed tightly over her chest, shoulders stiff with tension.

"*Circles,*" she repeated. "Round and round with the same question. How do we stop Denken? What's the point of this if none of us have the answer?"

"I never said we didn't have an answer," Purpurrot stated quietly. "I just said it's the plan that's still getting figured out."

"How about sharing either one with us mere mortals, then?" Finch snapped.

Both immortal beings stood motionless for a long time. Then the Gambler gave a heavy sigh and smiled thinly.

"Very well."

Chapter 21

Nature

"There are few things in the realm of humans that can combat us," the Gambler said. Morning sunlight streamed in through the living room window, highlighting subtle hues of red and blue in his pale hair. While Purpurrot had returned to the armchair in the corner, the Gambler had moved to the center of the room. "It's why the Rules have always existed. If we were not kept in check, we would be capable of immense and vicious power."

"Sounds familiar." When everyone's eyes turned to him, discomfort twisted through Gloucester's gut. "How are these rules supposed to be enforced?" he asked, hastening to move past his own flippancy.

"By me."

Gloucester would have been grateful to Purpurrot for drawing everyone's stares away if he weren't busy staring himself. Purpurrot remained calm and collected under their scrutiny.

"Hmph." Finch squared his shoulders and eyed Purpurrot stonily. As the Finches were well-read on the legends of the Brothers, perhaps the closest thing around to experts on them, Gloucester felt it entirely possible this was something he'd already known or at least suspected. "What are you gonna do to him, slow down time slightly?"

Purpurrot directed a long, flat look his way. To his credit, Finch raised his chin defiantly and didn't drop his gaze.

In his silence, Zane and Gloucester took over the line of questioning.

"How can you do it?" Zane asked.

"Why you?" Gloucester demanded at the same time.

Purpurrot huffed a dry laugh. Her eyes lowered demurely, hidden under her long eyelashes. She seemed to be contemplating her clasped hands in her lap. Finally, she raised her eyes with a smile that was old and full of memory.

"Because I'm his mother."

—

In the beginning, so they say, there was Nature. Green and growing, living and breathing, from the smallest blade of grass to the massive beasts lurking beneath the sea. Nature ruled over a world that was hers alone, and she was lonely.

From her capacity for creation, she gave birth to the Siblings, nature gods who exemplified the traits imbued in all sentient creatures. Conscious thought and creativity. The freedom to make choices, for better or for worse. The ability to love, to cherish, and to care. They were traits that had long existed in the world she had created, but now they had faces, voices, and minds separate from her own to keep her company. These were her children. Her responsibility.

But children can be unruly, and so they soon needed rules. Structure to live by, lest their power go to their heads. And Nature, creator of the children and their Rules alike, tasked herself with enforcing this structure. She alone would hold true sway over the nature gods. Throughout the ages, she would watch over them, protecting, guiding, and disciplining all in turn.

—

"Until the day you didn't."

The room hung onto Purpurrot's every word, so silent that Gloucester could almost hear his own heartbeat. All except Finch. He wasn't appeased by the tale.

"If you're really the guardian all of the stories talk about, what are you doing *here?* In Frettchen of all places. And what were you doing two weeks ago when this all went to hell? Where were you when *he* was taken?" He jabbed his thumb in the Gambler's direction.

Anger, hot and swift as fire, flashed in Purpurrot's eyes, but her voice was even when she replied. Dangerously so. "By *you.* And I was here. In Frettchen. In my pie shop."

"Purpurrot . . ." the Gambler started. He stopped when Purpurrot held up a finger.

"When you have lived through eons, you grow weary of things," she said, her eyes never leaving Finch. He was valiantly maintaining eye contact, but Gloucester could tell it was taking a lot of effort on his part not to flinch away. "You see how big the world is, and it suddenly seems too small. All the same. So you go hunting for the love and the passion for it all that you once felt. I found that here in this city. In the little lives of the little people who make the world seem big again."

For once, Finch didn't know what to say, silenced by the gravity of Purpurrot's words. Gloucester couldn't blame him. It wasn't every day you found yourself in the presence of divinity. He'd assumed Purpurrot was akin to the Brothers, a personification. Now that he thought about it, no one had said what she was the personification *of.*

Was Purpurrot really the one who had created the Brothers?

If that was so, then who had created her?

Maybe no one, he reminded himself. He'd never put much thought into gods before meeting the Brothers, but since then he'd sort of come to assume they simply sprang into existence alongside humankind. Did Purpurrot originate from before even that? He stared at the towering woman who remained so poised even as she spoke with thinly veiled venom. Despite her imposing height, unusual eyes, and undeniable beauty, she appeared human, more so than either Denken or the Gambler. Could she really be older than everyone? Every*thing?*

He cleared his throat and exchanged a look with Zane, who nodded her silent encouragement. "So, *can* you stop him?" he asked timidly. "How?"

It was the Gambler who answered. "Purpurrot has always had the power to . . . keep us in line. The Rules were a part of that. An agreement—unspoken, for the most part—between all of us, but set out by her. If we didn't follow them or caused trouble in the human world, Purpurrot was the one who could deal with us."

"So what's stopped you—?" Gloucester realized the answer before he'd even finished the question, and before Finch interrupted with a disdainful sneer.

"She doesn't have power anymore. Not really. Too long in the human world, eh, love? It's not good for your kind. Neglectful parents have a way of losing control over their children, you know?"

"I do know." Purpurrot's retort held the strains of a scornful symphony. "And if regret could solve problems, we'd all be home free right now. But it doesn't, so spare me your condescension, magician. Don't think I forget who caused all of this."

Finch was on his feet in a flash. "I am trying to right my wrongs. You think I don't wish every damn day we'd never agreed to work for the high minister? You think I wouldn't go back and change it if I could? My father *died.* But I didn't tell Denken to murder someone. I didn't make him do that. All this that's happening now, that's on him, not me."

His tone was adamant, but Gloucester wondered whether he truly believed his own words. Did he really feel no guilt, no responsibility for what had come to pass because of the Gambler's capture? He might have a point about not prompting Denken to kill the high minister, but could he really deny that he and his father had toppled the first domino, setting all of this into motion?

No. Finch had reached out to him that night in Hawke's Landing. He might not want all the blame, but Finch wasn't free of guilty feelings, nor was he as in denial about them as he pretended to be in front of the others.

"Stop it!"

Antimony, too, rose to her feet. Though she was shorter than both Finch and Purpurrot, her sharp impatience seemed to lend her an extra foot of height. Gloucester was reminded of the way Denken was able to expand his very presence beyond the physical limitations of his body. Finch and Purpurrot fell silent.

"While we all stand around bickering like children, the world is crumbling," she said, hands on her hips. "So from here on in, if you've not got something useful to say, shut up and let someone who does do the talking." Her hooded eyes focused on Purpurrot. "Purpa, what do you need to be able to stop Denken?"

Purpurrot sighed, her anger relenting. "My powers back. My full strength."

"And how do we manage that?" Gloucester asked.

To his great disbelief, Purpurrot actually looked embarrassed. "That's the part of the plan we're still working on," she said.

"Brilliant," Finch said under his breath.

"We'll figure it out." The Gambler crossed the room to place a comforting hand on Purpurrot's arm. "Purpurrot's powers aren't lost, just weakened. That which is weakened can regain its strength, given the right circumstances. We just need to figure out exactly what those circumstances are."

"Well, let's hope it's not seeing the whole world implode and get replaced by a crazy demigod's idea of home," Finch snipped, albeit without much heat.

"Has a demigod ever lost—er, weakened—their power before?" Gloucester asked, voice raised in a rather pointed way. Zane and Antimony were right; they were going in circles with all of this arguing.

"We grow weaker the longer we linger in the human world, away from our Pockets," the Gambler explained. "The Finches' enchantment kept my own abilities from atrophying, but those were not usual circumstances. Normally if we stay in the human world for more than a few months, life becomes . . . difficult. This world drains us."

"So Purpurrot has a Pocket too?" Zane asked, eyeing the goddess in surprise. "I never thought to ask. It seems . . . I mean, you never felt the same as them."

"I'm not," Purpurrot said. "But yes, I have my own Pocket. Or I did. Now . . ." She shrugged. Knowing who and what she was, Gloucester found it odd to watch her in moments where she seemed so human.

"Why'd you leave?" Finch asked, curt and direct. "You expect us to believe you just got bored of being an immortal goddess?"

Though clearly in no mood to answer any more questions from the magician, Purpurrot set aside her stung pride and explained with icy patience, "I *was* bored. Bored of being on the outside looking in at a world I created. I wanted to live in it."

"So you chose this?" Gloucester frowned as he mulled over the idea. "To get yourself stuck here?"

"Do *you* consider yourself stuck, Mr. Gloucester?" Purpurrot's stare was impossible to break away from. "All I wanted was an actual place in this world. Isn't that what everyone wants?"

Feeling like a chastised child and unsure what to say to that, Gloucester changed the subject. An idea was taking root in his head.

"Denken's building another Maze, right? He's trying to

rebuild his Pocket here in our world?"

Purpurrot and the Gambler nodded slowly, and Gloucester did his best to ignore the attention of the room once again focused on him.

"Could you . . . regenerate your powers in any Pocket or just your own?"

Understanding dawned in Purpurrot's eyes. "Our own space is best, but if we're invited in, another's Pocket can help, yes."

"I'd invite her to mine," added the Gambler, "but without her powers, she wouldn't travel well through the void between dimensions."

"We did all right," Gloucester pointed out. "When Denken took us to the Maze, I mean."

"Humans are different. You are essentially powerless, even the magical ones"—his head turned briefly in Finch's direction—"so traveling with you takes no effort. It's no more difficult than taking along the clothes on our backs."

"Er, right." Gloucester wasn't sure if this was insulting or just informative.

"My powers are weak, but I am still a personification," Purpurrot said. "We might look like humans, or near enough, but we contain a lot of power within us. Without control of that power, the void would rip me apart."

"So what you need is a Pocket that you don't have to leave the world for," mused Antimony, a rare smile spreading across her thin lips. "And Denken doesn't seem to have the whole 'by invite only' thing figured out yet."

"But does it have the same level of power?" Finch asked.

The nature goddess's mouth set in a stubborn line. "It will."

—

The conversation quickly spiraled away from Gloucester after that. Antimony and the immortals grew increasingly lost in thought, uninterested in continuing the discussion around the rest of them. Gear, uncomprehending of so much, soon grew bored and wandered off.

Gloucester, Zane, and Finch were left sitting in a corner, feeling distinctly on the sidelines. Zane watched the other three with a small frown. She seemed a little hurt about being left out of whatever the plan was. Perhaps Finch was as well, as he kept tossing Antimony, the Gambler, and Purpurrot very dirty looks when he wasn't staring moodily out the window.

Gloucester wanted to be annoyed, but it was growing increasingly difficult to care. Which was frustrating, considering all he knew was at stake. The short respite he'd been allowed since the escape from Denken had not been nearly long enough to do much good. His hand hurt, dulling the other aches and pains in comparison but certainly not erasing them, and his mind strayed with weariness. He found himself slouching in his seat, eyelids growing heavy.

A gentle touch on his shoulders stirred him from the falling veil of sleep. Though Purpurrot had worked wonders on the clawed cuts on his shoulder, they were still sore, and he flinched fully awake in an instant.

Grimacing apologetically, Zane retracted her hand. A second hand stayed put on his other shoulder, and when Gloucester looked over, Finch was also staring at him, some of his discontent tempering into concern.

"I'm fine," Gloucester told them, stifling a yawn and another wince.

Zane scoffed. "Yeah, okay. C'mon, let's get you lying down. Maybe in the morning, you can explain the giant monster in the basement?" she added as she and Finch pulled him to his feet and led the way out of the room. Antimony and the gods paid no mind to their departure.

They stopped first in the entry hall, where Finch gestured toward the door. "I should go," he said, tone business-like but gaze lingering on Gloucester, who was leaning more than he cared to admit on Zane's shoulder. The thin line of a frown furrowed between Finch's brows.

"If you need to stay here, I'm sure you can," Gloucester told him, glancing over at Zane for support. After a moment's hesitation, she nodded.

"If Denken's looking for you—"

Finch batted the concern aside with a roguish grin that was almost convincing. "I'll be fine, don't worry. There's a reason he had to lure me out. He's got his work cut out for him if he's planning on tracking a magician like me."

He winked, then turned toward the door.

Only to glance back a moment later, his hand on the doorknob but his eyes fixed on Gloucester. "I'm . . . I'm glad we got you back, Mikalai."

It still felt odd to hear his given name spoken by Finch, but Gloucester found that he liked the way it rolled off his tongue, lilting with his Islander accent.

"I'm glad you came to get me," he said in return. "Both of you," he added, perhaps a touch hastily as he glanced sideways at Zane. "All of you."

Finch smirked, the heavy weight of worry momentarily melting away, making him look abruptly much younger.

"Well, if you need me . . ." he started, then hesitated. Gloucester watched the smile grow on his face as he gestured to Gloucester's hand. "You've got my number."

He disappeared through the door and out into the morning sunlight. Gloucester squinted after his retreating figure. The sun had now risen high enough to shine over the rooftops of the houses across the street, silhouetting Finch as he strode away.

"He'll be all right," Zane assured him. She wrinkled her nose. "I doubt he's without some devious backup plan or another."

Gloucester snorted. "I think you're probably right."

It wasn't enough to banish the worry completely. That "probably" carried more weight than he let on. Would Finch be able to keep Denken at bay?

Zane led Gloucester upstairs and into what he assumed was the spare bedroom. It was, she mentioned, the bedroom she'd slept in the last time she and Gloucester had spent time lying low in Antimony's house, as well as being the room she'd called her own back when she lived there. Nonetheless, she was quick to insist he take it this time instead.

"I don't mind sleeping on the couch if I need to take a nap," she told him. "I'm not the one who was the prisoner of an angry demigod today."

"Lucky you." Gloucester groaned, lying back on the bed. He didn't care that he was on top of the covers and still fully dressed; sleep started to encroach on his mind the moment he let his eyes fall shut, and he scarcely registered Zane turning off the light as she left.

—

He wasn't sure how much time passed before he awoke. Pitch blackness surrounded him, and he was thoroughly confused before his eyes adjusted to the dark enough to realize it wasn't nighttime, but rather that someone had drawn thick curtains across the window, obliterating all but the faintest lines of light leaking through.

The weak light wasn't what had woken him, however. The culprit was a quiet ringing, one that Gloucester sleepily recognized as his phone. Zane must have brought it with her, he thought, and it sat on the nightstand beside the bed.

Who would be calling him? As soon as the question passed through his mind, he knew the answer. His caller was no doubt the same as the *last* time a ringing telephone stirred him from sleep.

"Hello?" he yawned into the phone, once he'd clumsily found it in the dark. "Cassus?"

"It's me," Finch confirmed.

"What d'you want?" Even half-awake as he was, it occurred to Gloucester that had come out a little blunt. "Are you in trouble?" he added in a softer tone.

Silence stretched out long enough to fan the flames of worry kindling in Gloucester's mind, but before he could ask again with more urgency, Finch spoke.

"Don't trust the Gambler."

Gloucester blinked. "What—"

"Seems to me he got away too easily," Finch cut him off. "How do we know he's telling the whole story? It just seems off."

"Why tell me this now?" Gloucester asked, dropping his voice to a whisper. He didn't bother trying to rebut the warning; the thought had occurred to him too. Would Denken really have been so easy to escape? "Why not say something before you left?"

"Never know who might be listening in that house. My phone's charmed to be secure."

"Oh," said Gloucester, rather impressed.

Perhaps it was evident in his voice because a smug chuckle echoed down the line. It was not enough to overshadow the grimness of Finch's final warning, however.

"Don't trust the Gambler," he said again.

Then he hung up with a click.

Chapter 22

Help From Above

Gloucester woke some hours later to the sound of raised voices.

Despite the noise, he stayed in bed a minute or two longer, reluctant to leave the bedroom's comfort and quiet behind. A half-formed memory chewed on the back of his mind, retreating into the shadows of his brain whenever he tried to focus on it. Was it a dream he'd been having before he woke? It felt like something he ought to recall, but whatever it was, it wasn't coming easily to the forefront of his mind.

Eventually, he could no longer ignore the voices downstairs, so he got up to investigate. He groaned at his many protesting aches and pains. Usually, he followed sleep with a regime of stretches, but there was no time for that now, and his body, stiff and sore, didn't feel up to the task anyway. As he trudged from the room—wearing the rumpled clothing in which he'd fallen asleep—he flexed his injured hand and winced when it still resisted with a dull twinge. It had a greater range of motion than before, at least.

He was halfway down the stairs when the voices became distinct enough to identify. One was easily recognizable as Zane, but the other proved harder to pin down. Masculine and sharp with annoyance, Gloucester was sure he'd heard it before. Unfortunately, no name was coming to mind.

"This is ridiculous! Don't you need a warrant or something?" Zane was saying caustically as Gloucester reached the bottom of the stairs. He followed her voice down the hall toward the sitting room. The sun coming through the front door's window carried the warmth of the afternoon.

"Not for him, we don't," said the other voice, snippy and impatient. Again the familiarity of it struck him, with more success this time.

Mulligan.

Despite the stiffness in his muscles, Gloucester picked up his stride. He rounded the corner into the sitting room.

Through the doorway, he saw several people standing in a loose circle. From her curly-haired head to her stubbornly planted feet, Zane radiated fury as she squared off against Mulligan, who countered her glare with a vehement one of his own. At first glance, he was impeccable in his neat navy suit and perfectly combed hair, but Gloucester could see the cracks in his facade almost immediately. The stern lines of a deep frown bracketed his mouth and drew his brows together. His hands were clenched into white-knuckled fists.

Not so easy running a city under siege from monsters. Gloucester felt little in the way of pity for the man.

The other two people were Antimony, who looked quietly scandalized, and the Gambler. Though the Gambler stood motionless in the far corner of the room, staring eyelessly at the politician, the icy stillness of his presence exuded a warning. His posture held the spring-loaded tension of a cat waiting to pounce. It would seem he hadn't forgotten all those who had been involved in his kidnapping. Mulligan, for his part, seemed to be putting a great deal of effort into ignoring the eerie stare.

"You can't just arrest people for no reason!" Zane insisted.

"We can if that person doesn't exist," Mulligan snapped. "There are no records of him still being alive. No open bank account, no home address, no identification. For all intents and purposes, Mikalai Gloucester is a dead man. And the rules don't apply to dead men. Aha!" He'd noticed Gloucester in the doorway. "Harrison!"

A figure lurking by the front door moved forward suddenly. Gloucester had been so focused on the goings-on in the living room that he hadn't noticed the tall agent until too late. Harrison clapped a heavy hand onto his shoulder, grabbing hold of Gloucester's arm with his other hand and pushing him roughly against the doorframe.

"Hey!" Gloucester struggled, aches and pains forgotten. "What are you doing? Get off!"

Harrison didn't reply, nor did he let go. Mulligan smirked at Gloucester, spiteful victory glinting in his eyes. Through the window behind him, Gloucester caught glimpses of black-suited figures lurking in strategic positions in the front garden.

Zane whirled around, eyes widening. "Hey!" Her fury blazing anew, she drew herself up to her full height. While that wasn't exceptionally tall, every inch of her seemed to expand in sheer rage, like a dog raising its hackles. Advancing in Harrison's and Gloucester's direction, she said, "Let go of him! Don't you bloody dare—"

"What do you want from me?" Gloucester asked loudly. He shook his head at Zane as best he could from his position. Harrison still had a hand on his wrist, locking the limb against the small of his back as he kept him pressed against the doorway. Gloucester's heart hammered against his ribs, and he drew in a deep breath. He needed to be calm.

Mulligan was anything but. He pushed past Zane, ignoring her squawk of protest, and strode to glare down at Gloucester.

Something lurked in his eyes. The same shadow of uncontrolled fear that Gloucester had seen in Harmony's eyes outside of Jeb's apartment.

Denken's influence.

"I want your cooperation, for starters," Mulligan said briskly. "Let's not make this more difficult than we have to, all right? I'm not opposed to arresting any one of your associates here."

"My cooperation for what?" Gloucester had no plans to go anywhere with Mulligan, but with Harrison at his back and a team of security agents surrounding the house, it didn't feel like he would have much choice in the matter. Not unless he could snap him out of Denken's hold. "What have I gone and done now?"

"Don't be smart." Despite his best attempt at a calm demeanor, Mulligan spoke through gritted teeth. "It's not what you've done, but what you *haven't* done. You and your . . . your *posse*"—he said the word with enough disgust that he might have been talking about gum he'd found on the bottom of his expensive leather shoe—"promised to have this mess cleaned up. It's been weeks and things have only gotten worse."

"So, just to be clear, you're going to arrest him for nothing, because he didn't do anything?"

A livid Zane stepped closer to Mulligan, and Gloucester, intimately aware of the agents watching from the window and what they were capable of, struggled against Harrison's hold.

"Zane! Stop, it's not worth it," he said. When she stared at him, affronted, he added, "Denken's got a hold of him."

Mulligan reared back. "What's that supposed to mean?" He snatched at the collar of Gloucester's shirt, ignoring Harrison's surprised warning as he pulled Gloucester away from the doorframe and out of the security agent's grasp. "How dare you—?"

Lurching out of Harrison's reach, Gloucester gave Mulligan a shove and then hastened into the living room, hands raised placatingly. He'd wanted to get out of the agent's hold, but he didn't want to spark a bigger fight.

"Listen to me," he said. *I seem to be shouting that at a lot of people recently,* an unhelpful voice at the back of his mind reflected.

Mulligan stumbled but was quick to recover. He swung a clumsy punch, which Gloucester dodged with ease. Reckless with fury, the politician tripped against Antimony's coffee table and nearly fell. Harrison hurried to his employer's side rather than pursue Gloucester across the room.

"Sir," the agent said. "Please, calm down. Maybe we should—"

But Mulligan pushed away Harrison's hand and his words alike. His face was red with rage, teeth bared. He took a step toward Gloucester—

The Gambler moved between one breath and the next. One moment he was on the periphery of the room, in the shadow of Antimony's covered harp, the next he stood between Mulligan and Gloucester. His hands rose, framing Mulligan's face. The politician went slack, fear skittering across his features before the Gambler spoke:

"Toby Mulligan, See with me."

He lowered his head, resting his forehead against Mulligan's in a strangely intimate position. No one in the room moved, not even Harrison. The agent gaped at the demigod. On the other side of the window, black-suited agents hastened toward the front door. Two of them burst in, dashing down the hallway and into the room with guns drawn. Gloucester reached toward Zane, wanting to pull her out of harm's way before the inevitable fight.

"Wait!"

The order came from Mulligan. The Gambler stepped away from him, hands dropping back down to his sides. Mulligan looked dazed, but unharmed. The anger had drained from his face.

"Wait," he said again. "I'm okay. It's . . . it's all right."

His agents stared from him to the demigod, weapons still raised, but no one moved to attack.

"What the hell just happened?" Harrison demanded, shock overpowering his usual professionalism.

"What did you show him?" Antimony asked, nearly at the same time.

The demigod took another step back, falling in beside Gloucester, who stared up at him. "I shared with him what I could of his futures," the Gambler said. "Not much, with so much unclear because of my brother, but what I could. And more importantly, my influence broke him free of Denken's."

Sure enough, Mulligan seemed more clear-headed as his daze fell away. He rubbed his brow, openly baffled, but when he met Gloucester's eyes, the unnatural fear and rage were gone.

"That was . . ." he said, then trailed off. "I don't know what that was. Please never do that again." Some of the fear returned as he turned his gaze to the Gambler, but it felt distinctly more natural. "You people are all mad," he grumbled, his face still bright red. This time, however, Gloucester suspected that embarrassment, not fury, was the culprit.

"Well," said Antimony, lightly clapping her hands once. "Now that's out of the way, how about we continue this discussion like rational adults? Mr. Mulligan, none of us are opposed to helping you, as long as you are willing to be *reasonable*."

For a moment, Mulligan looked like he was biting the inside of his cheek hard, vitriol gathering on his tongue. Then he glanced at the Gambler and seemed to reconsider. He coughed, straightening his suit jacket in a business-like way that was only slightly betrayed by the shaking of his hands.

"Fine," he said. "Fine, I am . . . willing to hear you out. Share information. I want you to tell me everything you know about what's happening."

"I'm surprised it's taken this long," Gloucester said, risking moving toward Mulligan in order to stand next to Zane. The anger had mostly abandoned her as well, and she wordlessly took his hand, giving it a squeeze. He offered her a tiny smile before turning his attention back to Mulligan. "I thought you'd be breaking down the door a week ago when downtown was burning."

"Yes, we suspected your involvement in that," Mulligan said.

"Involvement?" Zane's anger was back in a flash. "We bloody well saved the day, you ass! I didn't see *you* out there fighting a dragon!"

"Yes, well, there wasn't much I could do, was there? I don't have magic or magicians or . . . *that*." Mulligan gestured at the Gambler, who had returned to his spot on the far side of the room.

"No," said the Gambler. "You do not."

Despite his even tone and newfound distance from Mulligan, the Gambler's words carried a warning like the cold promise of winter. A chill filled the room.

Gloucester suddenly remembered Finch's call from earlier that day. That was what he'd been too groggy to recall when he first awoke, leaving it faded as a half-remembered dream.

Don't trust the Gambler, Finch had warned. Looking at the Gambler now, Gloucester tried to see something, *anything*, in his face that would hint at his motives.

There was nothing. Just that unreadable eyeless stare and an impassiveness like an unbreakable wall. The scratches on his face had faded to nothing.

Mulligan squared his shoulders, but Gloucester could tell he was unnerved. Whatever vision the Gambler showed him might have broken the hold of Denken's influence, but it hadn't done much to endear the Gambler to him.

"Is that a threat?"

"Merely a statement of fact."

Before another argument could start—likely one-sided in this case—Gloucester cut between them. "This isn't getting any of us anywhere. Mulligan, we're trying to work with you here. So can you please stop arguing with everything and tell your security agents to stand down?" He jerked his head at the agents in the doorway. Their guns were still drawn, and the lingering threat was playing on his nerves.

Mulligan glowered. "You're in no position to be giving orders."

"No, I'm not," Gloucester agreed. "But arresting me won't get you anywhere either. You want information, fine, let's all swap what we know. Maybe together we can actually *do* something."

Mulligan stared at him long and hard. It seemed like he was trying to bore right into Gloucester with the intensity of his gaze and see straight into his mind, searching for the trick. Gloucester held the eye contact steadily, ignoring the discomfort of it. He wasn't in the mood to be bullied.

"The monsters in the streets," Mulligan said finally. "The attacks. They're all because of Denken?"

The Gambler answered before Gloucester could. "By-products of his punishment."

"*His* punishment?" Mulligan gaped. "How is this punishment for him? Or is *he* punishing *us?*"

"Nothing so intentional," the Gambler said. "I imagine he's scarcely noticed the carnage."

Mulligan bristled, but Gloucester cut in again before he could voice his indignation. "You haven't seen him," he said quietly. For all that had happened, all the pain and fear and torment, he couldn't shake the look on Denken's unnatural face, the note of fright in his voice. "He's not in control."

"And that's supposed to make me feel better?" Mulligan was staring at him again, rife with furious incredulity. "Am I to feel sorry for him? He's a murderous . . . thing! He killed the high minister. He's unleashed monsters on the city. The death count is rising by the day. He has to be stopped!"

"Yeah," said Zane, unimpressed. "We know that. We're trying to figure out *how.* If you've got any bright ideas, we'd love to hear them. Otherwise, back off and shut up."

Mulligan drew himself up, and Gloucester prepared himself

for another bout of useless arguments.

But the new lord of Frettchen proved his expectations wrong. "Fine," he said tightly.

Zane was incredulous. "Fine?"

"Fine," Mulligan repeated. He gestured to his security agents, and they stowed away their weapons and retreated into the hallway. "We all agree he needs to be stopped. So, as you say, let's figure out how to do that."

Though Zane eyed him with suspicion, Gloucester didn't miss the flicker of Mulligan's eyes toward the Gambler as he spoke. He wondered again what the Gambler had shown him, but Mulligan didn't seem about to share.

"Back in All Saints Shrine, the magician Finch tried to kill Denken. Is there any chance he might have succeeded if he hadn't been stopped?" His gaze swept over all of them, but there could be no question who he was addressing.

"Yes," said the Gambler in his solemn voice, after a long moment's pause.

"So you lot can be killed . . ." Mulligan fell silent, rubbing his chin. The silence was not a comfortable one.

"If you're thinking of trying anything against the Gambler—" Antimony started.

"Don't be childish, Mrs. Jones. I know how to prioritize." He considered the Gambler. "Finch used magic against Denken before. And if my agents aren't mistaken, the magicians of the city have already been combating the monsters with it. Seems safe to say that magic's the key here. So . . . where is Mr. Finch?"

He peered around, but if he thought Finch was going to miraculously appear out of thin air, he was bound for disappointment.

"Not here." Antimony sounded rather vexed. Evidently, the childish comment had gotten under her skin. "Why don't you go burst uninvited into *his* home instead?"

"I would if I could find the bloody place," Mulligan groused. "Wherever it is, it's warded in some way. I had a hard enough time tracking *you* down."

Judging from Antimony's narrowed eyes and the unhappy set of her mouth, she wished he hadn't been successful. Hands on hips, she addressed the more pressing issue. "So, you'll fight with us against Denken? You'll leave Mr. Gloucester alone?"

Mulligan's face twisted in displeasure as if he were being asked to do something very unfair. "Yes. And no. Denken is the priority. All of Frettchen is in danger as long as he remains at large. But I'm not just letting you lot do as you please without my say-so. So I go where he goes"—he pointed at Gloucester—"to ensure that this isn't all some sort of trick."

Gloucester stared. Even free of Denken's hold, Mulligan had to be one of the most suspicious people he'd ever met. Had there ever been anyone he did trust? The high minister, he supposed. Mulligan seemed to be the only person who genuinely liked Frettchen's former leader.

"Some sort of trick?" Zane's voice bounced off the pale walls of the sitting room. "People have died. What trick could we possibly be planning?"

Mulligan shrugged, unmovable. "I've learned not to trust gods and those who throw their lot in with them."

"Suit yourself," Gloucester said.

When everyone turned to him with matching expressions of surprise, he uncomfortably avoided any eye contact. Instead, he picked a spot just on the edge of Zane's hair and focused his eyes there. He found it a good way to calm himself down and gather his nerves.

"I don't care if he doesn't trust me," he explained to the others. "Mulligan has the resources to help us. If we work together, maybe we can actually subdue Denken."

"As long as we're all in agreement, then," Mulligan said impatiently. "I'm assuming you have some semblance of a plan. So what is it?"

Antimony and the Gambler exchanged a look. "Complicated," she answered.

It wasn't a good enough answer for Mulligan. Huffing, he crossed his arms over his chest, creasing his crisp suit. "Working together implies we share information," he said shortly. "Just tell me—*What?*"

The sharp question was not directed at Antimony, but rather at Harrison, who had reappeared in the doorway.

"News in on the radio, sir," Harrison reported, clearly immune to the tone. He held up the small device previously clipped onto his belt.

"What is it?" Mulligan pulled a small leather-bound journal from the inside pocket of his jacket and prepared to take notes.

"Another attack. In the south end of the city. Reports are monsters gathering in an abandoned residential street."

"Abandoned . . . Shit," Gloucester swore, realization clicking into place.

"You know the place?" Mulligan asked. His pen scritched to an ink-blotted halt.

"If it's what I'm thinking, then yeah. Became acquainted with the place just recently."

Chapter 23

An Uneasy Alliance

The story was recounted as quickly and simply as possible. To Gloucester's relief, Antimony stepped forward to tell it. The scientist explained things with a cool-headed succinctness, though Gloucester noticed she made no mention of Gear or Hyena. He knew the former was out of protectiveness, and while the latter couldn't claim the same, Gloucester was glad for her discretion. He doubted Mulligan would consider Hyena anything more than an enemy to be destroyed.

His thoughts went to the giant beast in the basement. He hoped they were all right.

When Antimony reached the end of the story, Mulligan's brows were so knitted he looked like he might never untangle them. "He's building another world?"

"More or less," Antimony confirmed.

"Right on top of this one?"

"Pretty much," said Zane.

"And it'll spread and kill us all if we don't stop it?"

"As far as we know," the Gambler chimed in. "It seems prudent to prepare for the worst-case scenario. Then anything else that might happen will seem like an improvement."

It was almost a joke, and coming from the impassive Gambler, it sounded bizarre.

Gloucester expected Mulligan to sputter in disbelief a while longer, but the lord of the city-state was quick to pull himself together.

"If there are monsters congregating around this, this new Maze thing, then something must be happening. Which means we need to be there to stop it. One way or the other. Harrison! Assemble every agent who knows about all this. We're heading to the source of the latest attacks, but keep your distance until we determine how to proceed. Priority is getting civilians to safety. We don't want them underfoot."

Still stunned by Antimony's story, Harrison nodded and moved to leave. Then he hesitated and turned back. "Sir?" he said. "Are you sure you'll be all right? Perhaps I should stay and—"

"It's under control, Harrison," Mulligan snipped. "Get going."

Harrison didn't obey. He stood his ground, expression set. "Really, sir. I must insist. I can pass the point on to Agent Nesby. As Lord of Frettchen, you're too important to leave unguarded with these people."

He flickered a brief look of apology in Gloucester's and Zane's direction. The latter glared flatly back at him with such stubbornness that Gloucester felt a pang of sympathy for the agent. If he had hoped Zane might warm up to him, he was going to be pretty disappointed for the foreseeable future.

Incensed by this flagrant display of disobedience, Mulligan glared up at Harrison as ferociously as Zane, but he received only polite, stubborn silence for his efforts. Finally, he threw his hands up with an exasperated sigh. "Fine. Fine, you stay with me, then. Pass my orders along to Nesby."

"Yes, sir," Harrison said. "Thank you, sir." He turned away, speaking into his radio quickly and quietly.

"Let's get going, then," Mulligan said to the rest of them. He nodded at the door. "We might not be able to take down Denken yet, but I know you and your magician friends have been taking down his monsters."

With no help from you.

"It's not that simple—" Zane started, only to rear back indignantly as Mulligan waved aside her protest.

"We don't have any more time to argue about this. Get a hold of any magicians you can and let's go." Much to Gloucester's annoyance, Mulligan seized his arm and steered him toward the hallway.

"Let go," he snapped.

Any further protest was halted by Antimony stepping forward with a resolute expression. She tossed her golden braid over her shoulder and crossed her arms over her chest.

"Wait," she said, with an authority that made even Mulligan stop in his tracks.

"What?" he asked, exasperated. "Enough dilly-dallying! This is important!"

"You're right," Antimony said. "Which is why I have no intention of going in there empty-handed."

"What are you suggesting?" Zane asked.

"There are a few things I'd like to pick up. Not to mention a few people."

"We don't have the time—"

Antimony cut off Mulligan's repeated complaint. "We have time for this. Trust me."

From the look on Mulligan's face, this was asking a lot, but Antimony was already leading the others past him and out into the entrance hall. Perhaps recognizing that they were at least headed in the right direction, he didn't protest further.

"Come on," he ordered Gloucester instead, giving him a light push. Gloucester bit his tongue in an effort to keep his thoughts to himself.

They filed into the hall. Mulligan moved toward the front door, but he stopped short when Antimony headed in the opposite direction. Toward the basement.

"Hey!" he called indignantly after her.

"I need to get Gear," she said by way of explanation, blatantly ignoring Mulligan in favor of addressing Zane and Gloucester. The Gambler, Gloucester just noticed then, had vanished. He could only assume the demigod was scouting ahead.

Assume or hope? whispered the little voice of doubt in his head. It sounded a lot like Finch.

Sometimes you just have to trust people and hope for the best, he told it. This went against everything his brain had been whispering to him since his incarceration. Yet hadn't it proven a valid sentiment? He'd trusted Zane and Antimony in his hour of need, and they'd taken him in. And just the night before, he'd taken a risk and trusted Hyena, without whom he wouldn't be standing here now.

That last thought made up his mind, and he shook off Mulligan's hand and followed Antimony toward the basement stairs. If they were walking back into Denken's lair, he wanted to talk to Hyena first. He might not get another chance.

"Hey!" protested Mulligan, making a grab for him. Gloucester dodged out of the way.

"I'll be back in a minute," he said over his shoulder. Zane nodded, seeming to understand, and stuck her arm out to stop Mulligan from following him. Gloucester could hear them arguing as he hastened down the hall to catch up to Antimony.

The scientist was already on the stairs when Gloucester reached her. If she was surprised by his presence, she didn't show it.

"You're not asking it to come with us," she said. It wasn't a question, nor an order, but rather a simple statement.

Gloucester shook his head. "They couldn't wait to get away

from Denken. Hyena's terrified of him. I wouldn't ask them to risk their neck like that again. They shouldn't have to be involved if they don't want to be."

A small smile curved Antimony's lips. "Then they're welcome to stay here. Now, let's be quick."

—

Despite being the entire reason for his trip into the basement, the sight of Hyena still caught Gloucester a little off-guard. It was difficult to see past their monstrous appearance and sheer hulking size, especially seated as the great beast was in Antimony's lab.

Hyena sat in the middle of the room, long limbs tucked in against their sides. They gave off a distinctly uncomfortable air, clearly afraid any movement would land them in trouble. Considering the number of delicate instruments and equipment around the room, it was an understandable concern. Gear sat on a table nearby, swinging her legs idly. She seemed a lot happier now that the Gambler had returned. She grinned at the arrival of Antimony and Gloucester, waving an enthusiastic greeting.

While Antimony went to explain everything to Gear, Gloucester approached Hyena.

"Hey there," he said. He had to tilt his head back quite a bit to look Hyena in the eye. There were several to choose from. They cocked their head quizzically and waved a greeting. "Are you all right?" Gloucester asked.

Hyena nodded, letting out a single chortle. They held up their hands, which were wrapped in the same thick bandages swathing Gloucester's, then shrugged as if to say, *As well as I can be.*

"I'm glad you're getting healed," Gloucester said, offering them a smile. "Antimony and Purpurrot know their stuff, so I'm sure you'll be right as rain in no time."

He caught a glance from Antimony, who pointed at the clock on the wall. Gloucester nodded. To Hyena, he said, "We've got to go. I dunno if you can . . . I dunno . . . feel it? But Denken is gathering the other creatures like you. Something's happening where he's building the new Maze."

Hyena nodded again. Their bony shoulders were hunched, and Gloucester could see them shaking. They watched him expectantly.

"I think you should stay here," he told them. "We're going to go see if we can stop this, but it's going to be dangerous. You've already done so much. I would never have gotten out of there if it wasn't for you. And then you stepped in between us and that skeleton . . . I reckon you saved our lives. I just wanted to talk to you before we left. I—"

In a sudden and very alarming surge of movement, Hyena pulled him into a tight embrace. It was by far the strangest hug Gloucester had ever received, but he tentatively reached his arms up to return the gesture. He gave Hyena a couple of comforting pats on a spot as close to their shoulder as he could reach.

"There there," he said. "Don't, erm, don't worry." Hyena didn't seem to be planning on letting go. "I'll be careful, I promise. But we really do have to go now."

With a mournful giggle, Hyena sat back again. Gloucester did his best to smile up at them with a confidence he didn't really feel.

"I'll see you when we get back," he said. Again they nodded, but Gloucester wasn't sure they believed him.

—

"You should call Finch," Zane told Gloucester when he and Antimony rejoined the others in the upstairs hallway. She grimaced like she hated even suggesting it. "Something tells me he won't want to miss this."

"Something tells me he already knows," Gloucester replied dryly. Still, he pulled his phone from his pocket. Mulligan was glaring at the pair of them, clearly still annoyed by Gloucester's brief disappearance. He was soon distracted, however, when he caught sight of Gear at Antimony's side.

"What in the name of all the saints is that?" he demanded, forgetting his dignity for a moment as he pointed at her, gaping.

Zane smirked. "I don't know if the car ride is long enough for this story, mate."

Mulligan and Harrison both sputtered in confusion. This worked in the group's favor, as it turned out they were too flabbergasted to offer much of an argument when Antimony declared they needed to head to a pie shop of all places before confronting Denken's monsters. The kitchen phone started to ring as they headed out the door, but there was no time to answer it, so they left it to fill the silence of the empty house.

Chapter 24

Weapons and Warfare

When they pulled into the parking lot behind Purpurrot's Pies a quarter of an hour later, Mulligan was still scoffing at the story he'd just been told. He couldn't seem to wrap his head around Gear in particular. He kept craning his neck to stare at her from the passenger's seat, eyes lingering on the clear dome that formed the back of her skull.

With the exception of Harrison behind the wheel, the rest of them were crammed into the back seat. They had driven Mulligan's van, at his own insistence, which was larger than Antimony's sleek forest green sedan. On the bright side, this meant there was room for all of them, even if it was a little cramped. On the other hand, the lack of windows had Gloucester's nerves roiling with an unease dangerously close to panic. He tried to ignore the way the walls seemed to be closing in, the way Antimony and Zane squashed against his sides made him feel like a sardine in a tin. He told himself to focus on the important things, the things that *really* deserved his worry. When that failed, he simply tried to focus on breathing.

"It's not really alive, though," Mulligan said, narrowing his eyes at Gear. She stared back with a good-natured smile. "It's just a machine."

"She's a person, living and breathing," Antimony huffed. "Just a little different, that's all."

"A little different . . ." he repeated faintly. "You don't say . . . And she's really immune to the gods?"

"Seems that way," Gloucester said. "Lucky you," he added to Gear. Her smile dimmed, uncomprehending, so he explained, "It's a nice thing to be. I'd love to be immune to them too."

"Oh! Thank you." Gear beamed like he'd paid her the most gracious of compliments. "I'm immune!"

Mulligan sighed. "She has absolutely no idea what that means, does she?"

"She's not stupid if that's what you're thinking," Antimony said. "She just doesn't know about a lot of things yet. Right, Gear?"

The instant her eyes turned to the automaton, fondness, and pride replaced her curt annoyance. It was strange to see such an open expression on her normally stoic face, softening her angular features with the gentle curve of a smile and a rosiness to her cheeks.

Once the van was parked, they all climbed out into the open air of the parking lot, but Mulligan was determined not to abandon the discussion.

"How exactly is this"—he gestured at Gear with a skeptical sneer—"supposed to help us? One immune automaton . . . What's it going to do? Get close enough to blow Denken up?"

"I don't think that'd do much, other than hurting Gear," Gloucester said. The question had been directed at him and Harrison, and he felt a degree of bitter humor that Mulligan still unthinkingly treated him like a security agent. "I think Denken would just heal if he got hurt at all."

"Then how—"

"That's where Purpurrot comes in," Antimony said. "Gear is a . . . backup plan." The corner of her mouth was tucked into a miniscule frown. She wasn't pleased with the group's insistence that Gear not play a more central role.

"Riiiight," drawled Mulligan. "This so-called Goddess of Nature. Sorry, *retired* Goddess of Nature." He looked over at Gloucester and sighed again. "And I thought *you* were mad."

Gloucester rolled his eyes. "Mad's a bit relative lately."

A familiar figure loitered by the rubbish bins near the back door of the bakery, freckled nose wrinkling at the smell. As they approached, Finch peeled himself away from the wall and made his way toward them. Gloucester had called him on the way over, not long after they'd set out from Antimony's, and caught him up on the situation. He nodded greetings to the group and spared a smile for Gloucester as he fell into step beside him.

"Haven't lost my number yet," he joked.

"Couldn't even if I wanted to," Gloucester reminded him. The numbers inked onto his palm were still legible, but faded. He guessed the spell was at long last beginning to wear off.

"Well, I appreciate the call."

A large leather satchel was slung over one of Finch's shoulders, hanging heavily against his side. He appeared better rested than the day before, but a tightness still strained his expression.

"Enough flirting," Mulligan interrupted testily. "We're wasting enough time as it is."

"Ah, hullo there, Toby." Raising his voice, Finch smirked over his shoulder at the politician. It was strange to hear someone use Mulligan's first name, and Gloucester had to remind himself that he and Finch had worked together before. "Long time no see."

"Not long enough."

"Seconded," Finch shot back cheerfully.

"What was that about wasting time?" Antimony was already

at the door, foot tapping. Even as she reached to open it, it swung open seemingly of its own accord. That is, until a looming shadow spilled out onto the concrete of the parking lot like a red carpet unrolling in front of a dignitary's feet. Purpurrot stood at the door, easily filling the entire entryway.

"Come in," she said. "Quickly."

Inside, the pie shop was deserted, the closed sign hanging against the glass of the front door and most of the lights in the main area turned off. Only the lights in the kitchen and the hallway through the back of the shop were on, filling the air with a near-silent hum, like a fly just on the edge of hearing.

When Purpurrot led them into the kitchen, Gloucester discovered they weren't as alone as he'd expected. He'd thought perhaps the Gambler might have arrived ahead of them, and sure enough, he was sitting on the edge of a countertop near the fridge, silently nursing a cup of coffee. He wasn't the only one there, however.

Bleifrei the chef stood near the stove, leaning against the counter and conversing in very animated sign language with another woman. The stranger was a tall, willowy woman with a deep complexion and dark, hooded eyes. Her hair was very close-cropped, and large gold hoops dangled from her ears. Every now and then she nodded and signed in response to Bleifrei.

"Blei's wife," Zane murmured in Gloucester's ear. "They live not too far from where Denken's new Maze is starting. Purpurrot convinced them to stay here for now. She mentioned it this morning, while you were sleeping. Roundabout the same time Antimony was explaining how Murphy went to stay with her family up north. She didn't want to leave, but Antimony convinced her it was safest since she isn't magical at all."

"Seems like I missed a lot," Gloucester whispered back.

"If you'd slept a little longer, you could have missed a hell of a lot more."

Gloucester laughed hollowly. "Don't remind me. This could

have all been a bad dream."

"If only, if only," Zane sighed.

"Morning, interlopers!" Blei called over to them. Gloucester glanced at the clock on the wall. It was just past four in the afternoon. Blei continued to sign as she spoke, nodding at the newcomers before inclining her head to indicate her wife. "This is Lucienne. Lucy, you remember Zane?"

Lucienne nodded, waving hello and stepping forward to embrace Zane. Despite this friendly greeting, her smile wavered, leading Gloucester to the conclusion that she, too, knew how grave things in the city had truly become.

In contrast, Blei seemed completely unconcerned. "This is Gloucester—bloody hell, that's a long one to spell out, you need a nickname, chum—and . . . Finch?" She barely paused to let Finch nod before she was carrying on. "And this is . . ." She squinted at Mulligan. She had intense blue eyes, mirrored in the hue of her butterfly hairpin, and Gloucester got the feeling she wasn't someone with whom you wanted to end up in a staring contest. "Sorry. Got no clue who you are."

"I'm Toby Mulligan, Lord of the City-State," he said, miffed, his important tone marred somewhat by a sulky edge.

"*Acting* Lord."

Gloucester adopted an innocent expression when Mulligan's head snapped toward him.

Blei *ooh*ed and *aah*ed, suitably impressed, but Gloucester couldn't tell if she was playing it up or not. She was difficult to read but in a completely different way from her boss. Purpurrot disguised her thoughts and emotions behind an impassive facade, just as Antimony did, while Blei's sincerity was masked by an overabundance of sound and movement.

"Purpurrot's filled us in on what's what," she said, hands always moving to include her wife in the conversation. "The Gambler was just here too, though he's swanned off who knows where now."

Gloucester blinked. Sure enough, the Gambler had vanished.

I wish they wouldn't do that, he thought ruefully. An empty mug in the sink was the only trace the demigod had been there at all.

The others didn't seem fazed by his disappearance, save for one.

"He left? Isn't he going to fight the monsters with us?" Gear had been lingering at the back of the group, inspecting the kitchen with interest, but she pushed forward now. Blei gave a start at the sight of her.

"Oh, whoa!" she cried. "Wow, you must be Gear. Purpurrot's . . . um . . . mentioned you."

Gear's dismay temporarily faded. "That's nice of her."

Gloucester glanced at Purpurrot, only to find the goddess's back turned. Perhaps not wanting to compete with Blei's bluster, she led Antimony, Mulligan, and Harrison out of the kitchen to continue their own conversation. Their muted voices moved down the hallway and into another room. Gloucester was tempted to follow, but Blei was still speaking, paying the departure no mind as she rolled her eyes at Gear.

"Not really," she said. "Anyway, the Gambler's going with you, yeah. Dunno what he's up to at the moment, but he seemed pretty on board with the whole, uh, 'fight the monsters' thing. Unfortunately, that's more than I can say for Lucy and me."

"Did anyone expect you to come?" Finch asked, examining the kitchen warily, clearly anything but comfortable in this place.

"However!" Blei enunciated, apparently intending to ignore Finch by drowning him out. "That doesn't mean we can't help you. As you probably remember, Zane, Lucy's a hedge witch. Her specialty is in charmed objects." She tapped the butterfly in her hair, her grin wide enough to give Denken's a run for its money. In a sing-song voice, she announced, "We brought presents!"

"Oooh!" crowed Zane and Gear in a single breath, both edging closer to Blei. The chef spun to the counter and dug around in a bag Gloucester hadn't noticed. The confusion must have shown on his face because Zane explained:

"Hedge witches can use magic, like magicians. Only their magic is in their blood, not just learned from books. They don't do showy incantations and illusions, but they can spell things to be pretty powerful, brew potions, and make talismans, things like that."

Gloucester nodded slowly. Wondering what Finch made of this, particularly the somewhat critical take on magicians, he slid a look over at him. Finch didn't appear bothered. In fact, he was eyeing the bag with interest. Catching Gloucester's gaze, he lifted a shoulder in a lackadaisical shrug.

"My mum was a hedge witch, d'you remember me saying? Since Dad was a magician and raised me as one too, I'm sort of both." He grinned crookedly. "Makes me special."

"Gather round, children," Blei called, raising her voice even further. She didn't seem to appreciate sharing the spotlight, no matter how briefly. Once all eyes were back on her, she looked much appeased. "Right. Finch, we figured you're already geared up, right?"

"Of course," he replied. He looked a little more at ease now, and the snideness had left his voice. Gloucester guessed that he appreciated the presence of another magic user.

"And Gear, we didn't know you were coming. Sorry about that."

Gear's shoulders slumped, the gears in her head slowing as her excitement receded, but she offered a smile nonetheless. "That's okay. I'll be all right."

That was up for debate, but Gloucester's attention was pulled back to Blei as she aimed her grin his way. "Which leaves Zane, Antimony, and Gloucester."

Reaching into the bag, she pulled forth an odd assortment of items and set them down on the countertop. None of the objects struck Gloucester as particularly special: a few rings, a silver pocket watch, a handful of second-hand jewelry, some faded bandanas, and a couple of roughly forged knives approximately the length of Gloucester's hand. The sort of stuff that could be found at a yard sale or antique store. These were magical artifacts?

Blei picked up the pocket watch, swinging it on its chain. "We thought you might like this one, Zane," she said. "Seems right up your alley."

The chain of the watch was looped around, latched at both ends to the top of the watch itself, like an oversized amulet. Zane took it gingerly, holding it up for inspection.

"What does it do?" she asked.

"It's imbued with some pretty powerful protection spells." Blei was quick to translate for Lucienne, her spoken words only a beat behind the signed explanation. "Same as this little beauty here," she added, running the tip of her finger across the wing of the butterfly hairpin again, smiling fondly at her wife. "Antimony mentioned Finch cast wards on your mind, right? Think of this watch as a little extra *umph* to that. Long as you wear it, Denken's gonna have a pretty hard time having much of an effect on you."

Lucienne's hands moved and Blei laughed. "It's also got a charm on it so it'll always tell the right time," she added. Zane laughed too, a quick nervous chuckle as she slipped the chain over her head.

"Thank you, Lucienne," she told the hedge witch sincerely. "This is brilliant."

She gave Lucienne as bright a smile as she could manage and a double thumbs up. Lucienne returned the gesture with a smile of her own.

"That's not all!" Blei declared. "Protection's great, but it's not always what you need, right? For when you need to fight, there's this."

From the selection on the table, she picked up one of the knives.

"It's hard to find an enchantment powerful enough to hurt one of the Brothers," Blei translated, watching Lucienne's hands and face as she spoke. "This should do the trick, though. At least to slow him down and give you time to get out of there before he—ha!—eats you or something. Whatever it is that he might be into now he's gone feral."

"Eating people seems like a definite possibility," Gloucester said. Zane snorted in agreement, while Blei gave a mighty guffaw. Everything about her was overly animated and loud, in contrast with her silent and laid-back wife.

"So I've heard," she said. "These knives are enchanted to cut through just about anything, so handle with care. If they can hurt Denken, they can *definitely* hurt you. Though that's true of regular knives too, I suppose . . ." Blei scratched her chin, then cast the thought aside with a chuckle. "And don't you worry your curly little head, Gloucester, 'cause we haven't forgotten about you. From everything we've heard, you need all the protection you can get."

Gloucester did his best not to grimace. He hated how helpless he'd felt ever since he was thrown headlong into this secret, magical side of Frettchen. Everyone knew more than he did and seemed capable of doing so much more than he could ever hope to achieve. He couldn't throw magic around like Finch or Lucienne, nor understand the science and spells of an immune automaton. He certainly couldn't call upon the powers of sentient nature, like Purpurrot or the Gambler. Nettled as he was by Blei's patronizing tone, he couldn't exactly argue her point.

"First things first," Blei continued cheerily. "Here."

She held out the other small knife. Its outward appearance bore nothing of interest, really, its blade sharp and its handle carved from dark walnut. As soon as he took it in hand, however, Gloucester could feel the power within it.

"So the next time Denken tries any funny business on you, you can teach him what's what," Blei said, miming a violent stabbing motion. Considering the small size of the blade, and knowing what Denken was like now, Gloucester didn't feel all that comforted or confident in the knife's purported abilities. It was a gift, though, and a kind one. He murmured his thanks.

"As for less stabby protections," Blei went on, "we weren't sure what you might like, you know, style-wise and that sort of thing, so we went with something pretty simple. Hold out your hand."

Into his open palm, she dropped a trio of rings. As she'd said, they were simple in design, unadorned bands of silver. An equally uncomplicated pair of delicate chains connected the rings. Gloucester dangled them before his eyes, inspecting them.

Lucienne moved forward, eyes locked on him as she signed. Blei was quick to translate, but Gloucester didn't think it was really necessary. Lucienne's gestures made it pretty clear she intended to show him what to do with the strange jewelry. She waited until he nodded before taking his hand.

Holding his right hand gently in hers, she took the rings and slid them onto his fingers with care. One went on his pinky, one on his middle finger, and the last and largest on his thumb. The chains were long enough that he was still able to easily move his fingers and thin enough to add no significant weight to his hand. The brush of metal and the feeling of pressure around his fingers, light as it was, were things he would have to get used to, but it was worth it to be protected from Denken's influence.

"What exactly do they do?" he asked. "I don't have to say a magic word or something, do I?"

Lucienne and Blei shook their heads, the latter still translating for her wife. "No incantation necessary for either. The spells worked into the knife allow it to cut through that which wouldn't get cut otherwise. Metal, stone, Denken's skin, what have you." She flicked her wrist in a breezy way. "As for the rings, they're just as straightforward, only a little more interesting."

Like Lucienne, she took hold of Gloucester's adorned hand, but where her wife had asked first, Blei wasted no time on such pleasantries. "When something's coming at you that you need to block, all you have to do is raise your hand like this . . ." She guided his hand to face palm outward, arm extended before him, the universal sign for someone to halt in their tracks. " . . . and picture a wall right in front of you. Remember, magic takes concentration. No effort, no reward. You think you've got it?"

Gloucester didn't think anything of the sort, but Blei didn't give him a chance to answer before stepping back to Lucienne's side and dusting off her hands in a satisfied manner.

"And that's that for you two rascals. Good luck with the battling and saving the world and such! We've a few things to give to Antimony and then we're off."

"Off?" asked Zane. "Off where?"

The manic nonchalance fell away from Blei's face. When she smiled again, a strain around her eyes and mouth spoke volumes.

"We think it's a good time to take a vacation," she said. "Lucy has some family in Pesk."

Pesk was one of the South Cities, a mid-sized coastal city on one of the many peninsulas that made up that region of the Lower Lands. It was best known for its fishing trade and little else. It was also, Gloucester noted, very far away from Frettchen.

He offered the pair of women a tiny smile and nodded his thanks for their help. He couldn't hold it against them for fleeing the city. If they couldn't stop Denken . . . well, then maybe there was nowhere far enough away to escape the fallout. Yet Bleifrei and Lucienne had done what they could to help, and they deserved a chance at safety. Gloucester himself was still sorely tempted to take the next train to the Nordlands.

He could do more here, though. He knew it. This wasn't a fight from which he could simply run away. It had already destroyed the life he'd had. He wouldn't let it destroy anything else, not if he could help it.

Blei and Lucienne moved off in the direction Antimony and the others had gone, and Zane followed, but when Gloucester went to accompany her, he was stopped by Finch. The magician laid a hand on his arm.

"Wait a moment," he said when Gloucester cast him an inquiring look. He half expected more words of warning about who to trust, but Finch said, "I've got something for you too."

"And it's not even my birthday," Gloucester joked, curiosity and caution building in equal measure. He was never quite sure what to expect from Finch.

Zane was waiting for him at the kitchen door, but Gloucester waved her onward. "Go on with Gear and the others. I'll catch up. Just give me a minute."

She lingered reluctantly, but eventually gave in with a nod and disappeared into the hallway. Gloucester turned back to Finch, who was rummaging through the leather bag he carried. To Gloucester's surprise, he pulled forth a gun.

It was a pretty unremarkable handgun in appearance, similar to the model standard issued to the lord of the city-state's security detail. Finch offered it to him, and he took it. Upon closer inspection, he noticed subtle details marking it as more than a run-of-the-mill firearm. The muzzle had an odd sheen in places, and when Gloucester angled it to better see under the light, he saw that there were symbols etched into the metal. They traced along the length of the gun, a language foreign to Gloucester, yet not completely unfamiliar. He'd seen the same markings on the gun Finch pulled on Denken back in All Saints Shrine.

"You're giving me your gun?" he asked. He'd assumed the weapon was special to Finch, considering how powerful it seemed to be.

Finch let out a bark of laughter. "No, of course not. I charmed you one of your own. I figured it might come in handy, plus I know you can handle it."

Gloucester hefted the gun in his hand. Its weight was familiar, comfortable even. Finch reached into his bag again and tossed him a holster. He held the gun as Gloucester put it on, years of practice making short work of it. He preferred a belt holster or even a thigh one, but this one, which strapped around his shoulders so that the weapon nestled under his left arm, was not new to him.

"Thanks," he said. He took the gun back and stowed it in the holster. "You didn't have to—I wasn't expecting . . . um."

Bloody hell, when had he become such a stutterer? He'd never been particularly good at talking to people, and the time spent in solitary had only made that worse, but he'd thought he was doing all right in one-on-one conversations. Apparently, all it took was an unexpected gift to render him incoherent. Feeling quite foolish, he snapped his mouth shut before he could say something really stupid.

"It's no problem." A faint rosy hue colored Finch's cheeks. "It's just in case. It'll be handier in a sticky situation than that little butter knife the loud chef gave you. Speaking of whom, we should probably follow the dulcet tones of her voice and get back to the others before they leave without us. Tempting as it may be to let them."

Gloucester chuckled, giving the holster a final adjustment for comfort's sake and then following Finch out the door. Finch might have been joking, but Gloucester couldn't shake the very real instincts baying for him to do exactly that: let them leave without him. Get out while he still could. Even with magic on his side now, it wasn't like he was truly a match for the enemy, was he? He'd been trained to combat threats to the lord of the city-state, to guard his back and keep him safe from everything ranging from pushy journalists to would-be assassins. Magic had never featured in the job description, nor had gods. What was he even doing here?

Fighting. I might not know magic, but I was trained to fight. To protect.

So that was what he would do. The lord of Frettchen might no longer be his charge, but there were others to whom he'd pledged his loyalty. Others who needed protecting. Jeb. Zane.

The city as a whole. It had been his home for several years now, and it had become important to him. He wouldn't leave it behind.

"You've got your thinking face on," Finch commented, eyeing him sideways as they made their way down the short length of the hallway. "You're fretting, aren't you? Not that it's actually easy to tell. Your thinking face is pretty close to your default face."

Gloucester raised his eyebrows at him. "Maybe I'm just always thinking," he said, mustering up a bit of levity.

They reached the door at the end of the hall, and Finch let the subject go. Relief eased a knot in Gloucester's chest. He was hesitant to delve too deeply into notions of motivation and emotion again, not certain he knew how to articulate what he felt.

Inside the room, Purpurrot sat behind a handsome desk carved of polished wood. It was immediately obvious that this was her office. Even sitting down, she was tall enough to meet all of their eyes evenly. Mulligan stood against the furthest wall, scowling, one of Lucienne's enchanted rings on his finger. He fidgeted with it. As uncomfortable as the magic made him, he wasn't opposed to a bit of extra protection. There was no sign of Harrison, though Gloucester guessed he was nearby. He wouldn't stray far from Mulligan. Antimony sat on the near side of the desk, ankles crossed daintily as she inspected her fingernails.

No, that wasn't what held her attention, Gloucester realized. Antimony's fingers were reflecting the light, glinting gold each time she moved her hand. What he initially took for rings similar to Mulligan's or the ones he now wore, he soon realized were brass knuckles, fitted perfectly for Antimony's slender hand.

"That'll pack a punch," Zane observed with a grin.

Antimony returned the smile. "And then some."

In one corner of the room, Lucienne and Blei stood huddled with Gear, digging through the bag of items they'd laid out in the kitchen. Blei hummed and hawed to herself, not bothering to sign or even raise her voice to an intelligible level. If Gloucester were to guess, he'd say she was searching for something in their bag of enchanted goodies Gear could either use as a weapon or defense. Not for the first time, he wondered if the best thing for the innocent automaton would be to find her an escape route, not a weapon. With her soft smile and well-meaning nature, Gear would surely be torn apart by the imagination monsters within minutes.

Under his worried gaze, Blei pulled out an old silver key on a string. "This is for protection," she told Gear. She spoke rather slowly, as if to a child. "It should keep you safe as long as you wear it."

"I thought keys were for doors and things," Gear said, taking the key and inspecting it with avid fascination. "To open and close things."

Blei rolled her eyes while Lucienne hid a smile behind her hand.

"Well, this is a special key," the chef explained. "It's a necklace. Just wear it, would you?"

Though Gear didn't look like she fully understood, she obligingly slipped the string around her neck. The key rested against the pale blue fabric of her shirt.

"This is taking too long."

The low voice made Gloucester jump. He hadn't heard Harrison approach, but the brawny man now filled the doorway, expression strained.

This sort of impertinence wasn't approved of amongst security agents, but Mulligan didn't scold him. In fact, he nodded solemnly. "Those monsters could be up to anything. Even with the area evacuated, there's no end to the possibilities for trouble they could get into. Especially if all this about them being made of raw emotion is true. Unfettered imagination." He shivered.

Though he wasn't keen to admit it, Gloucester had to agree with him. They'd all experienced what the emotionally charged state of the city had caused even without the direct influence of the monsters. If they planned some sort of coordinated attack, the results would be catastrophic.

Purpurrot got to her feet, the top of her head nearly brushing the ceiling. "We'd better be off, then."

Like the Gambler, her face was unreadable. If she was scared to face Denken with her powers so weakened, she showed no sign of it.

—

As they made their way back to the parking lot, Gloucester found himself thinking about Hyena. Everyone was talking about the imagination monsters like they were vicious partners in Denken's plans, but were they really? Hyena had been reluctant to play a part in any of this and had run from it the first chance they were given. The skeleton they'd come up against in the false Maze had also willingly backed down once Hyena dissuaded it. Were there others who might do the same?

The fire dragon they'd fought had been so dangerous and out of control it was easy to assign it the role of villain. Zane had wanted to spare it, though, and had been upset at the prospect of its death. Gloucester wondered if she'd seen then what he'd now come to understand: these creatures were simply lost animals, scared and alone and desperate to return home.

And here we come to kill them.

Was it the only way? Maybe not. Maybe, just maybe, if they were given the opportunity to return to their home, they would.

He felt like there were a dozen pieces of different plans whirling around in his head, waiting to coalesce into a cohesive whole that could save them all.

Blei and Lucienne parted ways with them at the back door of the pie shop, heading for a cherry-red convertible parked nearby. Evening was approaching now, the sunlight rosy and cast low from the horizon. It reflected off the long hood of the car. The chef and the hedge witch waved as they drove away.

As he clambered into Mulligan's van, it struck Gloucester that this might be the last time he ever saw them. It surprised him how sharp the pang was, considering he scarcely knew either woman.

It had little to do with them, of course. He might die that night. They all might.

So, you know . . . he thought with a quiet sigh. *No pressure.*

Chapter 25

Monsters

The silence in the van was more uncomfortable than ever. Where the trip to Purpurrot's Pies had been filled with explaining Gear to Mulligan, now no one seemed to have anything to say. Gloucester almost missed Mulligan's disbelieving interruptions. They had at least helped stave off his fretful thoughts and the worst of his stifling claustrophobia. Now the sensation was worse than ever, especially with Purpurrot accompanying them, seated with comical grace on the floor of the van. If she was worried about their plan and the part she was to play in it, she gave no sign. Her eyes were closed, and not even Mulligan dared disturb her.

Without distractions to ease his mind, Gloucester had to rely on the training he'd received as a security agent. It wasn't as easy as it had once been to keep his heart rate down and his head clear, but he found after a while he could still manage it.

For the most part, at least. His hands moved of their own

volition, gently twisting the thin silver chains connecting the rings on his hand. The metal flicked this way and that between his fingers. Though they still ached, he was now able to move all of his digits without any noticeable stiffness. Under his arm rested the familiar weight of the gun. Physically he felt almost like his old self again, save for the aches and healing injuries. He wasn't sure he would ever feel like the same person in his head, however, no matter the lingering effects of his training.

With these thoughts whispering in his ears, he was almost relieved when they reached their destination. Harrison pulled the van over to the curb, but they'd barely stopped moving before Mulligan frowned at the security agent from the passenger's seat.

"Why here? We're not there yet, are we?" he asked. To his credit, his question didn't come across as accusatory, merely concerned and curious.

"The street is two blocks away. I didn't want to go too close in the van. Better to go on foot from here," Harrison explained. "That way we can watch each other's backs."

Gloucester nodded in agreement unthinkingly. The van offered them shelter, but it didn't provide visibility to anyone other than those in the front seats. Considering what they were up against, they were going to have to play this by ear.

They got out of the vehicle quietly. The street was deserted, even though the buildings on this block looked reasonably maintained and lived in. Recently evacuated, Gloucester surmised.

His feet had hardly touched the asphalt when a loud noise tore through the air, drowning out the muted traffic and hubbub of the city beyond the evacuated zone. It was a roar, almost high-pitched enough to qualify as a scream. An eerie, unnatural note threaded through it like it was someone's—or some*thing's*—imitation of a human in distress. Gloucester shivered. The tiny knife and rings suddenly seemed like very paltry protection. He was glad for the gun in its holster. If he was lucky, he wouldn't have to use it.

I haven't been lucky in a long time. Not really.

"Here there be monsters," Finch said at his side. The faint vibrations of magic brushed against his skin. He wondered if Finch was gathering it in preparation for what was to come. Could magicians do that? The sky gods worshipped by the Blue Church back home were said to swath themselves in storm clouds and rain lightning down on heretics. Was that magic?

They could use a little of that power on their side right about now.

"Be on your guard," Mulligan ordered. They nodded silently, though none of them needed the warning.

The inhuman scream petered out, but remnants of it echoed through the empty street. Gloucester couldn't tell if the sound was actually ringing in his ears or if it was only his imagination playing tricks on him. He'd always had a vivid imagination. Now, headed into the territory of a dangerously unstable personification of Thought, he could only hope his magical weapons and Finch's Blocking spell did their jobs. He refused to be helpless and at Denken's mercy again. He had a feeling that mercy had run out, anyway.

As the screams continued, Gloucester's stomach dropped. The noise wasn't his imagination, nor was it echoes of the mysterious call. They were replies, each slightly different in pitch, a pack responding to a scout's warning.

"I don't think we have the element of surprise anymore," Antimony whispered. "Brace yourselves."

They edged forward, ears open for any warning of an attack. Gloucester drew the gun from its holster as he moved silently to Mulligan's side.

"Hey," he said, voice as quiet as Antimony's had been. "Where are the security agents? The ones you sent ahead to evacuate civilians. They were still supposed to be here, weren't they?"

Harrison frowned. "Good question," he whispered from

Mulligan's other side. He also had a gun in one hand, and his radio in the other. He hissed names into it, calling for responses, but none came.

"Not the best, as omens go," Finch said in Gloucester's ear.

Gloucester shot him a look. Now wasn't the time for quips.

"If the beasts are congregating around the new Maze, then we should be heading this way," Antimony said. She strode down the sidewalk with a grim determination, Purpurrot looming at her side. Zane, Gloucester, Finch, and Gear followed after them. Mulligan and Harrison hesitated until they seemed to remember that they were supposed to be in charge of this mission, and they hurried to catch up.

"I should lead, ladies," Harrison said, his long legs carrying him forward with little trouble to fall into step beside Antimony. She ignored him. He glanced up at Purpurrot, but she didn't spare him an iota of attention, so after a moment he ducked his head and refocused on Antimony.

"Miss Jones, I must insist—"

"It's 'Mrs.'," Antimony said evenly. Despite her hip-swaying gait, she walked with purpose, back straight and head held high. Harrison didn't seem to know quite what to make of her.

"Mrs.—"

"Perhaps you ought to watch our flanks, Mr. Harrison," she told him. "Monsters rarely attack head on."

If Harrison wanted to argue further, he resisted. He nodded once and fell back. Following Antimony's suggestion, his eyes swept over the buildings on either side of the road, searching the dark windows and shadowed walls that towered over them.

The screams were getting louder. Closer. When Gloucester was young, growing up in the shadows of the Nordish mountains, the coyotes would call out in the night, yipping and howling to each other as they surrounded some unfortunate prey. This, he thought now, must be how it felt to be the rabbit.

Except that rabbits don't get weapons, he reminded himself, desperate for a bright side. The thin chains on his hand brushed against his knuckles, and his other hand gripped the gun steadily. He'd stowed the short knife in his belt, and though it was a far less comforting weapon than the enchanted gun, it was still something. A last resort of self-defense.

"How much further?" Zane peered all around with anxious eyes, one hand holding her own charmed knife aloft, the other clutching the pocket watch around her neck. "It's hard to tell in the light. What's left of it, at least. Didn't we blow the door down? You'd think that'd be easy to spot."

"It is if you stop trying to look with your eyes," Finch said. His hands were empty, held out in front of him as if he were walking through darkness and wary of running into a wall. "The spell I used on the door was basic in design, but powerful in execution. A big bang like that will have left magical energy lingering in its wake, even if Denken's redecorated since then."

It was heartening news because Zane was right: there were no visible signs of which building was the right one.

They walked on in uneasy silence, while all around them the monsters' shrieks came ever closer.

"Anyone else get the feeling we're being herded?" Zane voiced the question Gloucester had been thinking. "If they were properly chasing us down, don't you think they would have caught us by now?"

"Maybe they're friendly," Gear suggested with bright— though thankfully quiet—optimism.

Zane side-eyed the automaton. "I think it's more of a 'walking into a trap' situation."

"Our specialty," said Gloucester. Over his shoulder, the unseen beasts cried out. Even if it *was* a trap, what choice did they have but to keep moving forward?

It sounded like the monsters were practically on top of them when Finch stopped short.

"There," he said, pointing. "It's that one."

The house was nondescript. A shingled roof that had seen better days sagged above walls with peeling paint and a crumbling brick foundation. The front door, though as worn as the rest of the place, was intact.

"You're absolutely sure?" Mulligan asked. He'd dropped his voice so low that he was barely audible. Gloucester couldn't really blame him. The screams were now accompanied by heavy footsteps.

"Of course I'm sure," Finch retorted. "And I reckon we're better off in there than out here with whatever *that* is."

He'd gone very pale, and his pointing finger swung away from the door to Denken's domain and over to the mouth of an alley across the street. A shadow stirred there, stretching further and further into the street as whatever was casting it grew closer.

"Ah," breathed Zane faintly. "It *was* a trap. Well spotted, me."

The screaming stopped. In its place, something softer filled the air, a guttural, repetitive wheezing, like the breath of something gigantic. Several somethings.

"Run!"

Harrison's order was authoritative but almost inaudible beneath the boom of Purpurrot shouting the same thing. Her single word shook the rest of them out of their horrified stupor. Gloucester's feet didn't wait for orders from his brain before springing into action. He ran headlong for the house, Zane and the others hard on his heels. Harrison fell back to remain at Mulligan's side. Purpurrot swept along at the rear, her steps intentionally slow.

In contrast, the slim figure that emerged from the shadows ahead of them was quick as a flash. Cloaked and hooded, it might have been human, yet its scuttling movements were anything but. While more creatures approached from behind them, this one darted from the front, lunging at the group as they reached the foot of the porch steps.

Harrison threw himself in front of Mulligan with a shout, shielding him with his body. The creature's hood fell back as it drew close, and Gloucester's stomach turned. The bright black eyes and clicking pincers of a centipede stared back at him. He raised his gun, the etched symbols flashing with power, but he wasn't quick enough. The centipede shoved past him and Finch, hands with too many fingers pushing them aside with frightening ease. It went for Antimony and Zane, perhaps taking them for easier prey.

If that was indeed the case, the beast had made a grave miscalculation.

The creature struck at Antimony. Its clicking pincers snapped toward the blonde's throat, going for the kill.

Never to actually touch flesh. Antimony's fist plunged forward like a battering ram, and the impact of her brass knuckles striking the centipede in the flat carapace just above its pincers was deafening. Whatever spells Lucienne had worked into the brawler's weapon had granted it a lot of extra strength. The bug's armor cracked like brittle bone, and it reared back, hissing. Even without the added firepower of magic, it would have been an impressive blow.

Antimony swung like she'd had practice, her right fist shooting forward with a straight arm, her left pulling back to her side, into a position Gloucester recognized as the chamber. Her face was almost serene, a cold glint in her eye the only hint of her emotions.

"Yeah!" Zane cried, pumping her fist in the air. "Take that!"

The sympathy she'd expressed for the fiery dragon apparently didn't extend to six-foot-tall creepy crawlies. At least not ones trying to attack her.

The centipede lunged again, only to be rebuked by another swift punch. Antimony's fist moved so quickly it was a blur, punctuated by a sharp smack as it smashed into the centipede's shell once more. The crack in its armor grew, and Antimony's hand withdrew covered in thick brown pus, which gushed from the wound. At the sight of it, Zane stopped cheering and clamped her hand over her mouth. She looked like she was going to be sick.

"Great," she said with a hysterical sort of giggle. "Now I have a bug phobia."

The centipede writhed, agonized and furious, but it had run out of time. Violet-nailed hands clamped down on its thin shoulders from behind, and it screeched as Purpurrot hoisted it above her head. She threw it down into the street. Face thunderous, she swept her arms toward the house.

"Get inside, *now*."

Gloucester took the stairs up two at a time, skidding to a stop on the porch. When he snatched the doorknob and pulled, it was with a gut-wrenching feeling that he found the door locked.

"Out of the way!" Finch shouted. Gloucester threw himself to the side as the magician hurtled up the steps, the air electric around him. With a *boom* more sensation than noise, the door burst inward, nearly blasted off its hinges.

"Come on!" Antimony darted through the doorway alongside Gear and Zane, followed swiftly by Harrison, who was still using his height to shelter Mulligan. Finch called Gloucester's name in an urgent voice, and he stepped through the door after them, glancing back one last time.

Behind Purpurrot, he spotted the monsters that had been stalking them fill the street around the fallen centipede. Next to them, the bug was tiny. Each monster was different, yet they gave the distinct impression of a pack of wolves. Gloucester glimpsed wide eyes, snarling snouts, skin that flickered and flared like that of the dragon. There were yellowed teeth and grizzled fur and too-long necks. Every monster stared back at him, unblinking. Overwhelmed with horror, Gloucester dashed through the door, which Purpurrot slammed shut behind them.

When they'd been there before, the entrance hall to Denken's new lair was bright, blindingly so. That was no longer the case. The shadows that had pursued them down the halls had never dissipated. It was the sort of dark in which monsters lurked. Gloucester thought of the stories fishermen liked to tell down at the wharves, about the sharks and other hunters lurking in the dark beneath the hulls of their ships. He thought of Denken's terrifying smile, his staring eyes as black and impenetrable as the shadows encasing them. This, he thought, suited the god far more than towering church walls and bright light. He could be watching from the darkness even now, waiting to strike. Cold fear churned in the pit of Gloucester's stomach.

A moment later, the darkness was the least of his concerns. Scarcely after the door slammed shut, Purpurrot gasped. Gloucester jerked his head toward her, heart fluttering at the idea of something that could shock the unflappable goddess. She was clutching her head, her expression hidden in shadow.

"Purpa? What's wrong?" Antimony rushed to Gloucester's side and stared up at Purpurrot in concern. Purpurrot didn't reply. Even in the darkness, Gloucester could see she was in distress, curling in on herself in pain.

Then she was gone. Vanished, as Gloucester had so often seen her and her kin do in the last few days. And yet, something told him this instance wasn't voluntary.

Chapter 26

In the Dark

"**P**urpa!" Antimony cried.

But the goddess was gone.

"What the actual fuck just happened?" Zane's question quivered with panic.

"My best guess, entering a place this much like a Pocket was a wee bit overwhelming for her, after all this time in the human world," came Finch's voice.

He was barely visible, illuminated only by a faint light emanating not only from his hands but from Zane's pocket watch as well. She held it up like a lantern, making all of their faces pale ghosts in the dark.

"If we're lucky, she's still around somewhere, recuperating," Finch continued. "If not . . ."

"We're trapped in here without the single most important part of this damned plan of yours." Mulligan's glasses glinted in the magical light. "We need backup."

"The other agents would have to get past those things out there to get to us," Harrison said. "I don't think there's enough of them. They'd be slaughtered!"

If they haven't been already, thought Gloucester, thinking of the silence on the radio.

For a moment he fully expected Mulligan to say the risk didn't matter and order them to come regardless. It was what the high minister would have done. Yet Mulligan surprised him, sighing loudly but not pushing the matter.

"So we're on our own, then," he said. To Harrison, he added, "Try to reach Nesby again. Tell her to continue keeping civilians away. The least we can have them do is contain this if they're still in any shape to do so."

Harrison pressed the button on his radio and spoke quietly into it, but still only silence answered. Not even static reached their ears.

"Gonna take that as a big ol' no," Zane whispered.

"They'll know what to do," Harrison comforted her. He clipped the radio back onto his belt and drew his gun. "They're well trained."

"Let's hope they don't get in the magicians' way when they get there."

In contrast to Zane and Mulligan, Finch's voice betrayed no fear. Still, Gloucester suspected he felt it just the same. Everything he'd come to know about Cassus Finch in the last month made him question the unfazed, flippant air he projected. Beneath it, Finch felt as keenly as the rest of them.

"They know to look out for them," Harrison said shortly. "For now, I think it's best we just focus on our own problems. What's our next move?"

"Find Denken," said the Gambler, emerging from the darkness.

Gloucester jumped, heart racing, and he saw Zane do the same. Mulligan swore colorfully, hand pressed to his chest. Finch and Harrison both grew very still, as if their caution had turned them to stone. Antimony and Gear smiled.

"Gambler!" Gear cried. Antimony coughed pointedly, and Gear wilted. "Sorry," she apologized, dropping her voice to a more appropriate whisper. Her smile stayed as wide and bright as ever. "You're back!"

"I am."

It was strange to see the Gambler smile, but he did so for Gear. As the moment stretched on, it was Finch's turn to give a pointed cough. This time the automaton didn't look the least bit abashed, but she did refocus on the rest of them.

As did the Gambler. The smile was replaced by his usual melancholy frown. In the dim lighting, his face was even more unsettling than usual, the empty eye sockets nothing more than shadows, black and yawning.

"The magician is right. Purpurrot is still here somewhere, though I suspect she's struggling with the surge of power entering this place caused. Until she can get it under control, it would be dangerous to be close to her. But Denken's here somewhere too," he warned. "Not too close yet, but he'll sense us soon if he hasn't already."

"He probably has and just wants to play with us," Finch said.

"Thanks for the gloomy outlook, you ray of sunshine, you," Zane grumbled in return.

"Quiet," Antimony ordered.

They moved through the darkness as quietly as they could. It was an uneasy trek, all of them expecting Denken's vicious grin to appear out of the pitch black at any moment. Though she did her best to hold it steady, the glowing pocket watch swung in Zane's shaky hand, making the light bob and weave, shadows dancing across their faces.

"Where are we even going?" hissed Mulligan. It was impossible to say how long they had been walking. Gloucester felt like it could have been hours or mere minutes. "We should be outside, stopping the monsters. What good are we doing trudging around in the dark?"

"Potentially much," came the Gambler's voice. He led the group from several meters ahead, where his silhouette was barely visible. He didn't need light to see. "The beasts outside are symptoms, not the disease. The magicians and your agents will keep them under control. If we can stop Denken, the monsters, as you call them, will cease to manifest."

"They'll die?" Gloucester whispered. His thoughts were back on Hyena. Would the laughing beast just cease to exist? He didn't like that idea. They hadn't done anything wrong. They had, in fact, done quite a lot right, in his opinion. He would still be Denken's prisoner—or worse—if not for Hyena's aid.

"Not really," the Gambler said. He moved back into the light, an odd smile on his face. "Your concern for them is welcome, Mikalai Gloucester. I think it's safe to assume they will return to their base form." When they all stared at him, he patiently explained, "Raw imagination. As non-corporeal creative energy, they would probably have far more luck than Denken in returning to the true Maze."

"Could that explain why he has them gathering together?" Zane asked. "To build up enough of that energy to reopen the door for him?"

"It's possible. More likely, he would harness that energy to further power the construction of this new Maze."

Gloucester's fists clenched. "If the energy comes with their destruction, though . . . So he *wants* them to get killed? Or—or unmanifested or whatever? He's supposed to be their guardian, isn't he? He should be protecting them. That's what guardians do!"

His fervor was rewarded with a shush from Antimony and a derisive look from Mulligan. Gloucester fell silent but didn't grace Mulligan with a second glance. More and more it seemed to him the imagination monsters were as involuntarily caught up in this mess as the humans were, just trying to figure out what was going on.

Bear in mind they're doing that by hunting people down

and killing them, he reminded himself. It didn't seem like there was any right answer. The best option would be to get them and Denken alike back to the Maze, where the latter could heal and hopefully regain his sanity, such as it was, and the monsters could return to their proper places behind their doors.

Or would that just be returning them to prison cells?

He didn't know, and short of asking the Gambler, he had no way of finding out. He doubted the others would appreciate this line of questioning while the situation was so dire. It stuck with him, though, as they continued on through the dark. He'd spent enough time shut away behind a locked door to know it wasn't a good way to spend a life.

He could only hope there would be time later for pondering such things because he knew he ought not to be doing so right then. Denken could mount an ambush at any moment, and distraction could mean death.

Focus. If you want to get out of this alive, stop asking yourself pointless questions and just pay attention.

Easier said than done in this place. Despite the constant impending menace of the pitch-black corridor, its darkness was exactly the thing leading Gloucester's mind astray. There was nothing in the curtains of blackness onto which he could latch his eyes, like they were all simply floating in nothingness.

Was it just the dark, though? Denken was a manipulator of the mind. Considering all the things Gloucester knew Denken to be capable of, it would surely be an easy task for him to distract interlopers. Gloucester clenched his fist around the rings on his hand. What exactly did Lucienne's protective spells ward them from?

"We're almost there," the Gambler said, his voice drifting back from the darkness ahead. "The center of the Maze is close."

"All these years of knowing you, Joujou, and I never thought I'd actually see you blind."

The voice came from everywhere. Gloucester's blood ran cold. Zane, swearing audibly, spun around and stared into the dark, the light from the pocket watch swaying like a drunk man's flashlight.

Denken's overwhelming laugh greeted them. Gloucester fought the need to clamp his hands over his ears.

"And you brought friends," Denken crooned. Despite his omnipresent voice, Gloucester caught a flash of bright white teeth and the reflection of eyes behind Mulligan and Harrison.

"Look out!" he shouted, but too late. A hand shot through the air, and then Harrison was flying backward, crashing into a wall hidden by the darkness with a painful crack. He crumpled to the floor, stunned.

Denken stepped into the pale light, sharp-toothed grin wide and shining. He stared at Mulligan. "I remember you."

His sharp fingers were a hair's breadth from Mulligan's throat when another hand clamped around his wrist. The Gambler had moved silently and in an instant.

"Don't do this, Denken," he said. "Not again."

Denken's smile never faltered, but Gloucester could see the straining muscles in his arm. "Or what, little brother? You and the humans will stop me?"

"Yes."

Never had Gloucester heard so much sadness in the Gambler's voice. Tears spilled from his eyes just hearing it, and he hurriedly blinked them away. This was no time for blurred vision.

Denken's smile vanished. In the magic's paltry illumination, his face was gaunt and emotionless. "I see," he said.

For a moment he was very still. Then his foot kicked out, slamming into the Gambler's stomach with a force that would have driven a hole through a normal man. The Gambler flew backward. More graceful than Harrison, who was only now beginning to stir, the Gambler recovered midair and landed catlike on his feet. He pivoted to face Denken once more.

"Don't do this," he repeated, this time with an edge. "I don't want to hurt you."

"And I don't want to do any of this," Denken snarled. "Funny how things happen anyway."

He snatched for Mulligan again, but Mulligan had possessed the wherewithal to make a dash for the relative safety of distance. He retreated to Finch's side, no doubt viewing him as the most powerful ally. Finch's eyes were set on Denken, a fire burning within them. He didn't flinch when Denken's unnerving stare turned on him.

Dark eyes then flicked toward Gloucester, and Denken laughed.

"Dashing prince reunited with his agent-in-distress, I see. Nice of you all to gather in one place. Makes things a lot, well . . . I was gonna say 'easier,' but this would have been easy no matter what."

"Oh really?" Finch's tone was deceptively light. Even as he spoke, his hands were moving in a complex series of motions. "Just been dawdling, then, is that it? Can't think of another reason your big bad plan is taking so long. Not with it all so *easy*."

Denken stepped closer. He didn't need the massive shark of shadows now, not when his sharp teeth and black eyes moving through the half-light achieved the same effect.

Finch snapped the incantation to his spell, and a burst of heat and light made Gloucester flinch, shielding his eyes. At his side, Zane let loose a squawk of foul-mouthed alarm.

Denken swatted the magic away like a pestering fly. The spell never even touched him, the magic's trajectory changed with a breezy motion of his hand.

"Nice try, sunshine." Denken's hand flicked out again. A long tongue of light flashed in Finch's direction. Its heat burned Gloucester's face.

Before he could try to pull Finch out of the way, the magician was already countering. The attack rebounded off an invisible barrier that Gloucester could *feel* rise up between them and the advancing demigod. Its impact was blinding, the magic ricocheting upward, scorching a path through the darkness. White spots ringed in black danced across Gloucester's vision, and he blinked rapidly. Squinting into the dark, panic slammed through him as Denken's face reared into his vision, hurtling toward him. He threw his hand up instinctively, knowing that it was too late to aim his gun, too late to stop the imminent collision.

This turned out to be half-true. There was indeed a collision, Denken staggering back, eyes wide and teeth gnashing in furious confusion.

It wasn't Gloucester with whom he'd collided.

Instead, a wall, visible only by the light reflecting off of it, had risen up between them, shielding Gloucester from the attack. He stared at his outstretched hand. His fingers were splayed wide, thin chains stretched out between his digits. The rings emitted none of the glow of Zane's pocket watch, but he could feel the power in them, a vibration coursing through his hand and up his arm with mounting strength.

"Well, well," Denken hissed with a voice like acid. "Isn't that a handy trick? Someone's got a new toy."

"Yeah," panted Gloucester, hand shaking with the effort of keeping the wall in place. It felt like his hand and arm were buzzing with electricity, hot and cold all at once, and just on the near side of painful. "And it's not the only one."

He swept his other arm up, the gun reflecting light as he took aim. Channeling his intentions, the symbols carved into the metal flared with a light of their own, green like those that danced across the skies up north, illuminating an ancient language Gloucester couldn't read. He squeezed the trigger and felt the kick of the gun as it fired. A rushing in his head drowned out all sound and thought.

Something hot and bright orange flew through Gloucester's field of vision suddenly enough that he reared back. It slammed into Denken and knocked the demigod off his feet.

The Gambler rose like a phoenix, transformed. Standing over

Denken in a shroud of flames, he seemed to tower even taller than Purpurrot. All the color from his skin and hair had been stripped away and replaced with the angry orange and yellow of fire, which appeared to burn outward from his very flesh. It engulfed his clothing, licking up his arms and legs and pluming around his head like the halo of a furious angel. His usual benign apathy had hardened into a cold, stony countenance that contradicted the rest of his burning visage.

"Stop this," he ordered. His voice boomed like cannon fire, making everyone other than Denken and—Gloucester noticed—Gear flinch. The two words, simple as they were, contained centuries of emotion, of heartache and loss and consequential despair. Gloucester wasn't sure if the Gambler was speaking to him or Denken. Perhaps both.

"Why don't you?" Denken met him with a sharp parry, full of fury.

The unshakable allure that always laced his words was still there, tugging painfully on Gloucester's mind. He wanted to plug his ears, but that would involve dropping both shield and gun, and he had no intention of relinquishing either. At least the voice's pull wasn't quite as overwhelming as usual. He sent a silent word of thanks to Lucienne and Bleifrei.

"I'm trying," the Gambler told Denken in turn. The words tore at Gloucester's heart, and as he stared at Denken's nightmarish face, he saw the glimmer of tears on his cheeks.

"To kill me." Denken spoke in a near-whisper that nonetheless reached all of their ears. "Your own brother. You would really choose these humans over me, Joujou?"

"You're leaving me no choice, Denken."

Denken's laugh was cracked and dry.

"Oh, the irony," he said, then attacked.

Chapter 27

Mercy

The force of the clash drove all of them from their feet. Gloucester landed hard on his back, the weight of another body on top of him rushing the breath from his chest. The heat of an inferno turned the air dry, the darkness chased away by blinding light. Flames engulfed the Gambler. They mounted into a blaze that stretched to the distant ceiling, casting warped shadows of his form across the walls. The pitch black was replaced with unsteady, roiling light that grew and waned with the movement of the fire.

Like the Gambler, Denken was suddenly much taller than he had been before. The hall's remaining shadows surged around him, making the edges of his form indistinct and ever-changing. Only his face was still clear to see.

Gloucester wished it wasn't. Any humanity in the demigod was truly gone, burned away by his brother's fire. All of his features faded back, save his eyes and teeth, which glinted in the firelight. Both were impossibly large. He moved like ink dropped on wet parchment, smooth and unpredictable. It was a sharp contrast to the Gambler's movements, which were as quick and jittering as the tongues of flame around him. Their voices filled the air like fog horns, straining Gloucester's eardrums and bringing pained tears to his eyes.

"What do we do?" he shouted to the person lying atop him, too dazed to recognize who it was.

"We get out of the way." Antimony coughed, rolling away and to her feet in a flurry of white dress and blonde hair.

Gloucester forced himself to his feet as well. "You want to run?"

"No!" Antimony snapped. "I want to regroup and figure out what to do. If we stay here, we're going to be crushed or incinerated."

It was a valid point. Gloucester hoisted a gasping Zane to her feet and took a wild look around for the others. Everyone was in one piece, though the side of Harrison's bald head was red with blood and Finch now sported a bloody nose.

"Run!" Antimony shouted when they all took too long regaining their bearings. She pulled Gear to her feet and pointed in the direction from which they'd come. Maybe. It was difficult to tell, even with the reprieve from all-encompassing darkness. The light had revealed a passageway that wasn't at all familiar. For all any of them knew, the interior of the new Maze might have no consistent layout. Maybe it was always changing.

A trap we willingly walked into.

A fiery foot stomped down dangerously close to Gloucester, an unmistakable reminder of the urgency of the situation. He dashed after Antimony and Gear, shouting for the others to follow.

The last time they'd been there, the corridors were pale stone and towering. Now they ran through narrow, winding corridors lined in wood paneling and forest green wallpaper. The pitch black didn't return, even when they rounded a corner and left the fighting immortals out of sight. It seemed Denken had called all of the shadows to him, gathered like a swirling, seething suit of armor. Their absence left the corridors in a sort of half-light, with no discernible source and no shadows moving beneath their feet as they ran.

They'd only made it the length of a few corridors before a sound reached their ears. Not the crashing, roaring fight between Denken and the Gambler, but something closer, and gaining on them by the moment. They all slowed to a halt, breathing heavily and throwing nervous glances over their shoulders.

"Have they given chase?" Mulligan whispered. A crack ran down one of the lenses of his horn-rimmed glasses.

"Nah," Finch whispered, listening keenly. "I can still hear them at it. And the sound's coming from the wrong direction. That's something else."

"Purpurrot?" Zane suggested hopefully. Finch shook his head.

"The monsters," Gloucester said, staring back the way they'd come, searching for movement. "They must have gotten in."

"Nothing was ever really stopping them, if there weren't some already in here," Finch pointed out. He wiped the blood from his face with his sleeve and fell into a defensive stance, magic building in the air around him.

Gloucester expected dancing shadows on the walls to precede the arrival of their hunters. A creeping harbinger of an imminent attack. Instead, the creatures announced themselves only with great stomping footsteps and guttural breaths which could be heard even before they rounded the corner.

When they did, Gloucester fought the urge to cry out in dismay.

There were two of them. These were different from those they'd encountered in the street, but no less horrifying. The first was a great blubbery mass that dragged itself down the corridor on fat tentacles, like a grotesquely bloated octopus. No octopus had a face like this beast, though, with the gaping mouth of a deep sea fish, and bulbous, bloodshot eyes. It whistled angrily from a blowhole at the top of its head.

Where that monster had too much flesh, the second had none. It was a massive skeleton, the bones of its feet clattering with each step. It lumbered along on four legs, its feet splayed in long claws. Its skull was large and flat, with long, sharp fangs erupting from the rictus grin of its jaw, a bright blue point of light in each eye socket. Gloucester recognized it as the beast Hyena had faced down during their escape.

"By all the saints," choked Mulligan. He sounded ill. Then he cleared his throat, and when he spoke next, it was with the sharp bark of authority. "Ready your weapons!"

Gloucester needed no prompting. He aimed his gun at the octopus creature. He wasn't sure where to aim at the skeleton.

Yet he hesitated to shoot.

A gunshot cracked the air, but it was Finch who had fired. The shot hit its mark, and a long fracture split the skeleton's skull. It roared its displeasure. Clutching a clawed paw to its face, it focused its baleful glare on Finch, who promptly squeezed the trigger again.

This time the beast dodged, moving with alarming dexterity as it lunged to the side. The rattle of its bones across the floor was like dice rolling. Finch cursed.

"If only we had, oh I don't know, a seven-foot-tall goddess helping us out a little," he growled, firing another shot at the skeleton. Harrison was also shooting, though Gloucester guessed that his mundane gun would do little good.

Unlike mine. So shoot!

"Mikalai!" Finch's voice was suddenly closer, and Gloucester shook himself out of his thoughts to realize that the magician had backed up to stand beside him. His freckled face was pinched in concern. "Snap out of it! Shoot!"

Gloucester stared down the barrel of his gun once more, fixing his aim. The octopus was much closer now. It didn't seem to notice the bullets driven into its flesh by Harrison's gun.

Foamy strings of saliva slathered its many teeth, and its roar was more bloodthirsty than ever.

And yet still Gloucester hesitated.

"*Mikalai.*" A hand grabbed hold of his shirt and gave him a few hard shakes. Gloucester jolted defensively, but Finch held him fast. "Get a hold of yourself!" he said, voice firm but gentle in comparison to his clutching hand. "They are going to kill us."

The skeleton fell back. It took shelter behind the bulk of the octopus, while the flame in its eyes grew dim. Something twisted in Gloucester's chest.

This isn't the only way.

"I've shot this thing enough times to take down a giant!" Harrison shouted, jamming his spent gun back into its holster and pulling out another. "Nothing's slowing it down!"

Finch aimed his gun at the octopus and fired off several shots. Even the enchanted weapon seemed to have little effect.

"Tough bastard, eh?" Finch yelled. He stowed the gun away and whirled back toward Gloucester. The octopus was nearly upon them. "Time for a change of attack. Remember what we did against the dragon?"

How could he forget?

"Yeah," Gloucester said, nearly shouting to be heard over the creature's bellows. He wasn't sure how much he liked being a conduit for magic, but it had done the trick before. It was worth a shot now.

Reaching out with his free hand, he grabbed hold of Finch's shoulder.

"Harrison!" he called. "Get back with the others!"

"*What?* Why?"

"Just do it, secret agent man!" snapped Finch. His hands were already glowing with the blue-tinged light of magic. It flooded down Gloucester's arm, the itch of it spreading through his bones.

Harrison hesitated for a split second longer. Then a particularly frightful screech from the octopus made them all wince, and he swore, falling back to guard the rest of the group.

As when they fought the dragon, Gloucester felt the magic charging through him, filling his very blood, growing stronger and stronger with each beat of his heart. It built in his core and then spread to every toe and fingertip until he was afraid that he would explode, overwhelmed by its raw force. His thoughts spun with doubts and ideas alike.

In the heart of the storm, one idea sparked brighter than the rest, strong enough to cling to the forefront of Gloucester's mind. It seemed far-fetched, but he had no time to question it. Everything Gloucester had been feeling, all of the doubts and regrets coalesced into this singular, madcap notion. In the back of his mind, Finch's voice echoed: *You're a decent channeler . . .*

Let's put that to the test.

"Now!" shouted Finch.

Unlike the fight against the dragon, this time Gloucester didn't let go of Finch's shoulder. Instead, he pulled all of the power he could feel coursing between them and drew his mind back to the shield he'd created against Denken. He tossed aside his gun and swung that hand out in front of him, ringed fingers splayed.

"What are you doing?" Finch tried to toss Gloucester's hand off his shoulder, but Gloucester clenched his fingers around the fabric of his coat, refusing to relinquish the hijacked magic. He had no idea what he was doing, acting on intuition alone.

You're a decent channeler, but you've no training.

Luckily, the magic needed no incantation. Blue light barreled from his outstretched hand, but instead of the attack spell Finch had intended, it spread out wide, a super-charged version of Gloucester's earlier shield. The force of conjuring it threatened to fling Gloucester backward, but he planted his feet and braced himself.

The octopus shrieked, colliding with the wall. The whole building seemed to shake as it rebounded. Though its fury and surprise were obvious, it looked unharmed. Behind it, the skeleton sat back on its haunches, watching.

"You *idiot*." Finch wrenched himself free of Gloucester's grasp, glaring at him. "What are you playing at?"

Gloucester ignored him. He still contained enough magic to hold the massive shield in place. It was taking most of his concentration to do so, though, and what little he had to spare was focused on the creatures in front of him. They had both fallen silent.

"Listen to me!" Gloucester called out to them. In his mind's eye, he saw Harmony swinging their bat with fear in their eyes; Hyena with their anxious laughter; Mulligan with pride and stress controlling his actions. "*Listen*. No one needs to hurt each other. This doesn't need to go this way." He raised his voice for everyone to hear. He *needed* everyone to hear this. "You," he said, looking at the skeleton. "Do you remember us? You let us by before. You let us go. Hyena . . . the other, uh, the other creature . . . they vouched for us, right? They didn't want to be used by Denken anymore. They wanted to be free."

Please let this work. The beasts were still silent. As was everyone else. Gloucester could see Finch staring at him openmouthed. But no one interrupted. *Please, just let this work.*

"I don't want to die," he told the beasts. "And I don't want you to, either. I want to help you. We're going to try to get you all home to the Maze, all right? Away from this place where you don't belong. But please, to do that, you have to let us be. *Please*."

The skeleton and the octopus exchanged a look, the latter chittering in a distinctly questioning manner. Gloucester's breath heaved through him. His outstretched arm shook from the effort of maintaining the shield. He didn't know how much longer he could hold it, the magic he'd siphoned from Finch waning with each passing moment. If this didn't work . . .

The skeleton gave a single drawn-out cry and retreated. The octopus hesitated a moment longer, furious eyes locked on the humans, then it, too, moved away. In a cacophony of clattering bones and slapping tentacles, they disappeared down the corridor and around a corner.

Only once the sounds of them faded into silence did Gloucester finally release the spell. He lowered his arm, the shield's sudden absence enough to drop him to his knees. "Ow," he said, dazed.

A hand swatted across the top of his head. He glanced up to meet Finch's fiery expression.

"You utter, *utter* bastard," Finch growled. Then he pulled Gloucester to his feet and into a tight hug. "That scared the absolute shit out of me," he said into Gloucester's shoulder.

"Sorry," Gloucester said. "But it just didn't feel right . . . After Hyena and . . . and the way Denken treats them, I just . . ."

"You're unbelievable!" Stepping away from the embrace, Finch stared at Gloucester from arm's length. Then he ducked forward again and planted a quick kiss on Gloucester's lips. "Do that to me again, though, and I'll bloody kill you."

"I'm just glad it worked," Gloucester said. He crouched to retrieve his gun, fingers still tingling with the memory of magic. "I'm sort of amazed it did."

What are we doing here? he wondered. *We don't stand a chance. Not in the long run. Where the hell is Purpurrot?*

The goddess was surely their only hope. They had no guarantee that all of the monsters would prove to be so reasonable, and even if they were, it still left Denken. The Gambler could buy them time—perhaps he was even a match for Denken in strength—but Gloucester doubted he would be able to actually beat him. Especially after a year in captivity. Gloucester had only been imprisoned half that time, and it had taken a heavy toll.

As for Gear . . . well, more and more he was thinking Antimony's iron confidence in her creation was entirely misplaced. No, Purpurrot was the key. And Purpurrot wasn't there.

"More creatures are probably on their way," Antimony said,

breaking the silence. She moved to stand beside Gloucester, the others a few steps behind. "We can't hope to reason with all of them. We should keep moving before any more find us."

For now, the corridor was quiet, with no footsteps hurrying into earshot.

In fact, no sounds at all.

"I can't hear the Gambler and Denken anymore," Gloucester said as soon as realization dawned.

"Maybe they're farther away from us now?" Zane suggested, though she didn't sound convinced. "Maybe they were moving as they fought . . ."

Or maybe one of them has won. But who?

"So what now?" asked Mulligan uneasily. Gloucester wasn't sure if it was shock or fear or the fact that Gloucester had just saved his life, but he seemed to have forgotten to remain annoyed and disdainful.

"We need to get you to safety, sir," Harrison said. The blood on the side of his face shone black in the strange lighting of the corridor. "This was a mistake. We never should have come here, not this ill-prepared."

"Perhaps not," Antimony said. "But now that we're here, I don't think running away is an option anymore."

"What I'd like to know is what the bloody hell happened to Purpurrot. The Gambler said she's recuperating, but what does that even mean?" Zane said. "The plan, such as it was, sort of revolved around her. Without her, we're running around like chickens with their heads cut off."

No one had an answer. Purpurrot's disappearance had come without warning, and the Gambler's explanation had been, at best, a guess. She didn't seem like the sort to simply cut and run, but Gloucester was finding it difficult to trust most people these days. Let alone mysterious gods who came and went as they liked, vanishing the moment they were needed most.

"If we're on our own, we're on our own," he said grimly. "We'll figure something out. At least we're not defenseless." He hefted the gun in his hand. "We just need to work out our next step."

"I think we need to find our way back to the Gambler," Antimony said. "However his fight with Denken ended, it's the only place where we can end this. We need to face Denken."

No one looked eager to carry out this idea, but no one argued against it either, not even Mulligan.

"I agree," said Gloucester. "And I think I have a plan."

Zane's sigh was long. "If it's anything like all the others we've come up with, I'm sure it'll go great."

Chapter 28

The Knife's Edge

"The problem is that we aren't working together," Gloucester said.

"Yes, we are," Mulligan immediately countered. "We're all here together, aren't we? I trusted you lot, mad as you all are. Not that it's gotten us anywhere but in a worse spot than where we started. What more do you want from me?"

Gloucester huffed a breath, annoyed, but pushed on. "We're here together, yeah, but we aren't thinking like a team. Not really. We keep putting all our hopes on one person—Purpurrot, the Gambler—and it keeps biting us in the ass." He turned to Finch. "When you and the other magicians were fighting the imagination monsters, you were all working together, right?"

"Yeah, more or less. But that was a crowd of all magic users. Not . . ." Finch swept his hand around at the group. " . . . whatever this is."

"Gee, thanks," said Zane.

"Well, we work with what we have." Gloucester stepped between the two of them. "Remember the dragon, right, how we fought together? That actually *worked*. Because we were cohesive. A team." Instinctively, he looked toward Harrison, the other trained security agent. Harrison was nodding his agreement.

"Gloucester's right. We need to pool our assets. So what have you got in mind?" he asked.

Gloucester offered the man a quick smile, grateful for the show of support. "Right. Here's what I'm thinking. Zane and I have these"—he drew the enchanted knife from his belt—"plus Cassus and I have our guns. That's what we've got for weapons that might actually do something to Denken. Everyone has something from Lucienne that'll offer a bit of protection, too, right?"

Zane nodded and held up her pocket watch. Its light glinted off Antimony's brass knuckles, while Mulligan nervously tapped the ring on his finger and Gear smiled down at the key around her neck.

Gloucester held up his hand, displaying his own gift from the hedge witch. "I've got my shield as protection, and we've already seen that Denken can't get past it. Maybe I can use it not just as a defense, but an offense too. Use it to push Denken in the direction we need him to go—"

"Away from us, preferably," Zane chipped in.

"Exactly. And maybe into a trap of our own. The goal is to subdue Denken if possible. If we're lucky, Purpurrot will get a hold of herself and come save the day, and we just need to contain Denken until that happens. But we can't just bank on that. If necessary, we have to be ready to deal with this ourselves."

"You mean killing him," Antimony said matter-of-factly.

"If necessary," Gloucester repeated. "I don't want anyone to die, but there are a lot of lives on the line here. Maybe the whole world." He turned to Finch. "Cassus, you're our best bet in that scenario. You're the closest anyone's gotten to taking Denken down. If I can push him towards you, can you be ready? In case we can't hold him long enough for Purpurrot?"

Finch was already reloading his gun. "Been ready for weeks, Mik."

Though he said it with a cheeky smile, the darkness in his eye harkened back to the showdown at All Saints Shrine.

"We only shoot to kill *if necessary,*" Gloucester warned him.

"Yeah, yeah. Murder bad. So that's the plan?"

Finch, like everyone else, was looking to Gloucester for his response. He drew in a deep breath. "Pretty much. You and I take point on containing Denken. Zane has the other knife, so she can protect the others while they help the Gambler if he needs it. And everyone keep your protective items close."

It wasn't a great plan. Gloucester knew that, but with the Gambler's fate unknown and Purpurrot still vanished, it was the only one they had.

Antimony stepped forward. "May I suggest one addendum, Mr. Gloucester?"

Gloucester heaved an internal sigh. He knew what was coming. "If you're suggesting Gear—"

"Her immunity is no joke. If we gave her one of the knives, she could be our secret weapon." Antimony stood firm, even when the rest of the group scoffed.

"Gear. Really?" Finch gestured at the automaton. Misreading the motion, she offered him a friendly wave in return. "*Really?*"

"It's why she's here with us, isn't it?" Antimony pointed out. "She was always our backup plan."

"Not one we ever planned on using," Finch insisted. He whirled on the others, seeking backup. "None of us actually thought we would, did we? I thought we all knew that was just to appease *her.*"

He tossed his head at Antimony, who stared back at him imperiously. Gear watched over her creator's shoulder with anxious eyes.

"If I had one of those knives, I could hurt someone?" the

automaton asked. "Would that help?"

"No," Zane told her gently. "I mean, yes, you could hurt someone, but I don't think it would help. I'm sorry, Antimony, but I just don't think Gear has it in her to fight."

"And it doesn't feel right to ask her to," Gloucester said.

"Yet we ask it of the rest of us," murmured Antimony.

She argued no further, however. For a moment, silence held sway, broken only by the ticking of Gear's clockwork as she stared at the knife in Zane's hand.

After an uncomfortable beat, Mulligan spoke. "Well, I'd hardly call this a plan. Wandering through the dark *just in case* we can *maybe* get close enough to Denken to *possibly* subdue him. It's a lot of uncertainty."

Shoulders straight and emotions hidden away once more, Antimony gave a single, terse nod. "No point adding to it by standing around questioning ourselves, then. Let's go."

—

The group cautiously returned the way they'd come. An oppressive silence hung over the halls like a weight pressing down on their shoulders. The longer they walked, the heavier it felt.

It was also growing darker, as shadows slid back into place along the walls and chased their footsteps. Not a good sign. Eventually, they rounded a bend to find a corridor enveloped in a curtain of darkness.

"This again." Finch sighed dramatically. "Great."

Gear peered into the shadows, the inner workings of her skull clicking fretfully. "Does it mean Denken won?"

The group turned as one to regard her in surprise. She explained, "The Gambler doesn't seem to like the dark. That Denken guy does, though, and now the dark is back. Does that mean the Gambler lost?"

"I think it means the fight is over, one way or the other," Finch answered. He caught Gloucester's eye, and Gloucester knew what he was thinking. The fight could have ended another way, beyond a simple win-lose scenario.

Don't trust the Gambler.

"We'll soon find out," Harrison said. Though it looked like the last thing he wanted to do, he was the first to take another step toward the pitch black. Sighing, Gloucester fell into step beside him.

The corridor's remaining light fled all too quickly, and soon they were swallowed up by the darkness. Zane lifted her pocket watch like a lantern, as she had before, but its light could only spread so far. Everything outside its reach remained a mystery. Gloucester's imagination was only too eager to fill in the blanks with horrible possibilities. He clenched his fist around the chains connecting his rings, ready to conjure a shield at the first sign of danger.

Once again he became uncomfortably aware of how impossible it was to gauge the passage of time here. He guessed they had been walking in the dark for about ten minutes, but the more he thought about it, the more he wondered if it had been longer. Hours. Days. Months even.

He gave a start at the gentle touch of a hand on his wrist, but it was only Zane, her face lit by the watch held aloft in her other hand.

"I hate this," she whispered to him. "The silence. The dark. It's doing my head in."

Gloucester slid his hand into hers and gave it a comforting squeeze.

"At least we'll hear if more of the monsters come along," he murmured back. "Quietness doesn't seem to be their strong suit."

This earned a weak smile from Zane. "It really doesn't."

—

After what felt like several hours—or possibly mere minutes—Gloucester started to get worried. No matter the strange passage of time, he felt like they'd been walking for too long. Too far. Had they really put this much distance between themselves and the fighting demigods? Had Denken and the Gambler moved their battle somewhere else?

This is a maze. And no mere labyrinth, but one created by Thought itself. Something tells me there's a lot more to it than twisting corridors and dead ends.

For all any of them could tell, they might be walking in circles. Maybe this new Maze was designed to make them wander endlessly until they lost all hope.

We found Denken before. We can do it again.

Except we didn't find him. He found us.

So what were their options? Gloucester sorted through them, almost glad for the conundrum because of the distraction it provided. They could keep moving as they were and hope the path eventually led where they wanted to go. Or they could stop, hoping Denken and the Gambler would once more come to them, hopefully before another pack of monsters did.

He couldn't think of a viable third option. Moving forward was always better than standing still, in his opinion, so he kept walking.

At long last, something reached their ears. It was faint, a whisper in the dark, and it tugged at Gloucester's mind like an insistent child pulling on the hem of their mother's sleeve. He cocked his head in the vain hope of hearing it more clearly. Beside him, Zane grimaced. Gloucester gave her hand another squeeze, as much to comfort himself as to ease her mind.

The whispering slowly grew louder as they trekked deeper into the dark. Eventually, just as Gloucester could almost make out words, there appeared a break in the blackness. It was light, small and orange, like that of a lonely candle.

As they got closer, it became apparent that this was no small flame. Much bigger than Gloucester had initially thought, it grew and grew, until they drew close enough to make it out clearly.

It was the Gambler. Unconscious, he lay prone on the hard marble floor, spread-eagled and head lolled to one side. He was still alight, the flames encasing his body providing the light that had drawn them to him. As if it somehow knew its task was accomplished, the whispering faded, waning in pitch until it was a barely audible stirring in Gloucester's ears.

"Gambler!" Gear and Antimony spoke as one. The pair of them dashed to the Gambler's side, though both hesitated to touch him. It would seem even in her brief experience Gear had learned of the dangers of fire.

Gloucester and the others stared down at the unconscious demigod. His injuries were apparent: long gashes littered his body, deep enough they would surely have killed a mortal man. Though the bleeding was surprisingly minimal—little more than what usually stained the knees of his pants and was left in the wake of his footsteps—the claw marks' severity was obvious. His skin and clothes were torn back to reveal tissue and bones.

Guilt twisted its icy hand through Gloucester's chest. They had left the Gambler on his own against Denken. Would things have turned out differently if they had remained here?

Probably not. But glancing at the others, he saw the same feeling reflected in Antimony's and Zane's faces.

"Is it bad?" Gear asked Antimony, high-pitched with fear. "It looks bad. He's not supposed to look like that, is he? That's not how people are supposed to look!"

Doing her best to avoid the fire, Antimony reached over the Gambler to touch Gear's shoulder. In the flickering light, her face was even paler than usual. "He'll be okay. Don't worry. He's made of sterner stuff than that."

"I don't know what that means," Gear sniffled.

"It means he'll be fine, love," Harrison told her, stepping into the firelight from the back of the group.

Gear sat back, relieved, and even Antimony let out an audible breath. Something was bothering Gloucester, however, a niggling warning at the back of his mind.

"He's just healing slowly because it was another immortal who hurt him," Finch explained. There wasn't much sympathy in his voice, but Gloucester noted a hint of uncertainty. He doubted it had much to do with what he was saying and more to do with how this shook up his doubts about the Gambler's loyalty. "It'll take him a—hold on," he said, interrupting himself as confusion drew his brows together.

He and Gloucester turned as one to stare at Harrison. Then they looked over at the front of their little expedition. Harrison had been at the lead ever since they left the fight with the monsters. And there he was, staring past them in wordless bafflement at his doppelganger.

"What the hell—" Gloucester started. A flash of movement, and then the breath whooshed from his lungs in a single gust as something hard and heavy planted itself in the middle of his chest and sent him flying. The wall was a solid force against his back, and he slid down it, groaning. It wasn't nearly as hard a kick as the one dealt to the Gambler earlier, but it still hurt like hell.

Harrison loomed over him, grin widening to reveal sharp, triangular teeth. "Boo." His low, calm voice was layered with unmistakable power.

"What the fuuuuuck?" the real Harrison squawked, boggling at his second self. "I—What? How?"

Shrill and stuttering, he sounded almost as unlike himself as the imposter. The fake Harrison threw back his head and laughed. There was no missing Denken there.

Gloucester's gun was already in his hand, and he moved to aim it at the demigod. A foot stomped down on his wrist. Harrison's features shifted uncomfortably back into Denken's, and though he shrunk significantly in height, the weight pressing down on Gloucester's arm never lessened.

"Itty bitty humans, running around thinking you can do anything," Denken said, both amused and disdainful. "You're all meddling in more than you can manage—*Don't even think about it.*"

He pointed a clawed finger at Finch, who had started to raise his hands. Expression thunderous, Finch let his hands drop back to his sides.

"Good lad," said Denken, smirking. He ground his heel, and Gloucester gasped in pain. The personification of Thought looked around at them all. "I think it's time we all put this saving the world charade to bed, don't you? Before someone gets hurt."

"Someone's already gotten hurt!" Gear had been silent since the demigod's appearance, but her protest now was so loud and piercing that they all stared at her in amazement. Her kind face was livid with fury. She strode past Zane and thrust a patchwork hand toward the Gambler. "You hurt the Gambler! How could you hurt him? I thought he was your family."

Noticing Gear for the first time, Denken gaped at her, blankly shocked. Then he reined himself in and grinned once more.

"Well, well, well, you're a funny little thing, aren't you," he said. "Now where did *you* come from, Odd Duck?"

Gear said nothing, mouth drawn in a defiant line, but Denken's hand swung upward to point suddenly at Antimony. His eyes never left the automaton. "You've all got your cute little protection spells, but I can still hear your thoughts, Antimony Jones. The pride you feel over your little project here is stifling."

"I've a lot to be proud of," Antimony replied evenly.

"No doubt," Denken said with a harsh laugh. "Creating life where there was none. That's all you've ever wanted, isn't it? Ever since he died. Ever since you killed him."

Gloucester couldn't see Antimony well from where he lay, but her silence spoke volumes. Denken laughed again, reveling in cruel victory.

"Is it really pride when it's born out of guilt? You think a heart made of gears will make yours unbroken?" Denken finally looked away from Gear, sneering at Antimony. "Maes is dead and he always will be. He's never coming back, no matter how many times you wish it or cry his name in the night. No stupid machine will change that, either."

Angry glee crackled through his taunts like the flames encasing his unconscious brother. It danced in the darkness of his eyes.

Only to be extinguished a moment later. Gear snatched something from Zane's hand and lunged so quickly she was a blur, a snake striking at its prey. Denken reeled back. His weight lifted from Gloucester's wrist as he gawked down at the knife hilt protruding from his ribs. The wound was precise, Zane's blade stabbing into his solar plexus, right beneath his sternum. Denken's surprise soon twisted into pain, and his hands grappled at the hilt.

Gloucester wasted no time. Ignoring the pain in his arm, he rolled to his feet and pulled the second enchanted knife from his belt. This was their only chance now. He threw it to Gear. She caught it deftly, as if snatching blades out of midair was an everyday occurrence for her. Moving with inhuman grace, the key around her neck swinging on its cord, she took aim and threw.

Denken hadn't yet managed to pull out the knife driven into his ribs when the second one joined it. With the same eerie accuracy, it slid smoothly into the base of Denken's throat. He staggered back. Darkness gathered around the planted blades, shadows in the place of blood.

"Don't hurt the people I like," Gear said. The order was as cold and hard as the knives she wielded. Her clockwork clicked in the shocked silence, steady and mechanical.

"How . . ." Denken wheezed. Staring at the knives in disbelief, he sank slowly to his knees.

Gear reached down and snatched the knife out of Denken's throat before he could touch it, showing no sign of mercy upon his agonized gasp. She leveled the tip of the knife between Denken's eyes. He gaped up at her, openly amazed.

"You're immune," he breathed.

"I don't care," Gear said. "Make him better."

"Who do you think you are?" Though Denken's voice still conveyed pain, it roared with power like lightning through thunderclouds. Everyone quailed.

Everyone but Gear. She stood her ground, unflinching and unfazed. Gloucester saw now what had made Antimony so certain that Gear's immunity to the demigods was the key to combating one of them. Yet he felt little triumph at the sight of her standing over Denken. The firelight cast flickering shadows across her face, and she looked less human than ever, as unfeeling and metal as the gears turning in her skull.

She didn't understand death, he realized, doubt spreading its tendrils through him. And what she didn't comprehend, she didn't fear. Except that meant she didn't understand what it took to cause it, either. Innocence created the perfect killer.

"Fix him!" Gear shouted. The ticking from her head grew louder and more agitated as the gears spun faster.

"Gear," Antimony said, but for once her creation ignored her.

"Gear!" Zane repeated.

"Fix him now!" Gear ordered Denken, deaf to all else. "Fix him now or I will make you die."

The shadows leaking from Denken's wounds spread through the air like ink through water, but his expression was hard. "The word is 'kill,' machine. And even you aren't capable of that. Not with me."

"I don't care what you say!"

Gear brandished the knife with vicious intent. Gloucester's hand itched to raise his own weapon in response, but he hesitated. This was what they had come here to do. This was the plan, more or less.

So why didn't it feel right?

"You should."

The words rang like a symphony, beautiful and resonant. They all froze, transfixed.

Purpurrot moved out of the darkness with the same

dangerous grace and magnitude as Denken's shark made of shadows. Her exquisite features were serious, purple eyes steely as she took in the scene before her. Even Gear had fallen silent and still, though from her wide-eyed expression, it was more out of startlement than any thrall Purpurrot's presence exerted.

"Well . . . I don't," she said scathingly. But her certainty had fled. The clicking gears slowed.

"People will tell you that killing isn't easy," Purpurrot said, speaking like they were the only two in the hall. "And sometimes it isn't. But sometimes . . . sometimes it is. It can be as easy as breathing. As blinking. What's hard is what comes after. Tell me, Gear, what have you learned of regret?"

Gear didn't answer. Her eyes flickered to Antimony, but the scientist offered no answer in her place.

"What about remorse?" pressed Purpurrot. She stepped up to where Denken knelt, and the spreading darkness swirled around her, but she didn't seem to care. She didn't even seem to notice. "What about shame?"

"I don't know." Though the angry edge of Gear's words said a lot, the quietness of her reluctant answer said more.

"You won't come away from taking a life the same as you were before. It will break you, like clockwork out of line. Like it broke him." For the first time, she turned her intense gaze down upon Denken. He stared back up at her, dark eyes unreadable.

"Hello, Mum," he said. "Fancy meeting you here."

Purpurrot didn't grace the weak sarcasm with a reply. Her lips curved into a gentle smile as she held out her hand toward Gear. "You've helped, Gear. You did what the rest of them couldn't. Now let me do the rest. I am ready to end this."

"But the Gambler—"

"The Gambler will live." Purpurrot's voice held no doubt or question, only serenity, as if in the time since last they'd seen her, she had found some answer to which the rest of them were not yet privy.

Gear looked like she still had a mind to argue, but the

coldness was waning from her expression. After a moment, the clicking of clockwork returned to its normal steady pace. There came a single *tock,* louder than the rest, the warning before a clock's chime. Decision reached, Gear placed the knife in Purpurrot's waiting hand. The goddess took it with a smile.

"Thank you," she said. The look in her eye was the kindest Gloucester had ever seen her level at Gear. He wondered if she was beginning to change her opinion on the automaton.

Any peace to be found in the exchange was short-lived. With the cry of a feral animal, Denken snatched the knife hilt still in his chest and wrenched it free.

"I won't be talked about like some misbehaving dog brought to its master," he shouted. "Do not speak of me as if I'm not here!"

He swung his clawed hand at Purpurrot, slashing toward her throat. Then his hand froze like he'd suddenly changed his mind.

Except Gloucester could see the strain on his face. He hadn't stopped himself—he had been stopped.

There was no question of who was responsible. Purpurrot stared down at Denken, unperturbed. Nothing physical told Gloucester that magic was at work now. The only feeling he could sense was something deeper, some tug on the edges of his mind indicating there were strange powers at work.

"You've built up so much magic here, Denken," Purpurrot murmured. "So much like the Pockets. It feels nice to be in a place like this again."

Realization dawned, and the personification of Thought fought harder than ever to free his wrist. "No," he breathed.

Unlike Denken and the Gambler, Purpurrot didn't grow as her power mounted. Rather, a light had come on within her, one that wasn't seen so much as felt. Gloucester had the uncanny sense of standing next to a star about to go supernova.

The others felt it too.

"Should we be running?" Mulligan hissed. Harrison nodded

in adamant agreement. Even Zane and Finch looked like they would rather be anywhere else. Antimony's eyes were on Gear, tears running down her cheeks. No one answered Mulligan's question. As wise as it surely would be to flee, none of them could drag themselves away from the unfolding exchange.

"Mum," said Denken, in a voice that was small and broken. "Please—"

Purpurrot's hands cupped his face and the light within her surged, illuminating the dark corridor. Overwhelming as it was, there was something strangely peaceful in it. Gloucester wanted to close his eyes and let it sweep him away. He felt like it might burn him to ashes where he stood and, worse still, he would let it, bathing in its destructive warmth.

Forcing himself to keep his eyes open, Gloucester shielded his face with his arm. He wouldn't allow himself to be swept away by the magic of another god.

Denken's face was clear in the light cast by Purpurrot's aura, and it was starkly different from before. Where his confrontation with the Gambler had burned away any lingering humanity in his features, his mother's light had brought it back. Though his eyes were still wide and black, and his teeth still pointed, he looked more human than he had since the day he killed the high minister. He gave a great shuddering breath, caught somewhere between a sigh and a sob, and sagged in Purpurrot's hold like he was relaxing for the first time in a very long while.

"This needs to end, my Epiphany," Purpurrot said. "I'm so sorry."

The power around her continued to intensify, roaring like a windstorm. Gloucester clamped his hands over his ears, too deafened to hear anything else, though he could see Zane's mouth open in a scream. He thought maybe he was screaming too.

And then it ended. One moment Gloucester thought he would be crushed beneath the weight of noise and sensation, and then the next . . . nothing. A silence so complete he worried he'd gone deaf. His very thoughts were silent, the air so still that time itself may well have stopped.

Then a phone rang.

Chapter 29

The Oracle's Prophecy

After the rush of magic and roar of monsters, the ringing of a telephone was so mundane that it sounded entirely alien. No one moved, like players on a stage thrown off by an unexpected line change. Denken was unconscious, Purpurrot staring down at him in her arms, trance-like. The ringing phone was the only sound in the corridor.

Finally, Zane pointed at Gloucester. "It's yours, I think," she said, voice dazed.

Everyone was staring at him, expectant. Gloucester numbly searched his pockets for the phone. It was a miracle it hadn't broken, after everything. He'd forgotten he even had it on him.

"Excuse me," he murmured, at a loss for what else to say. He raised the phone to his ear, clicking to answer. "Hello?"

"About bloody time!" said a completely unfamiliar voice on the other end of the line, feminine and frantic. "Are you the only one there who actually brought his telephone, Mikalai

Gloucester?"

"Uh . . ." Gloucester managed. "Sorry? Look, whoever you are, I'm a little bit b—"

"Busy! Yes, I realize that! And I could have helped if Antimony bloody Jones ever answered her stinking phone!"

"Uh," said Gloucester again. "Look—"

"Don't 'look' me!" cried the voice. "Just listen. Tell Antimony—I've had a vision. Proper prophecy."

Gloucester's head was spinning. "Who—?"

The voice on the other end swore spectacularly. "Right, right! Bloody hell, it's hard with newbies. It's Orange Ianto. Antimony will know who I am." As if she could somehow tell that Gloucester had opened his mouth to speak, she shushed him. "Just listen. Listen and pass this on, all right? I had a vision of a sleeping city. Frettchen locked in time, all the clocks broken. The sky was full of shadows, swallowing everything. The darkness spread like spilled ink. And I woke up with words in my head, so clear they might have been written on the inside of my skull. *When the sheep return home and the doors once more seal . . . the false home is broken and nothing is real . . . Epiphany rises and the shark becomes king . . . creation, destruction vainglorious sing.* Got that?"

Gloucester gave himself a brief moment to reflect on how much he missed the normality of his old life. "I—I think so," he said, quite certain that he didn't have it at all. "I'll tell—wait, hang on . . . Epiphany?"

His eyes were on Denken, kneeling in a daze at Purpurrot's feet. Hadn't Purpurrot said something about an epiphany? Only a few minutes ago, he was sure of it.

This needs to end, my Epiphany, she'd murmured with soft regret.

"Epiphany is Denken," Gloucester said lowly. "It's a name for Denken."

"What?" said Zane, who was standing closest to him. On the other end of the phone line, he heard Orange Ianto echo the question. "What are you talking about? Who's on the phone?"

But Gloucester wasn't listening. "Epiphany rises . . ."

"They're gone," Purpurrot said. Her tone was dreamy, like she was in another world, oblivious to the rest of them. "They're returning to the Maze."

When the sheep return home . . .

"The monsters?" Mulligan asked, relieved. "They're gone?"

"The rest of this will fade soon too." Purpurrot pulled Denken closer to her chest. The personification of Thought didn't move, eyes still closed and mouth slack. "We should leave. Soon this will just be another run-down old house. We could all end up squashed in a wall, for all we know."

When the doors once more seal . . .

"I don't think this is over," Gloucester said. While everyone around him started to smile and breathe easier, he felt his heart beating faster.

Epiphany rises . . .

Denken stirred in Purpurrot's arms. The goddess's eyes were on the unconscious Gambler, however, and she paid the movements little mind.

"Listen!" said Gloucester.

"What's wrong?" Zane was the only one still paying attention to him. But Gloucester didn't have time to explain. He raised a hand to mutely point at Denken, just as Purpurrot cried out in pain.

Denken rose, growing bigger and bigger like a stretching shadow. Caught off-guard, Purpurrot fell back. Long gashes were raked across her face and arms. Laughter filled the air, a typhoon in Gloucester's skull. Pain flaring in his kneecaps told him he'd fallen, but he barely felt it, a minor discomfort in comparison to the crashing thunder of laughter.

Someone near him was crying. Or perhaps the wracking sobs were inside his head. He was suffocating, drowning in sound so heavy it was a physical thing. This was it. The end. It had to be. The last thing he would ever hear was this nightmare, pain coursing through him like liquid fire.

Something caught him around the chest, pulling him up from the floor. Bodies pressed against him at all sides, an elbow digging into his ribs, someone's foot scraping his shin, and a loud scream in his ear, barely audible over Denken's laughter. He felt an odd rushing sensation, and then they were all falling backward, but he could no longer see. He thought he must have squeezed his eyes shut instinctively, but try as he might to open them again, he saw nothing but darkness.

The shark becomes king.

—

Gloucester returned to consciousness slowly, his brain reassembling the world around him a little at a time. The first thing he noticed was that he was no longer being crushed against anyone else. Instead, he was lying flat on his back, pebbles digging into the back of his head and the smell of grass in his nose. He opened his eyes groggily. It was still dark, but in the natural way of nighttime, where the light of the moon cast enough gentle illumination to see vague shapes.

He sat up with a groan. "What just happened?"

His question earned someone else's groan in reply. From the pitch of it, he could hazard a guess as to the "someone," and sure enough, he looked over to see Zane sitting up. She, too, was rubbing her head. As his eyes adjusted to the dark, he could make out her face as she winced.

"Whatever it was, it was powerful," came Finch's voice from his other side. The redhead was propped up on his elbows, staring at the sky overhead. "A Transportation spell. And a mighty one at that. Look around. Is any of this familiar to you?"

Gloucester properly took in their surroundings for the first time.

Gone was the dark corridor lit only by the Gambler's fire. A night sky tumbled with stars spread out above them. They were lying on a grassy hillside, the silhouetted line of a wooden fence behind them and the bulky forms of buildings rising up at the base of the incline. They weren't the tall buildings of Frettchen, but rather what appeared to be a shed and, just beyond it, a house. In the middle distance, the shapes of trees formed a forest's edge.

"Where are we?" Gloucester asked, stunned. The air was warm, much warmer than it had been in the city. Frettchen didn't experience temperatures like this until the mid-summer when hot winds blew in from the Eastern Desert and rain stayed away for weeks at a time. "This feels like the south . . . How?"

"Like I said, Transportation spell," Finch told him, getting to his feet and dusting bits of grass and dirt from his coat. He rolled his shoulders and looked around again, his expression difficult to read in the dark. "Could be we're in the countryside near one of the South Cities. Looks like there's something that way." He pointed at the horizon past the crest of the hill, where the sky seemed lighter, perhaps from the lights of a distant city.

"You didn't cast the spell?" Zane asked, also clambering to her feet.

"Wasn't me. I don't reckon I could have cast even the most basic of spells back there, the way my head felt like it was going to explode. And Transportation spells . . . well, they're no small thing. I don't even know anyone who can do them. There are stories that say sorcerers could, but they've scarcely been seen since the Old Empire fell. The only other sort I know who can do magic like that now is—"

"The gods," Gloucester finished.

"Purpurrot," Zane said. "It must have been. Only . . . where is she now? In fact . . ." She trailed off, peering around at the hillside. "Where is everyone? Antimony, Gear, the Gambler. Even those government blokes are gone."

Gloucester squinted into the dark. Sure enough, there was no sign of the others. He raised a finger to his lips to signal for silence, but no amount of keen listening turned up any indication of their companions. All he heard was the wind in the trees and the calls of crickets in the grass. They were alone.

"What happened back there?" he asked. "What happened with Denken? Do you think he could have done this?"

Zane shook her head emphatically. "No. It has to have been Purpurrot. If Denken had grabbed hold of us, I think we would be dead."

Gloucester hummed in agreement, but inwardly he wasn't so sure. Denken had had plenty of chances to kill them. Especially him. He'd killed the high minister in an instant. Yet given ample opportunity to take the rest of them out, he had continuously managed to miss. Gloucester had to wonder how much of that was actually unintentional or bad luck.

Why did things have to be so damned complicated?

"What do you think?" he asked Finch. "You're the magic expert."

"I think Zane's probably right," Finch said, raking a hand through his short hair. "Purpurrot makes the most sense. And that might explain the separation from the others too. Not to mention the randomness of our current location."

"What do you mean?" Gloucester asked.

"Purpurrot was almost powerless when she stepped foot in that Maze. All of that power she used to try to take Denken down, it rushed back into her as soon as she arrived there. That was why she vanished, why she wasn't right there beside us the whole time. She was probably doing everything she could not to explode."

"So you think, what? That she transported us all out of there, but the spell went wrong? Left some of us behind?"

Finch shrugged with a grimace. "Scattered us, if we're lucky. With how things were going down back there, I don't think it would have been a good end for anyone left behind."

Gloucester was very tempted to sit down again. His head was spinning, trying to wrap itself around everything that had just happened. Half of their friends could be anywhere, in who knew what sort of danger. And they didn't even know where *they* were.

"What the hell happened back there with Denken?" he demanded again. "I thought we'd won! Purpurrot was winning!"

"That's a good question." Finch pulled his coat off and draped it over his arm, the wool no doubt stifling in the warm night air.

"Actually, Gloucester, I think you might be in the best position to answer that." Zane hung the magical pocket watch around her neck again, and it cast an eerie light across her face as she gathered her voluminous curls into a bun on the top of her head. He eyed her questioningly.

"Me? Wait—oh, you mean the phone call?"

Even in the paltry light, her impatience was clear. "Of course the phone call! What in the world was that about? You seemed to know something was going to go wrong before any of the rest of us did. Even Purpurrot."

Feeling quite put on the spot, Gloucester shrugged uncomfortably. "It was that—that Ianto person. Antimony's mentioned her before. I dunno how she got my number . . ."

Zane waved that aside impatiently. "Orange Ianto's an oracle. They're really powerful soothsayers. Finding out something like a phone number would be child's play to someone like her. What did she say?"

Gloucester frowned, trying to think back past the monumental whirlwind of happenstances that had just occurred. "She wanted me to pass a message along to Antimony. She said she'd had a vision. A prophecy, I think she called it?"

As Zane and Finch exchanged a meaningful look, Gloucester searched for his phone. He'd been holding it when everything went sideways, but his hands were empty now, with no sign of the phone in the grass around him. He even checked his pockets, in the half-hearted hope it might be there. All he found, however, was Denken's tooth, a key, and a crumpled address given to him by Jeb. That felt like an eternity ago now. He stowed all three back in his pockets. He must have dropped his phone when

Denken started to laugh.

"And?" pressed Zane.

"What was the prophecy?" Finch didn't sound as annoyed as Zane, but the question still had a definite keenness to it.

Gloucester wished he'd had time to write the bloody thing down. "It was some sort of rhyme. Like a riddle. Something about how when the doors of the Maze seal and . . . uh . . . Epiphany is vanquished . . . the shark will be king. That was definitely one of the lines. The shark will be king. And then something about destruction and creation, I think."

"Oh, very specific!" Zane snapped. Then she paused. "Wait . . . Epiphany . . ."

Gloucester glared at her. "Yeah. That's what tipped me off too. Purpurrot had just called Denken that."

"The Brothers have a lot of names," Finch said, managing to sound thoughtful and worried at the same time. "Epiphany isn't an unheard of name for Denken. They say he whispers ideas in people's heads. Gives them inspiration."

"That's a nice way of putting it," Gloucester muttered.

"So let me get this straight," said Zane. "By beating Denken, we actually made things *worse*?"

"Certainly seems that way, doesn't it? Maybe by sending all the imagination monsters back home, it . . . I dunno . . . released his true power or something?" He looked to Finch for clarification or confirmation.

"Nothing like this has ever happened before," Finch said with a helpless shrug. "Leastways, not in any record I've read on the Brothers. Which, trust me, is a lot. Judging from what just happened, I'd say it's a reasonable conclusion, though."

"Well, ain't that a kick in the pants!" Zane gave a sort of groaned sigh. Hands on her hips, she looked around at the dark hillside. "Next question . . . where the hell are we?"

"Our best bet is to head for whichever city that is and find out," Gloucester said, nodding toward the glow on the horizon. "Maybe we'll be lucky and the others will be there." He glanced askance at Finch again. "How far scattered do you think they might be?"

Finch's face was hard to make out, but from the tone of his voice, it was easy to imagine he was grimacing. "I hate to keep letting you down, mate, but I'm in the dark as much as you are when it comes to this. I reckon you're right, though. We're doing ourselves and the rest no good just dilly-dallying here like grazing sheep. Let's make for the city."

—

It was past dawn when they reached the city limits. The sky was an eggshell blue, tinged in the waning pink and orange of a mostly risen sun, which warmed the red-shingled roofs of the buildings that rose before them. In the distance to their left, the ocean sparkled, stretching out to the horizon. A sign beside the dusty road they'd been following for the last few hours proclaimed: *Welcome to Trident's Point!* More writing followed, but it wasn't in a language Gloucester recognized.

"Trident's Point?" read Zane wearily. She was sweating, her hair even curlier than usual, sticking to the back of her neck. "Where the bloody hell is Trident's Point?"

Finch looked out toward the sea, shading his eyes with his hand. He'd rolled his sleeves up, revealing the coiling tentacles of the octopus tattooed on his left arm. "If I remember correctly, it's one of the smallest of the South Cities. And just about as south as south goes. Unless you fancy swimming," he added, with a pointed nod at the vast expanse of water.

"Do you think Purpurrot meant to bring us here?" Gloucester asked.

"You mean, did she have some reason to think there's something in this Trident's Point that can help us?" Finch shook his head. "Seems like too much to hope. I don't think she knew any better than the rest of us what was going to happen. My guess is she was just trying to get us all as far from Frettchen as she could. Until we can get our hands on a map, it's hard to say exactly how far that is."

—

It didn't take them long to locate a map, but it wasn't much of a comfort when they did. It came in the form of a large sign outside a plaza filled with tourists, near a bustling train station. They'd been walking for about an hour when they came upon it, and with the sun now properly risen, they were all feeling the heat. Gloucester, who found summer in Frettchen bad enough, was trying to ignore the light-headedness the heat was causing. His head felt woolly, all his usual worried questions and thoughts spiraling sluggishly through it.

The three of them stood before the map, staring up at it. It covered the South Cities region of the Lower Lands specifically, but up at the top was the bottom half of Frettchen and its outlying hamlets. They looked from it to the spot on the map marked "Trident's Point."

It was a long distance.

"Please don't tell me Antimony and the rest could be anywhere between Frettchen and here," moaned Zane.

"I could agree and then just say nothing, but it's too hot for mean jokes," Finch panted. "So yeah, they could be. They probably are."

"What about Denken?" asked Gloucester. It was a daunting question, but one that had been rolling around in his head since they awoke on that hillside. The last they'd seen of the out-of-control demigod, he seemed to be *gaining* power, not losing it.

He didn't expect an answer. Finch and Zane had both made it clear they had no more idea than he did what had happened back in the New Maze. It came as a surprise, then, when Finch pointed down the street and said, "I think we might be about to find out."

A newspaper seller was setting up his stall little ways down, and already a crowd was gathered around him. Everyone yammered excitedly, making it impossible to latch onto what any of them were saying, but Gloucester heard the name "Frettchen" several times. Too many times to be a coincidence.

They drew closer to the newsstand. To Gloucester's disappointment, the gaggle of gossipers weren't speaking Frettchennian, but a rapid-fire dialect of the South Cities region. There were several, and Gloucester didn't know any of them well enough to identify which one this might be. For all he knew, it could be several at once, as beyond the occasional familiar word, it all sounded like gibberish to him.

He glanced over at Finch, hoping that he might have picked up some languages throughout his travels with his father. Sure enough, his attention was focused on the people gathered around the newspaper stand. He nodded vaguely along in apparent understanding. When he turned back toward Gloucester and Zane a few minutes later, his expression was grim.

"They're all aflutter about news just brought in on the early trains," he told them. "They say Frettchen's cut off all communications. No trains are coming out and no trains are making it in. Just dying on the tracks before reaching the city limits, no matter what the engineers try. A few of them are saying they tried reaching friends and family in Frettchen, but the calls won't connect."

A woman in a blue silk dress and matching headscarf snatched up a newspaper and began reading with avid interest, eyes flicking rapidly across the lines. Gloucester couldn't make out any of the words on the paper and doubted he would have understood anyway. Reaching the end of the front-page story, the woman shook her head and said something in an alarmed voice. A few people in the crowd laughed nervously. Finch glanced sideways at Gloucester and Zane.

"They're quick with their news here, but I guess everyone's been phoning in from the more northern cities in the region," he said slowly.

"And what is the news saying?" Gloucester asked, sensing further trouble. Possibilities tumbled through his mind, each one worse than the last.

Finch rubbed his chin. His stubble was growing thick enough to be the beginnings of a scruffy beard, and he looked starved for sleep. "There are reports from the people on the trains that broke down trying to get into the city." He was still speaking hesitantly like he didn't want to share what he had heard. Gloucester felt a twinge of fretful impatience, but Finch continued before he could put it into words. "They say dark clouds hang over the entire city like there's a storm only over Frettchen and nowhere else. And they say . . . they say that there's something in the clouds. That you can see a giant shape moving around. Like a shark made of shadows."

Creation, destruction vainglorious sing.

Chapter 30

The Sleeping City

Two days later, a cool north breeze blew into the city of Trident's Point, and with it, carried on the gusty air, came news.

The past forty-eight hours had felt like years, as the unfamiliar city buzzed with rumors and alarmist gossip. Finch and, as it turned out, Zane both spoke enough of the language—a South City dialect called Tomalti—to stay on top of the ever-changing word on the street. But Gloucester felt cut off and alone, more so than he had since the high minister summoned him from his cell the month before. He had to depend on his friends' translations to have any idea what was going on, and with none of them sure what was true and what was a tall tale, he felt like he was back in solitary confinement, wondering what was real and feeling like he was losing his mind.

That morning, the newspaper sellers were once again out in droves, hollering their headlines to a public eager for answers to the mysterious goings-on in the north. Even Gloucester, watching one of them from the window of the room he and his friends had rented, could tell something was different this time.

"Photographs," announced Finch, sweeping in through the motel door with a newspaper in one hand and a paper tray of coffee cups in the other. Zane came in after him, her hair wrapped in one of the colorful headscarves common in the area. When Gloucester had asked her about it, she explained it was an effective way to keep the sweaty curls from the back of her neck in the heat.

Fashion and its functions were hardly the first things on his mind now, however.

"Photos?" he repeated, accepting the steaming cup held out to him. "Of what? Frettchen?"

Finch nodded. He passed Zane her iced latte over his shoulder and tossed the newspaper onto the little table where Gloucester sat. "Exactly. And what a story they tell. A picture worth a thousand words indeed."

Gloucester scanned the front page. The entire top of the fold was taken up with a printed photograph. It showed the familiar skyline of Frettchen, the flat roofs of the harbor and warehouse district giving way to the high-rises of the business sector and the tall spires of the Old Cathedral and other remnants of the city's long history. The city was dark, nigh on silhouetted, the sky overhead shrouded in clouds too heavy and black to be natural. Visible amidst the darkness was a huge shape, one shadow darker than the rest.

It was difficult to make out a distinct form from the photo, but Gloucester's memories filled in the details with ease. What might have looked like nothing more than a strange blot in the clouds became a long torpedo body, tipped in teeth and a tail. He suppressed a shiver and searched the photo for other clues, not wanting to dwell on the giant shark.

He would have thought the photograph was in black and white, were it not for a shock of orange in one corner, rising from the ancient rooftops of the Central Library and town hall. It was a spire of flame, tall and thin. It looked almost like—

"Saints above! That's the Gambler," Zane cried, leaning over his shoulder. "God's teeth, he's giant!"

"At least we know he's alive, then," Gloucester said. "What's he doing, though?"

"Maybe he's stuck," Finch suggested. "Maybe he can't get out of the city any more than anyone else can. If Purpurrot couldn't get him out in time . . ." He shrugged.

"Why does he look like a man-shaped wildfire, though?" Gloucester asked. "You don't think he's lost control of his powers too, do you? Joined Denken's side?"

He didn't want to think about fighting two rogue demigods. One was proving impossible enough.

Zane shook her head emphatically, which Gloucester had expected. Finch did the same, though his denial was slower and far more reluctant.

"You know I had my suspicions," he said. "Now . . . I'm not so sure. The Gambler almost died. I don't reckon that was a trick. He was trying to protect us. Protect everyone." Spotting their expressions, he pulled a face. "Don't get me wrong, I'm not going soft on any of these celestial assholes. I'm just saying that my doubts could be wrong, that's all."

"I'm glad," Zane said. "Course, it doesn't answer the question of why he's tromping about all fiery. Maybe he's still trying to fight Denken. Judging from Ye Olde Sky Shark over there"—her finger tapped the shadowy sky in the photograph—"Denken's just as powerful as ever."

Gloucester stared down at the frozen image. "There was something the prophecy lady said. The vision she had. A sleeping city. Something about the clocks all being broken and the sky filled with darkness."

"Orange Ianto's head must be a fun place to live," Zane commented dryly. "I guess it could be worse. The city's not . . . not blown up or razed to the ground or anything. It's still there.

Just . . ."

"Sleeping," Gloucester finished. "So how do we wake it up?"

Finch stared at him, looking like he couldn't decide whether he wanted to laugh or cry. "I can't figure you out, secret agent man. Are you so determined to save the world because you have a hero complex or just a death wish?"

Gloucester frowned. Neither of those were very complimentary options. "I just want to do something. Seems to me we're in a better position than most, knowing everything we know."

"It won't be easy," Finch warned him. "If it's even possible. We don't know where the others are—"

"Yet." Zane smiled, determination shining in her eyes.

"—or what state the city's actually in—"

"It's still standing, at least," said Gloucester.

"—or where to even start with any of this."

Zane's laugh was anxious and tired and just shy of hopeless, but she clapped Finch on the shoulder and offered him a weary grin. "We'll call it an adventure," she said.

"More like a fool's errand," he retorted. He sighed, then relented just enough to reflect her smile with a faint one of his own.

In spite of everything, Gloucester chuckled. "Maybe it's both. Either way, giving up isn't an option."

"No," Zane agreed. Finch nodded beside her. "It's not."

Epilogue

The Burning Garden

Another place of timeless existence. Another impossible space. Beneath lush canopies of leaves as green as the height of spring burns a world on fire. The flames engulf a mighty garden, stretching as far as the eye can see. Glowing orange, fiery paths weave through the foliage, lined with flowers of all kinds and colors. As eternal as the fire burns, it never destroys. The garden grows in spite of it, impervious to all but the dancing light.

This is the Garden, as aptly named by its resident as the Crossroads and the Maze. There is one point within it to which all paths lead, and at this nexus of winding ways stands a tree. From a distance, it doesn't cut a majestic figure, with its slender trunk and carefully pruned branches. Were a brave—and foolhardy—explorer to draw closer, however, they would find their awe mounting with each step. What the tree lacks in bulk or wild majesty, it makes up for in magnitude. It stretches far past the reach of the flames toward a sky tumbled with storm clouds. Thunder rumbles and lightning flashes amidst the distant canopy. The tree's roots run deep, stretching throughout the entirety of the Garden. At the base of the trunk sits an iron-wrought bench, adorned in leaves and twisting vines.

No one sits upon it. This is a recent development. The god whose home this is sat there only moments before. Of course, in the absence of time, "moments" becomes a far more complicated term. They had been contemplating their actions for both an eternity and no time at all. This balanced out to about a day.

Timeless or not, a Pocket knows when its god isn't home. The lightning in the massive tree is more frenzied than usual. The fire crackles more loudly, and a hot wind blows along the garden paths. Things are changing.

Out in the Void Between Worlds, the personification of Love makes their way, mind fixed on a city frozen in time and swathed in shadows. It is time to join the game.

THE END

The gears turn, the hands move, and we are all driven by the ticking, carrying us ever forward.

Acknowledgments

A book comes into being by far more hands than just the author's. The biggest of thank yous to everyone who played a part in bringing The Ticking to life.

To my friends and family, a constant source of enthusiasm and support. Kate, Mum, Libby and Jess, Ginni, Sam, Dorothy, Mackenzie, Cindy, and so many, many more. Thank you for listening, reading, engaging, and just being the best group of people anyone could hope to surround themselves with.

To Susan Brooks and Literary Wanderlust, for once again taking on my creation, and for all the amazing work you put into making it what it is. It isn't easy out there for independent publishers, and I'm proud to be a part of LWL.

To Jennica Dotson, my stalwart editor, whose passion for my story and my characters is matched only by her keen eye and creative wit. Working with you has made this book so much better than I could have hoped for, and made the editing process so very rewarding.

To Craig Terlson, who designed not only the cover for The Ticking but also The Winding, and did such a brilliant job on both. Thank you for making my book so beautiful!

To my bookselling family at Manticore Books: Michael, Julia, George and Lillian.

And to my readers, past, present and future, who first took a chance on The Winding and then decided to keep reading Gloucester's story. Thank you for taking the time, and I hope you enjoy it!

About the Author

Ali Ives is a writer, artist, and daydreamer. She grew up with a love for reading and creativity that hasn't waned with adulthood. Working in a small indie bookshop near where she lives in rural Ontario has only made her love and appreciate the world of books all the more. Her first novel, The Winding, came out in October 2022, a fantasy novel about chaotic demigods, nefarious politicians, and one young man searching for answers.

When Ali isn't writing or surrounded by books, you're likely to find her drawing, wandering around her property with her dog, or covered in dirt and grass stains from her other part-time work as a lily gardener. The story that would eventually develop into The Epitome of Science trilogy started taking form all the way back in her teen years, with the characters filling up many a sketchbook and doodled on the edges of her schoolwork.

Instagram: https://www.instagram.com/aliiveswrites/
Tumblr: https://aliiveswrites.tumblr.com/